THE SWORD OF THE WORLD CONQUEROR

One of the colored stars in the roof of the tomb glowed with the same red as her Bloodstone. She reached up and touched it and it pulsed with the same warmth and light. Suddenly she could see the sword clearly, as though it were not wrapped and hidden behind the chamber wall.

Unhesitatingly she slipped her hand behind one of the pillars. As the tips of her fingers touched the long, slim blade, her body prickled with energy. Gently she slipped it out of the rocky crevice, and through its wrappings it felt warm and alive. The sword knew her. She could tell that no ghost was going to chase her down or call her thief. The exposed hilt was yellowed ivory and she touched it to her lips. . . .

I hold the fates bound fast
And with my hand turn fortune's wheel about. . . .

Ace Fantasy Books by
Joyce Ballou Gregorian

THE BROKEN CITADEL
CASTLEDOWN
THE GREAT WHEEL

THE GREAT WHEEL

Joyce Ballou Gregorian

WITH DECORATIONS BY THE AUTHOR

ACE FANTASY BOOKS
NEW YORK

For SCOTT, whose book is finally complete

&

in loving memory of JOSEPH FLETCHER
who first introduced me to Timur the Lame

This book is an Ace Fantasy
original edition, and has never
been previously published.

THE GREAT WHEEL

An Ace Fantasy Book/published by arrangement with
the author

PRINTING HISTORY
Ace Fantasy edition/April 1987

ISBN: 0-441-30257-2

Ace Fantasy Books are published
by The Berkley Publishing Group,
200 Madison Avenue, New York, N.Y. 10016.
PRINTED IN THE UNITED STATES OF AMERICA

"Lament not the revolutions of the vile wheel, for if it did not turn how else would poor men become princes, and princes poor men? In our age we have seen the Great Wheel raise Tibir Lord of Zamarra on high, and cast into the mud at his feet the Lords of all other lands . . ."

from *Tibir's Victory-Book*

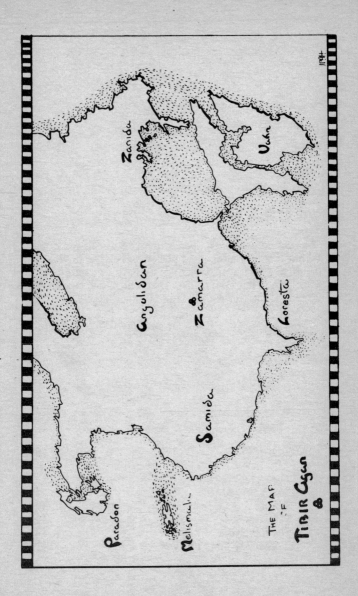

Paradon

Zanida

Usha

Angulidan

Zamarra

Lorestu

Melismala

Samida

THE MAP OF

TIBIR Cagan

Contents

The Great Wheel
Personae

I: THE TREDANANS

LERON,	king of Tredana
LINIRIS,	his wife
GERET,	his young son
ANITH,	his infant daughter
TAMARA,	the princess royal, daughter of Sibyl, Leron's first wife
GANNOC,	the royal steward
ALRIC,	the royal tutor, Gannoc's nephew
PARRIC,	ambassador to the Anguls
GLISSER,	governor of Villavac
HERRARD,	naturalist and traveler Known to the Karabdu as Rassam

II: THE KARABDINS

AJJIBAWR,	Karif of the Karabdu Known also as Clerowan
SHADITH,	a widow of the Tayyib, his lover
IBRASA,	a son of the Tayyib, his bodyguard
AMMAGEST,	an astronomer
HATTAM,	a surgeon

III: THE MELISMALANS

DANSEN,	surnamed the Learned, formerly of Tredana
ARROD,	his wife; one of the Dylalyr
DANYAS,	his son
TALYAS,	viceroy of the islands

IV: THE ANGULS

CHANAGA GAGAN	the first World Conqueror; dead 100 years
TIBIR AGAN,	the Fortunate Lord, Emperor, Conqueror of the World
SORIA AGANA,	the Empress, his chief wife
SUBI,	Sword-Bearer to the Emperor
TAAN,	chief historian to the Emperor
SINIM,	surnamed the Wise, last son of Chanaga Gagan
IBRIM,	great grandson of Chanaga, viceroy of Loresta
DALUN,	a daughter-in-law of Tibir, viceroy of Zamarra
SIKIN,	a son of Tibir, general of his armies
TAMMUSH,	a rebel mir of the northern Anguls
SOKTANI,	a loyal mir of the eastern Anguls
VARLAS,	father of Soktani; also the name of her son
TALA,	interpreter to Soktani
AKSU,	an ambitious mir
ZARDIK,	successor to Aksu

V: OTHER PLAYERS

VAZDZ,	Lord of Inivin; the Demiurge
SIMIRIMIA,	Queen of the Underworld
ARBYTIS,	High Priest of the Temple Ornat
PADESHI,	chief warlord of Paradon, former Master of Vahn
MARRICSON,	a traveling entertainer once named Odric
LERDAS,	son of Dastra and the Arleon

PROLOGUE

I: TREDANA

Tamara reined in her horse. Through a gap in the hedge of the castle's outer garden she could see her father the king, riding with her little brother Geret. Leron of Tredana had checked his horse's stride to match that of his son's little pony; Geret, always a worrier, rode with one hand on his father's booted leg for comfort. His high-pitched baby voice came clearly to Tamara through the branches.

"I'm having lessons with Tamara today. We're doing maps with Alric. He has new charts for An- Angul- Angulidan." Leron continued to smile, but his eyes were stern. Tamara kicked her horse forward and cantered around the bend, overtaking them in a spray of gravel.

"Look, father," she said. "I'm training him for the wars!" She sat back and her old gelding executed a creaky turn on the hindquarters while she waved her sword-hand over her head. Geret stiffened, and Leron frowned at his daughter.

"There will be no war if I can prevent it. In any case, it is unlikely even the great Tibir will be able to fight his way past the Karabdu."

"The Karabdu are our allies and friends," she answered. "We should march in aid of them. Then the Karif could give me a battle-trained stallion." She pulled her horse up on its hind legs in a shaky salute, but her father, gently disengaging his son's fingers, was not watching.

"It is nearly time for breakfast," was his final reply. "There will be no talk of war at the table."

Tamara's horse threw up its head in protest as she kicked its ribs and galloped back to the stables, angry tears in her eyes, feeling her father's disapproving gaze behind her.

1

II: ROSEDALE

"Notice," said Sibby, "the embossed seal of the Common-wealth, the cheap bond paper, the chipped lower-case *e*. Undoubtedly a genuine copy of Sibyl Barron Arleon's legal separation from her soon-to-be-former husband Michael."

Lynn shook her head as she handed back the papers. "I can't believe you finally did it."

"And I can't believe that I let you talk me into coming to a place like this." Sibby picked up a brochure from the table that was wedged between their wicker rockers, and read out loud. " 'Rosedale Campground: 1876—1976 One Hundred Years of Spiritist Fellowship.' I see the deceased founders of the community still vote at the annual meeting. 'The Loreley Woods: possibly the only stretch of genuine virgin forest in the region.' Possibly the most typical stretch of scrub in this part of Cape Cod. 'Daily Message Services (Guest Mediums).' What'll you pay me to go up to the hotel desk and ask if there are any messages for us?"

"Sibby! Give it a chance! You've only been here a few hours. The Message Services are really interesting. And there are plenty of mediums to choose from."

"Sounds like art school." Sibby riffled the pages of the brochure impatiently.

Lynn sighed. "Sibby! Just relax and get a feeling for the place. It will make you feel good if you let it. Remember, you're on vacation."

"How can I forget? I've got $120 to my name and for the next six days someone else is going to be teaching the little kids how to ride and pocketing my cut."

Lynn looked at her in horror. "A hundred and twenty dollars? But Michael's rolling!"

"We split, remember? You don't think I want anything from him now, do you? All I want is distance."

"How are you going to live?"

"I get free board at Laura's for the stable work and twenty-five percent on the lessons I teach. As long as I don't break a leg, buy a car, travel or try to save money I'm fine." Sibby waved the brochure in Lynn's face. "Now don't start on career planning and finances and health insurance. They're Mike's favorite subjects too. If I must take advice, I'd rather get it from the Other Side, if just for the novelty. C'mon, let's catch the noon Message Service. I'll be good, I promise.''

The Assembly Hall was built like a bandstand, open on the sides. It fit in comfortably with the narrow clapboard summer houses, the old hotel with the gingerbread front porch, the gazebos labelled Gifts and Literature. Sibby found it hard to concentrate on the service rather than on the fresh air outside, the bright Cape Cod sun, the rustling pines. A nice day for a trail ride. . . . Her eyelids drooped and then she snapped attentively upright as Lynn's elbow jogged hers. The Message Service was about to begin.

The hall seemed too bright, too dowdily respectable to be the proper place for communication with the Other Side. But up on the stage, between the upright piano and the ornately carved pump organ, a pleasant middle-aged woman and an aggressive older man with white hair were standing, ready to put the congregation in touch with loved ones gone before. The lady gestured to a man sitting alone on one edge of the gathering.

"Will you give me your voice, please?" Pink-faced, he cleared his throat and muttered hello. The lady smiled. "There's someone here from the mother's side of the family. I'm not sure if she would be your mother or grandmother, or perhaps an aunt. She had some trouble with her legs while she was on This Side? Her name is Anna— Amy—'' The man straightened up. "Agnes!" he said. "Aunt Agnes? What do you want?''

"She brings you love and blessings from the Other Side. She wants you to know you are never alone. Our loved ones are always with us. Aunt Agnes wants you to know that.''

The man stammered a thank-you and the lady turned her attention to a shabby little woman in a scarf and raincoat. For her, she brought blessings from a dead child, and the woman thanked her with tears running down her cheeks.

Sibby shifted uneasily and looked sideways at Lynn, who had been singled out by the white-haired man. "You're not here for word from the Other Side," he said. "It's news of this world you're seeking. You're troubled for a friend, are you not?" Lynn nodded slowly and Sibby went scarlet. "No one can bear another's burdens. Your own are more than enough. Remember that. Your friend, too, carries a burden not her own. She is going on a long trip, a trip from which she may not return. I see darkness ahead for her, a red-headed man and a black-haired woman. All you can send with her is your love. I'm sorry I cannot tell you more this morning." Lynn nodded and Sibby sat back in her folding chair, furious. A long trip indeed. Why not throw in a water crossing and a couple of tall handsome strangers?

Sibby glowered to no avail. The lady was now pointing in her direction; but this time she was no longer smiling. "There are several messages here for you today. But the one that comes most clearly is from your daughter on the Other Side. Tana— Tara— Tammy?" The medium did not seem to notice Sibby's reaction to this ridiculous fabrication; she was remote and listening. But what she said made no sense.

"She was a baby when you left her. Now she is a young woman. She wants you to know that she thinks of you still. But—" the medium faltered for the first time. "Apparently she is not on the Other Side? She is living, but with another family?"

Sibby looked at her blankly.

"Those on the Other Side are happy. Your daughter is not happy. Things are not going well. So of course she is with us here. It is my mistake. We cannot always tell whence our messages come. I take it she is with adoptive parents, that you do not see her? I think you should try and get in touch with her. She needs you very much. Her message makes no sense to me, but perhaps it will have meaning for you. She says 'Tredana' is in great danger. She wishes for your guidance."

Tredana.

As the small lady at the piano crashed and tinkled her way enthusiastically into the closing hymn, Sibby brooded over her bizarre message. With daughters she had nothing to do, but Tredana was another matter. It was a mystery word for a mystery place that had haunted her imagination since childhood. Confusion over Tredana and reality had complicated her teen-age years and practically flunked her out of Radcliffe—to say nothing of throwing her into the arms of Michael Arleon.

Once, as a child, she had thought of her mysterious Tredana as a refuge. Now it seemed to be after her: a sinister pursuing spirit. She would fight it off, if only she knew how.

THE SWORD-
BEARER

Chapter One

TREDANA

I

In the bitter spring of the World Conqueror's arrival on their continent, Tamara sat in the library with her father and brother, being instructed in maps. Now that Dansen the Learned made his home in Melismala, the royal tutor was Alric, a nephew of the steward Gannoc. In his youth, Alric had been wild and not much given to study. During the Regency he had even joined the outlaws of Clerowan, and taken part in many disreputable adventures before joining his uncle in exile, in Rym Treglad. But a spear through the shoulder had withered his arm and tempered his spirit and once unable to lift a sword or play the flute, he had sobered considerably and embarked on study under Dansen with as much enthusiasm as once he had taken to robbery in the woods.

Maps were a special love of his, as they had been of Dansen, and for him the horrors that trickled in to them of the Agan Tibir's campaigns were much tempered by the news of faraway lands and cities previously unknown. That many of these newly revealed cities lay smouldering in ruins as a result of the Conqueror's progress was a matter he addressed only when the lessons moved from mapmaking to history. Tamara often wondered at his singleness of mind.

From facts brought by the latest messenger from Treclere, Alric had added to his new "Extended View of the World," and this he unrolled for Tamara and Geret, their father watching over their heads, the baby Anith asleep on his shoulder. Although Leron's wife Liniris often warned that it little befitted his dignity to be forever seen with a baby in his arms, nothing could keep Leron from playing daily with his youngest. Tamara felt both the younger children were unnecessarily coddled.

"The extent of these provinces we cannot know for certain" Alric was saying, as he moved his finger along the broad new vistas of lettered parchment. "I have had to reckon my distances from the accounts of marches, and of course we cannot know for certain how much territory the Agan's army may cover in a week, or indeed whether the same speed is always maintained. I would guess that the distance varies and that marches may be either fast or slow, as ordered. Most accounts agree that there are numerous, indeed numberless, households traveling in the train of the Agan, and these many people must establish their tent cities and then dismantle them again as they move from place to place."

"Why does he bring so many people?" asked Tamara. "Wouldn't warriors alone travel much faster?"

"The Anguls do not consider their campaigns as war, nor do they consider their numbers an army. They are a family, a tribe—or a group of related tribes—and it is their destiny to find new pasturelands for their droves of cattle. At least, this is what I have read about the first great Angul conqueror, Chanaga Gagan."

"Maybe it was true about him," said Tamara, "but I find it hard to believe that this Tibir person doesn't know that he is conquering the world, and with a big army. All that business about pasturage sounds like an excuse. How did they feed their beasts before they left Angulidan?"

Alric's eyes met the king's in adult amusement. "Herds increase, my lady. Reflect on the fields that support the king's stud farm at Sundrat. There we have twelve hundred acres in grass, a few miles square, no more. And what do we support? Two hundred horses, before the grass wears thin. And we have the most favorable of climates—a cold winter, yes, but grass for grazing nine months out of the year, green and thick. Angulidan, from all accounts, is bare and dry and brown, a wide land but a cruel one, where fifty or a hundred acres may hardly serve to support a single beast! It is not surprising that from time to time they burst out of the confines of their high stony land and turn their neighbors' fields and cities into pastureland for their cattle. Thus it was in the time of Chanaga Gagan, and thus it will be with the new Agan, the lame Tibir. Or so I gather from these reports.''

Although Geret was too young to read fluently, he was clever and understood things quickly, and now he looked up from peering at the map. ''Did the other army come here too? That Chanaga man?''

''No,'' answered Alric. ''Vazdz protected us.'' He touched his forehead briefly and Leron frowned. He disliked seeing how superstitious his people were becoming: it was one of the few subjects on which Tamara had seen him completely lose his temper. ''He conquered all that you see here,'' Alric continued, ''establishing a four-part empire with kingdoms given to his various sons, but he did not cross the ocean to come into our land.''

Tamara tossed her head. ''It probably wasn't good enough for him.'' Alric's look of shock mirrored Leron's own. Tamara disregarded them. ''What have we got that they would want? We don't have thousands of horses. We don't have mountains of rubies or lakes of pearls and all those other things you have read to us about. One of the Agan's wives probably wears more gold around her neck than we have in our entire treasury.''

Tamara looked her father challengingly in the eye. ''You showed me the treasury, remember? You said our riches were in the civility of our government. Well, this Agan probably wouldn't rate that very high as plunder! And I don't see how we can offer much pasturage compared to that great continent Alric is showing us, no matter how much better our climate is. So I think what you should do,'' this to her father again, ''is find out why the Agan has come here in the first place. Maybe you won't have to fight after all. Although I, for one,'' now she was looking at her little brother, ''do not fear to fight.''

''You sound like your mother,'' said Leron reminiscently. Tamara flushed with pleasure. ''And your instincts may well be as true as hers. It will be interesting to see what answer our ambassador brings with him from Treclere. He should have met the Agan's forces there a month ago or more. We should be hearing from Parric soon.''

Tamara slid her eyes sideways toward her half-brother. ''Perhaps the Agan has had him flayed and stuffed with straw, and will send him back tied to a donkey with an answer pinned to his robes," she suggested wickedly. Lord Parric was a great favorite and, as she had hoped, Geret burst into tears.

She realized immediately that she had overstepped the limits: Alric's look of shock was unfeigned and her father was amazed to speechlessness. Even Geret, who always forgave her everything, looked up at her through his wet eyelashes and said, with exceptional vehemence, "Sometimes I just wish you would go away and leave me alone." Leron was slow to reprove him, and his considering look turned Tamara's guilt to a deep feeling of unease.

As it happened, it was Geret who was sent away—sent with Anith and their mother on a trip for which Tamara had wept and pleaded only a year before. The islands of Melismala were now in close touch with Tredana through trade, and on the next ship to come from the east there was once again an invitation from Dansen for the royal children to come and visit him.

The year before, Leron had resisted Tamara's pleas on the grounds that the warlords of Paradon posed too great a threat to the shipping lanes. Now this seemed a remote danger, in comparison with the approach of Tibir the Lame and his hordes. It was a chance for safety that Leron seized on eagerly, but he was not able to convince his eldest daughter as easily as he had his wife. She knew her mother Sibyl would not have fled. Whatever pangs Tamara felt—as she watched the ship unfurl its sails and bow and dip its way out of the harbor—were softened by the thought of finally having her father's undivided attention for the first time since she was six, and he remarried. Her eyes remained dry: the brown one that was darker than her father's, and the blue one that startled everyone who looked into her face for the first time. Alone with her father, she waited for news from the west.

Spring was turning into summer when the first word finally came. It was not their long-awaited ambassador who brought it, but a hard-riding messenger from the Karabdu, who left his sweated and shaking horse in the outer court and came stiffly in past the suspicious guards, his bright desert silks sweeping the cobbles. Hastily summoned, Leron met him in the small audience chamber with Gannoc and Alric, Tamara close behind. Tamara smiled with delight to see her dearest friend from among the Karif's bodyguard, but Ibrasa's pleasant face remained set and grim and he only nodded to her as he drew his letter from the bosom of his gown. It was sealed in red wax with the Karif Ajjibawr's familiar device of a two-headed horse: Leron broke it open and handed it to Alric to be read aloud.

I send this letter by the hand of Ibrasa, son of Adaba, former Mekrif of the Tayyib, on whose soul be peace.

Given in haste at our summer encampment by AJJIBAWR DARYOZILIMAN, KARIF of all the KARABDU, Mekrif of the Ziliman, Master of Harses and Lord of The Land, to LERON of TREDANA, Governor of Villavac, Lord of Sundrat and Rym Treglad:

Know that the outlander who styles himself TIBIR AGAN, Emperor of the Angulidan nation, who crossed the straits of Sembat this last winter as you know, bringing in his train a host that is said to number one hundred thousand mounted warriors or more, has utterly reduced the walled cities of Luntar and Vahanavat. For two months he invested the city of Treclere until Master Varys crawled before him in the dirt, by this abasement sparing the lives of those within its walls. These walls the Agan's company is presently dismantling.

While the armies of the Agan were encamped before Treclere, messages were sent to us in the desert, calling on us to submit and make clear the pathway of Tredana. To these we have answered neither yea or nay, sending back instead many rich and costly presents, including three hundred head of our finest horses. Knowing not what adventure it may please Vazdz to bring us here, we have caused this letter to be carried to you as swift as may be. Of council we have none. The sand which has been our shield these many years will not protect us now: if the Agan should so wish, he might set his men to pick it up grain by grain. It is his boast that rock, sand, river, ocean or ice are alike a highway for his men and not anywhere is there a voice of defiance to tell him that he lies.

LERON of TREDANA, farewell to you and yours: if we do not meet on earth again we will feast together in Paradise.

Tamara spoke as soon as Alric had finished reading. "Ibrasa," she asked, "what happened to your father?" Ibrasa

tightened his fingers a little on the silver dagger in his sash: his
eyes were very cold and blue.

"The messengers of the Agan met my father and his men
at the desert's edge. A company of mounted archers rode as
bodyguard to the Angul lords. They spoke insolently to the
Tayyib and demanded that he conduct them to the Karif
without delay. And although there was anger in the Tayyib's
heart, he did as they said because of the promise he had made
to the Karif. And a little way into the desert, the Angul
leader, a man named Aksu, demanded of the Tayyib that they
change horses, for he said that he had a mind to ride one of
the famous Karabdin breed before bringing any back to join
the herds of the great Tibir. To this the Tayyib did not
consent, and when Aksu laid hand upon his bridle the Tayyib
jerked it free with a mighty oath. Now among the Karabdu
one might expect such an argument to lead to the drawing of
swords, but among the soldiers of Angulidan it is not so. One
of them set an arrow to the string, and turning in his saddle a
little let fly with such speed that the Tayyib was knocked
from his horse and lay dead on the ground before any of them
knew that an enemy's bow had been strung. As the rest of the
Tayyib's men drew their swords, they too were struck down,
some wounded and some killed. I found them thus, prisoners
to the Angul lord, when I rode out to meet my father and
bring the Agan's emissaries to the Karif. And because of my
promise to the Karif, I had to let Aksu and his warriors live.
Vazdz willing, they will not live long."

"Our respects to your family," said Leron. "Your father
was a famous warrior."

Ibrasa bowed his head. "The Karif," he said, "was most
displeased." Gannoc raised his eyebrows at the understate-
ment. "If you wish to send a message back with me," Ibrasa
continued, "I will wait for it: if not, I will beg to exchange
horses here that I may return to my tribespeople as soon as
possible."

"See to our guest's refreshment, Gannoc, and tell the
stable master of his need. Then come and help us write our
answer to the Karif."

As Gannoc and Ibrasa left the room, Leron sat down
heavily in his chair. At his nod, Alric sat also, and in her
corner Tamara dropped her chin into her hands, quiet and
watchful.

"An army of one hundred thousand," said Leron. "It is beyond imagining; yet, it is only a small part of the Agan's forces, if we are to believe the tales. A little army for a small campaign on a poor, unpopulous continent."

"They are not honorable," said Tamara. "They shot the Tayyib with arrows when he had only his sword. If we are going to win against them, we will have to learn their rules."

Alric nodded. "The princess has touched the heart of the matter. If we fight them according to our own rules, they will laugh at our honor as they ride their horses over the bodies of our champions."

"What would you have us practice?" asked Leron. "The stab in the back? The attack in the night?"

"I would not have your majesty practice anything. I only wish it were possible for us to learn more of the ways of Angulidan before the Agan and his armies sweep over us."

Leron shook his head bitterly. "I have no wish to learn anything more about them than that they have left us. Alric, take your pen. We have a letter to compose."

When Gannoc returned, Leron read him the first draft, and the steward listened impassively to the king's words of support and resolve. "It may be that Tibir will leave the desert untouched," said Gannoc. "He has made it clear that we are known to him, that it is Tredana he seeks next. There is nothing in the desert if the Karabdu do not choose to stand and fight. His army might as well war on the wind. I think we underestimate this Agan if we think he must cross the desert to reach us. And everyone who has underestimated him has lived to regret it, though some have not lived long. The mountains that close our western routes, north of the desert, are not impassable. Arbytis the High Priest crossed them in his day, and Herrard the Traveler more recently. You have climbed those passes yourself, sire, when you left Arbytis in the peaceful valley. And wherever a man has once set foot, the armies of Tibir will not find it impossible to go."

"Should they cross the mountains," said Leron, they could fall upon Villavac without warning. Word must be sent to Glisser at once. He must set watchmen on the heights, as well as along the highway." He paused. "It is no doubt as you say. The Agan will not spend himself in foolish desert skirmishing. The Karabdu alone of all the peoples of this conti-

nent may yet avoid the Conqueror. We all may come to envy
them their isolation.''

As Leron thought out loud, Tamara narrowed her eyes in
concentration. She was well aware how much her father
wished he had been able to force her to go to safety in
Melismala. Perhaps if he were convinced that safety lay in the
desert, he might be persuaded to send her there for refuge.
Now it might be possible for her to fulfill the great dream of
her life.

II

Neither Leron nor Ibrasa gave Tamara any trouble. Her
father eagerly fell in with her plans, believing them to be his
own idea, as she had intended. And Ibrasa did not show
surprise when she asked him to be her guide.

Tamara had had Ibrasa under her thumb since she was three
years old and had traveled with her father to meet the Karabdu
in the pasturelands south of Villavac. He had been in the
Karif's bodyguard. Despite his dignity as a warrior, Ibrasa
had also been a gentle young man, well used to children.
After all, he was one of the Tayyib's more than forty sons.
While Leron and the Karif met in council, Ibrasa had taken
Tamara for rides on his horse and given her lessons in mounted
warfare, using a sheep he had roped from a neighboring herd.
Tamara had skinned her hands and her knees trying to learn to
cling to the side of a galloping, or at least a hurrying sheep,
and Ibrasa had seemed to her then the sum of all perfection in
mankind.

Later, when Tamara was seven, the Karif had come to
Tredana and once more Ibrasa had ridden in his attendance.
However, his lustre had been dimmed by the proximity of
Ajjibawr, his chief. It was then that Tamara had begun wearing her blue glass ring on a thong about her neck; not because
it was a token left from her lost mother, but because origi-
nally it had been a gift from the Karif to Sibyl, so many years
before.

At seven, Tamara had wondered how she could have been
so blind before not to see that in Ajjibawr the world's only
perfect man had been made. His face, his gestures, the way

he sat his horse, even the use of snuff—which her father disapprovingly referred to as a filthy habit. . . . Tamara had forced one of her servants to steal a snuffbox out of the Karif's room, and she still slept with it under her pillow whenever she felt in need of comfort. From time to time she would flick open the ivory lid and gently sniff the pungent contents, now dry and powdery with age.

To Tamara, the five years since that visit had seemed an eternity. She would never forget how kindly the Karif had spoken to her then, or more particularly how he had promised her a trained warhorse when next she visited him in the desert. Now, without actually lying to Ibrasa, she made it sound as though the Karif had been expecting her visit for many years. Knowing well the fascination of her odd-colored eyes, Tamara looked up at him from under her heavy dark lashes and watched his own eyes flick from her brown eye to her blue one. "You will have to ride like a warrior and not like a lady," he said at last when she had exhausted her arguments. "We will follow the new posting road as far as Villavac, then a Karabdin horse from the stables and into the True Land. God grant the desert is still our refuge."

The posting road was a recent creation of Leron's, and one of which he was particularly proud. The old rutted tracks that crossed his kingdom had been widened and smoothed, with stables and post houses placed every fifty miles. It made Tamara feel very important to receive from her father official communications to be delivered to each post master along the Villavac road; she was so excited that she impatiently pulled herself free of Leron's parting embrace, and did not remember to feel guilty until many hours later.

It was late in the afternoon when they left Tredana, and that night she enjoyed the casual freedom of falling asleep wrapped in a blanket on the bumpy ground. But if sleep came quickly, so too did the dawn, and they were back in the saddle and riding west again before she was fully awake. When they rose from breakfast after the second stage, Tamara's legs almost gave way. She did not say anything to Ibrasa, however; she only smiled and walked stiffly over to her new mount. Ibrasa was likewise silent, but instead of waiting for her to mount, he locked his fingers together and lifted her up with a gentle heave under her foot. As she sank into the saddle, she wondered if she could ever have gotten up there without assistance.

Tamara drowsed in the saddle, and when Ibrasa told her they could reach Villavac that night if she were willing to ride a little way through the dark, she wearily agreed. A bright moon was visible in the evening sky and as night fell the moon's white radiance filled up the landscape around them. Wildflowers glowed like stars, cupping the moonlight in their petals; they floated above the darker earth, blackness trapped under their leaves. As the round moon marched across the sky, it made her feel as though they were standing still, or worse—falling behind. The road glimmered before them; they trotted and cantered on, but the moon still slowly out-stripped them on its path toward the western horizon. Tamara was asleep in the saddle when they reached Villavac, and only woke a little when Ibrasa lifted her down and carried her into the governor's palace.

It was silence that woke Tamara next morning. Outside the big open window, the sky was red with dawn and filled with birds. Inside the big house it was oddly still. Usually, when Tamara lay abed in her room at Villavac, the air was filled with the bustle and clamor of servants opening shuttered rooms, dusting off furniture, banging doors. There would be faint laughter and sometimes scolding from the kitchen regions, and finally some young farm girl would be clattering in with hot water and towels, excited by the visit of the royal family and the opening of the usually dark and empty governor's palace.

Thoroughly awake, Tamara sat up and realized that her bed was unmade; a blanket had been thrown over the ticking for her to lie on, and another covered her up. The pillows had no covers, and the floor was dusty. Soberly, she got up and dressed in her well traveled clothes, then went out to the closet under the stairs where a hand pump brought up cold water from the cistern. She splashed her face, slicked back her curls, rubbed the dirt from her hands onto her riding trousers and went downstairs in search of breakfast.

There was no one in the state dining room, and dust sheets covered the banquet table and chairs. She could hear faint murmurs from below, however, and went down another flight to the cellar and kitchens. There was a small fire burning on the vast cooking hearth, and Ibrasa was just bringing a small pot of coffee to the boil. The steward of Villavac, Glisser, pushed himself up heavily from the table and bowed several times.

"You are welcome in Villavac, my lady. But even had we expected your visit, I fear we could have offered little hospitality. I have emptied the city for fear of this outlander's attack. We did not keep on a staff for the maintenance of this house."

"We're not staying." Tamara sank down on her heels by the hearth and Glisser plopped back onto the bench. "My father is sending me to stay with the Karabdu. He gave us a message for you. Have you seen it yet?"

Glisser gestured to some papers on the table before him. "I will do as His Majesty commands, of course, but the idea of an army passing over the northern mountains strains the imagination. Goats yes, or perhaps a solitary adventurer, but a force of men? With horses?"

Ibrasa poured out coffee and broke apart the day-old flat bread that was warming on the bricks. "You cannot judge the efforts of another by your own abilities," he said at length, and Tamara thought his gaze lingered on Glisser's pudgy form a little too long to be polite. "Our friend Rassam, whom you call Herrard, has crossed that range more than once. And it is well known that in the year of the destruction of the Great Queen Simirimia, Leron and Sibyl crossed those same mountains, taking with them Arbytis the High Priest to his final resting place in the Sacred Valley. Do you think the World Conqueror fears to follow in the path of children, in the steps of an old man dying on horseback?"

Glisser slurped his coffee noisily and swallowed a mouthful of bread. "The path of a solitary traveler, or two or three, is not the road for an army. I will post lookouts as the king has commanded, but still I say we must look to the desert. Your tribes will know of the Conqueror's advance long before we do, of that you can be sure." He punctuated his statement with another big bite of bread, and was still chewing it when Ibrasa was startled to his feet by the sound of men hurrying down the stairs. He had his hand on his sword when they burst into the room but Glisser only looked up complacently and motioned with his hand.

The steward's guards were farmers like himself, men who gave up a few weeks each year in service to the crown; their weapons hung on them awkwardly and their boots seemed to pinch. Tamara made a mental note to see about improving matters in the future. "Lord Glisser," said one. "The king's ambassador has returned from Treclere! He bears messages to Tredana! He has talked with the World Conqueror!"

Glisser frowned. "Is he wounded? Why does he not come directly to me?"

"He waits above. We have sent for the surgeon to attend him. He says he was treated well enough, but his feet are frozen from traveling over the mountains."

Ibrasa looked at Tamara and then at Glisser. Glisser's broad face reddened. "What mountains would these be?"

"The northern mountains, sir. But the Angul army has gone back. That is in the message. Let the ambassador tell you himself. He waits above."

Tamara rose and stepped forward now, Ibrasa behind her with his hand still on his sword. "I will speak with my father's ambassador," she announced, and let them follow her up the stairs, her only regret being that she was thus unable to see Glisser's face.

In the small audience chamber, two chairs had been pushed together to make a temporary couch, and on this Lord Parric half reclined; his cut boots lay on the floor and his feet were in the lap of an old man who was muttering and shaking his head in disapproval. He made as though to rise when he saw Tamara in the doorway, but she hurried over and put her hand on his shoulder, pushing him back. "My father is going to be very angry with you if you've let yourself get hurt," she said. "The only reason he let you go was that you promised you would be careful."

Parric laughed and fell back on his elbow, then grimaced at the proddings of the doctor. "I was as careful as any man might be, who travels with the World Conqueror. He is one, however, who knows not the meaning of impossible. His enemies charge that he never changes his course once it is set. And that accusation he takes as compliment. When he handed me these letters for the king, he said, 'Tell him that the Fortunate Lord has never turned aside his horse from any purpose. I have achieved what I started out to do, and Tredana will not interest me this year. After that, who can tell?' And, having crossed the most villainous mountains imaginable, he and his men rode out in a great circle and drove together the

sheep that pasture there in the high valley, to slaughter them
and feast before returning back over the mountains.''

Glisser interrupted. "My sheep? They ate my sheep?"

"If your sheep were marked with blue between the ears,
yes, they took your sheep, and by now the herd has vanished
into the bellies of the Angul army.''

Horror-struck, Glisser sank into a dust-sheeted chair. "Why
did they cross the mountains if they meant to go back again?''

"The Conqueror said it was to see me safely home. I think
rather it was to prove to himself, and to us as well, that the
mountains no longer form a shield around us. I also think it
may have been to seek out the hidden valley where Arbytis
sleeps. But the army is so vast I cannot tell you if they were
successful in that. I had to be carried much of the last way.
The Empress was very angry with me for not accepting felt
boots, such as the Anguls wear. I see now that she was
right.''

Tamara looked at him in wonder. "The Empress? There
really are women with the army?''

"The World Conqueror goes nowhere without his family.
The lesser wives and the small children stayed behind,
encamped about Treclere, but the old Empress rides like a
soldier, and was with us even passing over the mountains.
She made those descents on foot, where the Conqueror himself could not manage without being lowered by ropes, in a
woven litter. Of course, he is very crippled.''

"He really is the 'lame Tibir'?''

"I would not say it to his face. It is a term of contempt that
they used in Samida, before he conquered their empire. But,
yes, he drags his leg when he walks, which is never far. And
his right arm is locked at the elbow. You would not think it to
see him ride and manage a spear and shield.''

Suddenly Parric flinched and went white as the surgeon's
attendants placed a steaming cloth over his feet and ankle.
Tamara took a quick look and sat down on the edge of the
chair. "Why don't you show me your letters," she said,
"while the doctors look to your feet. Lord Glisser, fetch a
secretary. We will need to make copies for the Karif." Glisser
nodded and went out, and Ibrasa gave her a faint smile of
approval.

Parric undid the leather case stamped with Leron's device
and handed it to Tamara. She had often carried dispatch cases

to her father and had hung over his shoulder while he opened
them, but this was the first time she had ever opened one
herself. Her heart hammered and she felt very important, and a
little frightened. Inside there were several long, careful reports in Parric's familiar hand. The letter from Tibir was
different, traced in heavy black ink on a long, narrow piece of
parchment. Instead of the usual salutation, there was only
Tibir's name in gold ink at the top and under it, in letters a
little smaller, Leron's name in red. Although the style of the
letters was strange, Tamara could read it easily.

"Did he write this letter himself?"

"The Conqueror neither reads nor writes. However he
converses well in many tongues. And learned men travel
with his court, reading him history and science and the
study of the stars, which he discusses with them in the
evening. When he gives a letter he does so privately to
one secretary, then chooses another at random to read it
back to him. If one word is not as he said, he remarks
the discrepancy. His writers have learned to be accurate.
Whatever is in that letter will be exactly as the Conqueror
wished."

TIBIR AGAN, Lord of the Fortunate Conjunction,
to LERON, King of Tredana.

Given north of Villavac, in the mountains.
I have crossed the straits of Sembat as you know, and
caused the cities of Luntar and Vahanavat, which resisted
my coming, to be leveled to the ground. To prove that
my severity is only equaled by my generosity, I have also
caused these cities to be built again, and better than
they were before. The heads of the defiant are piled in
nine great columns at the gates as a warning to the future.
Treclere, which opened its gates to me, I have spared, and
Varys its prince has bowed before me and now coins money in
my name. Who challenges him, risks my wrath. Likewise, the
Karif of the Karabdu has not resisted my coming and has sent
me many fine presents. It would not be foolish for Tredana
to do likewise. Having found in the mountains that which I
sought, I return to the Heart of the World, leaving Varys to
be my spokesman here. When I have completed the task which

awaits me, I will return. Varys will inform you and the Karif of what tribute and levies are acceptable to me while you await my coming.

Tamara fell silent and looked at Ibrasa. He shook his head. "The Karif will not be pleased by this."

Tamara raised her eyebrows. "Neither will my father!"

Chapter Two

ROSEDALE

I

The cafeteria at Rosedale had not discovered health food. Over salty canned peas, salty pink pressed turkey, salty instant potatoes and watery coffee, Lynn and Sibby discussed their afternoon plans. Lynn forced down a swallow and spoke first. "What do you think all that daughter stuff was? A crossed circuit? Or something you never told me? I always thought it was pretty lucky you and Mike never had any kids."

Sibby laughed. "Luck had nothing to do with it. And no secret daughters that I'm aware of. But that Tredana stuff is something else. My psyche must scream it out all the time. Why, why, why?"

"Beats me. Let's visit one of the mediums after lunch. You can ask her."

"Only if she's cheap."

Lynn rolled her eyes and started quoting start-up salaries for office work.

Sibby made a rude noise. "Lynn, I know I only got serious about my riding to get away from Mike. It was just about the only outdoor sport he didn't like and wasn't very good at. But I more than like it. I love it. When I'm on a horse, I really feel free. There's space. I'm alive. You know, I don't think I will ever be able to live in a house again. The room over Laura's barn does great for now, but in another year I think I'll head west and see if I can get some kind of horse job out there. Even wrangling for an outfitter would be okay. I'd rather spend the rest of my life in a tent on the plains than ever live in the suburbs again. I lived in that damn hot fancy overstuffed box with Mike for eleven years! Never again!''

"What about books? Music? Movies?"

"My parents bought me a very expensive education. It may not have made me employable, but it did give me 600 years of English literature. I wasn't called the human tape recorder for nothing. There isn't an Elizabethan tragedy obscure enough for me to have forgotten it.'' Sibby raised a clenched fist and declaimed:

I hold the fates bound fast in iron chains
And with my hand turn fortune's wheel about
And sooner shall the sun fall from its sphere
Than Tamburlaine be slain or overcome.

"When I need amusement I can run through another play. In my head."

After lunch they wandered around the streets of Rosedale. Up Larch, down Ash, across Maple, down Elm. "I feel like I'm wandering through the letters of a gigantic Druid alphabet," said Sibby. "I wonder what these runes spell from the air?"

Lynn took it more seriously, scrutinizing each little house to see if this was the one with the right aura. Halfway along Elm, she paused. "I like the look of this one," she said. "What do you think?"

Sibby shrugged. At least this one didn't have a cement fountain, plaster gnomes, china cats on the porch roof and an "I Count None But Sunny Hours" sundial. It was sober red brick, with only a little crenalating over the parlor window. The card with the medium's name was businesslike, professionally printed, and gave a winter (or emergency? thought Sibby) address in Providence. "Sure," she said, and Lynn rang the bell.

Mrs. MacInnes welcomed them with pleasant dignity. Her parlor, a little outdated with its overstuffed furniture and looped lace curtains, was remarkable only for the extraordinary quantity of American Indian motifs. Not handcrafted objects from the American Southwest, but manufactured souvenirs of the American Twenties: bronze "Scout" bookends and a "Prayer to the Great Spirit" lamp, an "End of the

Trail'' metal ashtray, and, on the walls, rotogravures of men dressed in leather and eagle's feathers mixed with bright, childish oil paintings framed in odd assemblages of woven twigs, beads and braided gimp. Over the table at which she had them sit, the photo of a handsome, hawk-nosed man gazed at them through the camera's eye.

"That's Golden Cloud," she remarked cheerfully. "I'm very fortunate to have him as my guide to the Other Side."

Sibby spoke unguardedly. "How did you get the photograph?"

"I found the photograph, my dear. Golden Cloud led me to it, in an old issue of *Life*. Of course, it had been mislabeled." She had Lynn sit with them to improve the circle, then touched Sibby's hand lightly with her fingertips. As though shocked, she started backward, then touched her again more carefully. "But what power, my dear. You are a medium yourself. All you need is some training."

Taking Sibby's left hand in her right, she held her own left hand above it, palm facing palm. Sibby was immediately aware of a pulsing sense of warmth and energy, although the hand that actually touched her was cool. She met Mrs. MacInnes' eyes blankly.

"You feel that warmth, do you not? It is a sign. You are a healer. You have done very little with your gift, however." She cocked her head a little. "Some of the heat's more destructive powers have been used, I think. As for healing . . . with animals, perhaps? You have pets? Or a farm? I sense large animals."

Almost unwillingly, Sibby volunteered, "Horses."

"And when these horses are sick, you put your hands on them and they get better, am I right?"

"Well, I comfort them, of course. . . ."

Mrs. MacInnes shook her head. "You put your hands on them and you heal them, I can see it. Golden Cloud is showing me the picture."

Angrily, Sibby wished to repudiate Golden Cloud and all his tawdry works, but she could see the pictures too, clear in her memory. Hands placed on a horse's pain-filled belly, on a swollen knee, on a sweated, nervous neck. But surely that was nothing supernatural. Just the soothing touch of a horse handler. It was true they always responded, but wasn't that

just part of the general gift, the knack with horses? Not
according to Golden Cloud.

"You must develop this gift, use it. To heal is the greatest
gift we can be given. Never have I felt such heat in an
untrained hand. When you learn how to use it properly, you
will not even have to lay your hands on in the physical plane.
You will be able to send the healing with your mind. It is
well that you have moved out of that man's house. I do not
like to see a marriage break up, but there were no blessings in
that union. A warped spirit like his will oppress your gifts."

Mrs. MacInnes smiled. "You were wise to come to Rosedale.
This is a clear place. There are no shadows here. Absorb the
spirit and let the healing flow into your hands." She closed
her eyes. "Golden Cloud, be still. If she wants to know
more, she can come back later. This is quite enough for her to
deal with now." She opened her eyes again. "Golden Cloud
is full of stories for you. They sound quite fantastical, but I
have never known him to lie. To color the truth a little, but
not an outright lie." She picked up a box of black lacquer and
made Sibby meet her eyes. "Now you must tell me when in
September you were born. The twenty-second?" She chuckled at Sibby's blank amazement. "My dear, my dear, this is
my profession. If I can't tell a Virgo on the cusp of Libra
when she walks in, then perhaps I should be doing something
else. Now let me show you something you may not have seen
before."

She opened the box and took out the well-worn cards it
contained. They were not one of the commercial Tarot decks
familiar to Sibby from college, but a beautifully engraved
pack of cards, colored in rich, deep tones. "My mother
brought these from Russia when she fled, before the First
War," remarked Mrs. MacInnes. She shuffled with the ease of
a riverboat gambler, and the dexterity of her soft pink hands
was incongruous. "And here you are," she remarked, pulling
out a card and turning it over. "The Queen of Swords, which
is to say Virgo, and crossed by the Surrealist, or Mercury.
And what binds them together? The Great Goddess in her
doubled form, which is Virgo also. Now, if you were more
Libra in your temperament, I would have expected to see the
Empress there instead. Here is your foundation—the Emperor, how odd—he could be a man of the Scorpio sort, or
simply your own mind controlling the physical plane. You must
watch out for those Scorpios. What I could tell you about my

first husband, Dmitri. Now, behind you—of course, Temper-
ance reversed. We have already mentioned the failure of that
union. Was your husband born in May? I thought so. Taurus
is not for you, my dear. You need a more exciting combina-
tion. It has been a burden for you—or will be. Look, overhead, there is the Seven of Swords, Virgo and Mercury
again, this time significating a burden being carried, but to a
favorable end. And what lies in the immediate future?'' The
cards seemed to slip out of the deck into her fingers, in
answer to her rapid questions. ''The Chariot! Some call it the
Charioteer, and some the Conqueror. It is willpower; it is
Sagittarius, half-man, half-horse, all deadly archer. And what
is the greater future? The Wheel! A strange card. Some say it
has no astrological meaning, some give it one of those new
planets that the ancients did not know. I prefer to think it is
greater than that. The Zodiac itself, perhaps, turning slowly
through the ages. Aquarius approaches the equinox now, and
Pisces must give way after 2000 years of the rule of the
Hanged Man, the martyred god. Aquarius is the High Priest,
you know, the one who parts the veil of the temple. Now tell
me, have you ever before seen a horoscope using the Tarot?''

Both Sibby and Lynn shook their heads. As Mrs. MacInnes
scooped up her cards, Sibby greedily took in their images:
the Tzarina dressed in white, carrying a bright silver sword;
the ancient Emperor hunched under his tall gold helmet; the
Asiatic horseman, driving two galloping ponies, his short,
bent bow on his back. As the cards disappeared into their
black box, Mrs. MacInnes spoke brightly. ''Perhaps you will
come back again? If not for the cards, then for Golden Cloud?
I am sure he will want to tell you more.''

Fairly hooked, Sibby nodded. They paid and left in silence,
and walked slowly down the street toward the pond. There
were benches on the dock and they sat down side by side,
watching the ducks. The sunlight lay flat and glittering on the
water; one after another the ducks upended themselves and
waggled their tails in the air.

''You know,'' said Lynn, ''I first came here that year I
was trying to teach at Community College. You were busy
with Mike, fixing up your house, and Bob was busy getting
his practice going and I thought I was going to go crazy. No
one to talk to. Up till then I had really believed in the power
of literature. I thought I was going to transform empty lives,

and the kids just laughed at me. Not openly; they were pretty decent kids. But we'd go over something step by step and I'd think they were paying attention and then, bam! I'd ask a question and they'd look at me like I came from outer space. I didn't know that my course was supposed to be a gut course, for jocks. I didn't know they were afraid of getting low grades in Communication Electronics, so they covered themselves with Contemporary English Verse. One of them wrote me a whole paper referring to 'Under Milkweed' by Thomas Dylan. And it wasn't a joke."

Sibby smiled in sympathy. "But you were teaching all the weird writers. What's a kid in Lowell, Massachusetts, going to do with Auden or Eliot? You'd have done better with the seventeenth century, with Webster and Tourneur. Noises off, blood running from under the arras, screech owls, choruses of madmen. As far as I'm concerned, Eliot bombed on everything except funny cats and 'The Wasteland.' Remember when I memorized 'The Wasteland' in forty-five minutes, at that party? I won a case of beer for Mike. And I still remember the whole damn thing from April to Shantih."

Lynn wasn't really listening. "When I first came here," she said, "all I could see was the incredible bad taste. The lawn ornaments and the plastic ivy. Then the peace hit me and I began to relax and wonder if it was all some sort of test—you know how, in stories, the hero always has to look past things as they seem in order to understand things as they are? Well, you know, I think it's easier in lots of ways to be brave in the face of the frightening than it is to be courteous in the face of the ridiculous. Look at Sir Gawain."

Sibby laughed. "So Rosedale Campground is like the monstrous bride? It keeps a sleazy image on purpose, to weed out superficial visitors? What an embarrassing thought. No snob need seek spiritual enlightenment here. You could be right. I wonder how Mrs. MacInnes knew about my divorce. And my birthday."

"Maybe Golden Cloud told her."

"Maybe. But I don't know how much of his intuition I can afford. The hotel at six dollars a day is just my style, but Golden Cloud at fifteen dollars an interview will eat through my life savings in no time at all."

"I could loan you the money."

"I don't like to borrow what I can't pay back."

"Sibby, it's nothing to me, you know that."

"Yeah, but it is something to me. Look, you really don't mind loaning me ten dollars?"

"Anything you want."

"Okay, then I will borrow ten dollars. There's a hack stable just about a mile down the road, and I'd love to take a spin through these woods on horseback."

"Sibby, that is absolutely ridiculous. You ride horses for a living. People pay you to ride their horses for them. Why on earth would you pay ten dollars to ride some old plug while you're on vacation?"

"I wouldn't pay ten dollars of my own. But this is found money. And I need some time to think."

The Circle *R* did run mostly to plugs, and, as Sibby had feared, there was no such thing as an English saddle. The owner was pleasant however and his horses were neither thin nor sore. He chose for her a little chestnut gelding with one blue eye, and except for Sibby's fear of dragging her long legs on the ground she could find no fault with the selection. The animal still had some ambition and was not so thoroughly barn sour that she would have to spend her hour forcing him away from his companions and battling at every turn in the trail.

The woods were sparse and spiky, the ground sandy. Away from the edge of the road, the blowing papers and broken bottles gave way to thicker bushes and a carpet of leaves and pine needles. When they reached the first clearing, the gelding clearly indicated that this was the canter stretch, so she let him lollop across, enjoying his bouncy stride. They were halfway over the fallen log at the end before Sibby remembered the Western saddle and put her hand on the horn to protect herself. Now the little chestnut had got into the spirit of the thing and was beginning to enjoy the sensation of a rider who was neither timid nor a beginner. He shook his head, snorted and even gave a careful, playing buck. Sibby laughed and patted his neck. "Have fun, sweetie."

To the left, a narrow track rose up a rocky incline, leaving the main path to wander upward, and Sibby set her horse to the climb. He scrambled up happily, and at the top they came out on a bit of ledge that gave a panoramic view of the surrounding woods. She could even see the glitter of the Atlantic, far to the south. For a while they just sat and contemplated the view, then Sibby remembered her ten dollars ticking away on the clock and reluctantly turned her mount back down the hill.

On the way down another little track branched off from the first, and since it also led downhill Sibby chose it in order to cover a little more territory. At the bottom of this path however, they ran into a bit of forest fencing—rusty wire mesh, with a rickety gate across the path. The clock of a lesson horse was ticking in the little chestnut's brain, too, and his sense of direction was equally acute. He knew he was in the last half of his hour and that he was headed for home, and these two facts made him impatient enough to butt his chest up against the gate and refuse to stand still long enough for her to open it. It was hard to lean down past the stupid high pommel and lethal horn. Once more Sibby reached for the wire loop, and once more the chestnut bounced up against the gate, instead of turning sideways as she asked.

Telling him sharply to behave Sibby leaned forward once more, and in response to her warning shake of the reins the little horse suddenly threw up his head in panic, anticipating a jerk on his bit. His head rose just as her fingers reached the wire, and his hard skull smacked her neatly on the temple.

Letting go of the wire, Sibby helplessly clutched her horse's neck, while blue and white stars exploded in back of her eyes. Her equilibrium took a sickening roller-coaster lunge, and for a moment she thought she would fight her way back to the top, that her eyes would open and that it would be all right. Then she was plunging back down into the darkness again and the little stars glittered and went out.

II

The stars were glittering again when Sibby opened her eyes. They were far away and pale in a deep grey sky, and the throbbing in her head was so great that even those little points of light were too sharp to be looked at. She covered her eyes with her hand. So . . . her arms could move. She tested her feet and knees and neck, and finally pushed herself up off the ground. That the little horse was long gone did not surprise her. When she looked around in the starlight, she was however much surprised, for the woods were also gone.

She was standing in a desolate, open plain, blank and bare as far as she could see. The ground was gritty. She brushed the sand from her breaches and stooped over to examine more closely the rocks and coarse dark soil about her feet. It might have been the surface of the moon. The wind had a hollow, sweeping sound, and there was no rustle of branches, no smell of greenery, no animal sounds or bird noises in the night.

She put her hands to her aching head and took a few steps forward. The ground crunched under her boots. She had heard that a concussion victim might relapse after several seemingly normal days, or fall into a temporary amnesia. But she was still dressed in the clothes of that last ride in the woods. She rubbed her fingers down the well-worn inner surface of her boots and the cold, damp hairs of the little chestnut horse rolled up in her fingers. It did not seem that much time could have elapsed since her fall. Not much time, and yet she was now obviously far distant from the woods of lower Cape Cod.

The light continued to grow as Sibby walked. The dawn illumined a flat half-circle of horizon, above which there suddenly stood three suns. Sibby passed her hand over her aching eyes and looked again. She was sure that the lights on either side were optical illusions, sun-dogs, but they shone as round and bright and hard-edged as the sun in the middle. As they rose higher they merged together into one great sun and it was morning.

Sibby's thirst increased as the morning advanced. She tried to remember if ever before she had felt thirsty in a dream, and could not think of any other time. Under her feet the grit gave way to coarse sand, the sand to pebbles, the pebbles to small, smooth stones. Finally Sibby's boots, old and worn as they were, became impossible for walking on the rounded stones; she pulled them off with difficulty and stringing them together with her belt, slung them over her shoulder and went on in stockinged feet.

The single sun passed its noon and began a slow, circling descent. Sibby's thirst was very great. As her shadow lengthened ahead of her, her stride became shorter, her periods of rest longer. Suddenly she stopped and turned her head. There was a smell of water in the air, the claylike smell of water evaporating off of stone.

She changed course, following her nose and then her ears. There was a faint sound of trickling somewhere among the rocks. The sound increased, the smell grew stronger. A sudden burbling led her to the right and she stopped, bewildered by the sound of water under her feet. The water gurgled again and finally she understood its meaning. Around her, everything was rock—a sea of stones as far as the horizon, large and small, red, brown and grey. And somewhere under these tons of stones, this avalanche of rock and boulder, a stream still followed its ancient path directly below her feet, utterly out of reach.

Through the long day and into the night, she followed the sound of water flowing southward under the stones. Nowhere did the water rise to the surface. Midmorning of the second day, Sibby dropped to her knees for the hundredth time and put her ear to the ground. The sound came up quite clearly as did the maddening cool scent. It seemed nearer than before. She pulled out a few stones and others slid in to fill the gap again, most no bigger than small melons, but so many of them. She paused, then slid her narrow belt of stiff, cheap leather out of the boot tabs. Working carefully, she could push it in among the stones, gently chivying it past each turn and obstruction. If the water was less than a few feet down, there was a chance. . . . She pushed until only the buckle remained in her fingers, then slowly pulled back. The end was definitely damp. Now she tore off one of her cuffs and, separating the hem, tied it through the end hole of the belt. When she tried to push the bit of cloth down among the stones, it stuck immediately. She tore the rag smaller with her teeth and tried again. This time the belt went down all the way, and the rag, carefully withdrawn, was wet. Sibby squeezed the drops onto her tongue and relief swept over her. She closed her eyes and opening them again half expected to find herself awake and back in familiar surroundings. But she was still kneeling in the midst of rock desolation, in the strangely brilliant light of an alien morning.

Midafternoon, she found a spot where the rocky covering lay less than a foot thick. She was able to bring up enough water for real gulping swallows. Both sleeves were sacrificed at the shoulder, one for mopping up drinking water, the other for a washrag. Thirst satisfied, she now felt cold, and very hungry. That night, hunger and confusion of mind troubled

her sleep, filling it with strange sounds and visions and fre-
quent awakenings. Each time she closed her eyes, she told
herself the sounds were illusions, but still she startled awake
again hearing rustling, distant murmurs, the faint jingling of
bells.

She woke before dawn of the third day to find the sky filled
with a strange, low light that slanted yellowly on the stones.
The glow increased, then receded into full dark again. Panic
seized her. A hooded figure, dressed in brown, seemed to be
looking back over its shoulder at her from the south. She could
not bring her body awake as quickly as her mind. When she
finally jerked her head up and moved her arms, there was
nothing to be seen but darkness.

At true dawn she arose and walked slowly toward the place
where she had seemed to see the figure. She had not gone far
when the stones underfoot began to be mixed with pebbles
and the pebbles with sand. The edge of the rocky spill shone
clearly in the light before her, and where the last stones
spread out on the edge of the black sands, the water flowed
out silently from beneath them. At her feet, it spread wide
and golden in the morning sun. Sibby fell on her knees and
rested her face against the cold, quiet surface of the stream.

It was several minutes before her dulled mind began to
make sense of the marks in the sand. This was where the
animals came to drink. There were many marks, both cloven
hoofs and claws; somewhere there must be fodder growing,
green grass, bushes, trees. She braided back her long wet hair
and set out along the watercourse, barefoot, her boots slung
over her shoulder.

Through the long morning and the longer afternoon she
walked, and into the endless dusk. The low hills which she
had taken for her goal now seemed a little closer, and there
were dark patches visible on them that might be trees or
shelter. Her bare arms prickled with the cold, and finally she
stooped to pull on her socks, which she was carrying to save
from wear. As she straightened up, a pair of eyes met hers
unblinkingly; they were low and set close together and shone
with a reddish gleam. The animal itself was a vague shadow.

Carefully, Sibby stood up and slowly took hold of one of
her boots. "Who are you?" she asked softly, and her answer
was a startled blink and a sudden rush. "Stop it right now!"
she commanded in her best horse-scolding voice, and the eyes

blinked again about ten feet away. Now she could see it was a small, slinking, scavenger sort of animal, with heavy dark fur and skinny legs, a bushy tail and large ears constantly flicking forward and back. The jaws were heavy, and looked perfectly capable of crunching anything.

Again she scolded, and took a cautious step backward. Her loud voice seemed to intimidate it, yet it scuttled forward so as to remain the same small distance away. When she had retreated several steps, it was in fact a little closer then it had been before. Experimentally, she tried a decisive step forward; instead of fleeing, the animal rocked back on its haunches, growling and showing many interlocked, massive white teeth. It was not to be herded away.

The next time she stepped back it made a sudden rush at her feet, and she had to swing her boot at it to keep it away. It hesitated and she gained her original distance. Once more it made a scurrying rush and once more she swung the boot. It caught the toe of the boot in its mouth and shook its massive shoulders in a worrying gesture. She pulled the boot free, then banged it across the muzzle.

The beast lunged at the boot. As it sank its teeth into the stiff leather something whooshed past Sibby's right ear and thudded against the beast's skull. It was a falcon or small eagle, brown with white barring on its wings and tail, and its talons were sunk in the animal's forehead while its curved beak jabbed at its eyes. The beast screamed like a beaten dog, slapping at its face with its forepaws, shaking and lurching from side to side. The falcon beat the air with its wings but did not let go or cease its savage jabbing. Not until the beast had rolled onto its back did the bird let go, and even then it danced in the air above its victim, filling the air with feathers and harsh squawking until the animal had regained its feet and galloped lurchingly off into the gloom, blood running from its lacerated face.

At her feet the bird stood calmly in the dirt, grooming its feathers back into position. Sibby stood and watched it warily. Its wings in order, the bird carefully cleaned the talons of one foot and then the other. It smoothed its breast and stretched its neck several times as though to relieve a cramp, then turned one bright eye in Sibby's direction. She sank to her heels and met its eyes openly. "Thank you," she said at last, "I don't know why you did that, but I'm grateful." The bird made a harsh screeching sound that was remarkably like an ironic laugh, then bounded up into the air and circled around Sibby's head. Three times it circled then shot away toward the hills.

Sibby continued to follow the stream until her legs gave out; she was dizzy from lack of food and aching in every bone and muscle. She rolled onto her back, her right arm across her throat in an unconscious gesture of self-protection. The sky grew brighter as her mind dipped in and out of dreaming and her body dozed and woke again. Once more she heard the rustling and the whispering, the faint chiming of bells in the distance. From somewhere overhead a raspy voice came faintly to her ears. "Get up! Get up!" In answer she tried to raise her head but she was still asleep. "Get up! The hill! The hill!" The voice was closer now, harsher and more urgent. A shadow passed over her face and she felt the wind of a bird's close passing. Suddenly her eyes opened and she was awake. As she sat up she looked around for the speaker, but there was nothing to be seen, only the dark speck of a distant bird in the sky.

The hills were closer than she had realized. The nearest formed a smooth dark hemisphere against the pallid sky, and there was something triangular sticking out from its side. When she reached the bottom of the hill, the dark thing on its side was hidden from her. She stopped and caught her breath, confused by her unfamiliar weakness; then she made her way up slowly, circling to the right. She slipped a little in the scree and dirt, catching herself on her hands. When she rose she found herself staring into the empty eye sockets of a horse's skull.

from the Weekly Enquirer

HOSTAGE CRISIS A HOAX?— WHY CARTER CAN'T LOSE— UNDERSEA TEMPLE AN UNUSUAL FIND, SAYS PROF— ALIENS SIGHTED ON CAPE COD—CAN FBI STOP UFO??

"I was just driving home on Route 28," said Miguel San-chez, 37, a gardener at the famous Hoyt Estate, *"when all of a sudden there it was, hovering in the sky just like a giant cigar. 'O God,' I said, 'This is it!' I didn't have a chance to*

tell Julia how much she means to me. The lights were flash-
ing, red and blue and green, and I could hear it humming,
you know, just like a top. It got closer and closer and I closed
my eyes and I prayed. 'Sweet Mother of God,' I said, 'just let
me get home safe to my wife and my babies.' Then I opened
my eyes and it was gone, bam, just like that. I didn't tell
anyone, you know. I didn't want them to think I was crazy.
Then I heard about that girl disappearing in the woods, you
know, just at the same time, so I figured I'd better tell the
police what I saw.''

Chapter Three

THE DESERT

I

Both Ibrasa and Glisser expected Tamara to return home with Lord Parric. It was Lord Parric's health that gave her the best argument for going on, rather than returning. It had been clear to her from the moment she looked in his face that the doctor was a fool. He brought to mind Alric's long lectures on medicine that had so irritated her father. He had always talked about the wonderful abilities of desert surgeons, the need for young scholars to go and apprentice themselves to the great Karabdin masters. Tamara had paid scant attention to Alric's discussions on the advancement of science and medicine among the Karabdu, but she remembered his fervor, if she forgot the facts.

Glisser's doctor was detailing his treatment. Glisser was nodding gravely and Parric looked pale and resigned. Ibrasa stood a little apart, quietly scornful. Tamara went up to the doctor. "What do you intend to do?"

He smiled down on her blandly. "The whole of the left foot is frozen, and three toes on the right. They are black now, and left untouched mortification will soon be advanced, fevers will follow and the death of the patient will ensue. First we must drain the poisons of mortification from his body through cupping, then purify his fluids through fasting and sweating. Heat will be brought to the affected parts by immersion in boiling water, followed by the application of hot irons and wrapping in blue cloths, a color well known to promote healing. Vazdz willing, the patient will recover."

There was no mistaking the scorn in Ibrasa's face now. Tamara turned to him. "Ibrasa," she said, "how would your surgeons proceed?" She ignored the doctor's affronted exclamation and Ibrasa bowed gravely to her before speaking in reply.

"Truly," he said, "there is little frost in the heart of the desert. But I have traveled its northern boundaries in the winter, and often seen lambs and kids born before their time, suffering as our friend does now. It is the custom there to remove the frozen part with a sharp steel knife, well-boiled in an iron kettle and used still hot. The wound, if small, seals itself; if not, it is sealed with the black tar of Vahn, famed for its virtue of purification. And in accordance with the teachings of Ib'Sina, what is done for a sheep or a horse may be done for a man."

At these last words, the warmth of the doctor boiled over. "A sheep! Very well for a sheep to be hacked and butchered! It is what one might expect from the barbarians of the desert, from men in skirts. But we are dealing here with a man, filled with complex polarities of heat and cold, infection and cleanliness, things that must be balanced and treated according to ancient medical wisdom!"

Tamara laid a restraining hand on Ibrasa's sword arm. "Ibrasa," she said, "I think you will have to take us both to the desert. I am sure Lord Glisser can find a faithful courier to take the dispatches to my father?" She held Glisser's eyes with her own until he nodded slowly. "You will add in your own hand that I have taken it upon myself to bring Lord Parric before the physicians of the Karif. When his hurts have been attended to, we will return together to Tredana." She let her gaze dwell haughtily on the now silent doctor. "I think, sir, that you forgot before whom you were speaking. I thank you for your prompt attendance upon my father's ambassador, and pray that you will see him well bandaged for the ride that is before us." Her dignity had quite a shattering effect upon the two men.

For their last change of mounts, Ibrasa chose three wiry Karabdin horses from the royal posting stables. Before noon they were well south of Villavac. As they passed the southern pasturelands, Parric sometimes clutched at his saddle-bow and wavered in the saddle, but each time he caught himself and smiled at his companions with a word of apology. When they halted to let the horses blow, Ibrasa and Tamara stretched their legs but Parric stayed in the saddle, feet dangling. Although Parric was a much bigger man than Ibrasa, taller and heavier, the son of the Tayyib lifted him down easily that evening and helped him to the campfire. In the flickering light Parric smiled at Tamara.

"Whether the doctors of the Karif are successful or not," he said, "I have much to thank you for. Even amputation is easier to contemplate than immersion in boiling water." Then he smiled at Ibrasa. "And I also have much to thank you for, O Barbarian who wears a skirt."

Ibrasa threw back his head and laughed, and as Tamara snuggled down in her blankets, she was well pleased with the success of her plans.

The next night they were almost at the desert's edge and the stars shone very bright in a deep black sky, across which the waning moon followed a dim path. Ibrasa studied Parric's face, then spoke. "I do not know where the Karif is presently encamped. We have left our usual places for fear that they might be known to the spies of the Conqueror. I think it will be best to go to the valley and accept the hospitality of the Marajites. Apart from their fasting, prayers and penance, they are learned and wise. Thence I can ride in search of the Karif."

Tamara, also looking at Parric, agreed.

Next morning they set out and there horses, scenting the desert ahead, pulled eagerly at the bridle. The sand and the stones spread out all around them, and by noon they were in the middle of a perfect circle of whiteness, dazzling in its reflection of the sun overhead. Ibrasa pointed with his whip.

"That mark on the horizon is the nearest of the cliffs," he said. "It encloses what was once the Valley of the Dead Kings, and is now the Holy Hermits' City of Penitence. We will reach the back entrance by dark."

All afternoon Tamara rode in a daze of delight, marred only by Parric's suffering. The crunch of the sand and the jingle of harness, the wide white sweep of sand and wide blue sweep of sky, all was as she had hoped and imagined. From time to time she closed her eyes against the dazzle and felt as though she were flying in the sun-warmed dark. Then she would open her eyes again and see that the earth was really as vast and flat as she thought. It was the most beautiful country she had ever seen, and her spirits sang.

As they set their course northwest toward the valley, the sun was sinking on their left; bellied out along the sand's edge, huge and brilliant. There was only a lingering wash of red and orange in the sky when they reached the cliffs. Ibrasa led them on an intricate upward way, threading among the boulders and over ledges, turning right and left and right again as they climbed. When he disappeared into the cliff face Tamara was startled, even though she had known what to expect. Her teacher Dansen had ridden over the stone steps out of the valley twenty years earlier, when he had left with Tamara's mother, Sibyl. Sibyl had been just twelve years old. It was in this very valley that she had found the ancient ring, the one Tamara now wore on a thong round her neck. It seemed a favorable portent, and Tamara followed Ibrasa confidently into the blackness.

In the dark ahead she could hear a clatter as Ibrasa's horse slipped, panicked and was brought back under control. Her own horse threw up its head in alarm and behind her Parric's mount blew out its nostrils in loud, nervous snorts. "Halt," said Ibrasa and his brief command echoed on the rock walls. Here in the passageway no light came from outside; it was as black as a velvet bandage over the eyes. Tamara strained her ears and could hear Ibrasa slip down off his horse; his spurs jingled and his robes slithered on the stone. She heard an oath and the rasp of his sword unsheathing: it struck a spark on its scabbard that startled her eyes like a falling star. Then silence.

"Follow me," said Ibrasa at length. "I will lead my horse and tell you if there is any obstruction on the great stairway."

As they went on, from time to time Ibrasa would counsel them to move to the left-hand wall or to the right; once he spent some time ahead of them moving things in the dark. All the horses were now snorting and tossing their heads, so that the jingling of their bits echoed from wall to wall. Tamara noticed that there was something in the passageway that did not smell right—a sweet, sick odor that grew stronger, then grew less, but never went entirely away. The rock-cut passage made a final, right-angled turn and they came out into the grey light of early evening.

They were on a ledge high above the valley, above the head of the great statue of Vazdz that was cut out of the rock of the cliff face. Ibrasa led his horse forward and looked down into the valley for several moments, then cursed again, longer and more fluently. "Come and see," he said at last.

Tamara dismounted, then stepped out onto the ledge beside him. Almost two hundred feet below on the valley floor lay sprawled the tiny figures of men—dark blotches barely discernible in the growing dark, and here and there the larger carcass of a horse. To their right, where the cliff face curved around and the rock-cut tombs of the first nine Karabdin kings were engraved, the carvings had been mutilated and piles of rubble lay at the cliff base. The openings to the caves used by scholars and ascetics were clustered black with carrion birds.

Ibrasa turned to Lord Parric. "This has happened since I left the Land. Are you certain you left the Emperor in the northern mountains?"

Parric nodded, drooping against his horse's neck. "He has other armies," he said shortly. "And four of his own grown sons are generals."

Ibrasa helped Tamara remount, then led the horses across the high ledge and into the cliff passageway opposite. "Take care as we descend in the dark. You do not want to stumble on these stairs. I will go ahead again to clear the path. But I do not think there is anything left alive to oppose us." His inflection on the word *alive* was very slight.

Going down was much slower than climbing, the horses more cautious at the edge of each wide, flat step before stepping off into the dark. When the reached the valley floor it was not much lighter outside than it had been in the passageway, and Tamara was grateful not to be able to see more clearly the huddled figures of the gentle Marajites. Ahead, Ibrasa had stopped cursing and was repeating phrases in the Karabdin tongue. Twice she heard him speak in common Tregladen, "Accept these martyrs, Vazdz, who offer themselves to you."

It was barely a mile across the plain. Tamara kept her eyes fixed on her horse's shadowy ears, while the smell and the stillness made the hairs prickle on her neck. But before they had turned into the narrow cleft that led out through the mountains to the valley's front door, Ibrasa held up his hand for a halt.

He cocked his head, listening, and Tamara strained her ears

also but heard nothing. Then it came again, a faint murmur
off to their right, a hoarse whisper for pity. Ibrasa leapt down
and disappeared into the gloom. "Pity, pity." Ibrasa stooped
over a dark bundle. "O Lord, pity." He lifted it in his arms
and gently carried it back to the track where he laid it down,
pushing back the deep hood of the Marajite's woolen gown.

It was a young boy, not tall but powerfully built, a few years
older than Tamara. His face was swollen, blackened with dirt
or blood, and all he could do was move his head feebly from
side to side, murmuring "pity." Ibrasa checked him quickly
for bleeding wounds and broken bones, then tried to trickle a
little water between his lips, which only ran out again as he continued to murmur for pity. Setting the boy up on the front of his
saddle, Ibrasa mounted behind and took him in his arms. "Here
is another for the physicians of the Karif," was all he said.

Tamara rode through the dark tired, bewildered and hungry, hearing the soft groans of the boy ahead and the sharp
intakes of breath from Lord Parric behind. The desert had
turned its bleakest face upon her. Never had she felt so far
from human aid and comfort. With the hills that enclosed the
valley left behind, starlit space leapt out on every side and it
seemed as though they were riding into the sky. All around
them the stars burned with a meaningful clarity she had never
imagined. Twice in the night she saw Ibrasa sight a single star
high above in the northern sky, each time altering their course
a little. As the stars began to dim and the sky behind them
slowly filled with light, Ibrasa hurried their pace a little; at
dawn he waited for the sun to rise fully before sweeping the
distance with a brass sighting tube.

"The standard of the Karif. At last."

Tamara's heart thumped in her throat. She smiled at Lord
Parric, but he was unable to smile in return. In Ibrasa's arms,
the boy stirred and once more began his hoarse murmuring.
"Courage," said Ibrasa, and they rode on.

II

The Karif was not in his camp. That much Tamara absorbed
immediately as they dismounted and her companions were
taken to the tent of Hattam the physician. She was shown

to guest quarters and fell heavily asleep, and continued to be
lazy for the following few days.

The young Marajite recovered much more quickly than
Tamara would have thought possible. Hattam's diagnosis was
that he had been trampled and mistaken for dead, with a blow
to the head, cracked ribs and a separated shoulder. His spine
and legs were uninjured however, and with each passing day
his mind grew clearer and his body stronger. He remained in
some confusion concerning the actual attack and the hours
that preceded it, which, as Hattam remarked was quite natural. His name was Lerdas, and his age was twelve.

Lord Parric too did well, healing rapidly with no infection
or fever, as Ibrasa had predicted. The loss of his left foot and
half his right sunk him in a profound melancholy however, to
the extent that, for the first few days after the operation, he
did not even recognize Tamara's presence when she came to
sit on the edge of the bed and talk to him.

That first week in camp, Tamara wavered between fascination and boredom, worry and relief. Until the Karif returned
from his raiding party, she had nothing to do but keep out of
the way of others, amuse herself and comfort her friends. The
tent in which the patients lay recovering stood at right angles
to the Karif's, in the center of the encampment. Tamara's
eyes often strayed in that direction. The entrance to the great
tent was shaded by an awning of white silk, supported on
spears wound with ribbons of red and gold. On the carpets
that lay spread out in this square of shade, great hunting
hounds lay sprawled in graceful attitudes of sleep. They had
fine, narrow heads and long legs like deer, and they regarded
Tamara politely but without enthusiasm.

On the fourth afternoon Tamara sat as usual on the edge of
Parric's bed, holding his right hand in her own while with his
left he plucked at the short, fine hairs of his goatskin coverlet,
staring up at the dark tent overhead through half-closed eyes.
Although still depressed, he was beginning to answer when
spoken to, so for his sake as well as for her own interest,
Tamara began to ask him more questions about life among the
warriors of Angulidan.

At first his answers were short, but as he talked he became
more animated, his voice became stronger, and Lerdas sat on
his pillows to listen—his·temple bandaged and his arm supported by a sling. Hattam was so pleased to find them like

this he declared them ready for fresh air, and the next few mornings Tamara joined them for breakfast on a rug spread at the entrance to Hattam's tent. The silk awning was rolled back to allow the gentle warmth and pale light of the early morning sun to reach them. The sunlight more than anything else seemed to rouse Lord Parric from his depression, and his stories grew from curt factual answers to elaborate narrations in which he totally forgot Tamara's original questions.

Tamara learned about the composition of Tibir's army, their armor, weapons, tactics and morale. She learned that Tibir was not himself an Angul but a native of Almadun, "The Heart of the World"—a broad fertile valley bounded by rivers and mountains, lying south of harsh Angulidan. Tibir's family had a strain of Angul blood, a legacy from the days when Chanaga Gagan and his Angul army conquered the whole world, including Almadun, and it was Tibir's ambition to rebuild and even enlarge Chanaga's fabled empire. But the old Angul clans regarded him as an upstart and gave him more trouble than any outlanders. Parric had heard it rumored that Tibir was planning to march into the northern wastelands against some of the Angul clans that still defied him, before going on to conquer the mysterious northern island of Paradon, whose sorcerous warlords had never accepted his claim to rule the world.

"When I was among them," said Parric, "I heard mention of a talisman that Tibir is seeking: a sign from Chanaga Gagan that Tibir is to be considered his rightful successor. Some said it was a sword, some an amulet; others said that it was not a thing at all, but a priest."

"Do you think that's why he came here?" asked Tamara.

Parric raised his face to the gentle warmth of the new sun, speaking with closed eyes. "It is possible. More than possible, it is likely. The great Chanaga Gagan is said to have sent armies across the world, for no other reason than to compel the attendance at his court of certain wise men. Tibir may well have heard of Arbytis the High Priest asleep in his valley. It is a more likely reason for crossing those mountains than my return, or the slaughter of Glisser's sheep. Or perhaps he is looking for the Sword-Bearer of Chanaga." Parric chuckled. "If I had not spent so much time talking with the Empress, I might have learned more of important matters. It was from one of her ladies that I heard the legend of the Sword-Bearer.''

He opened his eyes and smiled at Tamara's expectant look.

"There's not much to it. Not much required of Tibir, either. It is called the legend of the Enku-dar, for in their language *enku* is sword, and one who carries is *dar*. It is said the Enku-dar of Chanaga will return with the sword of the great Gagan, to give it to the man who will become Lord of the World.''

Tamara sniffed. "The Sword-Bearer would have to be nearly as old as Arbytis. Tell me about the Empress.''

"She is old, strong, shrewd, loyal. What she looks like I cannot say: it is the custom of royal ladies to paint their faces pure white as a guard against cold, wind, wet and sun. Her hair is thick and straight to below the waist, worn loose or plaited, and so black it must be dyed. I have heard that she was a great beauty fifty years ago, when the young Tibir stole her from the emperor of Samida.'' Parric paused to refill his coffee cup. "She was one of the Samidan emperor's many brides, a gift from her father, who was a prince of Angulidan. She is of the house of Chanaga Gagan, and through her Tibir can claim a connection with the family—some say that is why he married her.''

"It might be why he married her, but it wouldn't explain her riding with the army fifty years later. Does she have many children?''

"No children at all. But Tibir has sent his sons and all his grandchildren to be raised by her rather than by their natural mothers. He has used her loyalty to stamp his whole family into a pattern of obedience. It was in the stealing of her from the Chama of Samida—that is how the Samidans name their ruler—that he lost the use of his arm and she scarred her hand. She is called the 'Shield of the Agan' because of that incident.'' Tamara raised her eyebrows questioningly, but Parric shook his head. "It is not a story I can tell you. Their standards of decency are not ours.''

"Then you may tell me the decent parts and leave the rest to my imagination.'' Parric flushed a little, and nodded.

"The 'Song of Tibir' tells how the young Tibir, then a poor warlord from Zamarra, in Almadun, journeyed to Samida in search of his fortune. The Anguls are all great players at castledown, a game they call sitranga and which their historians claim was invented in Almadun. Tibir was even then a mighty player, and at that time there was word of a challenge from the Chama, to pay great sums in gold to anyone who could beat him. So Tibir went to Samida to win a fortune in gold, and there he beat the Chama in three games, but won very little—and that in silver. However he saw among the court ladies a young princess of Angulidan and his blood was enflamed. Their eyes met, it says in the song, and their hearts began to beat as one.

"Of course, the ladies of the court were not unprotected. When they traveled in the streets of the city they wore heavy veils of silk, and their home was a garden enclosed within high walls, a place of flowers and scented trees and fountains, called the Zemama. It was also a place of many trusted guards, armed with swords. It was only by chance that Tibir saw Soria unveiled, when he was within the palace grounds. Any ordinary man would have realized they could never meet again. But Tibir is not ordinary.

"That night, it says in the 'Song of Tibir,' he spent the few coins he had won on a bath for himself and a song from a hired minstrel. And the words he gave the minstrel to sing were in the Angul language, and they asked Soria to stand by the tall white tree at midnight by the Zemama wall. And at midnight he left his boots in the street and climbed over the wall and met Soria alone in the Chama's own garden." Parric paused and coughed, and considered his next words. "A few hours later, when the guard surprised them, they were asleep and Tibir was not—not fully dressed. The guard thrust at Tibir's unprotected back and Soria, awakening, reached up and turned the sword with her hand, which was cut to the bone. You can see the scars yet. So the sword pierced Tibir in the right shoulder and he twisted around, seized the weapon in his own hands, and beheaded the guard in one motion. Thus they were able to escape over the wall, leaving a bloody trail. And they also left behind certain items by which the invader of the Chama's garden was identified."

Tamara raised her eyebrows and Parric explained. "The 'Song of Tibir' says that it is a good thing he had left his boots in the alley, since he was fated to leave his trousers behind in the garden." At this Tamara started to laugh and Parric joined her. They were interrupted by a strangled sound from Lerdas.

"How can you make light of these barbarians?" he cried, his pale blue eyes glittering. "What is humorous about a young savage debauching his host's wife in her own garden and then killing a soldier who was only doing his duty?"

"Young master," said Parric, "of course such a story is painful to you. You have only witnessed the severity of the Agan, whereas I have also experienced his hospitality. I beg your pardon." Lerdas muttered something under his breath and Tamara made herself look at him compassionately. He was becoming more and more difficult to like.

"Can you tell us something about your life with the Marajites?" she asked. "In Tredana we hear very little about the teachings of Maraj."

Lerdas shifted his arm in its sling. "I wasn't in the valley very long. When my mother died I wanted to leave home and there was a teacher in town, a holy man from the desert. He told me I could be his student and follow him to the valley. He was like a father to me." His lip trembled and his eyes seemed bright with tears. "When we traveled back to the valley we lived on the food people gave us and he told them about the teachings. He didn't own anything except his clothes."

"Is that the way all Marajites live?"

"That is the way they *lived*." Lerdas clamped his lips shut and Tamara tried to change the subject a little.

"My mother's dead, too. My father always says she went away, as though I can't face the truth. I never knew her, so I suppose I don't miss her . . . but in a way I do miss her because I want to know more about her. I read about her in Dansen's history and it makes me wish I knew more. Father says I'm a lot like her, only more so—whatever that means. Are you like your mother? How old were you when she died?"

Lerdas' mouth suddenly trembled with real sentiment. The change to genuine emotion was startling and obvious. "She was the most beautiful woman in the world. My eyes are like hers. She used to say that she had given me her eyes and that I should watch the world for her. But she had a terrible life. Everyone was jealous of her and conspired against her. She always told me I was her only friend, the only person she could trust." Tears clung to his sparse silver lashes. "When they tried to take me away from her she wouldn't let them, so they killed her. They said she was sick, but I know better. That is why I had to run away, so her enemies couldn't kill me, too.''

Parric leaned forward, shifting his bandaged legs. ''What enemies were these, lad? From what town did you come?''

Lerdas stumbled to his feet, even whiter than usual. ''I shouldn't have said so much. I'm an orphan now. You know—a man without a father doesn't have any friends.'' He turned on Tamara. ''What do you know about losing someone? You never even met your famous mother. And you still have your father. The great, wise, noble Leron of Tredana!'' He spit out the last words like poison and staggered back into the tent.

Tamara's heart pounded angrily in her chest while Parric patted her hand. ''My dear,'' he said, ''merely saving a man's life ensures neither liking on the one hand nor gratitude on the other. Do not let yourself be troubled.''

''I wish we'd left him there! For half a piece of bread I'd take him back now!'' She stood there shaking, ignoring Parric's kindly touch, so angry that it was several moments before she realized that the Karif's party was approaching camp. She pulled herself free with a startled excuse and dashed back into her tent to wash her face.

The Karif had been two weeks on horseback, in fruitless quest of the Angul warriors still harrying his outer encampments and those villages along the desert's edge that looked to the Karabdu for protection. Tamara pushed back the flaps of her tent and watched the Karif for several moments in secrecy. She had never imagined him tired, dusty and sweat-streaked, but it did not make him less attractive in her eyes. His blue eyes, with their odd gold flecks, seemed exceptionally bright in the pallor of his face. There were twenty horsemen with him who wearily dismounted and walked away toward the paddocks, their horses drooping behind them, noses almost to the ground. One warrior, slightly built, remained in the saddle. The Karif swung down easily from his own dark horse and walked over to his companion. First the other warrior handed down his heavy sabre, then leaning over placed his hands on the Karif's shoulders and slid down into his arms. He was lame, one leg dragging slightly, but he seemed to rest in the Karif's arms a fraction of a second too long, his short hair brushing Ajjibawr's shaven cheek. Then Tamara saw the lame warrior straighten up and toss back his head, and something in the gesture revealed him as a woman, dressed and armed like a man. An emotion Tamara did not understand suddenly tightened in her stomach.

Before going to the Karif's tent, Tamara brushed her dark hair until it shone like the sides of a horse on summer pasture. She washed with generous amounts of lilac-scented water and dressed in the nicest of the Karabdin silks she had been given. Both eyes wide open, the blue and the brown, she looked at her face critically in the dark mirror and wished it did not look so smooth and baby round. There had been interesting hollows in the face of the woman warrior: Tamara had to poke her finger into her cheeks to find where the bones ended.

When she stepped in, Parric was already talking to the Karif, propped up on cushions with his bandaged legs stretched out before him. Lerdas stood silently behind them, eyes downcast. The Karif had been squatting on his heels, holding a small cup of coffee while he spoke to Parric; he rose to his feet in a single easy movement and putting down his cup held out his hand.

"My dear," he said in his deep voice, "I could not believe my good fortune when Ibrasa told me. Welcome to the Land."

Tamara gave him a cold hand and a small smile; she was shaking and her coffee cup leaped on its saucer when he handed it to her.

"Lord Parric has been adding to Ibrasa's tale. I am honored that my surgeons were of aid to you, but I am more honored by the decision you made in Villavac. I know it is not easy even for a princess to set her will against those so much older than herself." Ajjibawr turned to Lerdas. "I rode through the valley two days ago, and we stayed many hours digging trenches and burying the slain. I did not think then that anyone could have survived. I am glad to be proved wrong. You are welcome among us."

He sank back on his heels, his head once more level with Lord Parric's. "And you must stay until our craftsmen can fit you with a wooden foot. Vazdz willing, you will walk and ride as well as before. But it cannot be done until the wound is firm and without pain." He paused, and drew out of his sleeve a little snuffbox of polished wood. Tamara felt a rush of tenderness as he took a pinch, sneezed, and rubbed his nostril with the edge of one long finger. His eyes met hers before she

could guard her expression, and this time there was no doubt
in her mind as there had been years ago in Tredana. The color
definitely rose in his face. She felt her own grow hot in
answer. Then the Karif smiled.

"Leron of Tredana will not thank me for keeping his daughter from him any longer than necessary, however. Especially
since he has sent the other children to Melismala. He will find
his castle cold and empty. Since it is clear the Angul army
has left us, for this year at least, I think it is my duty to
arrange for your safe escort home. But not until you have had
a chance to visit as once I promised, to hunt the gazelle and
choose a trained horse to take home." He turned again to
Parric. "It will be some months before you can follow her.
Ibrasa tells me you have studied the stars. I have a stargazer
here in camp who wishes very much to learn the Old Tregladen
names and qualities for them. Ammagest will share with you
our Karabdin knowledge in return. It should help your time
pass more quickly." He rose to his feet as fluidly as before.
"You must excuse me now. The Mekrifs are meeting in
council and we have much to discuss. Tamara, I will instruct
my horse master to be ready for your visit this afternoon. You
will see that not all our best beasts were sent to the Angul
lord."

Ibrasa conducted her to the paddocks late that afternoon.
The camp was quiet, just rousing from the few hours sleep
that customarily filled the hottest part of the day. That the
horse master and his grooms had enjoyed little rest was
obvious though.

Nine young stallions were tethered by the largest dirt paddock. Brushed to perfection, their silky tails swept the ground
and their white markings were spotless. Each was bridled and
saddled in the Karabdin fashion, with brightly dyed leather
embroidered in gold and silver thread, shimmering with silk
tassels. Any one of them would have been a fit mount for a
king, but one little chestnut turned such a round, sweet eye
toward Tamara that she had trouble seeing any of the others.
Because she was instantly enamored of him, she left him for
last.

Eight times Ibrasa held the stirrup for her, and eight times
she rode a wonderfully balanced, buoyant and flexible young
horse into the paddock, practicing his spins and halts, his canter
changes and simple leaps. None of them could she fault. But

the ninth shone brighter than polished copper, his iridescent hairs giving back all the colors of the sun; his little ears were pricked in her direction and his large nostrils fluted, savoring her smell. She caressed his neck as she mounted, and as she settled into the bright blue saddle his barrel between her legs was the perfect fit, neither too large nor too small. His back lifted strongly beneath her and his length of neck was just right for a comfortable distance of rein to bit. She urged him forward into the ring, almost dizzy with delight, and her happiness must have come down through her body into his own, because as she entered the riding area he suddenly dropped his head and exploded into an enormous buck of self-satisfaction, so violent that his tail came over Tamara's head and stung her eyes.

She laughed and pulled up his head, pushing him forward, and he came up into the bridle and moved with such power and precision that the other horses were completely forgotten. Tamara was dimly aware of the Karif coming out of a nearby tent to join his horse master and Ibrasa at the rail, but such was her pleasure in her little horse that her hero was momentarily ignored. She tried him with all the figures she had attempted on her old gelding back in Tredana, and even when he did not understand, the little horse responded to her weight and shifts and leg movement with eager compliance.

By the gate, she brought him to an almost square halt and saluted the Karif. He returned it gravely. "You have chosen well. May he bear you in safety and happiness for many years to come." He took the colt's bridle himself and held him as she slipped off. "It was twenty years ago I gave your mother her first horse. She surprised me then by asking its name. As you know, our horses are called simply the Bright One or the Roarer or some such title, and not even that until they are proven in battle. These young horses have no names or titles. They are waiting to earn them. Will you name this colt now or later?"

Tamara smoothed the colt's silky shoulder. "I've waited for him for five years. I knew you'd keep your promise. What is the Karabdin for promise?"

"Faras. The Promised One would be Ef'fras."

"I like the sound of Faras better."

Behind Ajjibawr, a husky voice spoke up. "Well-chosen and well-named." A slight figure was smiling at them, standing in the entrance of the tent from which Ajjibawr had come. It was the woman warrior, dressed in a long plain dress like a belted shirt, her fair hair ruffled around her ears. She wore no jewelry and her thin face was criss-crossed with fine lines of exposure to wind and sun. "I am Shadith," she said. "I knew your mother once. Welcome to the Land."

Ajjibawr looked at Shadith with an easy fondness Tamara could not mistake. "She has chosen the chestnut, as I said she would. I told you she has the eye. It is a gift and she was born with it."

"And is that so surprising?" asked Shadith.

Ajjibawr frowned at her and shook his head in silent warning, the sort of gesture a parent makes thinking it will not be noticed by a child. Tamara pretended to be interested in untangling a small knot in Faras' mane, but she was intensely aware of Shadith. A drab little woman, she would have liked to think, easily mistaken for a weather-beaten boy. But she could not ignore the power that lay behind the placid face. And she made herself smile politely in response to Shadith's invitation to join her the following morning on a hunt. Tamara thanked her demurely as she handed her reins back to the horse master, then followed Ibrasa back toward the center of camp, leaving Shadith with the Karif.

After a moment Tamara slid her eyes sideways toward Ibrasa. "Who is Shadith?" she asked, her voice perfectly steady.

"You have heard her name before. She was my father the Tayyib's youngest wife, a great hero in her own right before she married him and a greater warrior after."

"I'm sorry, I forgot her name. How was she crippled?"

"She was wounded by the Arleon, in the time of the Four False Kings. It bothers her now no more than his lameness hampers the Angul lord. I would not recommend crossing swords with her."

"My father won't let me train with a sword. I don't even know how to carry one properly. It's always archery, archery, archery. Nock, draw, loose, thunk. What fun is that? I want to use a sword."

"An arrow was enough to bring down the Tayyib, sword-master that he was. But I will tell the Karif your wishes. I do not think he will object to your learning the art of the sword."

Tamara had a radiant vision of herself on Faras, her bright, curved blade whistling overhead. "Thank you, Ibrasa," she said, and she adjusted the picture in her mind to show herself dressed like a warrior, riding at Ajjibawr's side, sword-bearer to the Karif.

Chapter Four

THE WASTELAND

I

The horse's skull was stuck on a post that protruded through the spinal cord's opening. Over the pole was stretched the horse's hide, a mousy brown dried rigid in the sun, the sparse mane standing erect and the wispy tail fanned out on the ground. This was the tentlike protrusion she had seen from the distance. Beyond it was another and another, nine in all, three bay, three chestnut and three parti-colored. The loosened jaws lay on the ground below the skulls. Sibby began to feel slightly better when she noticed that none of the horses could possibly have been under the age of twenty.

Sibby touched the nearest hide and rolled from her fingers the grains of salt with which it had been roughly cured. She turned back the flap of the throat, and still adhering to the sun-dried skin were shreds of meat like black leather. She ripped one free and started chewing: the salt tasted delicious. She began pulling the hard fibers free and cramming them into her mouth in a frenzy.

Back at the water's edge she washed down the salt with deep draughts of cold water. It was not until she was sitting on the sun-warmed rocks with her belly full that she realized what she had been eating. She thanked the horse silently in her mind and dropped her head back in a doze.

It was still midafternoon when she stretched and pulled herself to her feet, fed and rested. She set out slowly examining the rest of the mound. On the far side of the hill, her attention was drawn by more offerings on poles, grimmer than skulls or horsehides. On either side of the stream a series of stakes supported helmets and coats of linked mail, the scales made of overlapping bone. And as she feared the armor had not been empty when first propped up. She only took a quick look, then passed along as fast as she could, her scalp prickling.

At the base of the next and largest hill was ranged an honor guard of men on horseback, many of the figures still bizarrely upright, some indeed clutching rotten spears with rusted points. As Sibby circled warily, oppressed by the desolation and cruel ritual of death, her foot struck a helmet in the sand made of some bright, unrusted metal, inlaid with gold and silver. She picked it up and continued circling counterclockwise. On the far side of the hill was an opening, barred with a massive, timber door. Tumbled about before the threshold lay .vessels of bronze and iron; in some of them, traces of food or drink could still be seen. As she stood before the door, her heart pounded and the details before her sprang into sharp focus: green lichen on greyish wood, rusted iron spikes, incised lines of graining, sod sprouting withered grass overhanging the lintel.

The door gave way easily to her gentle push and showed her a beehive-shaped chamber, cut in half by the light of the opened door, swept bare and almost empty. There was a heavy wooden trapdoor in the floor; without a crowbar Sibby could see no way of moving it. Just inside the door there was a neatly folded pile of clothing. This she gathered in her arms and took outside to examine in the sun.

Although the clothing was perfectly clean, made of fine unbleached linen, closely woven and neatly stitched, Sibby had no doubt that these were grave clothes. Her own shirt was smelly and in rags, however, and the linen tunic was strong, clean and comfortable. In place of her sagging breeches she pulled on a pair of loose pants, with string ties at the ankle and waist. The third piece puzzled her until she realized that it must be to tie up the jaws of a corpse. A beautifully wrought gold pin secured its folds; she wound it into a sort of turban around her head and fastened the pin in front. There was a sash also, embroidered in red, with several rings of iron sewn onto one edge. She wrapped it around her hips several times and found that the rings hung low on one side, as though for attaching a pouch or perhaps a weapon. As she neatly folded her discarded clothing and placed it within the tomb where the grave clothes had been, she silently thanked the unknown occupants for her clothing and her new room.

The sun seemed to be sinking more quickly than usual. Either that, or she had spent more time than she thought in washing and dressing. As the light faded, the rustlings, squeakings, chimings and whisperings increased in the evening air. Sibby squared her shoulders and walked down to the stream, where she carefully cleaned her helmet and filled it with fresh water. With this beside her, and a handful of sun-dried meat scraps, she settled against the inside wall of the tomb on a pillow made of her dirty clothing, and kept an eye on the open door.

She did not find it easy to sleep. Nonsense lines ran through her head about glaciers knocking in cupboards and deserts sighing in beds. But she must have been asleep when the inner trapdoor of the tomb slowly lifted. Blackness came out of the hole, as obvious as the light that comes from a lantern. It flowed across the floor and rising covered her ankles, hiding them from her sight. She tried to move but could not, because she was asleep.

The blackness formed itself into many small hands, plucking at her clothing and hair. The muttering in the air increased. Suddenly the pale starlight of the doorway was blocked by the form of a giant hand, in which there shone a burnished sword, dark but brilliant as jet. The point of it lifted before her eyes while a voice spoke in her head.

"Thief, thief, for shame. You wear my clothes, eat my food, steal my golden pin. Come, join the other heroes below who thought that I was gone." Life suddenly flowed into her arms and legs, and as the apparition forced her back toward the black hole, she snatched up the helmet and tried to knock the sword blade away from her throat. Her hand and the helmet passed through it as though the sword were insubstantial, but next moment the blade drew whistling back, and as it slashed toward her she could hear and feel the wind of its passing. The sharp blade bit against her neck and she felt her head ripped from her body with a sound like a peach being bitten. As her head spun sideways and thudded against the floor, the chamber wheeled round before her eyes: she saw her bloodied and grotesque body slump back against the wall before her head came to rest in the middle of the floor, eyes open, looking up. The air was cold on her open neck. Then the bloody sword tip pushed against her cheek, making her head rock back and forth and the roof of the chamber sway above her. The sword tip caught on the golden pin in her turban. ''Thief, thief, I will have my golden pin.'' She could feel the tug on her head, then heard a flutter of wings in the air that grew and grew till it drowned out the voice of her attacker.

Her hawk was there in the doorway. She could just see the edge of the opening from where she lay. As he hovered in the doorway he seemed to grow, and the beating of his wings fanned the starlight into the room, driving back the dark. The sword whistled around and the starlight glittered on its black length as it swooped through the air. She tasted blood in her mouth as she tried to cry out a warning, but she could not make a sound.

As the blade cut into the hawk's neck, the brown bird seemed to peel away like a covering from a white bird underneath. And the white bird was large and brilliant, filling the chamber with such radiance that the blackness shriveled up like a drying puddle. What little was left flowed back down into the hole in the floor.

Now she was aware of the heat of the white bird. His feathers were edged in gold that was also flame. For a moment the dark eyes looked down into her staring ones, and a bloody tear formed and fell on her severed head. Like acid it burned her eyes and face and then the room was dark, with an ordinary nighttime blackness.

It was almost dawn when Sibby opened her eyes again and found herself lying sprawled on the floor of the burial chamber. She ached as though she'd been beaten and her head throbbed with pain. Although she knew it had only been a terrible nightmare, she felt her body all over with new appreciation. A lump of something warm lay on her throat. For a moment she thought it was dried blood and her fingers shook as she touched it. Then she held it up to the light. It was a lump of amber. As she pulled herself up onto her knees she saw that the inner trap was indeed open. A shudder convulsed her and she stumbled out into the greyish morning.

Sibby pushed the timbered door shut and took in the deepest breaths she could hold, then staggered down to the stream.

Nothing in the world would have made her go back in to the tomb, even to return the stolen clothes. After a drink of cold water, she wished defiantly that there had been more to steal. She opened her hand. In the daylight the stone glowed red and cast a dull rosy color on her open palm. Sibby told herself that she would be wiser not to take it, but her fingers seemed to wrap themselves around the stone of their own volition. It was a large lump of amber, red as a ruby, covered with inscriptions now mostly rubbed off with age. At one end it was pierced by a golden ring, just the size to slip over her disputed gold pin. She slowly unfastened the pin from her head scarf and started to thread the amber on it. Her fingers tingled with a soft sense of electricity and she almost cried out as the stone moved in her palm. It seemed to spring into place on the pin and she looked at it in wonder, feeling it warm and pulsing like something friendly and alive. It glowed as though lit from within. Still moving instinctively, she opened the fastener and pushed the thick pin through the cloth of her left shoulder, above her heart. She could feel the amber's warmth through her clothes, through her skin, through her flesh.

In search of a weapon she continued along the stream, determined to leave the large mound far behind. More mounds stretched out before her, lining the bank of the stream, and past the edge of the next she saw a flutter of wings. It seemed a good omen. The next hill was a smaller tomb than the others, and the earth seemed recently disturbed. At this Sibby shivered with apprehension, but a few moments' exploration showed her the natural reason. It was a recent burial, and here again nine horses had been offered, this time as living sacrifices. The wings she had seen earlier belonged to the vultures who were hollowing out the bellies of eight horses sprawled by the stakes to which they had been tied.

One grey mare still stood, legs straddled wide, head down, ears flopped to the side, in patient attendance on death. Even the heavy beating wings of the vultures could not make her twitch an ear or raise her head. Sibby walked slowly forward; the birds, heavy and glutted, ignored her. The mare was young, still a dark blackish grey, and small, with short sturdy legs and neat round feet. Her body was long, all ribs and protruding back and hips; her short neck was low-set and weighted by a large and heavy-jawed head. Even well-kept

she would not have been attractive, except for her eyes,
enormously round and dark. These eyes were veiled by long
white lashes, patiently dropped. The little horse had passed
beyond curiosity or any awareness of the world around; only
the fact that she still stood and that her flanks moved in and
out gave any sign of life.

There were piles of fodder just out of reach of the stakes,
bundles of cut grass bleached yellow and dry in the sun.
Much of the grass still carried heavy seed heads. Slowly,
Sibby shook out the grain into one of the bronze vessels
littering the ground and added water from the stream. She sat
and watched the grain swell, then ground it with a rock into a
milky paste, still adding water to make the thinnest of gruels.
She held the bowl up to the mare's nose. For a long time
nothing seemed to change. Then the white lashes fluttered
and the pinched nostrils twitched. Sibby stuck her finger in
the thin paste and opening the mare's lips rubbed a little of
the mixture on her gums. The inside of her mouth was dry
and yellow, her lips swollen and cracked. Moments passed,
the mare swallowed with difficulty, then for the first time
turned her gaze on her rescuer.

Sibby took another bit of the mixture and this time poked it
in between the mare's teeth, onto her tongue. This startled the
little horse into movement; her head lifted as she choked and
swallowed. Suddenly her ears swiveled round and her eyes
focused. Sibby held the bowl up and the mare touched her lips
to the food with tentative jerkings of her head and neck and
nervous plucking movements with her lips. Finally she took
in a little of the watery food and swallowed, then reached for
more. As she licked the helmet clean, her eyelids dropped in
exhaustion and Sibby felt tears spring to her own eyes.

She refilled the bowl with plain water and the mare slurped
a few swallows before relapsing into fatigue. Sibby searched
for a sharp-edged stone, then sawed through the heavy leather
strap that fastened the mare to the post. As it parted the mare
fell to her knees. She groaned for a moment, then let her hind
end collapse, dropping her head on the ground before her in
utter exhaustion. Sibby sank down before her and took the
mare's muzzle on her knee. She stroked the grey face and
caressed around her eyes until the little mare slept.

With food and care, the little mare blossomed. Sibby had
her stand in the stream while she massaged her legs to reduce

the swelling in the joints; the mare dropped her head onto
Sibby's back with closed eyes and groans of contentment.
Shaggy fur came out in handfuls under Sibby's vigorous
scrubbing, using twigs or dried grass for a brush, and the new
coat underneath glittered black and silver. As the mare regained her strength, she began to follow Sibby everywhere
like a large, loving and clumsy dog. Her head hung over
Sibby's shoulder and her foot was all too often on Sibby's
own. Sibby found herself calling her the Monkey.

While she waited for the Monkey to regain her strength,
Sibby established a camp for them on the far side of the hill,
out of sight of the other horses' remains, and well out of sight
of the mound where she had found her pin. She could see that
there were more resources here than food and vessels. Hair,
hides and bones—all could be useful. Sibby had only the
vaguest idea of what went into processing leather, but it was
obvious that the flayed horse hides could be useful. The
animals had been small and their skins were not much larger
than a camp blanket. At the first of the mounds she chose the
smallest and prettiest of the skins, a parti-colored hide blotched
red, black and white. She bundled it onto Monkey's bony back
and carried it back to camp. With wetting, pounding and
kneading, using a heavy thigh bone for a pestle and a hollow
in the rocks for a mortar, she made the skin noticeably softer
and more supple. A splinter of rib made a serviceable knife,
and strips of sinew were scraped and rolled together for future
use as thongs. Finally, she spent a long afternoon in the sun
braiding together strands of horsetail to make a prickly length
of rope.

Despite the litter of weaponry about the hill, there were no
saddles or bridles. From a broken belt Sibby fashioned a
neckstrap for the Monkey, and from several others linked
together she made an overgirth to keep the folded horsehide
in place as a saddle pad. The Monkey's back was far too
sharp and knobby for riding without it. Not that she would be
riding yet. When they finally set out along the stream, the
Monkey carried Sibby's collection of tools and supplies while
Sibby walked beside her.

II

It was Monkey who first noticed the horse approaching them. All morning, a rumble like distant thunder had filled the air: the ground had trembled and Monkey had trembled with it. The horizon was hidden under a thick and yellowish cloud. Now the mare whinnied a frenzied greeting and pulled against Sibby's firm hold on the neck strap. At last Sibby could also see the black dot that slowly grew into a galloping, shaggy brown horse, its rider crouched low on its neck. He was dressed in black, and some silver on his bridle caught the light. Both he and his horse were powdered yellow with the dust. As he drew near he sat up, slowing his horse. His whip, which he had carried clenched in his teeth, he took and raised in a salute of obvious respect, while pulling his horse down to a bouncy trot with his other hand. Three times he circled them, his keen black eyes flicking over every detail of her strange equipment. Then he saluted again and put his horse in a gallop back the way he had come. Sibby was left with a vivid image of his high cheekbones and narrow black eyes, his swinging pigtail as black and as long as her own.

Sibby turned in the rider's direction. Before them the haze was resolving into an enormous line of people, wagons and animals. At first she thought it was an army, but instead of soldiers she saw cattle, sheep and goats, tents, carts and oxen, horses and mules, old men and children, women with babies on their backs. She patted Monkey on the neck. "I guess we have company."

Farther back in the crowd, banners were being raised and waved, and tall poles were hung with colored cloth and horsetails, topped with bronze insignia. In apparent response the herdsmen began spreading their flocks out to the sides, shouting to small black dogs who nipped and circled and darted among the cattle, driving them away from the center. Whips cracked and bullock carts heaved to a stop with further shouts and the poking of goads and sticks. There was a sound of drumming hooves, and Monkey danced in place as forty or fifty small horses suddenly dashed past, pursued by riders who herded them with long, light poles like bamboo lances. All this Sibby watched as she hung onto her head-tossing horse, waiting the approach of the riders sent to meet her.

The young man in black was leading them, gesticulating with his hands and pointing dramatically at Sibby as if to confirm a story. Beside him rode a heavy-set older man with a thin, white beard, a heavy leather cuirass buckled over his long, dark overcoat. All three of the riders were dressed alike in loose baggy pants like Sibby's, over which they wore long overcoats of quilted felt. Their leather boots were soft and embroidered and their harness and weaponry glinted with inlay and fanciful decoration. The third rider was a woman, dressed like the others except that her coat was open to the waist, showing a thin, pleated shirt underneath. Her full breasts were covered with necklaces of silver, bone and coral.

Sibby reddened as the young man indicated her bare feet and stolen grave clothes, her packsaddle of folded horsehide, her club of bone. She wondered how this society treated its grave robbers—or its lunatics. But whatever they thought, they were certainly polite. Once more the young man saluted her with his whip, and the older man also raised his hand in greeting. The woman nodded and rode forward until her horse was almost nose to nose with Monkey. While their horses sniffed, muttered and squealed, the woman tried to speak to Sibby in what were obviously different languages or dialects. The sounds were deep and rather melodious, with harsh consonants, spoken from the chest with little expression in the mouth or eyes, but Sibby understood nothing. The woman looked at her keenly, then made the universal gesture for eating. Sibby nodded and smiled and the other smiled in return, a sudden warmth lighting her austere face. She beckoned as she turned her horse slowly back into the camp.

On either side the cumbersome carts were drawn up in orderly rows amidst a disorder of small animals and children. On one of the wagons, set a little apart in the center of the encampment, there rested an enormous tent nearly twenty feet across. The tent was of light brown felt over a wooden framework, hung with embroideries and wrapped with tasseled bands of cloth. Its heavy wooden doors stood open and smoke arose from the hole at the top of the dome. Along one side of the massive tent wagon were tethered the bullock team which drew it—twenty massive-shouldered animals tied by brass nose rings—engrossed in bundles of fodder.

They rode in under the fascinated stare of what seemed like a hundred eyes. A young man suddenly appeared at Sibby's elbow, carrying a goatskin bag of water and a bundle of green fodder, which he placed reverently in front of Monkey, offering for Sibby's inspection an ornamental tether of braided leather. At her nod he carefully placed it around Monkey's neck, then slipped away as Sibby's hostess approached, followed by the two men.

Inside the tent it was warm and smelled of spices. The pleasure of feeling really warm swept over Sibby in a rush. There were rugs, pillows, warm hangings and furs. By the big bronze firebowl two enormous white dogs lay asleep, each the size of three sheep and as woolly. In what room was left, a beautiful white fur spotted gold and black was spread out, and here it was indicated Sibby should sit. She sank down, suddenly weary, and let the fire beat on her face and neck. The old man went out and returned with a foaming bowl of what smelled like yoghurt; from his breast he drew out a small wooden bowl, which he first licked clean; then scooping out some of the liquid, he drank it with lip-smacking pleasure, an obvious indication of its safety and goodness. The others had taken out their bowls and licked them also, but waited politely for Sibby to take her portion first. She indicated that she did not have a bowl hidden in her gown and their consternation was great, creating a furious bustle behind the scenes until a bowl suddenly appeared and was put into her hands, shiny and still a little damp. Breathing a prayer for the health and general cleanliness of the bowl's former owner, Sibby dipped up some of the liquid and drank. It was delicious.

Her hosts now beamed on her fondly as though she had done something clever, and speaking a little more loudly than necessary, with exaggerated gestures, explained that she was drinking *masett*. "*Masett, masett*," said the old man, and the young man agreed, "*Masett*." Sibby smiled and repeated the word to their delight. Now the old man progressed to lesson two. Rubbing his stomach he pronounced, "*Masett hord-a*." This clearly meant that the drink was good, or tasty. Sibby repeated the gesture and the phrase and soon they were all smiling fondly on each other. As Sibby refilled her bowl, the room reeled a little and her eyes blinked, but it was not until she was sipping her fourth bowlful that she realized there was more in this beverage than diluted yoghurt. It was in fact spiked, and they were all well on their way to becoming drunk.

The arrival of dinner helped delay the process. Chopped lamb, mixed with hot spices and rolled in balls of fat, was arranged on a platter around piles of thin, chewy bread. The lamb was *oth* and the bread *shan;* Sibby assumed that both would be considered *hord,* but learned this was true only of the lamb; the bread was considered *hordit.* ''Your language would be easier to learn without gender,'' she told the old man, who nodded and agreed, ''*Shan hordit-a.*''

Sibby ate and drank until she felt sick, with the ravenous hunger of a wolf making its first kill in weeks. Nothing could have delighted her hosts more, and it was with great difficulty that she convinced them she was not merely being polite when she finally refused new helpings. Her bowl refilled with *masett,* she leaned back on the pillows and warmed her bare feet against the hot legs of the bronze firebowl. The young man brought her another fur to cover her legs, and when she smiled in thanks, he blushed and dropped his eyes. He sat down by the older man who Sibby now guessed to be his grandfather. The woman, possibly his mother, stood at the door of the tent speaking softly with someone outside.

Outside, a new voice was heard, and the headwoman stood aside to let another woman enter, a young girl carrying a baby. She had the sleeping infant in a sling across her breasts, and heavy silver jewelry was slung around her hips. It clanked as she set and arranged herself and her child. For a few moments she looked closely at Sibby, then asked her a question in a soft musical language. Sibby shook her head. ''I'm sorry,'' she said, ''but I don't think we have any languages in common.'' The other woman's face lit up. ''I speak a little of your language,'' she said, and Sibby looked at her in amazement. ''My name is Tala. When I was a child, then I was a slave in Vahn.'' Sibby continued to look at her blankly. ''I was taken by ship from Loresta. In Vahn I was slave two years. Then war came with Karabdu. The master ran away. New lord said, all slaves go home. Easy to say. Many months I was alone in Vahanavat—no food, no home, no friend. Then I saw great Angul lord, Sinim, and I threw myself on his feet. He gave me gold and letter of the Gagan.'' She touched an amulet case which hung from her silver belt. ''Letter I carry always. It brought me home to Angulidan.''

"Is this Angulidan?" asked Sibby.

Tala smiled. "This is the edge of Angulidan. Anguls come north in the summer, to place where spirits walk, where dark is dead. Now darkness grows again, we go home, go south, to pastures of Angulidan. Now tell me, lord, why do you ask these questions? Why do you speak in the tongue of Vahn? We have waited many years for you."

Sibby decided to ignore these implications. "My name is Sibby," she said. "You are Tala. What may I call these others?"

Tala gestured with her free hand, the other covering her baby's head. "You are in the *ardan*, that is, among the people, of Soktani Agana." Hearing her name, the older woman nodded gravely and Sibby dropped her head in answer. "Soktani Agana leads the ardan of her husband, who is dead. He was a prince among the Angul people. Her father is noble also, his name is Varlas Mir." The old man smiled at this. "Her son is also Varlas Mir, but he is called the little Varlas, the Mirik." The young man blushed. Tala looked at Sibby keenly. "Batur Subi, will you not tell us why you speak in the tongue of Vahn?"

"I do not speak in the language of Vahn," said Sibby. "If this is the language they speak in Vahn, they use it without my knowledge. I do not know Vahn. I come from far away." Then, to her own amazement, she heard herself add, "I come from the black sands of the north, where the water hides in the stones."

For a moment Tala did not answer. She urged her baby to nurse, and above the soft smacking noise she spoke softly and rapidly to the Agana and the two Varlas Mirs. The elder Varlas nodded several times, then pushed aside a rug which covered a small carved chest. Opening it, he took out a massive book covered in worn, woolly sheepskin. The pages were parchment, covered with black writing and diagrams decorated in blue, red and gold. Finding at last the page he wanted, he held the book away at a comfortable distance from his eyes, tracing the words he read with his gnarled finger. It sounded like solemn poetry, and at the end of each line he paused and looked first at Sibby, then at his listeners, with dignified emphasis. When he had finished he went back to the beginning and started over, pausing so Tala could translate each separate line. She listened carefully and chose her words with great care. At her breast, the smacking noise grew less, then lapsed into silence.

"He is reading from our great book, the history of our people. In the old days, when the Angul prince Chanaga became Gagan, that is to say King of all Kings, he caused men to write down everything that happened in a book, which was copied many times. Each mir has a copy and one of his duties is to study it. If he cannot read, then he must get a scholar to read it for him. There are many prophecies in this book, telling what will be. Some were made by wise men, some come from the stars and trees. This one is called the Enku-dar.

> *From grassland*
> *To wasteland*
> *The Wheel turns. He will come*
> *On a dead man's horse*
> *In a dead man's clothes.*
> *He wears the dead man's stone.*
>
> *Two horses he rides*
> *One living One dead*
> *The Wheel turns. He will ride*
> *One-colored*
> *Four-colored*
> *Looking for the sword.*
>
> *From grassland*
> *To wasteland*
> *The Wheel turns. He will come.*
> *To the Lord of the Age*
> *He will carry the gift*
> *The sword of Chanaga Gagan.*

"We have waited long for your coming, Batur Subi. You are the Sword-Bearer that was foretold. We have heard that Tibir Agan is returning from his victories in Vahn, leaving much of the east unconquered. The warlords of Paradon mock his victories, insult his honor and that of the Angul people. With the sword of Chanaga this would not have been. You have come in good time, Sword-Bearer."

Sibby wanted to stand, but the *masett* had loosened her

legs. She held up her hand in protest. "I know nothing of any sword. I have never heard of Tibir. You are making a mistake."

Tala laughed and pointed at Sibby's sash. "Did mistake bundle a royal Angul belt around your hips, to carry the sword of Chanaga? Did mistake pin the Bloodstone of Balaj to your shoulder? Did mistake bring you here, dressed in the proofs of your mission? It has not been well for us here in Angulidan since the great Chanaga died. The Angul lords have quarreled with each other as he prophesied. It has fallen to the lot of a lord from Almadun, a man not even of the pure Angul blood, to restore our fortunes. But Tibir must have the sword. You will take it to him. Tibir will bring the world under our feet and Angulidan will prosper as it did in the days of the Gagan."

Tala spoke again with the elder Varlas, and he reached once more into the carved chest. He drew out a bundle of dirty rags, which he unwrapped reverently to reveal a small statue, beautifully carved like a fine chess piece. He held it up before Sibby and she could see that a hooded figure was shown, holding a lamp in one hand and wearing a carved stone on its shoulder. The detail was clear, even to the tiny incisions on the miniature brooch. Tala smiled in triumph.

"This is the Hermit from Chanaga Gagan's own set of sitranga. Before he died, he broke up his set so no man could play again on his board, and he gave the pieces to the faithful lords of Angulidan. One was the grandfather of Varlas Mir. It is his greatest treasure. In the days of Chanaga Gagan that stone was worn by his own wise councillor, Balaj. It has been lost since. Now you appear with it on your shoulder. So too will the sword of the Gagan rise to your hand."

Sibby touched the tiny statue and felt the detail with her finger. The likeness was perfect. Her tongue and brain numbed with the *masett,* she nodded. "I will take the sword to Tibir. Where will I find it?"

III

For several weeks the Anguls moved slowly south and west. As news of the Sword-Bearer reached other groups, they hurried their flocks and carts to join with the people of

Soktani Agana. By the time the great mountains were in sight, five ardans were moving together, stretching in their tens of thousands from horizon to horizon.

Sibby had never dreamed it could be so comfortable to be a nomad. If she wished to ride horseback she could, but her hosts encouraged her to remain in comfort in the tent, as the cart that bore it creaked slowly forward. Other carts carried bath-houses, complete with iron cauldrons full of water waiting to be warmed at each halt by fires lit underneath. Even the poorest herdsmen had small canopied carts in which their old people and infants could be carried.

If Sibby was physically idle, she had never worked harder with her mind. Each day she sat with Tala and the elder Varlas, learning more words, trying to string together simple sentences while her teachers politely covered their smiles at her accent. Tala patiently translated for her their custom and history, laws, legends and recipes, names of the stars and parts of a horse and cart. And as her mind filled with Angulidan, life in Massachusetts receded. Unless she forced herself to remember the strangeness of her transition, she felt as though she were merely living abroad in another country far away, rather than in another world. She knew she was unimaginably distant from her home but she still felt comfortable—almost as though she had been this far away before.

The dusty plain gave way to a region of irregular foothills, and the wide line of Anguls fell back into a spearhead formation, the ardan of Soktani Agana in front. Now that the air was cleaner Sibby rode more often, on a fat and shiny Monkey who was quite unrecognizeably filled with bounce and willfulness. For several days they climbed slowly until they reached an enormous valley, more than twenty miles wide and several times that in length. The grass was lush here and the herds hurried forward out of control. Despite the impatience of the animals, the Anguls disposed themselves in camps as orderly as ever, and soon the beasts were sorted out and grazing in the sections allotted to each family. That night, Tala explained to Sibby that the elder Varlas would lead her up into the hills on the following day, to find the sword. She also explained that these hills were the vanguard of a great range of mountains, known as the Hills of Thunder, Bala-Balaj.

Next morning at dawn, Varlas and Sibby rode out through breast-high mist into a world of silver and green. For a while they rode along the side of the valley, then slipped into a cleft in the hills and began a slow and winding climb. Soon the valley was far below, and at one of their halts Sibby had a chance to see the whole panorama below, a vast, enclosed green valley dotted with fires and tents and grazing beasts—a city in the wilderness. Then their trail wound away into the heart of the hills and the valley was left behind. At noon they stopped again, in a sandy clearing filled with scrub and coarse, weedy grass. They ate bread and cheese and shared some wine from a skin, then Varlas unsaddled the horses and hobbled their legs with twisted rawhide, slipped their bridles and left them grazing. The upward trail from here was very narrow.

Despite his age and weight old Varlas climbed easily, his breathing unchanged, his face smooth and unflushed. When Sibby had to stop to catch her breath he waited politely, instantly ready to start again as soon as she got to her feet. Their way grew rockier; twice he led them across an angled face of rock so sheer that only with bare feet could they get enough purchase to cross safely. Sibby tried not to imagine how she would make her way back carrying something bulky like a sword.

It was late afternoon when they came out on the worn, eroded summit of the mountain. They looked down on clouds now covering the valley from which they had climbed: south and east the plain stretched away in full sun. The great knotted tangle of mountains continued west and north as far as she could see. Into those mountains Varlas pointed. "Bala-Balaj," he said, waving his hand to indicate the whole range of mountains. "Zamarra," he added, "Almadun," naming the city and the country of Tibir.

Now Varlas moved to the southern edge of the summit and without warning dropped himself over; it was as though he had jumped off the edge of the world. Sibby's stomach twisted and jerked. Cautiously she lay down and peered over. Below there was a narrow ledge, where Varlas stood smiling. Behind him, very far below, the great plains shimmered and wheeled around. Sibby closed her eyes and the gusting wind whipped tears across her face.

She opened them again at a stern word from Varlas. She wasn't sure what it meant, but she seemed to recall it being used on recalcitrant oxen. At least no one could accuse the

Anguls of coddling their god-sent heroes. Slowly she maneuvered herself around, and belly hugging the rock, she dropped
down onto the narrow ledge beside him. Before her, hidden
by the rock overhang, was a door. It was timber-framed,
studded with brass and iron, and Sibby had a delirious vision
of its portage to this spot from the valley below. Rain-worn
and sun-faded it still hung true and opened at a touch of the
hand. Thankfully she stepped inside, out of sight of the
clutching void. Varlas stepped quietly after.

Inside it was dark and cold. The terror of the tomb of her
nightmare froze her legs, while the frosty air raised bumps on
her arms and stung her nostrils. There was a faint red glow by
which she could see: the light came from her stone. Varlas
stood with his back to the door, and gestured with his hand.
"Chanaga Gagan," he whispered. "Gagana. Ashva. Enku."
He had named, in addition to the Gagan, his wife, his horses
and his sword.

Now Varlas had dropped to his knees, eyes closed, lips
moving. As in her nightmare, there was a dark square in the
floor at the rear of the empty outer chamber. Slowly she
walked forward toward the black void. She could not believe
that she was going to have to go further in. Even to look
down tested her courage to the limit. She more than half
expected a black hand to clutch her by the throat. If it had cut
off her head for stealing a pin, what would it do to preserve
the sword of the emperor?

She knelt at the edge and leaned over, and the Bloodstone brightened slightly, glowing on the ice below like a
multiple red eye. It was not very far below. She closed her
eyes and forced her heart to slow its pounding, her lungs to
pump more quietly. Then she sighed and lowered herself
down into the freezing blackness. The inner chamber was
filled with ice to within six feet of the ceiling, frozen solid.
Items of wood and metal projected from the ice, tree and
animal forms carved, wrought and inlaid, but frozen fast and
unobtainable. Wonder began to overcome her terror. But
there was no way to tell where in this mass of ice the great
Gagan lay, and what had been done with his sword.

At her feet a piece of fabric protruded—light-colored felt,
embroidered to show a snake with a green eye and a man on
horseback. She tugged at it gently but it was held fast. She
began a slow circuit of the chamber, allowing the Blood-

stone's light to choose what it would show her. The low roof overhead was whitewashed stone, domed at the center and pillared around the edges with false columns carved into the rocky walls. Gold splattered the ceiling in irregular blotches, blackish until the full light of her stone made its color leap out to her eye. There were also flashes of red, green, blue and white from gemstones set into the design, but it was not until Sibby had recognized the horned shape of the moon and the rayed face of the sun that she realized she was looking at a map of the sky.

One of the colored stars glowed with the same red as her stone. She reached up and touched it and it pulsed with the same warmth and light. Suddenly she could see the sword clearly, as though it were not wrapped and hidden behind the chamber wall. Unhesitatingly she slipped her hand behind one of the pillars. The gap she found would have been too narrow for a larger hand and wrist. As the tips of her fingers touched the long, slim blade, bound up in oiled cloth, her body prickled with energy, lifting her hair. Gently she slipped it out of the rocky crevice, and through its wrappings it felt warm and alive, pressing up against her hand like a loving animal. The sword knew her. No one was going to chase her down or call her thief. The exposed hilt was yellowed ivory and she touched it to her lips.

Gravely she saluted the ice that held the emperor and his household, then she gently raised the wrapped sword over her head and up onto the floor of the upper chamber. She pulled herself up after it and saw Varlas still bowed by the door, still murmuring, eyes still closed. Taking up her prize again she stepped forward and gently touched his shoulder. He looked up slowly, then kissed the bundle she held out before him. For the first time that day, he looked old.

Out on the ledge the wind had stopped blowing, and the air was hushed with twilight. Varlas stooped so she could use his back to step up onto the summit. She got herself up in a hurry and before she had regained her feet Varlas was beside her. For a moment they stood looking out over the world, all reddened along one edge where the sun rode low. Then they slithered down off the summit onto the trail.

They were still high up when the dark caught them, but the Bloodstone filled the air around them with a dim red glow. The bundle in Sibby's arms seemed to lift her up off her feet so that she walked in a dream, seeing the difficult path unroll away behind them without feeling it. They went slowly, and the dream cut off all sound; Sibby could not even hear the wind she felt against her face. Some time had passed, perhaps an hour or more, before Sibby realized that they were not alone. Their companion was tall and dark and hooded, and Varlas did not seem to be aware of him.

Ahead of her, Varlas disappeared around a pile of rocks. The hooded figure stopped in the trail before her and held up its hand. She could barely see it, but she could sense a smile in the blackness under the hood. A voice spoke softly in her mind.

"So, the moon's daughter returns to earth to carry a conqueror's sword? I would not have recognized you if it had not been for the Bloodstone upon your shoulder. Remember, you have brought the sword up from the Underworld; you will be responsible for its actions until it is returned. Touch the Kermyrag's blood when you are in doubt. You will find answers there. And when you meet Arbytis on your journey, take him the greeting of the Zenedrim."

The hooded figure stepped aside and Sibby walked on, still in a dream, and rounded the corner to find Varlas only a few paces ahead. How they crossed the rock ledges in the dark, Sibby never could remember afterward, but at length they reached the clearing where the horses still grazed and there they slept until first light—Sibby with her forehead bent to touch the sword that rested across her knees. As she woke her mind was troubled. She wondered that so light a burden could weigh so heavily on her soul. Now, when it was too late to change course, she wondered about the man whom she was about to confirm as Conqueror of the World.

They were saddled and riding downhill long before full dawn, and when they reached the valley floor it swam in the breast-high mist of early morning. The day before was all a dream and it was as though they had never been up into the mountains, but for her burden. She wondered what the sword would do, once it was placed in the Conqueror's hand.

from Balaj's Book of Chanaga Gagan

And it happened at this time that Chanaga Gagan was
troubled in his sleep by strange visions, and he sent for wise
men to come to him from every land, and he asked them the
same question, which was, Why should it be that I see the
lands of the world spread out beneath my sword, and yet I do
not see myself or any man I know? And no one could answer
him except an old man with white hair, bent with age,
one-eyed, hooded in plain brown with no marks of distinction
upon him. And this man spoke to him and said, The Sword of
Chanaga Gagan will rule the world, one hundred years after
his death. Do you mean that my sons will rule a greater
empire than myself?, asked the Gagan. The old man shook
his head and answered, Your sons will lose the lands you
have conquered, some through idleness, some through vice,
some through the treachery of their friends. The Sword of
Chanaga Gagan will be taken up by another, and with it he
will rule the world.

At these words Chanaga Gagan grew angry, but he held
his peace and spoke courteously, out of respect for the old
man's white hairs. How will my sword come into another's
hands? he asked and the old man smiled, and answered, it
will be brought from the land of the dead, by a hero who
wears a dead man's clothes and rides on a dead man's horse.
And it will be he who pays the price to the underworld, not
the Conqueror in whose hand he puts your sword.

When the Gagan had gone out I, Balaj, drew this old man
aside, and from him got as many answers as he would give
me. And these I have written below, for future listeners to
judge.

THE FORTUNATE
CONJUNCTION

Chapter Five

THE HUNTERS

I

Tamara caught only glimpses of the Karif during his first busy days back in camp. Lord Parric's days were taken with star charts and his evenings with stargazing. She had been avoiding Lerdas, but after a few days of loneliness she sat down on the edge of his bed and attempted to be affable. He was looking at the wall, the fingers of his good hand monotonously rubbing the scar above his right eye. His first words, spoken very softly, were startling.

"I know a lot about you. I've known about you for years. I never thought I'd meet you, though; at least not so easily. My mother used to tell me about you, and the Karif, and King Leron, and about your mother, Sibyl. I know more about your family than you do."

"What do you mean? Who was your mother? Where did you grow up?"

"I grew up in Rym Treglad. You've never been there. Good King Leron would never subject his heir to that hell on earth. Dry, baked land, shriveled crops, water rationed in the cisterns, the smell of fish salted and smoked hanging over the city."

"Alric told me it's a nice town. Father built it and lived there eight years, before he returned to the throne."

"Returned to the throne? Returned? He was never king. His father Mathon was king. And King Mathon named Ddiskeard to rule after him. But when Leron returned to Tredana the true King Ddiskeard was very conveniently murdered, and then Leron 'returned' to the throne."

Tamara shivered but did not get up and leave. The boy's voice was fascinating in its passion. She knew he was lying but she had to hear more. "What did you hear about Sibyl?"

Lerdas laughed. "Your lovely mother. Don't you know it was only the merest chance you were born in Tredana? By rights you should have been born here in the desert. You could have had all the horses you wanted, then. You'd have had to treat the Karif a little differently, though."

Tamara folded her clenched hands in her lap. "What do you mean?"

"I mean it's been fun watching you flirt and bat your eyes. You're such a baby that it has never occurred to you why he treats you so nicely. You're such a baby you don't even know what he does all afternoon while you lie dreaming about him in your tent. He's doing more than dreaming and it isn't all alone and it isn't in his own tent."

"The Karif's private life is none of your business."

"True. But Sibyl's private life concerns us both, and some of that includes the private life of the Karif as well."

"I don't understand."

"It's pretty simple. You don't have any right to the throne of Tredana. But you could make an argument for a higher position among the Karabdu."

Tamara finally stood up, her legs shaking. "Do you think my father would have treated me the way—" her words failed as she suddenly saw a composite picture of every tender glance Leron had ever given Geret and Anith— "would have brought me up as heir to the throne, if he were not—if I were not—"

"He doesn't do it for you! He does it to hurt me! To hurt me and my mother! When he learns that my mother is dead and that I've run away, he'll probably send word for you to stay here. He won't need you any more. He can bring his own children back to Tredana and leave you here in the desert where you belong, with your real father!"

Tamara's head hurt. She covered her dry eyes with her hands and felt the heat in her face and the pounding of the blood under the skin. She wanted to call him names, call him a liar, hit him, but all the little puzzle fragments of her life were falling into place as he talked. Finally she managed to speak. "Who are you? I don't know anyone in Rym Treglad."

"You've read those lying histories Dansen wrote. You

know how Leron went in search of the prisoner princess and rescued her from her enchantments. It was on that trip he first met your mother, when she was just a young sorceress, her powers not yet perfectly formed. But she was strong enough to turn him against the great lady Dastra, the princess for whom he had dreamed and suffered and fought. Later, when he was lost and thought dead, the lady Dastra was courted by his cousin Ddiskeard. They married and ruled together in great peace and harmony. It was eight years before Leron returned. Even then, the lady Dastra in her kindness could never believe that Leron had truly been so corrupted and bewitched. That is why she did not immediately summon the palace guards, that black night when he came sneaking back into the castle." Lerdas' voice was now hoarse and trembling with passion, and tears were running from his eyes. "She welcomed him into her chambers, to talk with him, to try and understand what had happened, and how did he repay her? Your good, kind, gentle, noble Leron? He killed her husband the king as he lay sleeping and then he grabbed my mother by the hair and threw her down on the same bed—"

Tamara found her voice. "No," she whispered. "No, no, no, no, no!"

"Oh yes, yes, yes, yes, yes!" mocked Lerdas. "He almost killed her. But she lived. Am I not proof of that? She lived to tell her story and to teach me the meaning of revenge. For am I not her son? The son of Dastra and Leron of Tredana!"

Next morning, the Karif ordered a hunt. Ibrasa appeared, leading his own horse and Faras, who was snorting and bouncing and looking around eagerly. For the first time she noted the seal of the Karif, branded on the colt's shoulder and embroidered in gold thread on the corners of his ornate saddle. She knew that Lerdas had noted it long ago.

The Karabdin noblewomen were unlike Shadith in the richness of their clothing and jewelry, the gleaming gold of their long, coiled hair. They rode in a group together, laughing and talking, sitting easily on their dancing horses while the sun sparkled on their rings and bracelets. Shadith was dressed as before in a long plain tunic belted below the waist, a light sword buckled over. She smiled at Tamara.

"The Karif has gone ahead with the hounds and hound masters," she explained. She held up her hand and there was silence. As she lowered her arm, her horse bounded forward and the other horses stopped their fretting, leaping along happily.

Tamara kept her horse's nose level with Shadith's stirrup and Ibrasa rode on the other side, by her shoulder. The wind blew through her hair and washed over her face and she stood slightly in the stirrups, letting Faras leap rhythmically beneath her, rolling up the ground under his feet and spewing it out behind, no worries, no memories, no concerns. His shoulders bunched, lifted, stretched and fell, his back swung up and down. Between his small incurving ears she watched the desert flow toward and under her, and found some peace.

All too soon they found their prey. A group of gazelle had been startled by the Karif's hounds and came cutting across in front of the riders, moving in great improbable jerks that seemed to defy the pull of the earth and allowed them to stand still in the air. The hounds were straining on their long silken leads, standing up like rearing horses with their front legs extended, their narrow jaws open and bright pink tongues lolling. At a nod from the Karif, the master slipped his leashes and the lead couple bounded after the gazelle, closely followed by the body of the hunt. It did not seem possible that even such swift hounds could catch the gazelle. They streaked in pursuit running low to the ground, their plumed tails flowing behind them, hunting by sight. They caught the first so quickly that it took Tamara a few moments to realize their prize had been a baby, barely half-grown, tired and confused. As the baby fell, a larger gazelle came leaping back toward them and stood up like a little goat, butting at the hounds with her small striped horns, only to fall almost immediately under their jaws. Trained as they were for the chase, none of the hounds worried their prey; they leapt and slashed and turned in search of new victims.

Leaving a gamekeeper behind to take up the kill, the master called in his hounds again and leashed them. The horses were blowing now, so the hunt trotted quietly in the direction the herd had taken, following the clear prints in the sand. At the top of a gentle rise the Karif signaled a halt, and there below them in a narrow ravine they could see the rest of the herd. The desert gazelle had coppery bodies the color of Faras, with black and white striping on their legs, faces and horns. The horns of the females grew straight and sharp, but the males wore massively twisted crowns on their narrow, bearded heads.

It was one of these bucks that suddenly sighted them. His leap alerted the herd, which had been scattered about the valley floor, panting and shaky-legged. Once more they bounded into flight, bouncing up the farther slope. The old male did not join them. Whether protective or confused, he came leaping up the slope toward the hunt. The hound master hastily uncoupled his hounds but they were confused by the gazelle's behavior and were still standing startled with ears flipped up and eyes wide as he crashed into them. His great horns tossed them yelping sideways. As his charge brought him level with the master, the man deftly dropped a leash over his horns and spun his horse around so the buck was pulled up onto his hind legs. Leaning down from the saddle, he slit its throat with a swift motion. The blood spurted out so violently that it was steaming on the sands in a bright red puddle before the buck's sides had stopped heaving. His eyes remained open, but Tamara had to close hers.

She opened them to find Shadith looking at her with a little amusement. "You do not hunt in Tredana?"

"Of course we do. It's just that he was so—so brave."

The Karif, riding over to join them, nodded at her words. "Brave indeed. His horns will be preserved in his honor." He looked at her face more closely. "If you cannot bear the sight of blood, best stay with archery and kill from a distance. Are you certain you wish to learn the sword?"

Tamara nodded, unwilling to trust her voice. As they turned their horses to home, sedately walking, she wondered what would make something gallop so blindly against the enemy, and die for his people. The Karif's next question startled her with its abruptness.

"What did they teach you in Tredana?"

"History. Music. Poetry—letter writing. Riding and archery. Manners. Things like that."

"No sciences? The progression of the stars and planets? Measuring and calculations? Anatomy? Languages? The making of charts?"

"Alric was starting to explain about mapmaking. But he doesn't get the chance to travel anymore. He has to wait for information to come to him. He wanted fa— the king to send men out on surveys for him, with instruments for making special measurements, but Leron said it was a waste of manpower. He said he needed the engineers for building in Tredana, not drawing lines on paper. We study the maps now, to learn about Angulidan; but Leron says it is necessary only in wartime.''

"He grows to sound more and more like his father, old Mathon. What histories do you study?''

"The founding and fall of Treglad . . . the rise of Vahn . . . Simirimia in Treclere . . . the defeat of the Four False Kings. . . .'' She choked as she remembered Lerdas' new version of the defeat of Ddiskeard, but the Karif did not notice.

"And what do they teach you of the desert? Of Angulidan and Samida? Do they tell you how sailors from the ancient empire of Samida founded Treglad as a trading port, long before the dawn of your own history? Do they teach you that an Angul observer has measured the distance around the earth? What do they say of the Karabdu?''

"Fa— the king has always spoken of you as a friend.''

"But he does not send his doctors here to study herbs or bone-setting or surgery. What would he do if you told him the measurement around the earth?''

"He would laugh and ask me what use it was.''

The Karif nodded. "I traveled once to Vahn, when I was young. I wanted to see a great city. Never before had I seen people in idleness. The rich, because they did not wish to work, the poor, because they could not find any work. Never before had I seen such hunger in a time of plenty, people starving in the streets of a city that was encircled by fertile fields, well-irrigated. And there for the first time I heard that my people, the Karabdu, were bloody and luxurious, primitive, without learning or culture, of interest only for their horses and their textiles. The men who told me this used Karabdin words when they named the stars, used Karabdin instruments when they charted their coasts, rode on Karabdin horses, wore Karabdin silks, walked on Karabdin carpets, preened in mirrors made of Karabdin glass. They fought with swords of Karabdin steel and sang love songs accompanied on Karabdin barakas.'' The Karif spoke with unusual vehemence. Suddenly he checked himself and shook his head. "Since the overthrow of Bodrum, that has changed. Odric and his brother have traded freely with us, in ideas as well as goods. Tredana has not. You will do well to enlarge your education while you are here. Perhaps you will have some influence on the king.'' He laughed. ''I little thought when I first met him, twenty years ago, that Leron of Tredana would prove so stubborn.''

''He's a good man.'' Tamara made the observation tentatively, but Ajjibawr agreed unhesitatingly.

''He is like his father, Mathon—kind, practical, more in love with song than science. He has sunk deep in familiarity. Perhaps the Angul danger will wake him up.''

Tamara searched for the right words. ''What would you say if someone—if someone said that Leron had been cruel? Or unjust? Could you believe it?''

Ajjibawr raised his eyebrows. ''Has he been cruel to you?''

''Never!''

''Well, I would say that I could not imagine it, except for that time long ago when he was under the spell of the Great Queen.'' A slight flush rose in his cheeks. ''And he was not the only one to feel her power.''

Tamara's heart, which had been rising, plummeted. ''Then if someone is bewitched, anything is possible?''

''If the bewitchment is sufficiently strong.''

They had reached the outermost tents of the camp. Servants sprang to their horses' heads but as before Ajjibawr held her horse himself. ''He pleases you?'' he asked, and she rushed to give him tardy thanks. They stood for a moment face to face, the Karif's eyes squinted against the sun, his pale hair far receded from his temples. ''You ride like one of us,'' he said softly, and abruptly turned away.

The sleepless night and morning's exercise sent Tamara heavily asleep that afternoon. In the early evening a message came from Shadith, offering her instruction with the sword. Tamara had thought it would mean actual practice, but instead Shadith brought her into her tent, where several different swords and daggers were laid out on the carpet, and for an hour or more Tamara learned their names and uses and the way they should be held. It was not until she left to wash before dinner that Tamara reluctantly admitted to herself that the faint familiar odor in Shadith's tent was the scent of the Karif's snuff.

Next morning Tamara worked hard at her first sword practice, and Shadith gravely complimented her. Again she brought Tamara into her own tent to wash off the dust and sweat of her exertions. Tamara soaked her red face in the cold, scented water, then flopped down on the cushions with a wet cloth over her face.

"How long does it take to get used to the heat?"

"You are doing very well. It would not take you very long." Tamara covered her face completely with the cloth and tried to sound casual.

"Did my mother like the desert?" The silence was so long that Tamara thought she would stifle under the wet washrag. When Shadith finally spoke, it was more curtly than usual.

"Not well enough to stay."

Tamara slowly rolled the cloth off her face and looked up at Shadith. "Why would she have stayed? She was on her way home to Tredana."

Shadith sat down cross-legged and leaned forward, her blue eyes burning into Tamara's. "Her home could have been here. So can yours, if you so choose."

Tamara closed her eyes. "The Karif wants to send me home to my father."

"The Karif has honored his promise to your mother. But do you think he would send away his only child if she wanted to stay with him?"

Tamara swallowed. "I have a duty to Tredana."

"The king has other children. Your duty is to yourself."

Tamara forced her tears back as they rose. "If I don't belong to Tredana, I don't belong anywhere. The Karif never sent for me. He only visited twice. If he is my father why didn't he want me?"

"Will you punish him for keeping his word to Sibyl? The call of the blood has brought you home. Will you return to those—those barbarians who hide in cities and wallow in ignorance?"

"Why do you want me to stay?"

Shadith looked at her soberly. "I want nothing but the happiness of the Karif. You hold it in your power. Think on it."

Tamara walked wearily back toward her tent, her shoulders aching from lifting the unfamiliar weight of a sword. The last person in the world she had wanted to see was waiting for her there, jiggling his arm in his sling.

"I told you it would happen! There's a messenger here

from Tredana. You can forget about ever seeing the sea again!''

She ignored his smirking and hurried over to the council area in front of the Karif's tent. There, sprawled on the carpets, was the familiar long-legged figure of Herrard the Traveler, grizzled and a little paunchy, draining a cup of wine and smiling fondly on the Karif. Parric was there also, propped up against one of the Karif's saddles. Herrard saw Tamara approaching and pulled himself to his feet; Ajjibawr rose also and indicated a familiar bright blue saddle, now resting next to his own on the carpet. She took Herrard's hand in both of hers and squeezed it, then folded up against her new seat of honor.

Herrard opened his leather case and handed her a folded letter. Tamara noticed another letter, its seal broken, lying by Ajjibawr's hand. As she split Leron's seal Herrard shook his head. ''The news is not good, my lady. Tibir has returned to his homeland, but he did not take all his armies with him. The soldiers commanded by Aksu did not stay in the desert after riding through the valley. While my brother Ajjibawr searched for them in the Land, they were riding north and east. It is a miracle you and Ibrasa did not ride into their arms.''

Tamara unfolded her letter. Father or not, Leron's strong, dark writing filled her with warmth and security. He asked her to stay in the desert until it was safe to send for her, and she could see nothing behind his words other than loving concern. He said more than once how deeply he missed her, and only in the letter's closing lines could she read any hint of her dilemma.

If I cannot have you here by my side there is nowhere I would rather have you be than under the protection of the Karif. He will see to your comfort, honor and safety as though you were his own, of that I am confident.

Always your loving father, LERON.

II

On the Karif's recommendation, Tamara resolved to study the stars. Parric was delighted and Tamara did her best to share his enthusiasm. She was one who liked to be up and doing, and she was more familiar with sunrises than the night sky. The first evening she accompanied him to Ammagest's special tent she felt sleepy and dull, filled with dinner and ready for bed. Then she looked up and her whole life was changed for ever.

Here, away from all the little lights of the camp, the sky was perfectly black overhead, so filled with a blaze of stars that her legs trembled at their beauty. In the eastern part of the sky, a broad pale highway of stardust crossed the heavens from north to south. How could she have lived so long and never seen the colors of the stars? Some were blue, some yellow, some red; each burned with its own secret fire and meaning. There were other stars much brighter, but one clear orange light drew her eye again and again. She turned to Ammagest and pointed. "What is that one? The orange one?"

"That is the Zenedrim, the Watcher. He stands in the head of the burning one, the Kermyrag." He indicated right and left with his hand. "To either side there are blue stars, do you see? They mark the wings of the Kermyrag. The bright white is his eye, and the small cloud is his blood that runs from his breast." He fell silent and Tamara traced the figure, seeing clearly the familiar shape of the firebird. But over and over her eye was brought back to the calm, brooding golden star above him. Then she looked down and to the right, where there was another glowing net of nearly related stars, three of which shone together in a brightly marked line, and one of which was dull and red.

"What is that figure, touching the Kermyrag?"

"That is the hero of the skies, the Sword-Bearer. Mark how the sword hangs from his belt. Can you see the three stars?"

Tamara nodded and said, "Isn't there a fourth star in his sword? A little one halfway down?"

Ammagest smiled. "Indeed there is, though few have the eyes to see it. Now look up, to the hero's shoulder, just below the edge of the Kermyrag's body. What do you see?"

"A dull red star."

"That star is called the Bloodstone. It spills, you see, from the blood of the Kermyrag, and pins the hero's cloak to his shoulder."

Tamara studied the two figures until her neck hurt, and

when she looked down Ammagest bowed and indicated she should enter his tent, where Parric already waited in his litter.

Here she had another surprise: the tent was walls only, high enough to protect the observer's charts from wind and sand, and to close out any distracting lower lights. There was no canopy overhead but the stars. On the table where he spread his papers, charts and calculations, there were several brass instruments for sighting and measuring, and a little lantern that could be completely shuttered.

Ammagest greeted Lord Parric. "She sees the colors and has singled out the Zenedrim."

Parric looked up at the night sky for a long moment, then shook his head. "They all burn white for me."

"For most they do."

Ammagest guided Tamara's line of vision from the Kermyrag, past the Sword-Bearer to another group of stars. "What do you see there?"

Tamara looked and her scalp pricked. "A greenish star—I don't know why, but it seems evil. There is a half-circle of little stars to the right, and then a crooked line of bigger ones. And a hazy patch, like a cloud but brighter. Why does the green star look so dangerous?"

"We call it Vaz-daz, which is 'the capriciousness of God.' Three days it shines as you see it now, then dims for a space of twenty hours. When God shuts his eye, anything may happen. The figure we call the Great Serpent, and those bright stars mark its length."

"Why is the eye of God in a serpent?"

"Some stories would have it that God was swallowed by this serpent. He is strong enough to keep its jaws open for three days, but when he tires the jaws snap shut, his eye is dimmed, and terror loosed upon the world. Others would have it that God has chosen the serpent's form, and closes his eye as it pleases him. In any case, it is not good to be born in the dimmed light of Vaz-daz."

Tamara looked at the baleful green star again and shivered, then looked back at the Sword-Bearer. "Does his sword point at the Serpent?"

"So it seems. Some believe he protects the Kermyrag from the Serpent."

Tamara's eyes stung as Ammagest unshuttered his lamp

and spread out some charts. The whole heaven was pictured there, with beautiful drawings outlining the indicated stars.

"Here are the figures you have learned tonight, the Kermyrag with the Zenedrim in his brow, the Sword-Bearer with the Bloodstone on his shoulder, his sword pointing at the Serpent with the Eye of God in its head. For two thousand years we have been in the Age of the Serpent, which is to say that each spring, on the day that dark and light are equal in length, the sun has risen in the Sign of the Serpent. But each year the sun's position has altered slightly, and now we are entering the Age of the Firebird. A new age is beginning—an age of different quality from the last. Some say the beginning was marked by the death of the Great Queen twenty years ago; Simirimia of Treclere, your mother's mother."

Tamara nodded, wordless. She had never thought of herself or her family as being part of heaven's pattern.

Ammagest picked up one of his instruments. "But before we look at more stars, there are many simple facts for you to learn. You must learn how to measure. You must learn how proportions remain constant, whatever the size of the figure. A triangle, for example. If you have two sides and one angle, or two angles and one side, you can calculate the missing parts. The proportions remain the same as in the little drawing on your paper, even though the space you wish to measure spans many miles." As he spoke Tamara yawned hugely and Ammagest nodded to Parric. "Enough for the first lesson, perhaps. Rest well tomorrow afternoon. You have only begun to see."

Next afternoon, Tamara obeyed Ammagest's instructions reluctantly. The conversation between Herrard and the Karif was becoming very interesting to her, and neither seemed to care that she sat and quietly listened. It fascinated her to hear how they spoke in a mixture of the Karabdin and common tongues: she had always known that Herrard the Traveler was well known among the Karabdu, but she had never imagined him dressed in robes and answering to the name of Rassam. They were talking about Arbytis, to her only a name in Dansen's histories, but to them a well-remembered friend.

When she excused herself to go rest, the Karif gave her an approving smile. "Ammagest tells me you show great promise. It is well."

She carried a little glow of self-satisfaction back to her

tent. She was still pleased with herself as she lay resolutely on her back with closed eyes, waiting wide-awake for sleep to visit her. The glow was dispelled by a harsh whisper from the corner.

"Tamara!" Lerdas was there, his Marajite cloak pulled over his head, hunched and frightened looking.

"What are you doing here?" she asked angrily, and Lerdas looked over his shoulder in a gesture of unnecessary caution, since they were alone in her tent.

"It's happened! That man from Tredana, Herrard! He recognized me! I used to see him sometimes in Rym Treglad. Now he's told the Karif who I am."

Tamara sat up and frowned. "If he did then they weren't too excited by the news. I just left them and they were talking about old times and the High Priest Arbytis. They never mentioned you."

"They don't know that I know. They don't think there's any need to hurry. When they want to make their move, they can just reach out and snap! I'm either in chains or *dead*."

Tamara's mild exasperation grew stronger. "Lerdas, nothing's going to happen to you!"

But he went down on his knees before her, his eyes glittering. "I've told you the truth! Why don't you believe me?"

"Even if I believed you, what could I do?"

"You could help me escape. I wouldn't be in this danger if it weren't for you. Just help me get away, you'll never see me again. That's all I ask!"

Tamara felt like reminding him that he wouldn't be alive if it weren't for her, but she held her tongue. One lesson Leron had always been very strict about enforcing was courtesy to those weaker than yourself. "How could you get away? There isn't any shelter for hundreds of miles."

"Yes, there is. The ravine where you found the gazelles. There's water there. I could hide."

"I'd just be killing you if I took you there."

"You'll be killing me if you don't! This way I have a chance." He buried his face in his hands. "I beg of you, help me."

Tamara knew perfectly well what her answer should be. But the thought of being rid of his sly face and painful stories was too tempting to resist. She supposed that if she grew to feel too guilty about him she could always send a search party in the right direction. "All right," she said. "This evening, when it's cool. I'll take my horse for a ride before dinner. You tell Hattam you need exercise and go for a walk—go east, out of sight of the tents. I'll already have ridden west. I'll double around under the cover of the big dunes and meet you. I suppose Faras can carry double as far as the ravine. If I get back too late, I can just say I got so busy looking at stars that I forgot about dinner."

Lerdas grabbed her hands and before she could pull away he was covering them with dry kisses. Her skin crawled and she pushed him back on his heels.

"Don't be stupid. Now just get out of here without being seen."

Lerdas skulked to the front flaps, peered around and slipped out, while behind him Tamara absentmindedly rubbed her hands clean on the edge of the mattress.

It was as easy as Tamara had thought. Faras pranced eagerly out of camp, protesting at the check of her legs and hand. He did not understand why she was so intent on conserving his energy. At the foot of the soft sand dunes he floundered and slithered in the loose sand, panting a little but still up-headed and eager. Once back on firm footing he half-stood on his hind legs in impatience, then startled and bowed sideways as Lerdas stood up from where he had crouched in a hollow of the dunes. Tamara said nothing, only giving him a hand to mount behind her. Faras sank a little in protest at the weight, then pulled himself together and strutted out valiantly, trying to pretend there was nothing unusual in the double burden. Tamara patted his neck and turned him north. Even though it was necessary for his balance, the feeling of Lerdas' hands on her back was repulsive to her.

The evening star shone clearly above the horizon to their left. As they rode the sky brightened along the rim of the desert in the last flare of sunset, darkening quickly above. The evening star was joined by others, their twinkle in brilliant contrast to its round, steady glow. In a few hours the golden Zenedrim would be up there, watching from the Kermyrag's crown, and on its heels would coil the Serpent, Vaz-daz, glowing green. Already the sky was beginning to seem familiar to Tamara, a place that could be signposted and explored, no longer just a deep, incomprehensible void.

She was so filled with these thoughts she failed to give any significance to the way Faras was flicking his ears, lifting his head, snuffing the wind. Half a mile from the ravine's edge, he stopped so suddenly both riders were thrown forward on his neck. Head parallel to the ground, ears pricked, nostrils wide, he stood and listened, momentarily aware of the people on his back. Tamara touched his side with her heel, gently at first, then with a hard kick. He squealed a little at that and despite their combined weight gave a little buck of protest. Then he trotted forward eagerly. A few yards short of the edge Tamara tried to halt him, but he thrust his head forward and continued walking right up to the edge. There he halted and cocking his head looked down into the shadows with great interest.

Tamara could see nothing. It was too dark and besides she was eager to be away. Lerdas slipped off and once more took her hand, murmuring his thanks, while she tried gently to pull free. Suddenly he closed his hand hard on hers and she was amazed by the strength in his fingers. She pulled back, harder this time, and Lerdas suddenly laughed and pulled in return, so hard and unexpectedly she almost fell off. As she slipped, the edge of her ornate stirrup hit Faras on the ribs and his sideways leap completed what Lerdas had started. Angry and amazed she picked herself up from the ground, only to feel Lerdas' hands on her once more, this time on her shoulders. He spun her around and pushed her to the ravine's edge, calling down into its depths.

"Lord Aksu!" he cried. "I have brought her as I promised." And a deep voice in the dark answered, saying that he had done well.

Chapter Six

THE HIGH PRIEST

I

Tamara knew the Karif would find and rescue her. In the presence of Aksu, the powerful Angul lord, she was as serenely contemptuous as she was with Lerdas. It gave her great satisfaction to see how her composure angered them both. After seeing her secure Aksu was soon content to ignore her, but Lerdas never gave up trying to get a reaction. While she jogged along on a shaggy Angul pony that was as smelly and unkempt as its owners, Lerdas paraded himself on her chestnut colt, jerking at the bit and using his spurs unnecessarily. Tamara merely looked away but in her heart she savagely wished him dead.

When the Karif's forces did find them nearly a week later, Tamara never even saw the attack. Aksu's scouts warned the Anguls of the approaching Karabdin force and they immediately fell into order—Aksu and his bodyguard commanding the center, with cavalry wings to the right and left. Tamara, Lerdas, women, children, prisoners and spoils were all forced far to the rear. Tamara would not have known who they were fighting, if a small group of Karabdin warriors had not galloped entirely around the Angul forces in an attempt to break their ranks. But the Anguls repulsed the desert horsemen, though they lost their leader in the fight. Despite the confusion and loss of morale, the Anguls kept their column together, marching safely out of the desert into Vahnian territory, their hostage and their booty intact. There they found that they had lost more than a leader. Their delay had also cost them a crossing back to Angulidan with the rest of the Emperor's forces.

They reached Vahanavat five days too late to join the general embarkation. The engineers who had been left behind to rebuild the city to the greater glory of Tibir were not very welcoming to these late, demoralized stragglers. At first it seemed that the Anguls might not even be able to find a vessel willing to take them home across the seas. Then Zardik Mir, who had taken command after the death of Aksu, produced his hostage and recited her pedigree, and the army engineers agreed that it was probably worth their while to see that she be sent along safely to Tibir in Zamarra.

The soldiers were bickering among themselves by this time. They had planned to sail for home as part of a triumphal army, and when they came to the nearly empty harbor, mere sullen discontent boiled over into rage. One group wanted to take Tamara themselves, to ransom or sell her privately, and it was with the greatest difficulty that Zardik Mir convinced them their best hope lay with the mercy of Tibir. Tamara hardly knew or cared that they quarreled over her. Tiredly she went on board and entered the stuffy cabin, to wait quietly through the long afternoon for the ship to set to sea.

A merchantman had been commandeered to take them at least as far as Dessa, on the southern tip of Loresta. Into the small ship pressed soldiers and camp followers, some wounded, some whole, all clutching booty either won in battle or scavenged from the streets of the ruined city. Tamara and Lerdas both, victim and captor, were put in the cabin claimed by Zardik Mir for himself; the rest made do in the hold, between the bales of goods and the picket lines for the captured blood-horses. Refugees crowded the decks. Faras was down there in the dark and stink of the 'tween-decks. Tamara did not think his case could be any worse than hers, in a tiny room with a gloating Lerdas and an Angul mir who dressed in uncured hides and did not wash, but dressed his skin and hair with rancid animal fats. And what made it worse was the realization that she was not going to be rescued. Until they went on shipboard, it had seemed at least a possibility. Now she could almost believe Lerdas' version of the fight neither of them had seen—that Aksu had killed the Karif before being killed himself by the Karabdu. What other explanation could there be?

The ship took the tide that evening, and soon after Tamara was allowed outside for air. The ship was more crowded than she would have thought possible. Homeless families were packed in between the railings, babies wailing, old people lamenting, children whining, mothers and fathers scolding. Several fires had been started with complete disregard for the dried timbers and tarry ropes nearby. Some families had chickens and a few had piglets. The smell was as bad as the noise.

The cabins were built high in the aft of the ship, and the passageway between them ended in a low parapet overlooking the deck a few feet below. Here Tamara leaned, resting her chin on her elbows, her eyelids drooping, bone-weary with despair. Then a pleasant voice spoke from below, and she looked down into a broad, good-natured face, framed in greying chestnut curls and edged with a darker and even curlier beard. "You must not tire now, little lady. The journey has scarce begun. Do you go only as far as Dessa?"

"I don't know," said Tamara. "I think I'm going to a place called Zamarra. I don't have any choice in the matter."

"Zamarra? The courts of Tibir? You are indeed fortunate. I have been told it is the most beautiful city in the world. I would like to see Zamarra myself, but I would fear to travel so far without protection. When the World Conqueror is on a campaign, the roads are not as safe as they are when he stops at home." He smiled. "But let me introduce myself. My name is Marricson. By trade, an entertainer. You have heard of me perhaps?" Tamara shook her head. Marricson swept her a long and courtly bow, and as he straightened he held, as though by magic, a ribboned baraka in his hand. "Then let me explain. Recently Marricson of Marricson's Famous Players, now Marricson the solitary minstrel. The late unfortunate events in Luntar and Vahanavat not only scattered my troupe, but also rendered what little audience remains incapable of being amused. I am hoping to find in Dessa happier times and people. And what of you, little lady?"

His warmth made Tamara smile back, but she answered cautiously. "My name isn't important. I'm—I'm a Tredanan. I'm the prisoner of an Angul Mir. Those are his soldiers down below decks. I think he's taking me to Tibir in Zamarra."

Marricson's eyebrows shot up and his heavy-lidded eyes suddenly opened ludicrously wide. "A prisoner! That explains the long face and the sighing. Tell me, do you think you are past being entertained, or would you like me to try and amuse you?'' Tamara blushed and shook her head, but Marricson's fingers were already on the strings. At the opening chords, some chattering family groups fell silent and turned to listen.

> *There was a lady in a tower*
> *Banorie o banorie*
> *There was a lady in a tower*
> *Wept and sighed from hour to hour*
> *"To fly away's not in my power—"*
> *Bow down o clouds of Banorie.*

> *There came a great bird from the west*
> *Banorie o banorie*
> *There came a great bird from the west*
> *He caught her up against his breast*
> *He flew to him that she loves best*
> *Bow down o clouds of Banorie.*

Marricson sang the song with a sweet voice and wonderfully exaggerated emotion, making Tamara giggle despite her weariness. He swept her another bow. ''Thank you my lady for proving that I am still an entertainer.'' For a moment, Marricson continued to smile at her without speaking. Then, easily for so bulky-seeming a man, he pulled himself up onto the railing and dropped to his feet by her side. He lightly touched her shoulders. ''I will walk you to your cabin,'' he said, and the warmth of his hands made her feel suddenly peaceful and secure. As if in a dream, she went back into the narrow passageway. At her door he bent his lips to her ear and she heard him speak as though from a great distance. ''Courage,'' he said. ''You are not without friends.''

Outwardly Tamara continued to droop during the long dull days at sea, but in private her spirits rose rapidly. Almost every night she managed to slip away to visit with Marricson and his friends. He fed her, listened to her, laughed with her, taught her silly songs. She began to feel like herself again, and as Dessa approached on the horizon she was ready to make her plans to slip away.

The tall palm trees of Dessa were the first things Tamara

could see. The whole coast was deep green—wonderfully
lush to her salt-stung eyes, shimmering in a strongly-scented
humid heat and filled with the cries of strange birds. There
were no familiar trees or plants, just the great, droopy-headed
palms with their prickly trunks, and everywhere masses of
outrageously bright flowers, their blooms as big as both her
hands together.

Dessa was built inland, at the mouth of a broad, muddy
delta. As the ship followed the winding waterway toward
town, the people on board, sick and weary from three crowded
weeks at sea, eagerly gathered their bundles and children
around them. Below decks the Angul soldiers, rested and
bored, simmered like a pot at the boil. Zardik Mir had his
hands full with controlling them.

It was nearly thirty years since Tibir had conquered
Loresta and destroyed the city of Dessa. His engineers had
rebuilt it on a grand scale, even to widening the channels and
rebuilding the docks in the harbor. Marricson had told Tamara how in the old days the narrow streets of Dessa ran with
filth, and how disease was common; now it was made up of
wide avenues with stone-lined, covered drains. To keep the
streets clean, animals of burden were not allowed within the
walls of the city itself. All portage was done by men who
carried padded platforms on their stooped backs.

Lerdas and Tamara were placed in the midst of the Angul
soldiery during disembarkation. Because of the horses they
brought with them they could not go into the city, but rather
had to march around to the stockyard area—slowly, because
of the weakness of the animals. There by the paddocks Zardik
had his men put up their tents. They would have to wait some
days for the horses to regain strength and balance. It was a full
month's march to Zamarra, and much of the way difficult.

The first night, Tamara was glad of a chance to wash with
unrationed water and rest on the motionless earth. She fell
asleep quickly. Next morning, she began to make her plans.
She wished she knew how big Dessa really was. Was it the
kind of city where a stranger could hide himself? Or was it
the kind where a stranger stood out like a signpost? She tried
to interest Lerdas in a trip to the great marketplace, but he
would not take her into the city without an Angul guard, and
the men were busy. So she had to content herself with visiting
the horses, especially Faras.

Like the others, Faras had dropped condition on the voyage. His coat was dull, his bones stuck out, his ears drooped. He recognized her without enthusiasm. She watered him and brushed him and saw that he always had a bundle of hay before him, and wondered how long it would be before he would be fit enough to help her escape.

Marricson came to their fires the second night. He did not greet Tamara except to wink at her when no one was looking, and he had with him several musicians, dancers and acrobats. The Anguls were pleased to be entertained and generous with their laughter and small change. They opened their wineskins and as they drank enjoyed the entertainment more and more. Before the music was over, she heard Marricson thanking Zardik Mir for the offer of his protection during the hazardous trip to Zamarra.

II

Two days later they left for Zamarra; the horses were not much fitter. Zardik Mir was still hoping to catch up with the Empress, however, and now Tamara learned the reason for his haste. Aksu had disobeyed the orders of the Emperor when he had kidnapped her in the desert. His job had been to guard the baggage train and the royal household. If Zardik Mir could rejoin the column before it reached Zamarra, he would be able to argue that he had done his best to fulfil the dead Aksu's duties. Then, in addition, he would produce a royal hostage. If Tibir were well enough pleased, Zardik might even be given a reward—might be made a *baturik,* or 'lesser hero.' A baturik had grazing privileges, herds of horses, weapons. It was a rank enjoyed by one man in a thousand.

Having Marricson and his entertainers travel with them put Tamara in a quandary. It was nice to know that there were people nearby who were kindly disposed toward her, but on the other hand, they were neither powerful nor headed in a direction in which she wanted to go.

A few days on the road improved Faras beyond recognition. The heavy damp heat which had made him puff and blow at first now bothered him not at all. He barely sweated, and the bloom was returning to his coat. Lush grasses grew thickly along the edge of the highroad, and at night the horses could hardly wait to be hobbled out at grazing. They had two weeks' travel before them to reach Loresta City, and from there the roads ran west to Samida as well as north to Zamarra. From Gagan-ala, in Samida, there were ships to Melismala. As Tamara made her plans, it seemed to her that her wisest course would be to try and escape just before they reached Loresta City. She would lay a false course back toward Dessa, then try and cut northwest through the jungle, toward the Samidan highway. It was a long chance, but her only one.

At first their way did lie through heavy jungle growth, plenty of game and water always at hand, but likewise filled with tormenting insects. Then the road lifted in a slow turning climb up out of the vine-covered trees and onto a broad, grassy plain. The air was dryer and cleaner, often with a cooling wind, and both humans and horses fared better. At night, large animals could be heard sniffing and growling out in the grasses beyond the camp, and Marricson described to her the giant cats of Loresta, large and more graceful than lions, striped gold and black, easily able to bring down a horse and rider with one leap. The Anguls kept their camp surrounded with roaring fires at night for protection, and Tamara began to wonder about the practicality of her plan.

On the grassy uplands, the night sky was as black as it had been in the desert. Since she had last examined the sky, the stars had progressed toward the west. The Serpent was now in the middle of the southern sky, and there were new groupings of stars to his left, which she did not understand. Marricson, noticing her sky watching, came to sit down beside her.

"Which stars do you watch? I have some friends who have studied with good masters—Sinim of Loresta City, Ammagest of the Karabdu—"

"Ammagest! Do you know him?"

"I have met him, yes. But I am not much of a scholar. I spent some time at Sinim's feet, though, several years ago. I was suffering from a personal sorrow and he argued me through it quite cleverly."

"I think Ammagest told me something about Sinim."

"Sinim's teachings have spread worldwide. He is as remarkable for his discoveries as he is for his parentage and his many years. Did you know that he is a son of the fabled

Chanaga Gagan? He was born to one of the younger wives, some months after his father's death. His uncle Ibrim—grandfather of Loresta's current ruler—took him under his protection and raised him to be a scholar and a man of peace. Sinim has lived to see the Great Wheel dash his family down, then raise it high again. He is fully one hundred years old. Perhaps when we come to Loresta City you will see him. I am told he is as keen in his mind as ever.''

Marricson had other surprises for Tamara. A little knowledge of the stars, some knowledge of history, a smattering of geography and a few words on the science of measuring. As she considered her new lessons, she wondered—with a pain she could feel in the pit of her stomach—if the Karif would ever know how much she had tried to improve her mind.

As her learning increased, her chances for escape dwindled. After passing through the grassy uplands, the road north wandered into the foothills of a long range of mountains, low at first, but rising into a mighty range in the far northwest. Marricson explained that these peaks were the spine of the Lorestan peninsula, and formed a shield which had always protected it from the Samidan Empire. Near Loresta City there was one pass west through the mountains, and one pass north to Zamarra. The ancient city that guarded these passes had only fallen twice to invaders—once long ago to Chanaga Gagan, and once to the lame Tibir. Northward they went, and the mountains along the west grew greater and more menacing. They were far enough away to be seen clearly; the tops were snow covered and often hidden by clouds. Their rocky sides were ribbed straight up and down, and the dirt tracks which led toward them ended in little villages built in the foothills.

From these the Anguls made a regular practice of commandeering food and wine. For them it was another form of hunting, no different in kind from the capture of deer and rabbits. It amused them to startle the peasants from their homes, to watch them run away, rabbitlike, before them. At one of the villages however, a little larger and more stoutly built with massive mud-brick walls, the headman of the village held the gates against them long enough to show Zardik the Seal of Chanaga given him by the Empress herself, only a week earlier. It had been in gratitude for the refreshment his people had shown her and her forces, and when he saw it

Zardik Mir became very serious and knelt in the dust of the gateway to kiss the signature of the Agana. Then he had them march on at a slightly quickened pace.

Although the season was high summer, dark came early because of the height of the mountains to the west; the sun was cut off while still a hand's-breadth high in the sky. Zardik Mir had them press on through the early dark, and soon even Tamara could tell that they were catching up with the Empress and her party. The circles of black ash where the campfires had burned were fresher, the hoofprints and droppings of the horses more recent. Then, a few nights later, one of Zardik Mir's observers gave a great shout and came galloping back into camp to tell of the fires he had seen burning up ahead. At once the Mir had his men take up their great horns and drums, and soon such a clamor was bouncing off the rocks Tamara clutched her ears. Again the horns boomed. This time it was rhythm that identified their army as belonging to Aksu, and once the echoes had vibrated into stillness, the answer came back to them from the hills ahead—the call of Tibir's household. It was shortly followed by a messenger on horseback, who only paused to identify Zardik and his company, then curtly ordered them immediately to strike camp and rejoin the column. The Empress, he said, was not overly fond of being kept waiting.

It was midnight before they reached the baggage train. The soldiers were shown to their billets, but Zardik Mir, his spy Lerdas and his prisoner Tamara were taken straight through to the Empress. She sat on a wooden throne, carved and gilded, raised up on the tailgate of a bullock cart. Crimson silk draperies covered the wagon and dark red carpets were on the ground around it. A large fire was roaring a few feet to one side, and in Tamara's tired eyes the whole scene was fantastically red, lit by the leaping flames. As Parric had described, the Empress was dressed in red also, and her painted mouth was a narrow red line in the cosmetic whiteness of her face. Zardik threw himself at her feet and Lerdas awkwardly copied the motion. Tamara stood stiff and straight.

The Empress raised her heavy lids, and her black eyes glittered in the firelight. "And in Tredana is there no courtesy shown a queen?"

Tamara flushed and made an awkward bow.

"Do not dislike me, little princess, for with my help you

will be a queen indeed, and in Tredana.'' She gestured to her
guards and they lifted Zardik and Lerdas up onto their knees.
''Now, tell me, Mir, where Aksu is hiding, and how he
explains the destruction of Tredana and the loss of the Tredanan
king.''

Tamara stiffened herself and waited to hear the worst.
Zardik spread his hands wide.

''Truly, Queen, Aksu must answer to the spirit of his
fathers and the great Gagan. As we hurried to rejoin you our
way led across the desert, and there we met with a small force
of men under the leadership of the Karif. The Karif challenged Aksu to combat, then slew him treacherously and
made his escape. We killed many of the Karabdu, and it was
our battles with them that kept us behind and brought us to
Vahanavat too late to sail with the fleet.''

''Then we owe the Karif an executioner's fee, for he has
saved the Emperor some trouble. Now tell me about Tredana.''

Tamara strained her ears as Zardik hesitated. He spoke so
softly the Empress had to command him to speak up.

''Lord Aksu believed that the Agan was desirous of humbling Tredana and making the Tredanan king his vassal or his
slave.''

''And yet I commanded him clearly to return with me to
Zamarra.''

''He thought—he thought he was doing the wishes of the
Agan.''

''It is the wish of the Agan that his men obey him.''

Zardik humbled himself in the dust again, then raised a
streaky face to the Empress. ''Truly, we did not know that
the Mir was making his own rules. We thought we did the
bidding of the Emperor. We marched east from the mountains
as far as Villavac. Villavac was mostly built of wood, a
flimsy place; we took a tribute from the governor, then fired
the town and drove away the sheep and cattle before us. Then
Aksu Mir sent a small group south to investigate the hidden
valley of the fanatic Marajites, where men practiced a secret
religion and there was rumored to be much gold. I went with
the main division to Tredana.

''As we approached Tredana we found that the farmers had
fled, but we burned the granaries and rode down the crops to
make sure the countryside would stay clear. We knew Tredana
was well fortified, but had not realized how it backs to the

sea; we surrounded the city on land, but the king and several of his court got away by water. We do not know whether they went up the coast, or across the ocean to Melismala. After we had knocked some holes in the walls, a man was sent to treat with us. But he would not give Lord Aksu the answers he wanted, so Aksu had him thrown down from the walls as a lesson to the others. Then the rest of the city surrendered.''

The Empress frowned. ''Lacking a king, with whom did Lord Aksu make his terms?''

''The chief of the merchant's league. He promised to proclaim Tibir.''

''And what did he give you? The treasures of the city?''

Again Zardik dropped his eyes. ''The castle was empty,'' he said softly. ''We took it down stone by stone, but it was empty.''

The Empress tilted her head slightly. ''I must be sure I understand this chronicle right. Aksu Mir's great march on Tredana has gained the Emperor a ruined city with no treasure, and the loyalty of a group of merchants?''

Zardik nodded, then went on hastily. ''We left Tredana and marched back to the desert, where we met the group who were sent to the secret valley. They destroyed the fanatics there, entirely.''

''And the treasure?''

''We found some strongrooms, built in the backs of caves, and mined them open. But all they held were scrolls and books. We burned them. And it was there they found this young man.''

The Empress slowly turned her black gaze on Lerdas. ''The clever spy? Learn this lesson well, boy: a spy is without honor abroad as at home, for his employers trust him no more than his former friends.'' Lerdas bowed as though he had been complimented. The Empress made a gesture of dismissal with her hands. ''I will hear the rest tomorrow. You may go.'' Two of her guards stepped forward to escort Zardik and Lerdas out of her presence. Likewise, one of her women stepped forward and touched Tamara's arm. Empress Soria's austere face softened very slightly. ''You stay with me. Behave yourself, little princess, and you will not find me unkind.''

Loresta City proclaimed a holiday at their arrival. The walls were draped with brightly colored flags and the guards on the walls blew silver trumpets and beat upon their drums.

Ibrim of Loresta unrolled the carpet of honor himself—a small, dark, clever figure dressed in yellow silk. He led the Empress into the central square, where tents of silk were already prepared. The Empress greeted him graciously as a cousin, and he responded with humility proper to one who had been placed upon his throne by the actions of Tibir.

Tamara was given a cushion to sit on, below the royal dais. Above her on the platform sat the Empress on her wooden throne, and the younger wives of Tibir were ranged on lower chairs beside her. The royal children sat on the floor by Tamara. Tamara was not allowed to mingle with them, and she looked curiously at their round faces, braided hair, brocaded robes and ornate silver jewelry. Some of the littler children smiled at her, but the older ones, better trained, looked impassively ahead. For some moments they all waited in silence, then the Empress arose from her chair and stepped down onto the ground. Four servants slowly entered, carrying a chair on poles at shoulder height. A small, frail hand lifted slowly from within the chair, and the Empress bowed her head in respect.

"Greetings, Uncle," she said. "Greetings and long life to Sinim the Wise, the son of Chanaga Gagan."

A dry laugh came from the litter, and as it was gently lowered to the ground Tamara could see within it an ancient old man, his face made up of wrinkles and edged with scanty whisps of white hair. "The greetings I accept gladly. Long life I have had already." His heavy-lidded eyes opened slightly, and he looked fondly at the Empress. "Child, as you can see from my finery, the Emperor has passed this way already. Despite the haste with which he returns to Zamarra, he stayed with me an hour and talked most courteously."

His eyes drifted away from the Empress and Tamara was shocked to find them suddenly fixed on her. They were small and sunken but very bright and very black. He laughed silently, a mere squinting of the lids, and beckoned her forward with one fluttering hand. She came and bowed her head awkwardly, standing a little behind the Empress. Sinim turned to Soria again.

"My child," he said. "My Queen, I beg your gracious permission to speak alone with the little Tredanan princess."

If the Empress was surprised she did not show it; Tamara, less well-schooled, started. The Empress simply nodded gra-

ciously and Tamara followed the litter bearers out of the great
hall.

Their way led along corridors into a small, sunny courtyard
filled with flowers; here the litter was set down in the sunlight, on a stone platform beside an ornamental fish pond.
There was a carved bench on the platform and on it an old
man sat, his face lifted to the sun. He had thick, long hair
and a turbulent beard, white with a few streaks of faded gold.
His expression was peaceful and his eyes were shut. Then he
turned his face toward them and his eyes did not open. The
lids were sunken and Tamara realized he was blind. He
smiled as though he could see her wonderment.

"Tamara!" he said tenderly. "I rejoice that the Empress
has you under her protection. Although we have not met
before, I knew your parents well. Your danger has been of
concern to me. Welcome to Loresta."

Tamara looked from one old man to the other. "How do
you know who I am?" she asked. "And how did you know I
would be here?"

Sinim looked grave but the blind man smiled. "I could say
the stars told me, or the leaves of a painted book. Or I could
say I overheard the chatter of a passing flock of birds. Does it
matter how I know?" Tamara frowned impatiently and the
blind man laughed. "You have your mother's temper," he
said. "It is enough now for you to know that I am bound to
serve your mother's house by bonds I cannot break even if I
would. As a priest I served your great ancestress; now, in my
last days, fate has brought me here to serve you any way I
can." He bowed his head before her and said simply, "I am
Arbytis."

Tamara felt her legs shake. She stepped over to the pond
and sat down slowly on its sun-warmed edge. "I learned
about Arbytis in my lessons," she said at last. "How he was
the high priest of the Double Goddess, and how he refused to
honor Simirimia when she forced the split from Rianna and
left old Treglad a ruin. I was taught that Arbytis wandered the
earth from that day on, a thousand years or more. But I also
learned that his journey was completed when Simirimia was
destroyed, and that he found rest at last in a hidden valley.
My own parents saw him laid to rest there, twenty years
ago."

The other nodded. "Leron of Tredana held me tenderly in

my weakness, and the child Sibby guided us through the mountains to my resting place. My resting place, child, not my tomb." He reached his hand toward Tamara and she put her fingers on his. His touch was warm and strong. "Tamara, I am older than you can imagine. I was centuries old when my friend Sinim was a baby. I was tired by the struggle with Simirimia. I had to rest, and I have rested twenty years. Now I am much refreshed, and I am ready for one last struggle." He squeezed her fingers and smiled into her eyes as though he could read her face. "Do you still disbelieve?"

Tamara looked away to Sinim, then dropped her eyes. "I don't know what to believe," she said at last.

"You must believe," he said firmly, "if I am to serve you. Matters are moving quickly now and we have little time for questions. Soon it will be the end of the Great Year. Do you know what I mean?"

"I think so. When I was in the desert I was shown some of the star groups—"

The blind man interrupted. "Who showed you, child?"

"A man named Ammagest."

He nodded. "Ammagest. A nice child. His father studied with me, or was it his grandfather? No matter. He comes of a good tradition. What did he say?"

"He said the Age of the Serpent was passing, and that the Age of the Kermyrag approached. Isn't that what you mean by the Great Year?"

The man who called himself Arbytis nodded. "Truly. I have studied the stars for centuries, but even before my time, when I was only a young priest in the temple, the Serpent had already ruled the skies for more than a thousand years. Now I have lived to see his end. I may yet have cause to be thankful for my long life."

"What do you mean by his end?" asked Tamara. "The stars won't fall from the skies!"

The blind man made a low circling gesture with his right hand, his left still firmly holding hers. "The figures Ammagest showed you in the desert were two of the twelve, the ones we call the Great Wheel. They follow a narrow pathway of sky, and turn around us—or we around them. To each of them we assign qualities, aspects of fortune, patterns of history. And each, in turn, rules a heavenly month two thousand years old. For two thousand years the sun has been rising in the sign of the Serpent, on the first morning of the new year. But the wheel turns. This past spring, the most careful measurements could not have told you whether the sun rose in the Serpent or the Kermyrag. Next spring there will be no doubt. The sun of the new year will rise under the sheltering wings of the Firebird. The reign of the Kermyrag will begin.''

Tamara had been watching his face while he spoke. She placed her free hand over his and pressed it gently. "You *are* Arbytis," she said. "I'm sorry I doubted. Will you explain another star for me? Who is the Sword-Bearer? Is he on the wheel?"

Arbytis sighed. "The Sword-Bearer! I remember when that sword was a flowering staff, and the Great Mother herself stood on the wheel, staff in hand. But before the Age of the Goddess could begin, Vazdz cast her down into deeper sky. She touches the Great Wheel but is no longer part of the circle. Her staff has become a sword, and now she holds the Serpent back from the Firebird. Soon her task will be done."

"I don't understand. Who is the Great Goddess? How could she become the Sword-Bearer?"

"Child, you will understand soon enough. I cannot tell you all in one moment. Now you must thank Sinim for his hospitality. Without his kindness we would not have met so easily. And there is more. On his word, I will be joining your party today, and on his word I hope to turn your steps from the north road to the west. Soon you will see Tibir, but you will not see Zamarra the Golden.''

"But Tibir is in Zamarra!"

"He is in Zamarra, but not to stay. Even the Conqueror of the World is bound to the Great Wheel's turning. He will have good reason for marching west, and we will meet him on the Samidan Highway, not far from the fortress city of Yokan. Did you think the Great Serpent would give up his house in the skies without a struggle? War is being planned in heaven; Tibir must not be late. Nor may we."

Arbytis rose, still holding Tamara's hand.

"Sinim, again my thanks. May we both be finished with these bodies soon, and meet again on the farther shore."

from The Book of Sinim the Wise

Conversations with Tibir

The last time I met with the World-Conqueror I was in my hundredth year and he himself was approaching seventy. We sat in my little garden in Loresta, he tottering from infirmity, I weak with age, and we laughed together that of all men alive in the world today I should be acclaimed most wise and he most strong.

He would not stay more than an hour, but in that hour our words ranged widely as usual. He spoke to me of his challenge from Paradon, and his belief that Tammush had joined forces with the Seven Warlords: then asked me about the Sword of Chanaga Gagan and whether I believed it would ever be brought to him. Before I could answer he changed again, and asked a question I never thought to hear from his lips, about the Marajites and what I knew of the teachings of Maraj. To my answers on this point he listened, but grew impatient. "If I wish to win a game," he said, "I must move my pieces. If I wish to give a feast, I must kill some beasts. If I wish to rule the world, I must slaughter my enemies. How can a man succeed at anything if he does not impose his will on others?" To that I could only answer thus, "How is any man to succeed at anything except obedience, when he is in the presence of Tibir?"

At this the Conqueror laughed, and drank more wine, urging me to do the same. "I have come too far to change," he said, "but note well that I have kept the laws of Chanaga: I will neither spare an enemy nor harm the one who surrenders. And to this I have added one that the heirs of Chanaga would have profited by: I will do no harm to my own flesh and blood. Disloyalty made public is punishment enough."
He went on, "If I fear death at all, it is only when I think of the sons of Chanaga Gagan killing each other and making war on their own nephews and grand-children. May such a day never come upon us again."

Chapter Seven

THE KING

I

When Leron awoke it was dark. His head hurt and the soft light of the lamp stabbed at his eyes. He shut them again and found he was groaning as he turned his face to the wall. Then the wall moved and dipped above him, more than mere dizziness. There was a sound of water slapping against wood, and a rushing sound of wind or ocean. He was not left to puzzle long; at a soft touch on his face he opened his eyes again, cautiously, and through the slits saw Alric holding a wet towel in his hands, slightly bloody. Alric smiled apologetically.

"My uncle hit you harder than he thought. You have been asleep these four hours. How do you feel?"

Leron tried to raise his hand to his throbbing head, but the effort made him sick to his stomach. "Was Gannoc trying to kill me?" he finally whispered, and Alric smiled nervously as he draped the cold cloth over his head again.

"Save you, rather," he said. "But you struggled and desperation must have weighted his arm—and the candlestick. Do you not remember?"'

Leron tried to shake his head, then whispered, "No. I remember—a messenger. From the Anguls. We held council— you were there. And Gannoc of course. And we decided— what did we decide?"

"We had no opportunity to decide anything. We were still talking when the trumpets blew in the distance, and we saw the horde approach. You do not remember?"

"No."

"They told us we had until morning. There was panic in the streets. You do not remember trying to talk to the crowds in the street below the gates?"

"No."

Alric dipped the cloth, rewrung it and gently smoothed Leron's bloody temple. "Then my uncle advised you to get away in one of the small ships we did not send to the defense of Vahn, to sail to Melismala and rejoin your family and Lord Dansen and others loyal to you."

Leron sat up suddenly, heedless of his splitting head. "Turn coward? Leave Tredana to her fate? Was he mad?"

Alric pushed him back against the pillows. "That is exactly what you said the first time. And that is why he hit you, and why we are now on board the *Sea Rose* sailing east."

Leron sighed and closed his eyes. "Truly, Alric?"

"Truly, my lord."

"Will you order the captain to turn back?"

"I will not, my lord." Leron started to get up and a gentle push from Alric was enough to make him sink back groaning, helpless tears streaming from his pain-shut eyes. "Truly, my lord, you are in no case to argue. Consider: Your daughter the princess is safe among the Karabdu. Your wife and younger children are safe in Melismala. These Angul savages come like the wind and like the wind they blow away again. With you and your family safe, we need only bide our time. Tredana will be as it always was, bad memories behind it."

"Where is Gannoc? Dare he not face me?"

Alric hesitated. "My lord—he is not here. As your steward he remained to oversee the defense of the city, and treat with the Anguls."

"And Mara?"

"She would not leave him."

"I suppose she can count herself fortunate he did not knock her on the head also."

Alric shook his head soberly. "My lord, it is a blow for which you will someday be grateful."

In the days that followed, Leron's head mended more rapidly than his temper. The captain was as respectfully disregarding of his wishes as Alric, and the blue skies and unvarying good weather only formed an ironic counterweight to his fears for Tredana and his people. At length he had no choice but to relax and await their arrival in Melismala, and he allowed himself to look forward to seeing his family.

The *Sea Rose* was not a fast vessel, and made the month's sail in a little over five weeks. Gradually they sighted the low cloud of islands spread along the horizon. As they neared land, steering carefully between the sandbars and rocky outcroppings, a delightful scent of fruit trees and spices came to them on the breeze. These first, easternmost islands were inhabited only by fishermen and farmers; apart from huts, there were no buildings except a few small, ancient temples built to Ruave, back in the days when men still worshipped her for her winds and tides.

It took several days of careful navigation to thread the way among the islands to Apadan, largest city of the largest island. The buildings there were low, built of brilliant white stone, climbing the green hillside above the quiet water. As they slipped in on the tide the depths of the dark harbor mirrored the hill beyond, so that Leron saw the city doubled, white on blue—as fair a sight as he had ever seen. They dropped anchor and watched as the harbormaster's boat approached to learn their business.

It must be a sign of these troubled times, thought Leron, that even the peaceful Melismalans should now bear arms. The harbormaster was dressed in typical island fashion—rough cotton loosely draped and caught at the waist with a rope belt, one shoulder bared and all his exposed skin bronzed dark by the sun. His long hair was dark and curly. But behind him stood two men in leather surcoats, helmeted and gloved, with small round shields and knives both short and long. Leron would have thought no more of it but Alric, standing near him at the rail, suddenly squeezed his arm in warning.

"Greet him as a merchant, my lord. Quick, while I warn the captain."

The sailors threw down a ladder, and when the Melismalans were aboard they welcomed the Tredanans politely to their island, in the name of Tibir, Conqueror of the World.

Leron could not entirely control his features. The harbormaster looked at him keenly and added, "We have only had the fortune to join the world empire recently. If you have been here before, you will find little changed. Our market is larger, of course, with a wealth of goods from Samida. And we have many soldiers here through the courtesy of Tibir Agan, to protect us from the possibility of attack.''

Leron chose his words carefully. ''I had planned to visit an old friend during my stay. I hope all is well with Dansen the Learned?''

''We must request our visitors now to stay at the harbor inn. You will be most comfortable there and have the chance to learn the news of all your friends here in Melismala.'' He pointed across the harbor to a new stone building built between two warehouses. ''You may tie up your boats at that dock; I will meet you there.'' And nodding farewell he went down the ladder as smoothly as he had come up.

Alric was all for having them take up anchor and sail away, but the captain pointed out that the wind was very light and their sailors too few for fast rowing. Furthermore, there was no way to tell what defenses the Anguls might have built around the harbor. Leron also turned on Alric bitterly.

''So, having branded me a coward as a king, you would also have me fail as a man and leave without learning the fate of my family and friends?''

Alric subsided.

An hour or so later they were tying up to the warehouse quay, Alric with pen and paper and notes, a proper merchant's scribe. Leron had dressed himself soberly and carried a heavy money pouch on his belt. They were greeted courteously and shown to a long room overlooking the harbor, given sweet Melismalan wine and bread and cheese and olives. Alric raised his eyebrows.

''I am glad to see that the niceties of life here have not changed.''

Leron touched the wine to his lips, unable to eat. ''I would rather have news than a meal.''

In answer the door opened, to admit not only the harbormaster but also a tall man with greying hair, familiar to both Tredanans from his years of serving as ambassador from Melismala to the mainland. Their eyes met, and Leron matched the blankness in Talyas' eyes with his own. ''Sir?'' he asked politely, and Talyas in reply introduced himself as the viceroy of the islands, welcoming him and his trade in the name of Tibir. Two Angul guards stood just outside the door.

''When you have concluded your business,'' said Talyas, ''I hope you will be able to do us the courtesy of taking a message back to the Tredanan king. Tibir wishes his victories to be known, but most especially the purpose behind them. Can you do this for us? Good. It will be of interest to your government to know that the Emperor plans a campaign against Paradon, and to that end has made Melismala an outpost of the empire. Here his ships will be supplied and refitted as they sail against the might of the Seven Warlords.''

Leron folded his hands. ''Lord Talyas,'' he said, ''I will be happy to carry your messages. Now what can you tell me of my old friend, the—the historian?''

''Lord Dansen's family and his guests are well.'' Talyas drooped his eyelids at the word *guests*. ''Lord Dansen will be sorry to have missed seeing a friend. But he is just now in Gagan-ala, the chief city of Samida, on a matter of state. Before you leave you must give me your messages for him.'' Talyas stood up. ''A guide will take you through the warehouses tomorrow. If you encounter any problems doing business, let me know. Before you leave our island we must do ourselves the pleasure of having a small meal in your honor.'' He made a formal smile of dismissal and went out, preceded by his Angul guards.

Alric took another bite of bread and pushed the plate toward Leron. ''When I was an outlaw,'' he said, ''I learned the first rule of adventuring; eat when you have the chance.''

Leron tried to smile in answer as he took a bite, but the bread was like dust in his mouth.

Leron did not sleep well, all too aware of the guards outside the inn door. By sunrise he and Alric were up, and within the hour an agent of the port had arrived to escort them through the warehouses. Their guide was of the league of wine merchants, red-faced like most of his brethren, but unusually serious. He made note of Leron's orders of honey and oil, raisins and spices, and from time to time checked his figures against the notes that Alric took, to make sure there was no misunderstanding of price or quantity. The Angul guards lounged sleepily against the sacks and bales.

At the price of raisins, Alric shook his head. ''Pardon, sir,'' he said, ''but I fear you are mistaken in your figures. If you sell one sack for a half-dunya, then a full load must be fifteen krahs, not twenty.''

The merchant looked at his notation, scribbled a moment with his pen, and nodded. ''A foolish error,'' he said with an embarrassed smile. "If you will cast your eye over these figures?"

He held the sheet up to Leron's face and there, in between the rows of calculations, he saw sentences in two different writings. "Danger here—go quickly—family well," was written first, in a strange hand. Below it, Alric had replied, "Tredana beset—fall likely—where safety—" and below that came the response, "Talk others—advise soon—" The merchant shrugged and Leron nodded.

"An easy mistake to make," he said severely, "but I trust it will be the last one."

That afternoon they were taken to examine the wines. Alric had eaten a hearty lunch, but Leron was filled with a restless impatience that stifled hunger. When the wine merchant held up his list of wines and prices Leron almost snatched it from his fingers, earning an admonishing grimace from Alric. In between the names of grapes and islands, years and makers, sizes of barrels and jars ran another note. "Friends warned—be careful tonight—make plans—"He looked up impatient for more news, and was handed a tasting cup, and after that, another.

"There is a dinner tonight in your honor," said the merchant casually as he poured out the third vintage. "You must not think we are not grateful for your business. I think there will be some other Tredanans there. Perhaps they can tell you more about our lovely islands."

Leron swallowed and choked and tasted another cask. To him they were all the same, and when he made his choices Alric shook his head in despair.

In Melismala the summer light lasted very late, and dinner was not served before full dark. Talyas himself escorted them to the park where richly embroidered cloths were spread upon the grass and fires burned in deep, sandy pits. The eating area was on a gentle slope above a quiet curve of bay, and it was sheltered by arbors hung heavy with grapes. Torches were stuck in the ground here and there, leaving areas of private, dark shadow.

Talyas gently steered Leron through the crowd, speaking quietly in his ear. "I see no guards tonight, but my friend be careful. Not all are as innocent as they look. A spy is often cheap to buy and the Emperor has much gold. Do not forget

you are only a merchant and that you know no one here."
Leron nodded, his eyes impatiently searching the crowd.

He saw Arrod first, as she went to the water's edge to greet
her kinfolk rising out of the sea. She had robes of light gauze
on her arm, which each of the Dylalyr casually wrapped
round himself after giving a quick, doglike shake. Seaweed
and foam clung to their narrow feet. Her two youngest children greeted their uncles with kisses, but Leron did not see
any sign of the eldest, a boy Tamara's age, Dansen's pride and
joy.

As he made his way to the beach Arrod turned and smiled
at him, distantly, as though he were barely known to her.
"The Tredanan trader! Welcome, sir. I am sorry my husband
could not be here to welcome you. But I think you are
acquainted with his sister? She is but lately arrived from
Tredana with her children." And her graceful hand indicated
Liniris, standing quietly in the shadow, a sleepy Geret cling-
ing to her skirt.

Leron trembled like a horse before a race. "Little Geret, is
it not?" he asked in jocular tone. "You have grown since I
saw you last!" He swung his son up and he felt Geret's body
shaking like his own, but the little boy maintained a better-
schooled face than his father's. Tears were rushing to his eyes
and he was grateful for the shade of the arbor that hid his
face. Liniris laid her hand on his arm and let the pressure of
her fingers speak for her. Briefly he covered her hand with
his own, and they both started at the touch. Someday, he
thought, we will talk of this and laugh.

It was Liniris who recovered first, shaping her features
with all her old Player's skill. "My brother will be sorry to
have missed you," she said. "He is always eager to hear
news of Tredana. Tell me, how is the city?"

Leron looked away from her eyes and tried not to think
about her mouth. "Soon," he said, "if not already, Tredana
will enjoy the benefits of Tibir's generosity. If Lord Gannoc
had not been so eager for me to come and trade with Melismala,
I would have stayed to watch how events turned out." He
touched the scar on his temple and Liniris frowned in sympathy.

"Perhaps the market in Tredana will not be good for you
when you return?" As he spoke, Liniris moved back slightly
into darker shadow and Leron gratefully followed.

"That is certainly a possibility," he said. She was standing between two massively twisting grapevines, centuries old, as big as trees, far from the light of any torch and sheltered from the stars. Risking all he pushed in next to her, and for a long, quiet moment they were pressed together, Geret muffled between them, body to body and lip to lip. Leron stooped to raise Geret up to their level and kissed him for the baby, and Geret promised to pass the kiss on that night when he went to bed. Then he hung on his father's neck, pressing kisses against his beard, until Leron gently pulled free and turned him round to cling to his mother instead.

As casually as they had stepped into the shade, they wandered back into the light, Leron's hand resting on Geret's curly head. Talyas greeted them with great curved shells of wine and nodded pleasantly. "I see you have found your friend's sister. Has she told you of his new employment?"

"I am afraid we were too busy with news of Tredana," said Leron. "What new project does Dansen now pursue?"

"An imperial one," said Talyas. "Here in Melismala we knew of his learning, but never realized how widespread was his fame. When the troops of the Conqueror arrived in our waters, Dansen the Learned was one of the very first they asked for. It seems the Agan values historians above all other scholars, and wished for Dansen the Learned to add to his library of knowledge. So he sent for him and his eldest son to come to Gagan-ala, not merely to instruct the scribes there with the history of your continent, but more importantly to tutor the Agan's own grandson, Prince Kladdur. Truly a remarkable honor."

Conversation was suddenly interrupted by a great gush of steam from the opened baking pits. "But come, my friend. Enough talk of serious matters. Food is at hand. Now you will see why we are famous for more than our wines!" Talyas drew Leron along by the arm to sit with the company of merchants, and no more personal business was spoken that night.

Leron paid for his purchases the following day, under the watchful eye of an Angul tax collector, who took the empire's portion and gave receipts to both seller and buyer. Then boats and men had to be hired for loading the ship, and when this was done Talyas came down to the docks to oversee the packing and give his approval. "My friend," he said, "surely with matters in Tredana so unsettled, you would find better markets to the east? In Gagan-ala they pay half again as much as any Tredanan merchant, especially for our wines.''

Leron raised his eyebrows. ''But what of the messages you wished to send to Tredana?''

''God willing, the news I have for the Tredanan king will reach him.''

Leron smiled. ''My captain is not familiar with the journey.''

''I will give him the charts myself,'' said Talyas. ''The way is easy. A safer road, surely, than the one you purposed to travel. Furthermore, your profits from Gagan-ala will bring you back here again to buy more of our goods. What do you think?''

''I think it is good advice.''

With the charts and sailing notes, Talyas included several personal notes and messages, but they had no more chance to talk. Leron wrote a cautiously worded letter to Liniris with no signature or salutation, which Talyas promised to give her. He had assured Leron that her identity as Dansen's sister was unquestioned on the islands. As the *Sea Rose,* heavenly laden, left Apadana behind to the west Leron went below. Unable to bear looking back, he stood with his note from Liniris crumpled in his hand. At least when he returned it would be as a known trader. Presumably he would have greater freedom on his second trip. He thought of the dark under the grape arbor and sighed.

II

Once they were well on their way to Gagan-ala, Leron felt more comfortable. He had discussed with Alric the possibility of returning to Tredana, or better yet Rym Treglad, but they both agreed they had more chance of free movement in a settled portion of the empire than on the frontiers. Moreover, Leron felt keenly the need of Dansen's counsel. Events had moved too fast, his world had enlarged too quickly; he felt like a child again and he wanted his teacher.

In happier times, Leron would have been excited to think of seeing the imperial city of Gagan-ala. However Tibir might style himself now, it was the Chama of Samida who had been the true Great Emperor, and his father's fathers before him, for nearly one thousand years. The city was famous for its extravagance and ornament, its mechanical wonders and gardens of amusement. It was famous as well for its great island library and the stone observatory from which the chama's wise men kept watch over the movement of the stars. Dansen had often spoken with longing of the library there; it was likely that the imperial command from Tibir had not been entirely distasteful to him.

Nothing Dansen had told him was preparation for the entrance to Gagan-ala. Leron was not an untraveled man. He had been to Treclere in the time of the Great Queen, to Vahanavat and walled Luntar. He had made a journey north to visit Shirkah in his palace of ice, and traveled in the desert with the Karabdu. But all the wonders of his own world dwindled to insignificance by comparison with the city of Chama.

A giant stood astride the harbor, on legs so long the tallest ship could sail safely beneath him. He was built of stone, covered in bronze, and carried uplifted in one hand a wreathed serpent, in whose open mouth a flame burned perpetually. As the *Sea Rose* passed beneath the Giant of Samida, the shadow of his thigh lying on the water was greater than the length of the ship.

Now they were in a narrow channel, marked by floating barrels. Here the harbor seemed as narrow as a river, and hills rose steeply on either side, covered with houses and planted fields. Leron had never even imagined so many people living so closely together. A final curve and the harbor broadened to surround an artificial island, where the great library stood. A small thing compared to the guardian, and yet the largest building Leron had ever seen. Its sheer walls went up and up, three or four times the height of a great castle, unbroken by windows or battlements or ornamentation. Overhanging the top, scaled to the same gigantic size as the guardian, a bronze bird spread its wings, sheltering the library and seeming to peer down into the water below, ready to snap up an unwary ship in its beak.

As they slowly passed the island, Leron's captain suddenly called to his sailors to ship their oars. A great stone causeway barred their way, joining the island to the shore. The far side of the island had already shown itself impassable, filled with shoals and jagged rocks whose points lifted above the water.

Then they heard the sweet note of a trumpet, and to their amazement the causeway split open before their eyes. Like the drawbridge on a moat it lifted, but many times more vast, and with no chains pulling it up. As their ship glided through, the captain touched his forehead and murmured an ancient invocation. Behind them the causeway clanged heavily shut with a clamor of iron plates.

Beyond the causeway, the harbor widened out again to form the inner bay of the city. Here at last was fabled Gagan-ala, and Leron and the others exclaimed and threw up their hands to shield their eyes. The walls of the city were covered entirely with bits of glass, and the city dazzled the air like the noonday sun, too bright to be looked at directly.

By imperial decree, foreign merchants were free within the walls of Gagan-ala, but permits were required to travel out into the Samidan countryside. Strangers were not greatly noticed in the city. Leaving the stolid captain in charge of unloading their wares, Leron and Alric set out to explore.

The various brotherhoods of merchants and craftsmen each had control of a group of warehouses and markets, and gave the flavor of their trade to their particular neighborhood. Slowly strolling, they passed from food sellers through bakers and wine merchants into metal workers. Here the noise was terrible—thousands of hammers shaping hundreds of vessels in silver, copper, bronze, iron. The smiths were next, then the armorers. At the goldsmiths' stalls Leron lingered, his eyes as dazzled as they had been outside the walls. One Samidan workman had on his bench as much gold as a wealthy Tredanan merchant might expect to see in a year. And the gemstones came in more colors than he had ever imagined.

Each of these merchants' areas was very large, and there was much to see. Gradually they worked their way around to the southeastern end of the city, nearest the causeway that led to the island library. This was the quiet end of the city, a place of green gardens and reflecting pools filled with colored fish, shaded by tall, ancient trees. It was a place of schools, and the few shops sold only paper and parchment, ink and slates. In many of the gardens, classes could be seen reciting, and the gentle hum of students saying their lessons could be heard from open windows and courtyards. Samidans typically dressed in long, sashed robes over loosely fitting shirts; but whereas the ordinary citizen favored bright colors and embroidered designs, the students and teachers were all dressed alike in cloth dyed a dull pomegranate red.

By one of the courtyards Leron hesitated, and met Alric's eyes in puzzlement. Some of the words in the lessons being spoken sounded familiar. They listened a little longer and finally it was plain that the students were studying Common Tregladan speech. The grammar was impeccable but the accent worse than poor; it was unrecognizeable. It was Alric took matters by the throat.

With an exaggerated bow of courtesy, Alric stepped into the shady courtyard—startling the young men at their lessons and drawing a frown of displeasure from their teacher. "Your pardon, noble sir," he said, speaking with unnatural clarity and precision. "Hearing the sounds of my homeland I could not pass by without speaking. How is it that you speak my tongue so well?"

The master smiled in pleasure, and gestured for Leron and Alric to come in. With difficulty, Leron understood him to bid them welcome and beg them to stay and listen to his students. His students looked embarrassed and dropped their eyes, as well they might, Leron thought grimly. But considering the quality of instruction, they really did not do too badly.

"Twegaad iza ohdess zity ona conninenta Vahn," chanted the students in unison. Smiling fatuously, Leron and Alric nodded their approval. Then Alric boldly pushed on with the more important question. "I have heard," he said, seeming to chew his words and spit them out, "that one of our greatest scholars is here in your noble city. Dansen the Learned, famed in Tredana for his histories. Is it true he studies here at the library?"

"Dasson the Lunned! Ituz twoo, ituz twoo."

Alric sorted this out, then nodded encouragingly. "We would like to greet this famous man," he said, then repeated the words twice as slowly.

"Noting isyar," said the teacher. He dismissed his students with a wave of his hand, then patted the grass beside him for them to sit. "You stayir, drink alittawine, soon Dassonir, you greetis famuzmun."

In response to his gestures a silent servant appeared from somewhere within the school, carrying a small, round tray set with wine and glasses. They toasted each other, Gagan-ala, the library, Dasson the Lunned. Leron was finding their host easier to understand.

Food followed the wine and more wine followed the food, sweeter this time, with a trace of honey flavoring. Leron began to wonder vaguely if he had misunderstood the *soon*. It was not until evening was darkening the air, and the little bats had begun to flit about their heads, that the teacher shrugged and stood up, dusting the crumbs from his red silk robe. "Dassun wocks latonight. Come, I will sow you libry."

They followed him into the alleyway and as they turned the corner onto the main street, the stone pillar nearby suddenly roared with flame. Leron and Alric gasped, but the teacher smiled and gestured encouragingly, as though to a startled horse. Along the street other pillars, evenly spaced, were likewise catching fire. Each started with a great upward burst, then settled down into a clear steady flame, unnaturally white. No one else in the streets so much as looked up, and Leron felt foolish. At the end of the street one pillar did not light, and presently a man came along who climbed up nimbly and peered into the basin at the top. Taking a small instrument from his belt, he clicked it together in one hand and a tiny white spark jumped from its end, which of a sudden burst into a great flame. The man watched it burn for only a moment, then went off down the next street, presumably on a tour of inspection. Hurrying to keep up with their guide, Leron nevertheless kept trying to see what it was that burned so fiercely in those stone basins. He could see no wood or cakes of fuel, he could smell no oil.

Pillars of light framed the street all the way, until it ended at a great archway built within the city wall. Doors of metal plate inlaid with designs in gold and silver filled the archway. A small door next to the main gate led to a passageway through the walls, and at the far end Leron could see twilit sky glimmering on water.

The rock-cut passage through which they walked was narrow, and in places there were gaps along the sides where metal gates had been pushed back out of the way. Long tubes of metal were mounted along the roof, and at intervals these turned down into tiny metal basins shaped like leaves, in each of which a very small light burned bright and white like the great pillars outside. It seemed to Leron that these lights made a hissing noise.

From the causeway looking east, the lights of Gagan-ala were enchanting. Still warm with wine, Leron stood and looked in muzzy amazement until Alric gently took his arm and pushed him along the pathway. Their guide was a few steps ahead of them, and Alric took the opportunity to whisper in Leron's ear. "Sir, we must think clearly. Remember, Lord Dansen does not know our case. He does not know of Tredana's besiegement or the necessity of your disguise."

Leron nodded agreement, but his mind was already taken with new wonders. They were crossing the section of causeway that lifted, and here the stones gave way to iron grillwork underfoot, through which he could dimly see the water moving far below and shadowed against it, indistinct shapes of wheels and metal scaffolding.

They were almost at the library doors when the sound of a great explosion made them turn. A burst of blue light shot up from the center of the city and fanned out into a spray of stars that scattered and winked away into nothing. It was followed by another in red and a third in gold, accompanied by a crackling so loud, the noise echoed off the walls of the library behind them. Despite the beauty of the sight Leron felt a cold fear clutch at his stomach, but their guide burst into laughter.

"Ituz goo', vewy goo'," he exclaimed. "Tibir Agan is comin'. Two weekz and he will be-ir. Hiz mezzenga is-ir." Still chuckling he went up to the massive door and pushed it open, while behind them new explosions of color rattled and banged in the evening air.

It took a few moments for their eyes to adjust to the dimness within. Here too there was artificial light, but only the tiniest flames, like those in the passage through the walls. The library they found to be built in the shape of a great hollow tower, and the entranceway led them right through the whole width of the wall into the central garden. This center was open to the sky, and looking up they could see balconies and passageways and windows interrupting the inner walls all the way up through the various levels. Their guide pointed upward. "Hiztowy," he said succinctly, and they followed him up the stone stairs.

History occupied all the third level of the library. There were jars of scrolls, boxes of manuscript, shelves of books, cases of letters. On tables and benches, material lay in various states of repair or copying. Disdaining the artificial light,

on a bench placed so as to catch the last light of the sky, a
familiar figure in brown stooped over his manuscript. "Dassun
the Lunned!" their guide remarked happily, and Dansen looked
up from his work with squinting eyes.

Reckless from wine or simple emotion, Leron stepped
forward with his hand outstretched. He did not even notice
the other scholar, stooped in the shadows beyond Dansen's
shoulder. He shrugged off Alric's warning hand on his arm.
"Dansen my dear," he exclaimed and Dansen rose from the
bench, only to sink to his knees before him.

"My lord!" he said, bowing his head and behind him the
other historian looked up alertly, pen poised above the ink.
Before Leron could raise Dansen to his feet, the other man
had risen and stepped forward.

"There is only one man to whom my stiff-necked friend
here would show so much respect," he said cordially. His
accent was flawless. "I take it I have the honor of addressing
His Grace, the King of Tredana?" His eyes met Leron's and
he bowed with ironic courtesy. "You are welcome to Gagan-
ala," he went on. "You have saved me a long sea journey.
My grandfather the Agan has been most anxious for us to
meet."

Chapter Eight

THE CONQUEROR

I

On the road to Zamarra Sibby rode at the head of the leading ardan, the Bloodstone pinned to her shoulder and the Enku, still in its wrappings, on her hip. It had been clear to her, even before Tala translated the instructions of the elder Varlas, that the sword was to be unwrapped by no one but the Conqueror himself. Riders sent out ahead had returned with the news that Tibir was expected to make a triumphal return into Zamarra before the end of the summer, bringing with him the riches, spoils, curiosities and captives of his campaign. He had laid waste to walled Luntar, destroyed Vahanavat, reduced Treclere and made the free-roaming Karabdu pay tribute. There was no mention of Tredana.

It took great effort for Sibby to send her memory back to before Angulidan to the predictions made at Rosedale, a scene unreal and very far away. Her "daughter" had said that Tredana was in great danger. Presumably, the "daughter" was now in better spirits, Tredana having been spared. All that remained was to find out where Tredana was, and who there claimed her as mother. Had she lived in this world before, in a lifetime now forgotten? Why had the word "Tredana" haunted the life she did remember, the life in Massachusetts? It was not just answers she needed. The questions had to be formulated first.

The confederation of Anguls intended to camp in the plains northeast of Zamarra, in the shadows of the mountain chain that almost enclosed the country of Almadun. Almadun, explained Tala, was the "Heart of the World," a beautiful region of green fields and fruit trees and wide, calm rivers. Zamarra the Golden had always been its chief city, sitting athwart the major trade routes west to Samida, north to Angulidan and south to Loresta, and from Loresta across the waters to Vahn and the continent beyond. But in the last thirty years Zamarra had been even more ennobled by the riches brought home by Tibir. Tala's eyes glowed as she tried to describe the marketplace, the buildings, the gardens. The other Anguls, who had never lived in cities, regarded her enthusiasm with amusement.

The first signs of entering Almadun were the planted trees along the highway. In the course of one day's ride, the broad, sprawling trail had narrowed down to an avenue only a few hundred feet wide, lined on either side by poplars. That the trees were maintained was clear from the fact that any dead trees had been replaced by saplings. Despite its generous proportions, this highway was much too narrow for the multitudes of Anguls: gradually, the different ardans split up and moved off into the grasslands on either side to graze their beasts and wait for news to be sent back to them. Each family designated a leader to stay with the ardan of Soktani Agana, and to attend Sibyl when she was presented to the great Agan. By the time they were a week's ride from Zamarra, Soktani's ardan had also settled down, and Sibyl rode on attended by Soktani and Tala, Varlas Mir and the Mirik, five other Angul lords and several servants.

Two days' ride from the city, gardens and planted fields lined the sides of a much narrower highway. At night there was no open space in which to camp. They were forced to stop in the mud-walled courtyard of a teahouse, where enormous copper tea urns bubbled on charcoal fires and fresh bread was being baked in domed brick ovens. It amused Sibyl to see how soft and fussily dressed these settled people were, and to see how they shrank from their booted, shaggy guests. The tea was good though, and the tough, chewy bread was delicious. A special treat that evening was fresh honeycomb on the table, and a platter of pomegranates. They glutted themselves on the sweetness and the fruit and lay down under the stars well satisfied.

Across the road from the teahouse stood the public baths, and there they went the following morning to make them-

selves presentable for the courts of the Agan. The bath attendant cooed and cuddled Tala's baby while the three women
scrubbed themselves in cold water, rinsed in hot, oiled their
skins and lay down to dry on marble slabs in the fierce heat of
the drying chamber. Through the thin alabaster wall that
divided the bath, they could hear their male companions
laughing and shouting as they threw each other—and, apparently, the bath attendant—into the hot-water soaking pool.

Meanwhile, in the adjacent courtyard their servants were
busy beating and airing the garments of felt and leather,
washing their linens and drying them on hot stones. While
they waited for their clean clothes to be brought, Tala carefully washed her baby and oiled his round pink limbs, wrapping him in fresh swaddling, careful not to disturb the good-luck
coral beads around his fat neck. Their linens returned to them
smelling of rosemary, and their heavy outer clothing of cloves.
As they made ready to remount, Monkey turned a damp and
disgusted face to her rider: even the horses had been scrubbed
clean of the dust of the road for the entrance into the city.

Soon they could see the walls of Zamarra in the distance.
Tall green trees showed their tops above the sandy brickwork;
glazed tiles sparkled blue and gold in the sun. It was a
multi-colored ornament set in a ring of emeralds, for all
around it the flat fields were irrigated and glistened a brilliant
green. Away to the west, a broad blue river wound along the
edge of the fields, spanned by a handsome bridge of many
low arches, embellished with pierced work and inlay. The road
that led from Zamarra to the river bank was lined with stones
on which people had spread their washing to dry in the sun,
while brightly dressed figures dotted the river bank, soaping,
pounding, chattering. Blackbirds circled in the peaceful sky.

Sibby had supposed they would ride into the city, but at the
gates they turned right, entering a narrow lane lined with
massive twisting grape trees that were trained up and over the
road, to make of it a long, green, fragrant tunnel. Grapes
were already bunching on the stem, some purpling and some
staying green. The birds were busy in the foliage around
them. "Tibir does not stay in the city," explained Tala. "He
has many palaces, for himself, for his families. And even in
these he does not live. He builds them for their beauty, but he
lives as always in a tent, which is pitched in the garden. His
gardens are the most famous in the world. The Chama of

Samida could not rival them. When the Almashar palace was built, the builder lost his horse in the gardens. He did not find it again for half a year. Almashar means Heart's Rest. It was built for Dalun, an Angul princess, the wife of his eldest son. Her husband is dead, but she is the mother of two of Tibir's grandsons.''

The arbored lane led them along the walls of Zamarra for about a mile, then turned straight across the green fields, spanning several ditches with sturdy, ornate bridges of hewn stone. As the Almashar gardens developed on either side, Sibby found it easy to believe the story of the builder's horse. The plantings, walks, hedges, roses, arbors and lawns spread out for miles and miles on either side of the main approach. Two browsing elephants, knee-deep in wild grasses, made Sibby stand in her stirrups and crane her neck for a better look.

"Twenty pair, Tibir brought from Loresta," said Tala. "When they are not with the army they pull great stones for the builders here. In these gardens many beasts are kept for the Conqueror's amusement. He brings them home, and also trees and grasses and flowers so they will not be lonely."

A little further on some pine trees bristled in the sun, and in their shade two reindeer were flopped on their sides, panting with lolling tongues. A wide, deep trench lined with sharp spikes separated them from the neighboring garden, planted with bamboo as tall and incongruous as the pine trees. There the first thing Sibby could see were the partial remains of a horse, lying on its back, half eaten. The meaning became clear when a gap in the bamboo revealed a glorious tiger also lying on his back, asleep, legs sprawled wide, round belly full of horse. As they neared the palace, the animal park gave way once more to flowers and the air was filled with the unmistakable, harsh lament of peacocks.

On a little rise ahead stood the Almashar, gleaming white in the sun. Broad steps ran down from its upper terraces to a walled courtyard, where several enormous, bright silk tents were pitched between the pink roses and splashing fountains. At the first gate they drew rein, awaiting the guards of Princess Dalun who were riding up to meet them.

The royal guards wore steel helmets inlaid with gold and silver; their sword belts and short daggers were of similar workmanship. Over their shining mail they wore loose surcoats of thin scarlet silk, embroidered with a figure of three small circles, touching. This same mark was inlaid on their weapons and branded on the necks of their fine-blood horses. "It is the sign of Tibir," murmured Tala. "He is the Lord of the Fortunate Conjunction—the three planets that met to mark his birth."

The guards greeted Soktani Agana politely, and escorted them into the courtyard where the princess was encamped, awaiting the return of her father-in-law and older son from the foreign wars. At the inner gate they left their horses, servants and weapons, to enter the royal household on foot. Cushions for them to kneel on were placed in the carpeted space before the great reception tent of blue and yellow silk. They were kept waiting only a few moments. Lady Dalun entered, attended by several ladies, and seated herself on a low dais before them. Since Sibby could understand almost nothing of what was being said, she greedily took in every visual detail.

Lady Dalun she judged to be little older than herself, mid-thirties at most. Her black hair was thick, straight and shining, held back from her face by a gold and silver circlet of wrought leaves. She was dressed in white silk, with a plum colored overdress heavily embroidered; rings covered all her fingers, but she wore no other jewelry. Her ladies were almost as richly dressed as she. At her feet, Soktani was pouring out a gift of river pearls and bright red amber beads. Dalun nodded acceptance and motioned to one of her ladies to take up the gift. Her face remained sober and her eyes, deeply shadowed, remained half-hidden behind dropped eyelids.

Suddenly Tala's baby made a fretful noise and clutched his mother's dress; Dalun looked up in surprise, revealing large and brilliant eyes. She spoke, and Tala in answer brought her baby over and knelt with him in her arms. Dalun leaned forward and placed her hand on the child's head, seeming to murmur a blessing. As she did so, tears began to sparkle in the corners of her eyes. Sibby looked away, suddenly uncomfortable, fingering her dull red amber. As she rubbed it, it grew warm under her fingers, and slowly in her mind's eye an image grew of a little boy lying in bed, wide-eyed, and sweating, dying of fever. And now in her mind's ear she heard again the words of foolish, faraway Mrs. MacInnes, naming her a healer.

Heedless of protocol, Sibby leaned forward and whispered

to Tala. "Ask if I can see her little boy. I know he's very ill. I think I can help him." Trembling, Tala relayed her words and Sibby saw a desperate hope light the princess' face.

As Sibby followed the royal ladies through a maze of fabric corridors linking several tents together, she was uncomfortably aware of the odd picture she must present, dressed like a male warrior, and a shabby one at that, with a cumbersome, wrapped object hanging from her sword belt and an unformed bit of amber pinned to her shoulder. Now that she was no longer touching the Bloodstone, the image of the child had faded and she felt sickeningly unsure of her mission. Then the ladies were standing aside and indicating that she should precede them into the room ahead.

It was hot, dark and stuffy in the inner chamber. Two shallow saucers of oil with floating wicks gave only the faintest of light. On sweat-soaked quilts in a nest of cushions lay a little boy of four years, twitching and shaking, eyes wide open. More quilts were piled over him, and as he tried to fight himself free his loving attendants relentlessly piled them back on, eyes brimming in sympathy.

Sibby touched his head and her fingers jumped in surprise that flesh could be so hot. Now as her eyes adjusted she saw a ewer of cold water standing by a shallow wash basin. She pulled off the lightest coverlet and hurriedly soaked it through, then, pushing off his other coverings, lifted him in one arm and wrapped the cold blanket around his body. With urgent gestures she made it clear to the women that more cold water was needed. With one corner of his wrapping she gently smoothed his scarlet face and squeezed the drops on his lips. When the basin had been refilled she wet another coverlet and wrapped it over the first, this time lapping it round his head and throbbing neck as well.

His face began to return to normal color, but his limbs were jerking more wildly, interspersed with violent shivers. Although it went against every natural instinct to make the sufferer cold instead of warm, Sibby did not unwrap him. But as she cradled him in her arms, moved by an instinct she did not understand, she unpinned the Bloodstone from her shoulder and held it against his forehead. With the stone in her hand, once more the images returned; she shut her eyes and dropped her face against the child's sweaty hair. His jerkings grew less in her arms, his breathing quieted. . . .

She was standing in the wasteland, where the water was trapped under the stones. Ahead of her the rocks were piled up into a long, rough wall. Although the sun shone brightly where she stood, it was shadowy on the far side of the wall, darkening rapidly toward a black horizon. The little prince was walking along the top of the wall, looking at her. From time to time he would stop to smile, then playfully run a few steps and pretend to fall, then catch himself. As she watched, filled with concern, his foot did slip and he almost fell into the dark. He caught himself again, squared his shoulders and frolicked on. She tried to reach up and catch him, but he was playing with her once more.

Now the wall was a dike, the side of a rocky, earthen dam; black water rose on its far side to within a few inches of the top. Before she could warn him, the child slipped again. Helplessly she watched him slipping down into the black water, until only his terrified face and clutching hands were visible. Making a tremendous effort, she threw herself onto the wall and reached over to grab at his arms, which were limp and cold in her grasp. The water clutched at him as strongly as mud or quicksand, and for a few moments she thought it would pull her in also. Then they were free, tumbling back onto the hard ground on the sunny side of the wall. He was heavy in her arms, cold and inert, but breathing.

As she opened her eyes in the prince's room and looked down on his quietly sleeping face, she knew that all was well.

II

With the recovery of Dalun's little son, Sibby found herself doubly welcomed among the nobles of Almadun: as the Batur who brought the sword of Chanaga Gagan to Tibir, and as the hero who had brought Tibir's grandson back from the Land of the Dead. Soktani and the other Angul lords were made welcome in tents pitched on the grounds of the Almashar. Each night they were feasted and entertained with songs, wrestling, acrobatics and shows of conjuring. Wine was poured so freely that Sibby was amazed any of them were able to get up in the morning; but the natives of Almadun, no less than the wilder Anguls, seemed to have great capacity.

Their generosity was also great. Soktani's gift was returned the following morning, multiplied nine times over. In addition, they were each given long silk shirts, embroidered overclothes of felt, leather and multi-colored wool, coats of mail engraved with animal designs, silver-mounted sword belts and heavy necklaces of coral, ivory, jet, turquoise and pale yellow amber. As Tala explained the significance of this last gift, Sibby finally understood the meaning of the poem with which Varlas had identified her as the Batur. The four colors of the world were its four corners, yellow for the west, blue for the north, white for the east and black for the south. Red was the color of the center, Almadun: their necklaces were the battle honors of the armies of Tibir, who had successfully returned from campaigns in each of the cardinal directions.

Sibby also learned that Dalun's dead husband had been the favored son of the Conqueror. He was the child of Tibir's first wife, whose death, before he was twenty, first sent him out wandering in search of fortune. This son had been called Dunagan, King of the World, and he had died in battle only a few weeks before the birth of his youngest son, who was said greatly to resemble him.

All was not peaceful as they awaited the Conqueror's return from the savage lands of the east. In Tibir's absence, Dalun stood in his place as regent; messengers rode to her daily from every part of the empire. She had known of the approach of Soktani Agana long before the Anguls had reached the outer borders of Almadun, and now she was hearing of another muster of Anguls coming down from the northwest. These were not ardans friendly to Tibir, but rather the hordes of the treacherous Prince Tammush. Sibby had heard the story of Tammush told several times and could well understand the disquiet caused by this latest piece of news.

Tammush had been tricked out of his inheritance when only a young man, and had come to the courts of Tibir for protection, shortly after Tibir had defeated the Chama in Samida and placed on the throne one of his own grandsons, a prince named Kladdur. Tammush had been welcomed as a member of the old Angul nobility, given men, arms and horses; he had received instruction in the art of warfare from Tibir himself. And this was done for him not once, not twice, but three times over, before he was successful in defeating the usurpers and taking back his position. Once reinstated in the far north, he had forgotten the meaning of gratitude. He had challenged the rule of Tibir and twice had menaced the great Samidan highway, destroying over a range of hundreds of miles all who opposed him and stood firm in their loyalty to the Agan. Each time the armies of Tibir had followed him north, destroying his own cities in retaliation; but each time they had lost him in the farthest north and returned dissatisfied. Now, while the great Tibir was still a month's march away, the armies of Tammush had been seen gathering a week's ride to the north.

Days passed, and soon, from one of the slender towers that flanked the Almashar, Sibby could see the dust of Tammush's army. There was no word from Tibir. The household of Dalun moved into the city, peasants fled their homes in the northern fields, engines for withstanding a siege were readied and the army was gathered in from all its far-flung outposts. Never had any threat to Zamarra itself been imagined; the armies of Tibir patrolled the borders of his empire, not its center.

Silent, vast and menacing, the armies grew along the northern horizon. Sun glittered on their standards. Several miles distant, Tammush encamped, surveying his prize. He had not been there long when riders carrying his demands approached the walls of Zamarra, demanding entrance.

Dalun received them in the courtyard of the great hall built by Tibir to commemorate his conquests. Like all his structures, more attention had been given to the gardens and the courtyards than to the interior, which was cold, high and drafty. The courtyard was filled with profusely blooming roses and with fountains; colored tiles inlaid around the walls showed scenes from thirty years' campaigning. Tammush's emissaries did not bow before Dalun, but stood impassively, hands resting on their sword hilts, while her secretary read their master's message.

His demands were simple, to the point, and modeled on those of the great Tibir. She was to give up her son and herself to the mercy of Tammush, open the city to his men and have her armies lay down their weapons. Only thus could the city and those within its walls be spared. Dalun's lovely brows drew together briefly, then her wide black eyes met those of the messengers. "The city of Zamarra is the bride of

Tibir,'' she said at last. "She may be taken by force or killed. But she will not willingly offer herself to the unclean jackal who now barks at her feet." From the faces of the messengers, Sibby had a lively sense that the phrase "unclean jackal" was a little stronger in the Angul language than it sounded in Tala's softly whispered translation.

The messengers flushed and one, in contempt, spat at the regent's feet. Dalun gestured to her guards and the messengers were suddenly taken by the arms. "Fool," she said. "Having refused what little mercy your master offered, what need have I now of your good will?"

Despite her words, she did not kill the messengers as Sibby expected: she contented herself with having them stripped naked for the long walk back to Tammush's camp. And despite the threat of utter destruction that hung over their heads, the guards at the wall hung over the parapet and laughed at the messengers as they limped with tender feet over the stony ground, two dwindling, small pink figures. After they had been dismissed, Dalun sent for her son, and sat back on the royal dais fondling him to her breast. Still weak from his long illness, he lay quietly against her, twisting a strand of her hair between his fingers.

"I know Tammush," she said at length. "He has studied well the ways of Tibir. He will not wait until tomorrow. He will attack tonight, in the dark." Her generals nodded agreement. "See that the liquid fires are ready, the archers on the heights. Reinforce the barricades. Have water ready, and sand. There is nothing else we can do but wait." They bowed again, and respectfully left her alone with her councillors, her ladies and the Batur Subi.

Dalun turned her bright eyes to Sibby. "I had thought you would offer the sword of Chanaga Gagan to Tibir in feasting and celebration. Now we must hope that he will arrive in time to claim it from you in battle."

"He is on his way?"

"God willing. But he was far when the news of Tammush reached him."

It was full dark when Tammush attacked. His armies had crossed the intervening plain in silence; then, as they reached the base of the walls, they suddenly lit torches and bonfires, beat on drums and brass gongs, blasted on horns, beat on their shields and screamed. The noise and light was inhuman, and even though she had been expecting an attack, Sibby felt the hair rise on her arms and the back of her neck; her heart pounded, her palms and armpits were cold and wet. Dalun, who had once more sent for her son, merely stroked his head and soothed him when he cried out at the noise. Tala and her baby were with them also, but Soktani Agana had put on armor and joined her father and son and the other Angul lords up on the battlements.

Silence followed the first onslaught of noise and light. Finally the wait was over, and arrows began to whistle and thud against the walls, some flying over and striking within the city, some carrying flaming rags. The fire attendants were kept busy with their sand and wet quilts. Two of the five great gates began to vibrate as the armies of Tammush drove their battering rams against them. He had chosen gates at opposite ends of the city, forcing the defenders within to divide their forces.

Catapults were brought into play, and heavy stones crashed against the parapets, knocking off several of the guards, some stones even landing on the streets inside. All through the night guards rushed in to report to Dalun from each part of the city: damage done, defenders lost, fires started, repairs made. A little before light the first onslaught had ceased, and by dawn the defending archers on the ramparts had no targets they could hit. The armies of Tammush had withdrawn beyond bowshot.

For several days the fight continued in this manner, the armies of Tammush destroying in the night, the defenders of Zamarra rebuilding during the day. They were ill-equipped to withstand such a siege. The wells within the city were small, mere supplements to the river without; neither were there large granaries within the walls, nor was there room to cleanly dispose of the dead. With each night's attack the walls grew more ragged, the great gates lost their strength. On the fourth day Tammush did not retreat at dawn. His men continued to undermine the walls, protected from the archers above by wide, woven screens, which were kept wetted in the river to prevent firing by the city's defenders. Fully engrossed with their imminent success, all of Tammush's forces were concentrated on their prize like a pack of hounds bringing down prey. And thus it was that the watchers in Zamarra were the first to be aware of the return of Tibir.

Sibby did not have to understand many words of the Angul

language to realize what was happening. She was pulled up onto the ramparts by the younger Varlas, who gestured dramatically to the south. In the distance, shifting and floating in the heat-distorted air, wavering lines of men in sparkling armor began to appear along the edge where sky met sand. Out the lines spread, wider and wider, until by comparison the armies of Tammush seemed nothing but a handful of men. It was not until the ranks of Tibir's army had filled in half the distance from city to horizon that Tammush and his generals looked up from their work and saw beyond it their destruction.

Tammush was trapped; his only natural defense was the city against which his army must now set its back. But those very walls were filled with his enemies also, only too ready to rain down fire on his head. For a moment it seemed as though he would try to feint right or left, but the wings of Tibir's cavalry had separated from the center and were galloping out to the sides, enclosing their city and the army which had so foolishly attacked it. The generals of Tammush blew their horns and signaled with their standards: the ranks closed order and prepared to meet Tibir.

From the heights Sibby watched in comparative safety. The only danger to Zamarra now was the occasional missile thrown by Tibir's army that had overshot its mark. The right and left wings of the Conqueror's army in their encircling movement were, for the most part, out of sight, but the center was directly ahead of the gate by which she kept watch. Marking the heart of the army's center was a golden spear shaft, hung with a white horse tail and surmounted by the three golden circles of Tibir. Under it a solitary figure sat on horseback, the dust all but hiding the glittering gold of his armor and the red and white silks that crossed his chest and fluttered in the wind.

All morning he sat there in the center, while the fighting rolled back and forth between him and his city. The armies of Tammush fought desperately but without success. Behind the Agan stood his spear-bearer, but Tibir sat silently watching, touching no weapon. So, too, Sibby watched him, and as she observed the Conqueror of the World, her fingers touched the Bloodstone on her shoulder, cold under her hand.

The battle continued into the afternoon. Tammush's men were fewer. Still Tibir sat and still Sibby watched him through the shouting and the haze. Slowly under her fingers the stone began to glow, and in her mind she suddenly saw Tibir bent in the saddle, falling under the blows of the enemy, reaching out his hand for a weapon that was not there.

Below, in the streets, Dalun's army was beginning to issue forth from the gates, picking off those of Tammush's men who strayed too far from their dwindling ranks. Irresistibly moved, Sibyl ran down the ladder and threw herself onto one of the riderless horses milling about in the streets. She battered her heels on its sides and pulled it around, forcing it out through the gates as they opened to let out another group of soldiers. Then she was through, out in the heat and sun and noise and smell of the fighting.

Sibby clung to the shaggy neck, ducking and wincing as swords slashed the air around her. The dust was her only protection—thick, yellow dust that hid the warriors from each other, painted their horses a uniform dun color and dulled the brightness of their armor. The noise was more horrible than she had ever imagined—clanging and clashing of metal on metal, the shouts and groans of the wounded, the grunts and curses of the fighters, the gasps and whinnies and gurgling screams of the horses. Riders thudded into each other and horses were knocked asprawl, legs flailing, eyes rolling, then screaming as sword or spear was driven into the unprotected belly.

In the midst of the slaughter the Conqueror sat his motionless horse. Dreamlike Sibby saw an enemy champion suddenly burst through the Conqueror's bodyguard, whistling a two-hand broadsword over his head. Slowly the Conqueror stretched back his hand for his spear. And as in a vision Sibby saw that the spear-bearer had fled, that the Conqueror of the World stood unarmed.

Grimly, Sibby bent further down on her horse, forcing it forward. Ahead of her, the champion had reached Tibir and his blows were denting the golden helmet Tibir bent before him. Wrenching the sword of Chanaga Gagan from her belt, she threw herself off her horse and ran up to the side of the Agan and fell on her knees, holding it up in both hands. "The Enku," she cried. "The Enku of Chanaga Gagan." Tibir slumped under his enemy's blows, letting the heavy sword run harmlessly down his armored back. He reached unquestioningly for the preferred hilt, and as his hand closed over the yellowed ivory, the blade pulled free of its wrappings, leaving both sheath and rags in Sibby's hands. It was bright and slender and shone like a light, and had pierced the enemy warrior through his unprotected armpit before his massive sword could be raised for yet another blow to the Agan's head.

Tibir jerked the blade free, and his attacker fell dead just as his bodyguard arrived at the gallop to tardily encircle him. Tibir kissed the blade and held it up before him, then returned it to its sheath in Sibby's hand. His black eyes took in its ragged covering, her clothing and her gem.

"You are welcome to us, Batur," he said, and gravely inclined his arrogant head.

from Ammagest's On Stars

We must look beyond the Serpent, whose age is passing. Behind him lies our history—before him lies our future. For we are now in the Great Wheel's third quadrant. Before there were men, before there was learning, love or war, the Wheel turned peacefully through long ages under the sign of the Tortoise, the Dolphin and the Cock. Then the world was formed, the great beasts lived, filling the forests and the seas. Mighty birds clove the air. It was a good time, violent, yet full of the innocence of the beasts. But the Wheel turned, and at length the Cock crowed no more at sunrise in the spring.

The Great Wheel's second quadrant was the time of the Eagle when man rose from among the beasts, the time of the White Stag when man's power spread across the world, the time of the Grey Wolf when man strove with man for mastery. It was a time of violence and honor, hope and despair. Black, brown, yellow and white, men came to rule their several quarters of the world, and all would still be well if the world had been larger, or men fewer. It was in the age of the Grey Wolf Treglad was destroyed and the first Arleon fled its ruin to found Tredana.

The Age of the Serpent brought us into the Wheel's third quadrant, and with it arose the power of Vazdz. But his age too is passing. The destiny of gods is like the destiny of stars: one rises, another falls.

IN
OPPOSITION

Chapter Nine

THE HORSE PASTURE

I

The entry of Tibir's army into Zamarra lasted many days. Dalun's court moved back to the Almashar, and in its vast gardens bright pavilions sprouted as the household of the Conqueror established itself. It was the sixth triumphal return Zamarra had seen in the last forty years; everywhere Sibby heard enumerated the marvels of the five previous processions, and disappointment that the baggage and spoils had been left behind in Loresta, not to be seen for many weeks to come.

Tibir had learned of Tammush's latest treachery when he was still far south of Loresta City. Leaving the royal household and the baggage train behind him, he had brought the cavalry forward in a forced march of such extraordinary speed that the rest of his forces would not arrive in Zamarra for at least five weeks. After a grand review of his troops in the streets of Zamarra, the Conqueror returned to the gardens of Almashar to be with Dalun and his grandson, go over the records of his kingdom, see to the writing of his latest histories, and wait for the rest of his forces, his family, his baggage train, his desert horses. He did not rest; that was not his way.

The Batur Subi he dressed in the colors of his honor guard, and she was expected to attend him at all times, sitting on his left hand or riding by his stirrup. On the day she went to be fitted with body armor, she was casually taken by the arms and steadied by two guards while the master armorer pressed small block of glowing metal briefly against her skin, just below the collarbone. She did not feel the pain until it was over and the mark of Tibir was permanently branded on her breast. It was explained to her that few heroes were so honored; the honor kept her in extreme discomfort for more than a week until it healed. On her hip, the sword of Chanaga gleamed in its newly cleaned scabbard of black leather laced with silver wire.

As a Batur of the Agan, Sibby found her knowledge of the Angul language and the affairs of its government increasing rapidly. Each night Tibir spent several hours discussing the natural sciences with his scholars, history with his chroniclers, morality with his advisors. Tibir was more concerned with the philosophy of history than its records of events. A constant argument between him and his chief chronicler, Taan, was that the writers used language too ornamental for simple people to understand. "I was successful" he would say in his quiet, deep voice. "I have always been successful. There is no need to say anything more. What need do I have to boast?" And the offending passage would be reworked, its passage of praise removed, only to turn up a little later, grafted onto some new incident. Even his recreations were serious. Each afternoon he played a complicated, chesslike game with his advisors, a game at which he was reputed world master. Its name was sitranga and Tibir gave generous rewards to whoever could keep him from winning too easily. Taan told Sibby how Tibir often spent the last hours before a major battle sitting quietly in his tent, playing at sitranga with a son or grandson, no more likely to lose the game than the battle.

Tibir did not read. Each day he waited for Dalun's son to receive the petitions and letters brought before the emperor. Walking stiffly, chin high, the little prince took the documents and bowed before his grandfather before placing them in his hands. Tibir gravely accepted them with drooping lids, and then had the child take them to the secretary for opening.

Time passed and the Conqueror grew restless with neither family nor spoils to amuse him. His famous patience in battle was unmatched by any similar patience at rest. When word was brought from the west that a group of stragglers from Tammush's army had been found near the Samidan Highway, east of Shakar, Tibir did not show any outward excitement.

He simply ordered his bodyguard to be saddled within the hour.

Sibby was already feeling the strain of riding at the side of the World Conqueror. She had been disheartened to hear that during forced marches Tibir had himself carried forward in the night, by litter, so that no time would be lost for anything so trivial as sleep. She was quite certain no one carried the bodyguard. She could only hope that it would not come to forced marches too soon, before she had the chance to toughen up a bit.

In much less than an hour they were riding out of the city. Their way led south to join a broad highway, the Great West Road, which passed the fortress cities of Tokan, Shakar and Yokan on its way to Gagan-ala and the sea. Tibir had with him only his personal cavalry, fewer than a thousand men, divided as always into a center and two wings. Reinforcing the center rode the company of heroes, baturs and baturiks—men who had earned their special honors through personal feats of daring. The wings would be reinforced along the way by men from standing armies at outposts along the highway.

Sibby's place in the march was not with the other baturs but with the members of Tibir's household. Normally this would have included some of his wives and children; without his family, the household consisted only of historians, attendants, advisors, scientists and seers. They were as interested in Sibby as she was in them, and questioned her politely at every opportunity. In return, they were free with their own knowledge and filled Sibby's head with songs, histories, legends and lore.

Few of them were Angul by birth. They came from all parts of the empire, some drawn by the fame of the Conqueror, others made captive in the course of his campaigns. The surgeon was a black man from icy Zanida, where the people were famed for magic and medical knowledge; his name was Sharkim and he had joined with Tibir voluntarily, being eager to see the world. He had brought with him his three children, his wife being dead, and had recently married a girl of noble Samidan background. He told Sibby that Tibir had insisted he remarry, that he would not have anyone in his household who was not "happy as nature intended." Then he laughed and rolled his large expressive eyes and warned her that she would have to start making her choice, if she did not want Tibir to make it for her.

The historian Taan was Samidan—a small man, strongly built, with skin the color of yellowed ivory and long, narrow eyes. He dressed in dull red silk and often shook his head in dismay at the crudity of Angul customs and clothing. He was constantly writing and rewriting, making notes, memorizing texts, giving orders to his assistants and then changing them, only to change them back again a few minutes later. Two of his assistants were also Samidan, young men learning the craft, but the third was a slave named Danyas from one of the islands that lay across the western ocean. He was the youngest of the scribes and also the most learned; he was sad, bitter and moodily silent by turns. Taan worried about his continuing ill-health and fretful anger. "He is a great scholar," he told Sibby, "but he will be no use to me dead. Soon I will ask the Agan to let me send the boy back, or at least as far as the library of Gagan-ala. If it was just his temper I would not be concerned, but look at him! Every day he is thinner!" And, indeed, to Sibby's eyes Danyas looked pathetic even when angry, his bones sharp under his greenish white skin, his hair and eyes as pale as she had ever seen.

Once they had passed the mountains encircling Almadun, the character of the country changed. It was fierce and barren, broad salt flats shining in the sun. East of Tokan they joined the Great West Road and the country began to soften. First just a tinge of green, then sparsely planted fields, then lush ones. Tokan lay in an oasis of small streams, wooded hills and cultivated land. No sign had been seen of Tammush and his retreating army; Tibir did not waste time with ceremonies, but rode directly through without stopping, accepting the homage of the people impassively as though the city did not exist.

From Tokan to Shakar the land was wild and strange and beautiful. The road lay as level as the engineers of the Agan could make it, but the country undulated on either side, broken in low, rocky hills, glistening with streams and misty with waterfalls. Trees shadowed the road and the air was bright with colorful birds. To Sibby this was beautiful, as it was to the Samidans. But the Anguls found it oppressive country, damp and close and crowded. They called the picturesque wooden villages "people stables" and laughed at the way the buildings were huddled together.

As they neared Shakar there was still no news from the scouts ahead. But the scouts sent out to patrol the rear came riding in with broad smiles on their faces. They had met the forward guards of the royal household, the Empress and the baggage train. Tibir drew rein immediately, and as the army made temporary camp by the highway, Sibby thought she saw a slight smile on his face.

It was nearly a day before they saw the dust of the household's slow approach. Tibir's five younger wives rode in canopied bullock carts, painted and gilded and sumptuously hung with fabric. The Empress Soria rode a fat white stallion that puffed and sweated as it pranced along in the dust. It did not look like a horse used to hard campaigning. The smile in Tibir's eyes died away as his glance passed from his family to the guards riding behind.

"You do not ride well protected," he said. "The army of Aksu was to have joined the column. Has he gone with the spoils to Zamarra, or do we still wait for our tardy general?"

Soria reined her horse around so that he stood side by side with Tibir's, and they spoke privately—unheard by anyone except the emperor's Sword-Bearer.

"We wait for him no more, my lord. He compounded disobedience with folly, and paid for it with his life. I have had the full tale from his captain, a certain Zardik, who brought me the men who survived and who now humbles himself in the dust before you."

Tibir frowned. "Tell me all."

"It seems Aksu Mir was informed by a spy that the daughter of the Tredanan king had been sent to the desert for safety. Fearing your displeasure for his manifold disobediences, he took it on himself to bring her here, a hostage to win your favor. And indeed he did lure her into his hands without the knowledge of the Karabdu, and came upon his way well-satisfied. But the Karif tracked him down and challenged him at the very edge of the sands."

"Did he turn coward as well as disobedient, that a few desert savages could hinder him?"

"Not cowardly, but foolish, one we are well rid of," said Soria. "At the desert's edge he drew up his men and faced the Karif's forces. A single rider came forward and they all supposed a messenger was approaching. A hundred paces away the warrior suddenly drew his sword and galloped straight at Aksu and the other generals, crying the name of some Karabdin lord who had been killed by Aksu in an earlier meeting. And he and his horse had scarcely been dropped by the archers when the Karif himself rode forward, drawing his own sword and saluting in formal challenge. Aksu drew likewise and rode forward to meet him between the lines. There they met and addressed each other, and as Aksu turned his horse to prepare for the opening charge, the Karif hurled his sword like a spear and killed him in the saddle."

"Have the Angul archers forgotten how to avenge their leaders?"

"The Karif was struck several times, but he and the Karabdu disappeared back into the desert, and did not stand and fight. It seems that Aksu's men were already in fear of your displeasure. They decided tardily to obey your commands, but as they marched out of the desert the Karabdu harried them from ambush, killing many. That is why so few are with me now. I told them that the hostage they have kept will buy them some forgiveness for their errors."

Tibir's heavy frown lessened slightly. "So we have the daughter of Tredana still? It is well. I cannot but wonder what it was drove a famous warrior like the Karif to stab his enemy in the back. I had not heard he was dishonorable."

Soria shrugged. "Who knows what such barbarians use for honor? The captains tell me, however, that the first lone warrior, the one they killed, was a woman armed and dressed like a man." She looked at Sibyl and her eyebrows seemed to twitch. "It seems, my lord, that such is the latest fashion."

II

On the hills above Shakar, the army of Tibir encamped and celebrated the arrival of the royal household with a great hunt and feasting. For two days the Agan was not to be seen, for he disappeared among the carts and tents of his family. His captains knew well how to enjoy themselves in his absence. The wings of the cavalry were sent galloping outward for a period of several hours, then turned at a signal from their leaders. They made the Great Circle, and then the closing of the circle commenced.

For a while Sibby stood looking down onto the plain below, and watched the first few frightened animals dashing in toward the mounted sportsmen who sat in the center, spears and arrows poised. The master of the hunt had a pair of hunting cats on leashes, long-legged skinny animals, like cheetahs, except that they were striped rather than spotted. They were named Gagan and Gagana and were great favorites of Tibir. Sibby had never seen them work before. It was hard to compare the taut, eager animals straining at their leashes with the sleepy cats who lay rolled on their sides by the feet of the Agan, hoping for a caress on their heads or a scratch on their bellies.

As the huntsman bent to slip his cats' collars, Sibby turned away. She could hear Taan's students reciting and went in search of them. It was the Angul custom, when time permitted, to erect windbreaks in the form of woven barriers, marking off courtyards and stable areas next to the carts and tents. The yards of Tibir were hung with silk and carpeted with rugs and cushions; his household enjoyed similar luxury. Near Taan's group of wagons the historian had set up his schoolyard, hung with the blue and yellow colors of Samida; red was conspicuously absent. Sibby slipped in under the tasseled archway and sat down quietly, propped against a cushioned saddle.

Most evenings, when Taan read history for the Agan, he dealt with the history of the Anguls and Almadun, the empire of Samida, legends and tales of heroes. But today he was listening, not teaching, and the pale young scholar from Melismala was reciting stories of his islands and of Paradon.

As Danyas spoke of the simple life on Melismala, Taan listened carefully, from time to time checking on the notes his scribe was taking. There had been little on Melismala that could be called history, nothing but crops, trade, natural disasters, and festivals until the development of power on Paradon. Sibby had heard mention earlier of the Seven Warlords of Paradon; now she heard in more detail their raids on Melismala and the continent of Vahn. She noticed that it was only Taan who used this last term, however; Danyas always referred to Treglad. Taan continued to correct him, then lost hold of his volatile temper.

"Boy, boy, why do you persist in using an ancient city to name a continent?" Danyas looked him straight in the eye. "Why do you persist in using an irrelevant one?" Taan bounced to his feet and slapped Danyas on the cheek, and ordered him to keep a respectful tongue in his head. Danyas was rocked back on his heels, and Sibby thought that even for a teenager he was overdoing his reaction. Taan asked him to continue and there was silence. Angrily he bounced forward again then stopped as a horrified expression came over his kindly face. "My child," he said, "forgive a foolish man. Truly I had forgotten." He pushed back the hood from Danyas' face and gently took the boy's chin in his fingers, turning his face to the sun. The entire print of his hand was there on the pale skin, a deep black bruise spreading out to cover half the face. The left eye was already beginning to shut. Sibyl sprang to her feet. Danyas managed a shaky smile.

"I will be all right. I'm used to it. Most of my friends are land people."

Taan continued to cluck sympathetically as he wet a kerchief and draped it over the boy's face. "Nevertheless, my boy," he said sternly, "the fault for which I made the reprimand remains. Explain yourself and I will endeavor to keep my temper leashed."

Danyas shrugged. "You have taken Angul usage, something which makes sense for them but not for a Samidan. The Anguls knew of the Tregladan continent only from raids on Vahn, the chief city of its western coast. Thus they named the continent and the language for this city. But Vahn, like Treclere and Tredana, is a late child of the continent's first city, Treglad, on the eastern seacoast. When ancient Treglad was destroyed, wanderers from that city settled in various places, and those settlements grew to all the cities we know there today. Old Treglad is gone, but Rym Treglad, or new Treglad, stands near the ruins of the old. I know much about it, though I have never been there, for my father planned the city and I have seen all his drawings. And for those of us in Melismala or Paradon or Samida, Tredana and Rym Treglad are the cities by which we know the continent, not Vahn. Until King Leron of Tredana and his cousin Sibyl journeyed west, in the year of the destruction of the Great Queen, no one on the eastern shore had even heard of Vahn."

Sibby had been watching the bruise spread on Danyas'

face, wondering how to ask what he meant by land people. She was barely attending to his explanation until she was jolted by the sound of her own name. Danyas continued, "These facts are known by me to be true. My father Dansen the Learned accompanied the king's party, and returned to Tredana with Sibyl. He wrote all these things from his own observation and the firsthand observation of others. It is not like the stories that the Anguls call history." There was an unmistakable edge of insolence in his voice.

Before Taan could explode in another reprimand, Sibby interrupted. "Who was this cousin of the king—Sibyl?"

Danyas caught the look on Taan's face and bowed politely. Taan sighed and gave him permission to answer. "The king of Tredana is Leron, son of Mathon Breadgiver and the lady Leriel. Leriel was twin to Armon, who perished with his army when it marched against the Great Queen of Treclere, Simirimia. Sibyl was the daughter of Armon and of Simirimia, sent away from our world as an infant in order to complete the prophecy whereby she would help encompass her mother's destruction. Then she went away as mysteriously as she had come, only to return eight years later. That was during the reign of the Four False Kings, when Leron was in exile in Rym Treglad. The cousins were married, and at year's end Sibyl and Leron had a child, who is now the princess royal. But Sibyl went away a second time and Leron of Tredana has married again. Until the Agan sailed into Vahn, the powers of the continent of Treglad were four—that is, Leron in Tredana, the Karif of the Karabdu in the desert, Varys the Master of Vahn and Treclere, and, in the far north, Shirkah of the Zanida. Now that the Agan has visited Treglad, who can say?"

Sibby bowed to Taan. "I crave your indulgence. But this young man's stories interest me. Is it the usual thing in your chronicles for people to appear and disappear?"

Taan raised his eyebrows. "Not in the histories of Samida. Nor among the Anguls, primitive though they may seem in many respects. But this young man has given you an accurate rendering from the histories of Dansen, a man whose scholarship none would question. Now if you will excuse me, Batur Subi, there is a question concerning the career of Varys I would like to discuss with this young man—"

Sibby took the hint, smiled and withdrew. She would talk with Danyas later.

Once outside Taan's little court, the noise of the hunt could be heard plainly. Too plainly. Sibby shuddered and went once more in search of quiet amusement. Some of the riding horses had been turned out to graze, wearing leather hobbles, in a grassy depression bordering a stream, high among the rocks above the camp. Sibby climbed slowly and the shouts and cries died away below her. The herdsman saluted her as she passed, then stepped down from his post so that she could look out over the herd. Monkey was being her usual antisocial self, grazing apart from the group. She did not notice Sibby until she was quite close, then looked up, decided that nothing of importance was happening, and plunged her face back into the thick grasses. Sibby walked over and rubbed her between the shoulder blades for a while, then grabbed her muzzle and kissed her on the lips, getting covered with green slime for her trouble. Monkey gave her a quick caress, then returned to the serious business of eating.

"I've never seen a warrior do that before!" announced a voice behind her.

Sibby turned and found herself being measured by the fascinating eyes of an unkempt, skinny young girl. The eyes were odd colored, brown and blue, and they were set in a face that looked sulky, proud and clever. "I'm not exactly a warrior," replied Sibby, "and I kiss horses frequently."

"You're a woman!" The girl examined her more narrowly. "And you're not an Angul. What are you? A spy?"

Sibby shook her head. "No. Are you?"

The girl collapsed in a leggy heap. "No," she said in a dramatic voice, "I'm a prisoner." She tossed her head in a way that would have been more provocative had her hair been clean. A chestnut horse that had been grazing near her came over and nuzzled the top of her head, and she rubbed her face against his muzzle. "This is my horse, or was. Now he's a prisoner, too. He is one of the trained war horses of the Karabdu."

Sibby looked at the little horse and saw something that very much resembled the desert horses of her own world. He was neatly made, strong in the legs and feet, with a gleaming coat and kind, intelligent eyes. She patted Monkey's underslung neck. "This is my special horse. She was supposed to be an Angul sacrifice. I saved her life."

The girl, who had been looking at Monkey rather coolly, sprang to her feet. She hugged her around the neck. "You poor thing," she cried, "you poor, poor thing." Monkey sighed in agreement and closed her eyes; Sibby grinned. "In answer to your other questions, I am not an Angul nor a warrior nor a spy. I am called Subi, and I am traveling with the Agan as his Sword-Bearer. I come from very far away. Who are you?"

The girl sat down again. "My name's Tamara. I'm from Tredana, a prisoner of the Emperor. But the Empress says Tibir will let me go home soon." She shook her head. "The Empress has been very good to me but I don't think she realizes how ruthless Tibir is. The way she talks about him he sounds like some ordinary man. Perhaps he has not let her see his atrocities." Her face lit up. "If you're his Sword-Bearer, you must have seen many battles and encounters."

Sibby shook her head. "I have only ridden with Tibir a short time. I know he is a great king, and I have heard he can be terrible, but I have not seen it. I know he is good to his own people. And he loves his family."

Tamara rolled her eyes. "You should have seen them this morning. I thought that when I finally saw the Conqueror of the World he would be covered with jewels and walking over the bodies of his captives, with kings on chains and an army stretching to the horizon. Or at the very least sitting on his horse, dignified, like the Karif. I couldn't believe it! I was called in to be presented to the Agan and there he was, practically naked, sitting on some pillows and sharing a bowl of wine with the Empress, and she had her hair all down her back to the floor and it's practically all white now and she wasn't wearing too much, either. I was so embarrassed. And they spoke with me as though kings and queens always sat around in silk shifts receiving their subjects. My father would never believe it."

Sibby sat down next to Tamara in the grass and they selected stems to chew on themselves, while their horses grazed in closer and closer to them.

"I know nothing of the history of Tredana," said Sibby at last, "but I was listening to an interesting story a few minutes ago. It was about the first wife of your king—I believe her name was Sibyl?" Tamara bit through her grass stem. "Taan, the chief historian of the Agan, is adding to his knowledge of your continent. He has a young scholar instructing him, a prisoner like yourself."

"What is his name?" Tamara was leaning forward, odd eyes bright.

"Danyas. He—"

"Danyas? The son of Dansen?"

"I believe so. I don't remember all the names I heard. But his father is a famous scholar—"

"Danyas a prisoner! Does that mean Tibir has taken Melismala too?"

"I have heard that there is no land left for him to go, excepting Paradon."

Tamara burst into tears and stumbling to her feet went over to her horse and hung on his neck. As she cried into his mane, the little horse looked at Sibby with round, reproachful eyes.

"I'm sorry," said Sibby. "I didn't mean to upset you. Danyas seems well. Or, I should say, well treated. I must say he doesn't look very healthy to me. Has he always been sickly?"

Tamara wiped her hand under her nose and smoothed back her hair. "He's always been healthy, as far as I know. Dansen says it's the strength of a complete outcross, like horse breeding. His mother isn't one of us. She's Dylalyr."

"What are the Dylalyr?"

Tamara looked at her in amazement. "Don't you know anything? The Dylalyr are the undersea people, the sea-born ones. They can live with us but they don't enjoy it. I have always really wondered what it is about Dansen that made it worthwhile for Arrod to change her life so much to live with him. I mean, it's not as though he were the Karif, or anything heroic like that. He's just very nice."

Tamara's easy tears had dried and Sibby decided to press on rather than risk another overflow. "Is the Karif a great hero?" Tamara's face lit up and her wordless nod was eloquent. Her hand had left a trail of grime across her face and Sibby felt an odd maternal surge. She patted the grass beside her and Tamara folded herself up again onto the ground. For a while they sat wordlessly in the bright sun, then Tamara flopped on her back, arms outstretched, in imminent danger of being stepped on by a wandering horse. It was very peaceful and Sibby closed her eyes, thinking about Tredana.

Chapter Ten

THE HOSTAGES

I

The rythmic tearing of horses' teeth through the grass, the humming of insects in the heavy air, Tamara's light breathing as she lay sprawled on the ground—it all seemed to be the sound of the sunlight lying over them. Sibby drooped her head forward onto her knees and flipped her braid over her shoulder, so the sun could beat down on her neck. Her thoughts grew vague. She was almost asleep when she heard a thunk in the distance.

Beside them, Monkey suddenly lifted her head, her clever ears swiveling forward. The herdsman was lying sprawled on the ground by his rock. Sibby shrank in close to Monkey's chest and peered around her shoulder. Black and featureless against the bright sky, a man was standing on the rocks above them. He held a short curved bow in his hand, and a bunch of arrows.

"Stay down," she hissed at Tamara, whose eyes had opened. "He has arrows. I don't think he's seen us yet." Above, on the ridge, a second man had joined the first. Sibby drew the knife from her belt and rolled over in the grass toward Tamara's horse. He watched with quiet interest as she sawed through his rawhide hobbles, snuffing her neck. "Keep him between you and that ridge," she said. "Go slow as you can. When you reach the path, wait. I'll make a diversion so you can swing up and get out of here. Go as fast as you can for help."

Tamara did not argue. On hands and knees she wormed in

among the horses and her chestnut stallion minced along after
her, sniffing her feet in great interest. He was going no faster
than a horse in hobbles; there was nothing to give him away
except the free swing of his gait. Long minutes passed and
Sibby risked another peek. The men were slowly descending,
making no move or sound to startle the herd. The chestnut
stallion was near the fallen herdsman now, approaching the
path to camp. Sibby sawed through Monkey's hobbles and
grabbing her mane, pulled herself aboard. She clapped her
heels to the affronted mare's ribs and turned her in a wide
circle, as though to gather the herd and turn them for home.

This certainly drew the men's notice. There were three of
them now. She could see from the corner of her eye the man
with the bow nocking another arrow to his string. She hooked
her arm over Monkey's neck and tried to hang over one side,
but she was so long-legged she threw the small horse off
balance and made her stumble. She had no choice but to pull
herself up on top again, and as she did so she felt a blow to
her back so hard it seemed to come out through her chest, and
she fell to the ground. Monkey stopped and turned but the
other horses did not see her in time. Clumsily hobbled hooves
flurried around her head and over her body, the ground
shook, and she felt five or six distinct blows as heavy as the
first on her back and legs and neck.

The horses passed and she lay still, eyes closed, barely
breathing. Spasms had started in her legs and back, but her
brain seemed unnaturally keen. She could hear the men as
they walked toward her through the grass, and she could feel
it when they stood between her and the sun. One of them
soothed a horse with words she did not understand and she
sensed that several animals were being haltered and hobbled.
Then, weirdly, she heard the voice break into song, in words
she could understand.

> He stole two hundred horses
> The Clerowan stole them all—

Above her, a deeper voice spoke peremptorily in the first,
unknown language, silencing the singer. One word stood out,
perhaps a name: Ibrasa. Then the third man spoke, a harsh
light voice speaking a strange Angul dialect. "Why take just
the desert-breds? There is no hurry. We can bring them all

back to Lord Tammush. Tibir the Lame is busy with his indulgences.''

''They may not follow us for six horses,'' said the deeper voice, speaking Angul in clipped, precise sentences. ''They will certainly have our heads for sixty. Make sure you have left no blunted arrowheads on the ground as clues for the soldiers of Tibir. Now come away before these men awake.''

''Why let them wake at all?''

Sibby's scalp pricked as she felt her knife being drawn from her belt. She wondered if her arms and legs still worked, if she would be able to roll over and defend herself.

Above her the deep voice spoke again, more urgently. ''Come away. They have raised an alarm.''

One of them kicked her as they turned away, and his foot dug into the place on her back where the blunted arrow had hit. She started to be sick and then passed out.

Sibby woke to the taste of spiced wine rinsing her mouth clean. The bowl was being held to her lips by Sharkim, and at first all she could see was the deep red surface of the wine, the silver edge of the bowl, the gloss of the physician's black skin and clean pink nails. Gradually the greyness receded and she could see the tent within which she was lying, the pillows and sumptuous hangings. Sharkim's skin had a pleasant spicy odor and his touch and voice soothed her into closing her eyes again. She snapped them open at the sound of the voice of Tibir, suddenly realizing that she lay in the Empress's tent.

Sharkim's long fingers gently palpated the knot at the back of her neck, but it made a strange clicking noise as she turned to face the Agan. He was dressed much as Tamara had said, in a loose white shirt left open to the waist, sashed in red. She had not seen him bareheaded before. His long coarse hair was tightly braided, evenly streaked in red and grey, lying over one shoulder. It was knotted at the end with a plain silk cord. His sinewy arms were bare; he was remarkably smooth-skinned for an old man, lightly dusted with freckles and red hair, terribly marked with scars. Under the open edge of his shirt Sibby could plainly see part of a large tattoo—a falcon with spread wings and grasping talons that seemed to cover most of his right shoulder. The Empress held a wine bowl in her hands and reclined against his knee.

''Drink, Batur Subi, and tell us what you have seen.''

Despite Sharkim's restraining hand, Sibby heaved herself upright. Her right arm hung heavy, dead and dangling and the pain in her hips made her gasp as she talked. "Three men, my lord. One was Angul. He spoke of Tammush. They took six horses. Desert horses. They need many more. They thought to do it in secret." She had to stop for breath, then gasped again as Sharkim began manipulating her right arm back to life. Tibir stroked his long moustache.

"Tammush has never been clever enough to gain by secrecy what he might lose in open competition. His mind has only one narrow course, no wandering sidestreams, no waterfalls, no channels. Who were these men who were not Angul?"

"I could not see them. I do not know their language. But I think one was named Ibrasa. And he sang a few words of a song I could understand, something about a man named Clerowan stealing two hundred horses. When he spoke it was in a different language."

Taan was there also, taking notes. He looked up at this and Tibir invited him to speak. "The outlaw Clerowan? That is a legend from Vahn. And during the time of the Four False Kings, there was a real outlaw who called himself Clerowan and became a popular hero. He was Karabdin, and some people think it was the Karif himself, in disguise. What was the name you heard?"

"Ibrasa, I think."

"Ibrasa. That has a Karabdin ring to it. But surely this is impossible. Karabdin warriors fighting for Tammush, half a world away from home?"

Tibir shook his head. "To a brave man nothing is impossible. I am glad that Tammush has found allies to make his last battle more interesting for me."

He nodded to one of his attendants and his overcoat was brought to him; it was of embroidered felt, inlaid with patterns in precious stones. As he was helped into it, Sibby saw for the first time how little he could raise his right arm, and she had a glimpse of the terrible wounds that had nearly severed his arm so long ago. He was raised to his feet and, right leg dragging, helped out to where his litter was waiting. Sharkim gently eased Sibby back onto the floor. "Roll over my little hero," he said teasingly, "and show us how brave you can be. I am about to realign your back." Taan came over and watched with great interest as Sharkim explained

what he was doing; both of them politely ignored Sibby's
gasps and tears. When he had finished, Sharkim patted her
head and drew the covers up to her shoulders. "Rest now.
Your bones are too hard to break easily, which is good, but
your sinews are too tender to take these insults lightly. If
Tibir needs to chase after Tammush tomorrow, tell him to
carry his own sword."

Sharkim must have mixed sleeping drugs with his wine.
Sibby slept heavily and woke from time to time with a brief,
heart-fluttering panic, a sense of being drugged and unable to
move. She wondered later if Tibir had come back to his
wife's tent in the night, and if that had influenced her dreams.
They had an erotic tone, and she saw herself in the arms of
the deep-voiced horse thief, lying under him at night, seeing
his head dark against the sky and hearing his voice close to
her ear. In the dream she knew his name, but when she woke
it was all gone, except for a sense of mingled loss and shame.

At dawn she finally forced her mind to clear and her eyes
to open. There was no movement from the inner chamber,
only a sound of quiet breathing. She got to her feet with
difficulty, then halting, dragging one foot, she limped toward
the bath house.

The fires were roaring and the steam room ready. The
attendant made sympathetic noises as she helped Sibby un-
dress; her back and legs were a lurid map of the last day's
adventures. In the soaking pool she half sat, half floated, her
hair making a wide circle around her.

"If you'd haul your hair in there'd be more room," Tamara
announced, squatting on the wooden lip of the tub. Sibby
tried to twist it up using only her left hand. Tamara came to
her rescue, deftly braiding it up and then tying the braid itself
into a short firm knot. Then she slid in beside her, a long,
pale child with no hint yet of any female development.

Her eyes flickered over Sibby's body and Sibby had no
trouble reading her expression. "Don't be in a hurry," she
said. "It happens to everyone sooner or later."

Tamara plunged her head under water and came up shaking
like a dog. "I'm in no hurry. Shadith told me it can destroy
your sword-arm. If they get too big, I mean. She told me I
would be glad of staying small." She pulled in her chin and
looked down, where the water ran off her collarbones over
the arch of her ribs. "Within reason, of course."

"Of course," Sibby agreed, and Tamara started to scrub her hair vigorously.

"I'm glad you didn't get hurt too badly yesterday. And I'm glad they didn't take your horse. That was quick thinking."

Sibby laughed. "I don't think my horse was ever in much danger of getting stolen. Her virtues don't exactly leap to the eye. Your horse is more like what they were looking for."

"Do you think so? The Anguls seemed to like them broader."

"Yes, but these horse thieves weren't Anguls. The archer was. But the other two were Karabdu."

Tamara dropped her sponge and retrieved it. "Did anyone see them?"

"No, and I couldn't understand what they said. But one of them called the other Ibrasa. I guess that's a Karabdin name. I just find it hard to believe that anyone would travel halfway round the world to steal back some horses, no matter how nice they are. You know something about the Karabdu. Are they that fanatical?"

Tamara continued her vigorous scrubbing. When she spoke her voice was a little breathless. "Not about horses. But they might come halfway round the world for something more important."

II

Sibby knew that if she did not keep moving she might get too stiff to move at all. Later that morning she joined one of the search parties spiraling out from the encampment to look for tracks. By the time they had returned empty-handed, Tibir's cavalry and the royal household had already packed up and were on the highway west of Shakar, heading for Yokan and Gagan-ala.

The baggage and spoils had been sent under guard to Zamarra; even so, the size of their procession was larger than two typical ardans. The chief difference was that the flocks were mounted warriors, not sheep. At times the Empress rode with the household, but more often she was to be found near the front with Tibir and his generals. She had a small body-guard, and with his group Sibby often saw the child Tamara.

She was glad to see her under the protection of Soria; she looked much too young to be out on her own.

The forward guards brought back word of Tammush before evening. A small village in the hills ahead had been raided and burnt; not an uncommon occurrence in troubled times, but something no warlord other than Tammush would have dared with the Emperor so close. If any further proof was needed, one of the horses stolen from the Emperor was lying dead in the mud, foreleg broken, throat slit. The Emperor listened impassively, then quietly gave orders for the center and most of the left wing to continue on through the night. The right wing remained behind with the royal household, to follow at a normal pace.

As the bodyguard prepared to mount up after their brief supper, Tibir's chief steward touched Sibby on the shoulder. "Pardon, Batur, but the Emperor requests that you stay with the bodyguard of the Empress. He will wear the Enku himself."

Sibby reluctantly unbuckled the sword from her hip. She was as awkward as she was reluctant, for her right arm still had no strength and she had to let the steward help with the buckle's stiff leather flap. She wondered if she were being left behind as a liability. She thought of touching the Bloodstone on her shoulder, but it would have required supporting her right elbow with her left hand in order to reach it and she did not make the effort.

A herdsman took Monkey from her as she stiffly limped back toward the royal carts. It had been much more comfortable on horseback, and she dreaded the thought of lying down, or rather of getting up. The Empress once more gave her a sleeping place in the antechamber of her own great tent, and Tamara joined her there with quilts and a small pillow and no intention of sleep. As Sibby tried to stretch out her cramped legs and find a position that was not so excruciating as totally to prevent sleep, Tamara chattered non-stop. She seemed a distant relation to the sulky child in the horse meadow.

She answered Sibby's increasingly sleepy questions with enthusiasm, talking about the history of Tredana and Melismala and relations with the undersea people. Sibby had unpinned the Bloodstone from her shoulder and she held it in her hand as Tamara talked to her. When she fell asleep it was still in her hand, curled up against her throat as she lay huddled on her side.

The amber lump remained cool in her hand, but her dreams were hot and disturbing. The deep-voiced horse thief was in them again; the blood from a horse's slit throat was splashing his boots. A woman was in his arms: not a woman, a girl—not any girl, but Tamara. Several times in the night she awoke and changed her position to one a little less uncomfortable. She reassured herself that all was well as she listened to Tamara's quiet breathing.

As the household followed the highway west, messengers rode back and forth between them and the Emperor's party. As days passed, the messengers had to force greater and greater pace from their mounts; by normal reckoning, the Emperor's party had pushed itself more than a week ahead of them. West of Shakar, the road swept straight across a long, featureless plain for many days. Then gradually it climbed the slow, undulating foothills of the last mountain range between them and the western forests that stretched to Gagan-ala and the sea. The pass was guarded by the fortress city of Yokan, a citadel of fantastic complexity and strange beauty. It dominated the skyline for three days once it came into sight, and Sibby heard several times over how Tibir had spared the city thirty years ago in return for unconditional surrender. Of all the great towns and wonders of Samida, only Gagan-ala and Yokan had avoided destruction; only Gagan-ala and Yokan still showed purely Samidan taste and design.

Yokan was built into the cliffside, unapproachable from above or below. One narrow causeway served as both entrance and exit. Its domes and turrets were enameled in bright colors, decorated in gold, silver and inlaid mirror-work, in contrast to the severe and massive stonework that supported them. Tibir had turned northward some days previously, going cross-country on the trail of Tammush. But as the household approached Yokan, a rider from the Emperor rode up with word for them to await his return in the fortress city.

There was no room within Yokan for more than a small portion of the Empress's retinue. Part of the army she sent ahead to make camp on the far side of the pass, while the bulk of her retainers were settled in the valley just below the citadel. Leaving the lesser wives and the children to follow,

Soria took her bodyguard and personal servants up to the gates for her entrance into Yokan.

A deep, broad, viciously tumbling river separated the walls of Yokan from the highway. The causeway that spanned it was delicately arched, with carved figures of wolves, hawks and monsters along each side. It was wide enough for three horses to ride abreast. Tamara's chestnut stallion snorted at the water rushing under his feet and leaned against Monkey's flank as Sibby and Tamara crossed side by side. Several paces ahead, the Empress's charger arched his neck and pranced, apparently enjoying the echo of his hooves on the smoothly worn pavement.

Halfway across the river the causeway angled to the right and, with curious abruptness, brought them into the shadow of the cliff—the afternoon sun was cut off like an extinguished lamp. Monkey's pricked ears almost touched at the tips, and in the suddenly chilly air Sibby shivered. The streets of the fort were narrow, too, completely overshadowed by the height of the stone warehouses on either side.

Yokan was a merchant's depot, an army garrison, a center for outfitters and caravan leaders. Sibby knew that there were no civilian residences within the walls, but even so it seemed strange that so few people had come up from the villages to see the Empress's arrival. There was a hawk sitting on the carved lintel of the gate. As the Empress passed beneath him, he stretched his neck and even at a distance Sibby was aware of his bright, unblinking eye. She was equally aware that they must not enter the fortress. She closed her legs on Monkey's sides and the little mare shot forward, feet sliding and clattering over the stones. Their sudden departure made Tamara's horse throw up his head in surprise and balk, blocking the riders behind him as he turned nervously sideways. Sibby managed to push her way through a few of the bodyguard, but in her excitement she could only think of the Angul word for warning, and the soldiers' first response to this was to close ranks behind the Empress, pushing her further into the citadel.

Sibby pulled her mare around in a circle, half rearing, and standing in her stirrups she shouted across the inner courtyard to the Empress. Soria half turned in the saddle and her horse backed several steps, bumping into her bodyguard. Sibby called again, and the Empress slowly rode back across the square toward Sibby and the open gateway behind her. A third time Sibby called out, this time forming a complete, intelligible and urgent Angul sentence. But she was not able to finish. Behind her an iron gate fell crashing onto the stones, closing the gateway, and from the walls on either side dropped swordsmen, two or three for each of the bodyguard who had made it within the gates.

Sibby had not taken another sword upon surrendering the Enku to Tibir; she had only her knife and her wits. She spun Monkey around like a cow pony, and managed to knock one of her attackers off balance, but the other jumped up and grabbed her around the throat and she could not shake him off. Monkey spun again, slipped and fell on her hip, tumbling them both onto the stones. Before Sibby could push herself back up off the ground, her opponent had taken a grip on her hair and placed his knee against the small of her back. As his knee dug into the deep bone bruise on her spine Sibby felt her legs lose their strength and her head spin. She collapsed under his weight. With a jerk on her hair he pulled her to her knees, then her feet. Some of the Empress's bodyguard lay dead on the stones, some had their arms clipped behind their backs. The Empress herself sat impassively on her horse, the bridle held tight by a triumphant Angul warrior. Other soldiers were pushing shut the great brass-studded wooden doors of the city.

The Empress acknowledged Sibby with a slight nod. The other warriors might not have existed. "My thanks, Batur," she said. "You have saved most of my household this temporary inconvenience.

Sibby tried to respond but her captor's fingers had dug so hard into her throat she could barely swallow and had no voice. Sibby was pushed behind the Empress's horse along the narrow street that led from the gate to the large central court. On a fur-covered throne Prince Tammush sat stiffly upright, his unsheathed sword across his knees. For a long moment his eyes and those of the Empress met. Then Tammush smiled.

"It is long since a player has been able to capture a queen from Tibir. Perhaps the old man should try some simpler game."

"Any game you could win, Prince, would have to be simple indeed. If I am your prisoner, so are you, too, a prisoner, trapped on the Agan's gameboard. How do you intend to leave Yokan? My men are without, and soon the Agan himself will be here.''

Tammush shook his head. "The Agan chases phantoms north. And your safety will ensure my own." His eyes moved slowly over Sibby and his broad face lifted in humorous lines. "The Emperor's Sword-Bearer! Yes, Batur, your fame has reached me. But where is this famous sword?''

Since Sibby was unable to speak, she chose to look defiant rather than injured. She was thrown to her knees for her trouble, and her shins banged on the stones.

"Are we to understand that the Emperor dares to wield the Enku of Chanaga himself? Gods have been knocked down for less. Perhaps it will be written in the future days that Tibir lost his last fight with the great Prince Tammush because the God of the Anguls could not bear to see the sword of the Gagan in the hand of a half-breed from Almadun.''

The Empress looked quickly ahead at a point a little above Tammush's head, and Sibby tried to match that impassivity on her own face. Tammush polished a fingerprint from his sword blade with the edge of his hand. He was plainly dressed, in a quilted felt overcoat that showed the effects of hard campaigning and a rapid flight cross-country. But his armaments and those of his men were well maintained, clean, oiled and sharp. A narrow golden circlet in his thick, braided hair was the only mark of rank. He seemed to have about fifty men, unless there were others hidden in the walls.

"Help the Empress alight, Sword-Bearer. Alas, we cannot allow any of her other retainers their lives. Yokan makes a perfect prison, but we are not jailers." His men threw the Empress's remaining soldiers on the cobbles and killed them with little noise or fuss. Sibby closed her eyes while Tammush laughed softly. "Freely I admit it," said Tammush. "I have learned many things from the great Tibir. But when he spoke similar words outside of Dessa he held a thousand men at swordpoint, not seven." He nodded graciously at Sibby. "Someday you must go and see it. Their heads make a tower outside the city, enclosed in brick. It is fifty feet high. The Empress and I will have time to share many such pleasant reminiscences, while we wait Tibir's return. But I need some token to send him so he understands his position.''

Sibby had taken the bridle and held the Empress's stirrup. The old woman stepped down slowly, with perfect dignity, and did not seem to notice the bodies of her men on the stones, their blood running and puddling in the cracks. Then one of Tammush's men gave her a shove forward, and if Sibby had not been able to catch her sleeve, she would have fallen at Tammush's feet.

"You should fall at my feet in shame," he said as he rose, taking a firm grip on his sword. "A great princess of Angulidan, the bride of the Chama himself, consorting with a red-haired barbarian, rejoicing in his domination of the Anguls as much as his destruction of other barbarians. Even his Sword-Bearer is a foreign sorceress—an evil woman of impure blood handling the Enku of Chanaga Gagan, your own great grandsire!"

One of his men grabbed the collar of the Empress's long robe, while another ripped free the long coils of her hair. Tammush slashed with his sword and her hair slithered to the ground, part of it resting in one of the many small pools of blood. The tip of his blade tore a long rip in the Empress's clothes.

"You should have shaved your head for shame long ago. Now go and sit in the chamber I have prepared for you, old woman, and consider your many sins."

Soria looked very tiny without the great mass of hair on her head. But her expression never flickered. She looked down at the pile of her hair and back at Tammush. "You are sending Tibir the material to make a rope," she said. "Shall I tell you how he will use it?"

From The Secret History of Tammush

The goose has not been hatched whose feather can yield a quill capable of being made sharp enough to etch on parchment the depths of horror and bloodshed and iniquity which the self-styled Emperor loosed on the world he conquered. The passage of Chanaga Gagan a hundred years earlier now seemed like a gentle ray of sunlight over the land, in comparison with the winter-chill of Tibir's forces.

Where there had been peace, there now was ruin; where there had been fertile fields, now wasteland; where there had

*been the voices of children, there were no longer left alive
even the mothers to mourn them. Blood was more common
than water and death more often encountered than life: wherever the Conqueror encamped the merchants held lively trade
in death and heads were sold in basket-lots to the officials of
the Agan.*

*Only in the north was there any word of defiance. Only
among the true Anguls of the Blue Ardan was there a prince
to defy the false Emperor. Tammush, with the support of the
lords of Paradon, dared risk the wrath of Tibir, secure in the
knowledge that fortune favors the just.*

Chapter Eleven

THE LOVERS

I

The Empress and Sibby were shown to a dark, cold chamber at least forty feet on a side, with a group of three narrow windows overlooking the river far below. It was a haven for bats and starlings and spiders at the upper level, and rats and beetles on the floor. Along one wall was piled refuse from long years of storage: broken pottery, rotten fabric, clumps of packing straw.

As the doors shut behind them Sibby slumped against the wall, but the Empress stood with her arms folded against her chest. "In the first year after I married the Agan," she said, "his enemies in the service of the Chama surprised us in a village of Almadun. We were made prisoners in an underground stable while our captors waited for instructions from Samida. It was colder than this, and smaller and much less clean. Praise God his luck did not desert him then. It will not fail him now." She pulled off her heavy traveling robe, then dropped it onto the floor. "Sleep now, Batur Subi. I may need your strength later." Sibby did not argue.

For the next two days they were left alone, except for an occasional flask of water and handful of dried fruit. They could hear the sounds of stones being shifted and timbers dragged and hammered into place as Tammush reinforced his stronghold. The Empress maintained her calm faith and unvarying good humor and chided Sibby for her restlessness. In the dark of their long lightless evenings she told Sibby stories of the campaigns of the Fortunate Lord.

The morning of the third day no one brought them food, but Soria leaned serenely by the window looking out, the wind ruffling her short fine hair. "It will not be long, now," she remarked softly. "Tammush has never learned any of his lessons well. He has already forgotten how quickly the Agan can travel when there is need." She patted her flat stomach. "Hunger teaches us the pleasures of eating, as adversity does the uses of success."

Sibby was spared the necessity of framing a philosophical answer by the entry of Tammush. He was looking much more relaxed, and one of his men was carrying a chair so that he could sit as soon as he entered. His men had put aside their helmets and coats of hardened leather and mesh; all were dressed in Angul fashion except for a tall, lean warrior dressed in a belted tunic of dark blue homespun, worn over coarse brown hose and shabby boots. The boots were bound with strips of cloth to keep them from falling down, and his weather-beaten face was pale in contrast to the Anguls, with high cheekbones and a straight narrow nose and brilliantly blue eyes. His pale hair was a mix of blond and grey, lying unkempt on his shoulders. In contrast to the smooth faces and long moustaches of the Anguls, his face was roughly shaven; the stubble added to his look of tired desperation. He walked with a limp.

Tammush was once more repeating the long list of indignities that Tibir had served upon the Angul people, but as Sibby listened she was distracted by the bright angry gaze of the tall warrior. Wherever she looked she could feel his eyes upon her, and something about his arrogant face haunted her.

"You can see," Tammush was saying, "how this civil war has wasted our people. It is not only the Agan who is forced to surround himself with men from Vahn and Melismala and Zanida. It is not only the Agan who relies on the assistance of an outlander for his chief Batur." He swept his hand back toward the blue-eyed warrior. "With my best men slaughtered by the forces of the Agan, I had no one to help me organize my retreat. Then fate brought me a champion from the deserts of Vahn, the famed Clerowan." He leered at Sibby. "A more useful present from fate than an outlandish sorceress."

Sibby spoke before she could control her tongue. "Useful, if all you need is six horses stolen. It has been many years since Tibir needed so trifling a favor. The Agan can use six horses in a day himself, if he hurries, and so can each of his hundred thousand men. You should have taken this outlaw's six horses and gotten away when there was a chance. You are surely doomed now.''

Tammush got slowly to his feet. ''At last the Sword-Bearer speaks. But you disappoint me. I was hoping for some display of your magical powers. Am I to guess that your hold over the Agan is of the more usual sort?'' He gripped Sibby's arm and dug his fingers into her tensed muscle. ''And yet you have neither youth nor beauty to recommend you. Tell me, how is it that you amuse the Emperor?''

His breath was on her face and the heat of his body felt sickeningly close. She set her jaw and stared him down with a great deal more success than she had had with Clerowan.

He dropped his eyes to the open throat of her shirt and pushed it back to reveal the edge of her brand. ''The true mark of a Batur,'' he said softly. ''By what passage of arms did you earn this?'' Then, insultingly as before, ''What other marks of the great Tibir do you bear on your body?''

Sibby's control snapped. She was tired and hungry and her body ached almost everywhere. And despite Soria's calm she did not herself believe they had any chance of survival. She brought Tammush's gaze up to meet her own, and without dropping her eyes or warning him in any way she raised her knee in a truly satisfying thrust and shove. As the prince's head lurched forward, mouth sagging, she grabbed her weakened right wrist in her left hand and brought up the two fists together onto the point of his chin. Tammush fell at her feet.

Her triumph was too short to be enjoyable. Three of the Angul guards threw their heavy, muscular bodies on her, pinning her winded and bruised to the floor. Their hands and legs and hot breaths were everywhere, and there was no way she could get out from under their weight. Clerowan called them off, even as he helped the shaken prince back into his chair. Reluctantly they pushed themselves up off the floor, with unnecessary handling of her body as they did so. She closed her eyes and tried to think of suitable last thoughts.

Tammush gasped a few moments before speaking. ''She will not be ransomed. We can buy our safety with the Empress alone. The Agan has no dearth of amusements. He can spare us this one.'' He straightened in his chair. ''Batur

Clerowan, examine her. You have told me of her sorcerer's powers. As yet we have seen nothing. Examine her so we may plan accordingly." He managed a breathless laugh. "We call for a duel. A duel between the outlander baturs of Prince Tammush and the Agan Tibir." The Anguls laughed as they hauled Sibby to her feet and pushed her through the door. Partway down the corridor another storage room stood open, the twin of the room she had left. In there she was pushed, and after her came Clerowan, shutting the door behind him.

Sibby turned her back on her enemy and walked to the window. The view here was the same as it was next door. The damaged muscles in her back were in spasm again, and sharp pains of intolerable intensity were shooting down her legs. She did not see how she could possibly survive any physical confrontation. Clerowan did not look like the sort of man who was driven by lusts of the body or the desire to kill, but he was in the service of Tammush. He was tall and lean and hard-muscled. If I were a puppy, she thought, now would be the time to roll over on my back. Clerowan's first words were not promising.

"Sorceress," he said, and his low voice shook with passion. His voice was deep and familiar from her dreams. "I never thought you would prove so much your mother's daughter."

Sibby passed her hand over her face and tried to make some sense out of what he was saying.

"I tell you this, sorceress, and I promise with my blood: if you try to make your daughter the inheritor of your mother's powers, I will kill you with my own hands." He sounded completely serious. She turned to face him and the harsh morning light deepened the set lines on his face and showed up the darkness under his heavy-lidded eyes. Sibby laughed in his face.

"If I were a sorceress I would not have to stand here and be beaten, starved and yelled at. My mother is a nice, ordinary lady of no special gifts, enjoying her second husband and life in Florida. I do not have a daughter." She raised her hand and pointed at his face. "And just who the hell do you think you are?"

Clerowan took a half step back. "I know who I am," he answered. "Have you forgotten who you are?" His nostrils twitched. "You even smell like an Angul."

Sibby suddenly felt light-hearted. She sniffed her own shoulder ostentatiously. "Everyone sweats," she said, "and your prince has not provided bathing facilities. That other smell is just the sheepskin. They dry it in the sun. I'm surprised you haven't got used to it by now."

"I only ride with the Anguls. I do not sleep with them."

"Maybe you should try it. It might make you more civil. And one of them might lend you a razor." She tried to turn back toward the window, but his hand closed hard on her shoulder and pulled her to face him.

"Do not laugh at me, witch. Vahn and Tredana are destroyed, the Karabdu are scattered, but I am still alive and so is Leron the King. Do not think we will fail to pay you what you are due. In the valley of the Marajites you slaughtered without mercy unarmed scholars and men of peace. In Tredana your forces threw down the steward Gannoc from the walls and laughed at his death—a man who had treated you like his own daughter when you were little. They tore down the walls of the castle where you lived as queen and bride and mother. In Treclere your Anguls made Varys crawl in the dust and abase himself while they laughed at his disgrace. Varys, Odric's beloved brother—once your friend. And in the desert the Anguls murdered the Tayyib and stole his horse, took from me my finest horses, stole my daughter, killed my lover, slaughtered my bravest warriors—" His hand pulled open the front of her shirt, exposing her breast and the mark of Tibir above her heart. "Can you deny this infamous brand? Were you already with the Angul cause when we last met in Tredana? Is it here you came when you left us so mysteriously?"

He pushed her against the window and unluckily the protruding edge of the sill caught her in the damaged center of her back. The pressure made her legs suddenly fail and she fell forward into her enemy's arms. Her head spun as she lay briefly against his chest, filled with confusing images. He was a stranger to her, angry and dangerous, yet in her mind she saw him in a hundred different and familiar poses. She closed her eyes and let her head rest momentarily on his arm. "I used to know your name," she said softly.

There was silence.

"Do you swear you do not know me?" he asked at last, and she looked him straight in the eye before letting her lids drop again. "There is no way I could know you," she said. "I don't belong to this world. Some power brought me to Angulidan, a few months ago. I have been with the Anguls ever since. I have never been in your part of this world.'' Her legs were supporting her again and she pulled herself free of his arms. She shook her head. "I think," she added truthfully.

Clerowan's confidence seemed shaken. He gently pulled the edges of her shirt together and patted it closed. "Tell me your story," he said at last in a softer voice, "and I will tell you mine."

Sibby sat down awkwardly, arranging her bruises against the hardness of the wall and the floor. Clerowan squatted on his heels beside her.

"My name," she said at length, "is Sibyl Barron Arleon." Clerowan startled at this but did not interrupt. "I am thirty years old. I have lived all my life in Massachusetts, a state in the northeastern corner of the United States of America. I am a graduate of Harvard University, an ancient and respected center of higher learning, also in Massachusetts. My field of study was English literature, especially poetry. I have been married to Michael Arleon, also of Massachusetts, for the past ten years. We have been separated for one year and I am in the process of getting a divorce. I do not have children. Since leaving Michael I have earned my living by teaching children how to ride horses, a popular amusement in Massachusetts. Two months ago I was riding a horse in Massachusetts when I struck my head on his by leaning forward at the wrong moment. When I woke up I was not in Massachusetts, and I haven't come close since."

She dropped her head back and slowly retold her wanderings in the wasteland, the meeting with Soktani Agana, Varlas Mir and the Bloodstone, the Enku, Dalun and her baby, the defense of Zamarra. She described Tibir and the meeting with the Empress. When she came to the raid in the horse pasture, Clerowan startled again and shook his head. "Tamara was there?" he asked. Sibby nodded.

"I sent her to safety. But your friend with the bow might as well have had a point on his arrow." She half turned and pulled up the back of her shirt, aware that by now the bruise looked as bad as it felt, swollen in the middle, jet black and still spreading.

"I almost stood by and saw you killed," was his only comment. "You lay at my feet and I did not know. And

Tamara was there!'' He sighed and Sibby went on with the tale, bringing it up to date, to the walls of Yokan. ''Tamara was behind you on the bridge?''

''She is safe with the royal household. Now you have my story. It's your turn.'' She looked at him more closely. ''What are you to Tamara? Why do you think you know me?''

Clerowan dropped his face in his hands and laughed. ''I have been more than a friend to you both. But my story is longer than yours, and somewhat more violent.''

He paused to search out the right word, and as he did so there was a clatter of hooves on the causeway below. He helped Sibby to her feet and they looked out together. A single figure sat his horse on the narrow bridge, unmistakable in his golden armor and surcoat of red and white silk. The bright sword of Chanaga Gagan winked in the sunlight as the Emperor made his formal salute of challenge. No one could have told that the arm lifting it was crippled. Clerowan raised his eyebrows.

''Tammush will be needing me. My story must wait. I would like to make one small test before I go. I have your permission?''

He took her face in his hands and touched his lips to hers, lightly at first. But she clutched his arms and pulled him closer and he opened his mouth in answer, kissing her until she had to pull free to breathe. He smiled, and twenty years dropped from his haggard face.

''Now there's no question in my mind,'' he said. ''And you never tasted better to me.''

II

All day Tibir challenged Tammush from the causeway. He galloped his horse up to the gates, wheeled and checked, trotted back, turned and galloped up to the gates again. He raised both sword and shield above his head and rode with his weight alone, the reins lying loose on his horse's neck. No answer came from Tammush. It was madness for the old man to make a personal challenge, with his hundreds of thousands of mounted troops behind him; a madness typical of Tibir.

Sibby leaned her elbows on the windowsill and wondered how Tammush expected to be able to get his demands to the Emperor.

She was interrupted in her reverie by an Angul guard who hurried her along to the central courtyard. Soria was there, arms folded, chin raised. Tammush was there also, sitting in his chair, face dark, no armor on. "He dares call me a coward!" he exploded as Sibby approached. "Old fool. Crazy old fool. I should let him ride up and down until he dies of old age. But I will take pity on his grey hairs. My Batur will meet him hand to hand."

Behind him, a group of Anguls were putting together pieces of armor to cover Clerowan. Even the helmet was a poor fit, gapping critically at the neck. No part was long enough; the cuirass so restricted the movement of his shoulders that he dropped it to the stones and took a heavy leather surcoat instead. The sword at least was his own, lean and whippy; he also carried a curved sabre on his back. As he took off his helm and turned up his leather collar to partially protect his neck, his eyes met Sibby's. He shrugged and smiled, then eased the helmet down over the collar's edge. The horse he mounted was also one of his own, stolen back from Tibir—a heavy-muscled grey with a long light neck and noble head. Before he turned and rode to the gate he saluted Tammush, but his eyes swept over Sibby as he turned.

Sibby's heart sank as he rode out. She did not even know his real name, but she wanted very much to have the chance to find out. Soria's arms were pulled roughly behind her back and an Angul soldier did the same to Sibby before walking them both onto the ramparts above the gate. Tammush joined them, breathing audibly. At the far end of the causeway Tibir turned his horse. It was wet with sweat, all foamy where the edge of its hardness rubbed. Before the gates of Yokan, Clerowan sat with a stillness that rivaled Tibir's usual impassivity. His horse stood quietly chewing the bit, waiting an attack.

Tibir saluted and his horse leapt forward, hooves clattering on the stones. He held his sword over is head. Clerowan did not even draw until Tibir was halfway across; he waited, and at the last moment wheeled his horse in a tight circle, ducking the blow and landing a slash on the Emperor's armored back. In the little space by the gates they circled each other, just twenty feet below the watchers on the walls. It was soon clear that they were as well matched in horsemanship and sword-craft as they were mismatched in equipment. Time and again Clerowan's sword rang on the Emperor's armor; time and again the Emperor's sword bit through Clerowan's shabby covering.

Sibby felt tears sting her eyes. Watching the fight, it was clear that no quarter would be given. There was blood now in the slashes on Clerowan's body, and he handled his sword a little more awkwardly.

Suddenly Tibir faltered, and his sword arm seemed to fall sideways. The Enku dropped from his hand. At the far end of the causeway Tibir's baturs surged forward, and two of them set foot on the edge of the bridge. Tibir's short sword was on his back, but his arm would not raise high enough to reach it. Clerowan reined back his horse and saluted. Then he reversed his sword in his hand and held out the hilt to the Emperor. Slowly the Emperor took it, and saluted in return as Clerowan drew his second sword. Then they closed again, slashing faster and more fiercely.

Tammush cursed as he watched the fight below. "We will never have such a chance again. He is done for now."

Seemingly in answer to his words, Clerowan fell forward in his saddle, his shield arm hanging useless. He managed to heave himself up for a final thrust that skidded across the smooth metal of the Emperor's greaves, and possibly pricked him low in the side by the hinge of his belt, but the Emperor brought his sword around in a cunning thrust to the armpit. Sibby was reminded through tearing eyes of her first sight of the Emperor, but this time the Agan held his thrust and the blade did not go in more than a few inches. It was enough to knock Clerowan out of the saddle and he sprawled, bleeding, under the hooves of the Agan's horse. Both sides waited for the death blow but Tibir backed his horse away, to the midpoint of the bridge. A flick of his sword point summoned his baturs to him; at a word, they picked up the Enku and returned it to him, then took his borrowed sword and laid it by Clerowan's outstretched hand. One of them then rode forward to the gates and hammered with his mailed fist on the doors.

"Tammush," he cried, "take up your champion. The Emperor has defeated him as he defeats all who oppose him.

Open your gates to us and you may find mercy. Yokan will not protect you long. Look!'' The warrior gestured widely with his hand. ''Tibir has changed the river in its course. Who now dares oppose him?''

Sibby looked up from the huddled figure below and saw that the batur spoke the truth. The river was no longer roaring. It was shallower and calmer, more brown than white, and the stones over which it ran were showing their tops in great black clumps. The Emperor rode back across the altered river, followed by his baturs, leaving Clerowan bleeding on the stones. Tammush went slowly back down into the courtyard, but made no move once there to bring in his fallen champion. It was the captain of his soldiers who finally took it on himself to open the gate and drag the warrior in. Tammush looked at him briefly as he walked away. ''Take up what armor we can use, and the swords. Dispose of the rest.'' He did not spare a backward look, but the captain who had dragged Clerowan in saw to it that the stripped body was thrown in the same storeroom as one of the prisoners, rather than over the walls.

Tammush kept Soria with him, while Sibby and Clerowan were once more locked up. The batur's long legs sprawled limply on the floor; his ripped shirt was soaked with blood at hip and waist and shoulder. From under his sword arm the blood still flowed, but sluggishly, and there was a streak along the side of his neck that would have been mortal had the leather of his collar not managed to turn the Emperor's sword blade. Sibby dropped to her knees and wondered where to begin. He opened his eyes.

''If we do not tie up my arm I may bleed to death, and that is not part of my plans.''

His eyes dropped shut for a moment, then he gave a grunt and heaved himself up to a sitting position. His face was white. Sibby helped him peel off his tattered shirt and rip it into sling and bandages. His upper body was a lurid mass of scars, mostly old, but several deep ones were recent. ''I can see you've been through this before,'' she said a little shakily.

His pierced armpit was the only major wound, but the other slashes were dirty with bits of crumbled leather from his coat, and there was no water with which to clean them. Sibby covered them with the cleaner bits of shirt and took off her sheepskin vest. It was not broad enough through the shoulders for him to wear but he accepted its covering gratefully, shivering with fatigue and shock. Under its cover she put her arms around him and tried to give him a little of her warmth. For a few moments he let himself slump against her, then he sighed and straightened up.

"Our problems have only begun," he said. "I have managed to avoid killing the Emperor of the World, but he is still out there and we are still here. More to the point, the Empress is below and Tammush will use her safety to threaten Tibir. I do not think we can trust the prince to honor the terms of combat."

"Wasn't it your idea to capture the Empress?"

"I did not know Tammush so well then. I assumed he would honor the dignity of his hostage." He threw off the vest and fell forward on his knees and free left hand, then he slowly got to his feet. The effort made fresh blood spurt from under his arm. He lurched to the window and looked down. "We do not have much time. The river is almost gone and Tammush will be in a panic. Did they bother to lock us in?"

He dragged himself to the door and Sibby looked around for something with which to pry open the central crack. The warehouse's doors were not made for opening from within. They were hung in pairs, hinged on the sides and barred together across the middle, opening into the rooms. She did not remember having heard the bar fall into place outside, but she could not get her fingers around enough of the edge to pull. Then Clerowan returned from a poke through the rubbish on the floor, holding a well-worn horseshoe of the Angul type, a round, solid plate, half-cracked from overuse. He eased it between the doors and teased at the edge; the doors creaked open.

At the end of the passage they stopped and listened to the shouted conversation below. One of Tibir's grandsons sat his horse outside the iron gateway; the inner wooden doors were pulled back and just inside the gate Tammush sat defiantly in his chair, arms crossed. His men must have been on the walls with their few arrows, for a short bolt struck the young prince on his helmet and snapped his neck to the side with the force of its flight. He did not fall from the saddle however, and with a calm worthy of his grandfather stretched his sword to right and left.

"Tibir has turned back the river," he called in a strong

young voice. "We will take these walls down stone by stone if need be."

"You will build your grandmother a fine burial mound!"

The young man saluted. "The Agan says we will build her a mountain in the north of Angulidan, a mountain made of the skulls of the people of Tammush."

Tammush rose to his feet and walked out of sight of the archway, to where Soria waited under guard. She was too old and small to resist them as they forced her up to the inner side of the gate. Head shorn, shoulders bare, gown ripped and dirty—she folded her arms and stared straight ahead with no emotion on her face. Outside on the causeway, the young prince dismounted and kneeled by his horse. "The greetings of Tibir to his queen," he said and Soria nodded in return.

"And mine to him. Ask the Great Agan to do one thing for me." She half turned and looked at Tammush. "Ask him to take apart Yokan and spread it down the mountainside, so that in days to come no man will know where it once stood. And no man will know how far the bones of Tammush lie scattered."

"It will be done." As the prince remounted and turned away, Soria pushed past Tammush and sank in his chair.

He looked at her, at the gates, up at the sky. Then he drew his sword and took two paces forward. As Tammush touched his hilt Clerowan slipped down the stairs, silent in his worn boots. Sibby followed as silently. By the time he had his sword clear of its sheath, Clerowan was less than fifteen feet away. In the chair Soria had dropped her face forward on her hands and was quietly waiting for the end. She was startled upright as Tammush's sword came skittering along the stones past her feet, closely followed by Tammush—with the bloody and desperate figure of Clerowan fastened to his back. Sibby grabbed up Tammush's sword and presented the point to his throat, and Soria smiled.

With only one arm, Clerowan could not work the mechanism for the gates, so he took the sword and held Tammush at bay while Sibby struggled with the stiff wheel and lever. A roar went up from the army outside as the gate opened, and the young prince turned his horse on its haunches and sprang into a gallop as he returned. At the gate he saluted Sibby, then threw himself off his horse and led it inside to where the Empress waited. As he lifted her on its back, he gave her such

a squeeze of delight she gasped and scolded, but she patted
his head as he walked her out of Yokan.

A chief batur and two other royal grandsons followed, to
take Tammush in charge and dispose of his men. Horses were
brought for the two shabby heroes, and Sibby felt weakness
wash over her as her horse was led slowly back across the
causeway. The stones of the river glistened below, with just a
little water running between them. Tibir had turned back the
river indeed, and Sibby had no doubt Yokan would soon be
destroyed.

All she wanted to do was wash and sleep, but the Emperor
would not allow it. He received the heroes of Yokan in his
own tent, sitting under the long, bloody plait of hair from
Soria's head, looped on his battle standard. Sibby was raised
to her feet by one of his grandsons, who did the same service
for Clerowan, now paler than ever. Tibir spoke to him first.

"I give you your life, batur, although you have served
Prince Tammush. Serve me faithfully and I will give you
honor as well. For now, I give you the freedom of my
encampment, horses, clothes, armor." A flash of humor
briefly crossed his face. "Armor that fits. For the rest, time
will tell. You may go. My surgeons await you." Then he
turned to Sibby.

"You must take up the Enku again, Sword-Bearer. It is not
for me to carry it. If there is anything I can grant you now,
ask it."

Sibby dropped her eyes. "I am your Sword-Bearer, but I
am not a warrior," she said at last. "Grant me a bodyguard."

Tibir nodded. "How large a group do you require?"

"Only one. The Batur Clerowan."

Now Tibir smiled broadly, his narrow eyes almost hidden
under his brows. "He will be assigned to your quarters," he
said, and he was still smiling as he dismissed her.

III

Sibby slept well in her new tent, buried deep in silk-covered
lamb's-wool cushions, her body bathed, oiled and massaged.
The tent was not large but very elegant, striped in the Emper-
or's colors. In the small antechamber there was just enough

room for a single guard to sleep—amid a litter of saddles and weaponry. And there, presumably, Clerowan slept as well as she. He was certainly quiet.

At dawn she awoke and admired the way the sunlight illumined the silk above her head. She heard Clerowan cough and change his position, and rolling silently onto her feet went to the inner hanging. Or she thought she had gone silently, but he spoke up the moment she hesitated.

"Good morning, Batur."

She lifted the flap and he was propped up on his unbandaged elbow, his right arm tied neatly to his side. He looked very rested and her heart lurched in her chest.

"The surgeons say I will live. Would you care to check their handiwork?" He started to push back the covers and Sibby took an involuntary step backward. He grinned and spoke more softly. "Surely," he said, "you cannot be afraid of a one-armed man?"

Sibby laughed and sat down by his feet, safely out of range. "You don't need an arm for everything," she said primly. "When we were interrupted yesterday you were about to tell me your story. And your name."

He closed his eyes and leaned back. "It is too much of an effort," he said. "I am not well enough to speak loudly. You will have to come closer." Her heart lurched again, pleasantly. She slowly got up and sat down by his waist. He heaved a sigh of relief. "That's better," he murmured. "Now you must lean down." Laughing softly, she leaned over and was not surprised to be caught in the hard circle of his free arm. "This is where we were interrupted," he said, and brought his mouth up to hers.

Despite the lightness of his words, his heart was knocking violently in his chest and his body trembled. She was scared by the depths of his passion and pulled herself free. "This is very nice," she said quellingly, "but I still don't know who you are."

He took her hand and held it as he dropped back against the cushioned saddle he was using as a pillow. "You do not remember," he corrected her. "Once you knew me well." He did not look in her face as he softly spoke of the desert and the Karabdu; sometimes he closed his eyes as he searched for a word. His voice dropped lower and lower as he talked about his past life, and hers. She dropped against his chest and he held her quietly while he spoke into her hair, almost in a whisper.

"I don't know why I believe your stories," she finally said. "I don't remember any of them. Did I call you Ajjibawr?" He murmured *yes*. "Is Tamara really mine?" she asked, and he tightened his arm in answer. "And yours?" He squeezed her again. She pushed herself up and examined his face more closely. "When we were on the ship," she asked at length, "did you stain your face brown?" He nodded. "I could see it in my mind's eye," she said. "A single image. The others must be there, too."

She closed her eyes and let her face drop onto his chest. He held her quietly for a moment, then tightened his arm around her not in passion but awkwardness, as he used his teeth to tug a ring from his finger. As she pulled herself free, he laughed and rubbed the thin silver band between his fingers until it shone. "I have owed you this a long time," he said. "Will you take it from me now?"

She took it without looking at it and kissed him gently. As she trailed her lips across his face, he groaned with pleasure and tightened his arm again. Past his head the pommel of the saddle stuck out, bright with twisted silver wires. There were shields and swords piled at his side and a tangle of uncleaned harness. The thought came to her to go inside where there was more room and comfort, but she did not have the chance to speak it. He held her with his legs and arm and mouth and she gladly let herself be made his prisoner.

When she woke she was still in the circle of his arm, lying on his chest. Outside she could hear the morning bustle of cooking and cleaning, but no sound of tents being struck or oxcarts loaded. Clerowan gently shifted her weight to one side and sat up by her. He buried his face in her unpinned hair and kissed her shoulder.

"It is time to get up," she said. "I have to wait upon Tibir."

Clerowan laughed and moved his lips down her arm and across her chest. "The Great Tibir is very human," he murmured against her skin. "I suspect that at this very moment he is busy, much as we are. He will need no attendance from us this morning." He started to pull her down on top of him again, but this time she did pull free.

"Come inside," she said. "We will only cripple ourselves even more by staying here."

The inner room glowed with light and striped their bodies red and silver. Clerowan arranged himself against the cushions with a grimace. "You will have to come to me again, my love, for I am in no state to support myself on one arm."

Sibby laughed and shook her head as she looked at his battle-scarred body. She turned so that he could see all of her bruises full. "It's just as well," she said. "I could not possibly lie on my back. We make the perfect couple." She lay down gently against him and he traced the marks on her back while she examined the scars on his chest, arm and hip. "These do not look like lovers' bodies," she said at last.

His hand slipped along her back and caressed her legs, then pushed them apart. "Then I suggest you shut your eyes," he said and smothered her laugh with another kiss.

The day lasted forever, but when it ended it had been much too short. They lay wrapped together exhausted and exhilarated, soaked in sweat and the smell of each other's bodies. Utter fatigue made them sleep like the dead during late afternoon; utter hunger woke them later that evening. Sibby woke first, and as she washed herself her stomach gurgled and growled. She dressed quickly and then returned to her sleeping hero to wash his face. He groaned and stretched out his arm and legs, then lifted his chin so she could wash off the angry wound along his throat.

"Are we finished so soon?" he asked mildly. "I was just beginning to find my pace."

She laughed and gave him a quick kiss. "Is that what they call it here? Where I come from, they call it fading fast."

With sunset came the coolness of a fall evening. Cooking fires roared in the dark and the area by the tents of the Agan were a blaze of torches, little lights and fires. Still buckling on her Enku, Sibby approached the tents, marveling at the way her bruises and soreness had all been scoured away by the day's activities. Her bodyguard walked behind, and even his limp was less. They could smell the lamb and the bread all over the camp; in the courtyard before the tent of the Agan, sumptuous carpets had been spread, covered with platters in gold and silver and enameled copper. There were great bowls of masett and bowls of wine, platters of bread and lamb. Melons and grapes had been gathered fresh from the surrounding countryside and were piled along the center of the carpet. Tibir sat on his dais and beside him sat the Empress, his other wives ranged on either side, one step lower. Soria's headdress of ornamental gold and silver leaves was so ornate that it hid her hair entirely. Both the Empress and the Emperor looked tired, but pleasantly so; Sibby smiled sympathetically.

The need to eat took first precedence; Sibby suddenly realized that her last meal had been a handful of dried fruit two days ago. Her batur ate no less eagerly, and made her laugh by gravely sampling her wine and her masett. As they ate, Sibby's eyes searched the crowd for sign of Tamara, but none of the younger children were present. After the food came stories and songs, dancers and musicians. For a while Sibby noticed Tibir's hand resting lightly on Soria's shoulder, the first time she had ever seen him touch her in public. She waited for Marricson to appear, but there was no sign of the Empress's favorite singer. She assumed he was probably enjoying the feasting too much to feel like performing. Certainly, he was not missed. Song followed song, dance followed dance, recitations covered the whole broad sweep of Angul history. Clerowan touched her hip and whispered a suggestion in her ear. She laughed.

"Brave words. But can you prove them? I'm willing to wager that you are done for today."

He pulled her to her feet and no one noticed their leaving.

Back at the tent she laughed again as he tried to unfasten her clothes using only his left hand. He fell back against the pillows, shaking his head.

"Perhaps you are right," he said. "But I've always managed to get at least as far as the undressing."

She carefully unbuckled her sword and laid it behind her pillow, then slowly leaned over and opened his coat at the throat. "I still have two hands," she said. "Let's see how far they can get."

The suddenness with which his passion returned surprised them both, and when they fell asleep for the night they were still in a tangle of clothes. There were no further awakings that night. They slept like the dead, and when Sibby awoke it was to find her lover trying to remove his boots without disturbing her, using only one arm.

After they had their bread and masett, Sibby left Clerowan

cleaning his old weapons and examining his new ones. She
went to wait on Tibir but was turned away from the royal
tent. He was still with the Empress in private. She found one
of the Empress's serving women, however, a nice girl who
had treated Tamara as well as the royal grandchildren. When
she asked for the Tredanan hostage, the girl shook her head.

"You must speak with the captain of the household," she
said. "While we awaited Our Lord's return—after the capture
of the Empress—the child disappeared. The captain is looking
for her now. We did not notice at first, you understand. We
were too concerned for the Empress. Speak with the captain,
he will tell you more."

The captain of the household was not that easy to locate. It
was several hours before Sibby found him, just returned from
a brief attempt to isolate the tracks of the escapees. It was not
just Tamara; Marricson the singer was also gone. The captain
shrugged.

"I do not relish telling the Empress this. But it must be
done. The whole thing is without sense. Where would they
go? I have sent messengers back as far as Shakar. We ourselves will soon be in Gagan-ala. There is no place else to go,
unless they flee into the wilderness. It is without sense."

"When was she missed?" asked Sibby.

"She came back and raised the alarm when you were
taken," he answered. "And she spent that first night with the
Empress's women. The next night she was gone."

"It has only been three days. How far could she go?"

"A hundred miles or more—or less, much less. There is
good cover in these mountains. She might even be close at
hand. It is with God."

Sibby fought back her first impulse, which was to ride out
and see for herself. As she returned to her tent and her
personal bodyguard, she thought how little she was accus-
tomed to sharing her problems or taking advice from anyone.
Now was the time to start learning. Clerowan was sitting in
the sun in front of the tent, a new sword pinned across his
knees by his bandaged right arm, while he ran the stone along
its blade with his left. He cursed softly as his cross-handed
clumsiness brought his thumb in contact with the newly sharp-
ened edge. At her approach he looked up and smiled, squinting against the sun; his face was washed so free of tension he

looked nearer twenty than fifty. She sank to the ground at his feet.

"She ran away," said Sibby. "Three days ago. And I don't think she's alone. That friend she made, the singer, is missing too. The Empress does not know yet, but the captain of her household has been out looking for them."

Clerowan carefully placed his whetstone back in its little box and propped the sword against the wall of the tent. His heavy lids veiled his expression. "That child," he said at last. "She must always act first and think afterward. Who is this singer? Is he young? Old? Trustworthy?"

"I liked his looks," said Sibby. "But I never spoke with him. And when I liked his looks I wasn't thinking of it in terms of being the right man to take care of a twelve-year-old girl."

"Did she ever speak of escape to you?"

"To me? The Emperor's Sword-Bearer? No."

She dropped her head against his thigh and he gently rubbed her neck. "There is one thing," she said. "She knew you were nearby. After our near-miss in the horse pasture, I told her the whole story, and mentioned hearing the name Ibrasa. At the time I did not realize she recognized the name. She covered herself well. I asked her what the Karabdu were like, and she said they might go to any lengths for something important. Could she be looking for you?"

"If she suspected I was near, yes. And more to the point, she may already have found Ibrasa."

"Where is he?"

"Tammush left him in charge of the men in the hills above Yokan. There were not many—fewer than twenty. And none of them could Tammush trust. That is why we two outlanders were able to rise so far so fast. The men will have fled by now, but Ibrasa would stay at hand to see me through. She'll be safe with him, as safe as anyone might be who is not under the protection of Tibir. Dear God," he said on a rising note of passion, "how can I have come so close only to lose her now?"

Sibby took his hand and held it. "She's not just any little girl. She is smart and tough and knows her own mind. She's the daughter of the Karif of all the Karabdu, and she has more energy than ten horses in race training. Fate hasn't brought us this far to play a cruel game now. Trust in it—and trust her. Your blood is in her veins.''

''And yours,'' he added softly. ''Who knows what games fate plans to play with you, or with your daughter?''

Chapter Twelve

THE RUNAWAYS

I

Nothing in her life had prepared Tamara for the confusion that reigned in the royal household outside Yokan. A personal threat to the Empress was unimaginable, the baturs and captains stood helplessly by, with Tibir so many days away. Messengers were immediately sent to the Emperor, but an attitude of helplessness prevailed in camp. No one except Tamara seemed to be mourning the loss of the Emperor's Sword-Bearer. Now more than ever she wished that Arbytis the High Priest had been allowed to stay with the royal household. She had not seen him since the two armies had been reunited and the Emperor had taken him into his private circle of advisors. Without him for counsel, or the Batur Subi for companionship, she felt quite lost in the growing disorder of the camp.

The refuse lay uncollected, the cooking pots were left rancid and unwashed, the water in the bathhouses grew cold. As Tamara miserably moped around on the second day after the capture of Soria and Subi, she fell into the arms of Marricson, quite literally, tripping over a tent rope. As he closed his arms around her to keep her on her feet, she found to her embarrassment that she was crying, and he held her tenderly and patted her back. When she was done he wiped her face with a large and relatively clean handkerchief, which he produced from his sleeve like a man doing a magic trick. Then he made her smile by making outrageous faces at her.

No one stopped her from accompanying Marricson back to

the entertainers' camping area. The atmosphere here was far less disturbed. Fires were burning, food was cooking and all around singers sang, dancers danced and tumblers tumbled as though no deadly insult had been offered to the Emperor of the World. Marricson went away and returned with bread and masett and a handful of purple grapes, and he stood over her and made her eat like a watchful mother. Then he picked up his battered baraka and strummed a little. When he handed it to Tamara, she carefully picked out one of the tunes her father had taught her when she was little and he had still enjoyed playing. After he married Liniris, he had insisted that she be the one to perform if there was to be any dancing or singing. For she was one of the players, and he but an amateur. But Tamara had never enjoyed listening to Liniris, and after that time she herself had played very little. Now her fingers were awkward.

Marricson was complimentary, however, and showed her how to make some new chords and runs. "Do you know this one?" he asked, and began to sing very softly. As soon as she heard the opening words, Tamara joined in.

> *It was summer in Tredana*
> *and the false king in his hall*
> *he swore that our Clerowan*
> *would be hanged before the fall*

> *Far to the north in Sundrat*
> *from paddock, field and stall*
> *He stole two hundred horses*
> *The Clerowan stole them all.*

"My tutor used to be an outlaw," Tamara remarked proudly. "He rode with Clerowan, and he taught me lots of Clerowan songs. But he never told me who Clerowan really was until years later. It's hard to imagine someone as dignified as the Karif playing all those tricks, and being so reckless. Alric has told me some stories that aren't in the ballads—you can hardly believe them."

"Alric," said Marricson. "That would be poor—Lord Gannoc's nephew? When I heard of him last he was studying with Dansen the Learned. So he took his teacher's old position?"

"You know Alric?"

"Not as well as I knew Dansen. Or Clerowan." Tamara stiffened, then her eyes grew wide as he went on, "Does the name Ibrasa mean anything to you?" He smiled at her expression. "It has come to my attention that there is a blue-eyed outlander by that name who has come some distance to see you."

"I knew it! I knew he was here!"

"However, for obvious reasons he does not feel comfortable about coming to visit you. You will have to go see him." Tamara was already on her feet. "Careful, little one. We do not wish to attract undue notice. This expedition must be very casual. It is true that the captain of the guard has other things to occupy his mind just now than the fate of one small hostage. If you agree, I will find you a change of clothing and this afternoon we will go for a short walk in the hills to gather herbs—a fat man and a little girl, nothing suspicious."

Tamara looked up stricken. "What about my horse?"

"Ibrasa has already promised to see to him. The horse master is almost as distracted as the royal guard."

Tamara strolled out of camp that afternoon dressed like the child of an acrobat, in a brilliant tunic and leggings that clashed violently in color. Her heart was hammering. Marricson carried his baraka in one hand, looking as unconcerned as a youth out berrying. They had to climb a steep bit of trail to leave the mass of the encampment behind; even with the bulk of the army absent, all the valley about Yokan was filled with Tibir's men.

Ibrasa had found a clearing among the rocks, with grass, a stunted tree and a trickle of water down the rock face. He had two horses, also: one of the six that he had recently stolen from the Emperor's horse pasture, and a more recent acquisition—a familiar chestnut stallion. Faras was delighted to see Tamara, but he insisted on showing her how frightened he had been by blowing up his nostrils and plucking at her with his lips. He sidled in alarm as Tamara stepped back from hugging his neck and threw her arms around Ibrasa's.

"Ibrasa! Didn't the—are you all alone?" His eyes smiled fondly at her but his face was tense and drawn. As he briefly recounted the terrible events in the desert after her kidnapping, she had to bite her lips hard to keep her face from crumpling. There was worse to come, however, as she learned who it was that served Tammush as champion.

Until that moment she had not realized how much she had come to identify with the cause of the Emperor. It was absolutely right and proper for the Karabdu to fight Aksu and his men, but for the Karif to serve Tammush against the Agan upset her terribly. Ibrasa tried to soothe her.

"The Karif has no interest in these Angul causes. We have crossed these thousands of miles with only one purpose, to find you and make you safe. To serve Tammush served ourselves, for a while."

"But what now? When the Karif comes back, are we going home? What is happening in Tredana? And the desert?"

"One hears many things," Ibrasa said evasively. "I cannot tell you the Karif's plans. Perhaps you can convince him to return to the Karabdu."

"Convince him? I don't understand. Why wouldn't he return to his people?"

"I have described the last battle," said Ibrasa. "Aksu had accepted his challenge. The Karif should have fought with him, not killed him by surprise. He feels dishonored before his people, unworthy to be Karif."

"But they killed the Tayyib dishonorably. And they murdered Shadith."

"That explains, it does not excuse. The Karif has never before broken the laws of combat. He is unhappy within himself, and that makes him difficult." Ibrasa patted her shoulder. "To see you here, safe, will do much good. It will not be long now. Tammush will have to negotiate the release of the Empress with Tibir, in return for his safe conduct north. We already know the route Tammush will take. We are to set out and be ready to meet them northeast of here, in the wilderness. The Karif will join us there, after he has given Tammush the slip." He frowned at her expression. "Why the long face?"

"I was wondering—do you think that the people with the Empress will be safe? I almost rode into Yokan with them. There must have been ten or twenty of her special cavalry inside when the doors fell shut."

Ibrasa shrugged. "It is possible that they will be killed. Tammush has very few men left. He might feel safer with them out of the way. Did you have a friend among them?"

"Not with the guard. But there is a woman who has been very nice to me. A warrior—well, not like Shadith, but she is a batur. She is the Emperor's Sword-Bearer."

"The mysterious sorceress from the north, with the sword of Chanaga Gagan? There have been many rumors about her. She is trapped in Yokan?" Tamara nodded. "She may come out safely again, but that is one thing I would not care to predict. Tammush has many scores to settle with Tibir, and he may choose to settle them against a batur, since it would not be at all safe to settle them on the Empress."

Tamara felt sick.

It was not easy for them to work their way through the hills and safely out to the edge of the northern plains. It would have been impossible had not Ibrasa just skulked through the same area with Tammush and his men. As it was, they had difficulty avoiding the wide sweep of Tibir's army hurrying toward Yokan. "The ransom of the Empress is approaching," Ibrasa said with a smile, but Tamara could only wonder if she was also seeing the ransom of the Batur Subi.

Once the last of the vast panoply was out of sight, days after they had first sighted its approach, their little party became very cheerful. A walking pace was all that could be managed, since there were only two horses and three riders, and one of them a heavy man. Sometimes Marricson and Ibrasa alternated rides; sometimes Marricson grew footsore and Ibrasa walked through the day. But it was clear that they would have to find another horse soon if they were to meet the Karif as planned.

Fate brought them horses not long after they had entered the wasteland north of the Samidan highway. Ibrasa first noticed the dust along the horizon and altered their own course accordingly. That night he scanned the range of their fires and decided that they were seeing an Angul army of relatively small size. "Perhaps Tibir has sent to Zamarra for reinforcements," he said. He looked at Marricson. "Here are the horses we need. Our wants are modest. Two will do us well. And only one need be up to any weight."

Marricson smiled but looked worried. "I dislike putting my head into the lion's mouth more often than necessary."

"Just this one time," said Ibrasa cheerfully, "and then we will have the wherewithall for a hasty escape."

Small by Angul standards, the army was large enough to be

easily followed and they kept course with its progress for
several days. Then, early one evening before it was too dark,
Ibrasa led them into the main encampment, offering his sword
in a formal gesture of submission to the guard who stopped
them. They were led to a captain, who granted their request
for food and drink, and accepted, with scant good humor,
their offer of a little entertainment for the officers.

They may not have amused the captain, but the men enjoyed Marricson very much. Even more, they enjoyed his
little troupe's lack of talent. The men laughed loudly as they
plied them with food and rough red wine and rude suggestions; the laughter was at its loudest when a tall figure dressed
in dark armor came and stood just outside the circle of
firelight, silent and unnoticed at first. Tamara looked up from
her attempts to keep time on the drum and tambourine and
felt her heart sink in her boots; for a moment she was sure
that she was looking at Tibir. Then the others noticed him and
he stepped forward; a younger man than the Emperor, but
obviously his son or grandson. He was the general of the
army; his name was Sikin. He sat down next to the banquet
trays and made a gesture with his hand for Marricson to
continue. Like Tibir, his complexion was pale and his hair
red, and like Tibir he wore it in a long braid down his back.
He was lithe and muscular, however: he moved as one would
think Tibir might have moved before so many crippling wounds.

Marricson had spent much of his time among the Anguls
learning their songs; he sang a lovely melody in praise of
Zamarra that brought a slight smile to the general's face.
When their songs were over for the night, Sikin commanded
that they receive a generous amount of flour and dried meat
from the stores. Tamara began to feel bad about stealing
horses from people who treated them so well. Then he nodded to one of his servants, who came over and gently took her
by the arm. "You have found favor," he said. "The general
has chosen you to look after his children and teach them the
customs of many lands."

Tamara froze in horror. She was being raised to her feet
willy-nilly while her companions watched in disbelief. Suddenly she tore herself free and ran to embrace Ibrasa. "Would
you take me away from my brother?" she cried, and the
general did not answer for several moments. Then he gestured
to another servant, who went to Ibrasa's side. "You may

serve the general also," he said. "He has need of another groom."

Marricson seemed too stunned to move as Ibrasa and Tamara were courteously ushered away. Then Ibrasa was led off toward the picket lines, while Tamara was hurried through the dark to find light, warmth, luxury and utter pandemonium.

The general's family traveled in a large tent set on a bullock cart. But the children of three different mothers made this space even smaller, and to make it worse the two surviving wives also shared the tent. There was no privacy, no separation of families. The seven children were all under the age of eight.

They fastened themselves on Tamara like kittens on a string, pulling at her hair, fingering her clothes, pointing at her odd-colored eyes and laughing. Soon they were quarreling with each other about who had the first right to touch her, then fell to crying and slapping each other. Their mothers sank into an exhausted heap against some cushions in a corner and Tamara looked about with disbelief and horror.

The next few days would have passed like a bad dream, if Tamara had ever had the chance to sleep. The children were spoiled beyond belief. They kept no regular hours, sleeping and waking as they pleased, so there was always a number of them awake and ready to be amused, eager for Tamara's company. They were only quiet when their father came to visit. Then the tears dried and the whines ceased. The prevailing atmosphere of tension persisted however, and it was particularly evident in the relationship between Sikin and his wives.

From the children, Tamara soon understood that none of the girls or young women brought in to help care for them had lasted more than a few months. They did not tell her what had happened to the failures and Tamara did not ask. With any one or two of them she could have had a good time and maintained some sort of control, but as a group they were impossible, and their mothers offered no help. Tamara wondered if the two living wives ever envied the one who had died.

By the end of the second day, Tamara made up her mind to make a run for it. She had not seen Ibrasa and had no idea of where in camp he might be found. And she did not know what had happened to Marricson. She was given her chance by one of Sikin's little sons, however, that afternoon as she tried to sing him to sleep.

"I want to go see that new singer," he announced loudly. "Why can't we go? Everyone else has been." He started to cry softly and two of his brothers joined in. "Why can't we go?" "We never do anything!" "I wish we had stayed in Zamarra!" "Don't like staying in tent." Tamara covered her ears.

One of the mothers had silently witnessed this interchange, and she must have spoken to her husband, because that evening the children were washed and scrubbed and dressed in their finest clothes, to join their father and his lords at dinner, and to stay up afterward for the entertainment. Their pretty round faces were golden skinned, with bright pink cheeks from the scrubbing; their smooth, dark hair glistened from brushing and oiling and hung in long plaits. Tamara felt a certain grim satisfaction as she got the last one cleaned and dressed in embroidered sheepskin and beaded boots. It was time for them to be gone, but one of the wives made the guard wait while Tamara hastily washed and dressed in the nice clothes she had been given, clothes of the same quality as the children's.

The smell of dinner cooking hung in the air. It made Tamara's mouth water. But it was a meal she would never taste; somehow, in the short distance between the tent and the banquet area, one of the seven children disappeared. She had counted them herself as they went down the steps, and she counted them again as they entered the circle of light by the fires. Seven coming out, six coming in.

The excitement was slow to build, but quite violent once it was underway. A guard was sent out looking, then two, then three. Then the bereaved mother was sobbing quietly, then crying, then both of Sikin's wives were crying, beating their breasts and wailing. The other children, thrilled by the noisy emotion, cried or screamed as it suited them best. The men looked horrified, Sikin angry and embarrassed. Tamara shrank back out of the way.

As if this confusion were not enough, the horse master's men came running in to report that the group of officers' remounts had been stampeded south along the watercourse, and were now out of sight. The herdsman had been knocked unconscious and the master of horses himself was missing, possibly off in pursuit.

At this news Tamara stopped worrying about the safety of the child, and concentrated on getting away herself. She remembered what Ibrasa had taught her about classic diversions. The horses were galloping south along the watercourse; she must make her way north. She slipped away into the dark among the tents, and no one noticed her.

Clear of the tents she went more slowly, trying to find her way in the velvet dark. She held up her hand before her eyes and proved the truth of the old saying: she could not see it. The watercourse lay to the east, however, and direction was something she could feel in her bones. She went slowly, tripping less and less frequently, and the water that lay among the stones caught her eyes in the blackness, glowing with what little light there was to be reflected.

She had not gone far when she sensed something moving in the dark near her. Her muscles tensed as she stepped softly out onto the worn pebbles of the river bed, but she waited quietly. Then her heart leaped as hands closed softly but firmly around her throat from behind. She could not speak. Her captor passed his hand over her Angul clothes and finally touched her face; then she was released. "Pardon," whispered Ibrasa. "Your clothing startled me. Come." She took his hand and he led her north along the watercourse, so fast that one would have thought he could see. They had gone at least a mile in this fashion before they came to where Marricson waited, with four horses and two prisoners.

Sikin's horse master was bound hand and foot, dressed only in his shirt. The missing child had Marricson about the neck and was giggling, pulling at his beard. "It is time for you to return, sweetheart," he said softly. "You are going to be a great hero and bring back one of Daddy's missing horses, and his missing captain too."

The beginnings of a pout were immediately erased. "A hero?"

"Indeed, for you have accomplished what no one else in camp could do."

The horse master's legs were untied and he was bundled onto one of his animals, his arms still fastened behind his back. From the way his head lolled, it was clear he was still suffering from a blow to the head. The horse's reins were passed to the child.

"Stay on the watercourse and the horse will lead you home. See, I have loosely hobbled his legs so he cannot pull away from you or go too fast. He knows the way. Walk with him, and you will bring him and your father's captain home. Can you do that?" The child nodded and marched off happily.

"Now we must hurry," said Ibrasa. "Let me see this famous horse. I warrant he'll look his best tonight in the dark." Marricson swung himself up onto a heavy chestnut and Ibrasa nodded. "Well done. Now my only question is this—" he paused to lift Tamara onto Faras—"how did you manage to best a group of Angul officers at castledown?"

"Nothing easier," said Marricson, smiling sweetly. "I cheated." He nodded to Tamara. "A fine horse was the stake," he explained. "I am not one to trust to luck alone when so much can be won."

Ibrasa judged they had about an hour before the child could reach camp. Then the Anguls would know in which direction to search. He knew that Sikin was under orders to proceed to Gagan-ala immediately, but he well might send out a small band to hunt them down. Therefore, the safest choice was for them to circle east and come up behind the army and off to one side, parallel to Sikin's forces.

They rode very carefully for the next few days. Ibrasa would go ahead and scout, then return for the party, leading them from cover to cover. From the last of these forays he returned looking very grave. "I met a fugitive," he said. "One of Tammush's men. He is trying to make his way home alone. If he tells the truth, all our plans will have to be reworked. Tammush, if he still lives, must be a prisoner of Tibir. Yokan has been destroyed—not one stone remains on top of another. He spoke quite wildly; he said that Tibir had commanded the river to stop flowing so that his army could walk across to besiege the city!"

"What about the Karif?" cried Tamara.

Ibrasa suddenly looked evasive. "He was not certain," he said at last. "All he would say for sure is that Tibir has made Yokan disappear. When he took a last look down from the heights, the city was being dismantled." Ibrasa suddenly sat

down and dropped his head in his hands. "Now we are on
our own. I am sure of nothing anymore, except that we are
very far from home."

II

Tibir's journey to Gagan-ala was delayed several weeks by
the destruction of Yokan. His engineers undermined its walls
and dismantled its buildings, spreading the rubble along the
damp bed of the diverted river. In the end, huge blocks of
stone, piles of timber, smashed heaps of tilework and ornamental inlay covered the natural river course for more than a
mile downstream from the city's site. Then up in the hills
above Yokan, Tibir's men shifted the great rock dam they had
built so hastily at his command. The river was no longer sent
to spill over into the valley where it had flooded out more
than one unsuspecting village. It roared and bucketed down
its traditional course, taking up the lighter bits of debris and
totally covering the rest. By evening of the last day of work,
the river was as it had always been, except that there was no
causeway and no Yokan.

The puncture under Clerowan's arm mended quickly despite his carelessness for his body. Unable to use a sword
until it healed, he joined in some of the horse breaking
instead. Sibby watched in disbelief one day as he repeatedly
pulled a rank colt over onto its back, stepped off and jumped
back up again, one-handed. This behavior won him the high-
est respect among the guards of Tibir and the royal household. They nicknamed him Ajur, a term meaning moon-crazy
that was most often applied to the sort of young warrior who,
in his first battle, saves the lives of his companions by
running full-tilt into a nest of spears. For so old and experienced a man to be termed Ajur was a very great honor.

By the time Tibir had gathered his forces to take to the road
again, Clerowan Ajur was on intimate terms with the captain
of the royal household, and knew as much as could be learned
about the escape of Tamara and the singer from Vahn. Furthermore, a lucky chance brought his skill at the game of
sitranga to the Agan's attention. One night a week he was
taken into the Agan's presence to give him a game, and

though he rarely succeeded in winning a game from the Emperor, he was able to prolong each contest late into the night. Tibir was pleased and he rewarded Clerowan accordingly.

The third time Clerowan was called to play at sitranga he stayed very late. Deep in the night, Sibby was surprised to be shaken awake; it was more typical of him to go to great lengths not to disturb her, even to sleeping outside with the saddles and weapons, where there was no longer a bed. She yawned and curled up in his arms, and he pulled her into a sitting position and made her listen to him.

"While I was with Tibir tonight, his son Sikin reported. He has brought the rear guard from Zamarra to join the main army again. We were in the midst of the game, so I was left to study the board—for all the good it did me—while Tibir received his son's report. He had not come by the highway, but in a circle down from the northeast, across the salt plains. Of a sudden Sikin looked up and saw me, and in a moment he had his sword's point at my throat."

Sibby jerked fully awake at this. Clerowan's arm tightened around her shoulders. "As Tibir told him to put up his weapon, Sikin asked how the brigand—myself—had come into the Imperial Presence. As Tibir answered, Sikin looked at me more closely, then sighed and apologized—not to me, he never so much as spoke to me—and said that the man he had encountered on the way was much younger. To him, all blue-eyed outlanders look alike; I quote his very words." Clerowan's whisper rose in intensity. "Then Sikin went on to tell the Emperor about the misadventure he had had near the edge of the salt desert, with a blue-eyed outlaw, a singer and a girl."

"What misadventure?"

"I could not follow exactly. They spoke a dialect of Almadun, and with allusions known only to themselves. Still, it was clear that they had tried to interfere in someway with this group of people, and had been embarrassed by the quickness with which the blue-eyed brigand struck and fled." He paused a moment. "Ibrasa has a subtle mind, for a son of the Tayyib. And Tamara is with him."

Sibby pressed her face against the warmth of his throat. "He has kept her safe, as you hoped. What else happened?"

"I lost the game." He wriggled out his clothes and they put their arms around each other gladly.

Sikin took his forces on ahead of Tibir, to ready Gagan-ala for the Emperor's welcome, and to scout out an area north of the city for a winter camp. From her place at Tibir's side on the road, and at his feet in the evenings, Sibby now learned as much about Paradon as she had earlier about Angulidan. Taan told her more in private, and read to her with great relish the exchange of letters between Tibir and the warlord Padeshi.

Tibir had had no interest in the island of Paradon until Padeshi sent him his first letter. He had not even shown any interest in the riches of Melismala—nothing, at least, that was known to Taan and the other chroniclers. As Taan had remarked to Sibby, it was often difficult to know Tibir's true intentions, since he had no ministers and kept council only with himself and his sitranga board, and possibly the Empress. But certainly no mention of any campaign against the islands had been made. Then Kladdur, in Gagan-ala, received a ship from Paradon in the harbor, with an ambassador for the court of the Agan. It had taken months, but the man from Paradon had finally reached Tibir in Dessa, just as the Agan prepared to cross over the water in his assault on Vahn.

Taan had been there when the warning letter from Paradon was opened. "It was even strange in appearance," he said. "The top third of the parchment had the names of the Seven Warlords drawn in gold and silver and illuminated in different colors, with Padeshi in the middle. Then, underneath this, the name Tibir, no titles, no colors, written small and black. And the language! Never in the history of the world has anyone ever written such a letter to such a ruler!" Taan chuckled. "Do I need to tell you Tibir's answer? He wrote immediately to say that Padeshi and his allies should look for him to arrive in a year or less, as soon as he had attended to matters abroad. And he ended his letter thus:

> As there is one God above, so there
> should be one king below. If Vazdz claims
> to be that God then it is time he
> welcomed Tibir the King to visit him in
> his house.

And since that time he has already conquered Melismala and started gathering a fleet there to sail on Paradon."

"We are not returning to Zamarra?"

"Not this year, Sword-Bearer. We go now to build a city north of Gagan-ala, and gather the great army. Paradon the Mysterious, Inivin the Hidden: soon Tibir will expose their secrets. When this campaign is accomplished there will not be any place under the sun that has not acknowledged the might of Tibir."

Sibby shared her lessons with Clerowan, and he continued to tell her about the world she had once known, and the events in which she had taken part. Curious and inconsequential images came to her as trivial portions of her memory returned, most often as she lay in his arms, contented and half asleep. Sometimes these memory exercises called to them at inopportune moments. When they were on the road there was no possibility of privacy, and the impatience with which the two baturs occasionally awaited the pitching of their tent inevitably attracted some amused notice. Sibby did not realize how much notice, until the Empress mentioned it to her.

They were only a few days from Gagan-ala when Soria asked for Sibby to attend her. She received her in the privacy of her inner chamber, offered her a bowl of wine and had her sit at ease. She herself had taken off her elaborate headdress, and her growing hair curled charmingly around her ears. They drank in silence and Soria smiled at her husband's Sword-Bearer. "It is not known to many," she said, "that the great Tibir has one unending regret. His sons have brought him joy, sorrow and pride; his grandchildren much pleasure. But of his daughters, not one has lived to see her first year complete. I myself—" her voice dropped slightly—"I myself bore the Emperor three daughters. One lived a week; the others less than a day. By now the eldest could have made me a great-grandmother; by now the youngest would be about your age."

Sibby kept her eyes lowered, embarrassed by these uncharacteristic revelations.

"Tibir thinks well of you, Batur Subi. More than well. He has plans for your future and it is not in his nature to discuss his plans with anyone." she smiled. "But I know him a little after these fifty years. Let me tell you a story, Batur. There was a wrestler once whom Tibir admired. So he gave him for a wife a young girl of great beauty and good humor whom he had noticed among my servants; a girl, moreover, from the same village as this wrestler. And he gave them many pres-

ents, a tent and flocks. And a few weeks later he saw this girl
in camp and she was not smiling. 'What is wrong?' asked
Tibir. 'Has your husband not brought you pleasure?' 'Lord,'
said the girl, 'truly he has not. For all that we share the same
tent, we might as well be brother and sister.' Tibir was not
pleased. He summoned the wrestler to him and asked him an
explanation. And the wrestler told him how, when he had
started training, his master had said to avoid certain things,
and that included the pleasures of women. And Tibir gave
him a choice. He could treat his bride as a husband or visit
the Emperor's surgeons, 'to have removed that which he did
not need.' A few days later the young bride smiled and I
believe she still is happy, even though her husband is no
longer a champion wrestler.'' Sibby took another sip and
waited for the moral.

"Batur Subi, Tibir is always Lord, in benevolence as in
wrath. He thinks well of you and soon he will reward you. He
will reward you as he would reward a daughter of his own
flesh. I am speaking of marriage, Batur, and marriage with a
great prince—a king, if he can find one suitable: not with a
landless hero twice your age whose only fortune is his horse
and sword.'' She smiled at Sibby and urged her to pour out
more wine. ''Do not look so lightning-struck, little one. I am
not telling you to send your batur away. Not yet. But you
must prepare yourself to receive the generosity of Tibir. And
he will be generous, and you must receive it. There is only
one will in the world, Batur, and that is the will of Tibir.''

As they approached Gagan-ala, Sibby tried to put Soria's
words from her mind. Almost she convinced herself that she
would be able to show Tibir how suitable a choice Clerowan
could be, if and when the time came that such a choice was
inevitable. She did not tell Clerowan himself anything of the
Empress's words.

Stirrup to stirrup with the Fortunate Lord, Sibby rode into
Gagan-ala, the Enku on her hip. The city amazed her with its
exotic complexity, but she felt stifled by its walls and parks
and massive buildings, eager to be away and out in the wind
again. She assumed Tibir must feel the same, but his calm
mask never varied. He received his grandson, the guild chiefs
and the elderly master teachers in a large square central to the
city. Much of what they discussed was unintelligible to Sibby;
they spoke softly and in a dialect with which she was not

familiar. Bored, she kept her face impassive but let her eyes
wander discreetly. She was startled to find herself the object
of unbroken scrutiny from a man who had accompanied
Prince Kladdur. He was rather attractive, with dark eyes and a
curly black beard and hair; he looked on the young side of
forty. But she had trouble examining him because he stared
so at her. Her eyes were constantly meeting his, then sliding
past in embarrassment, to try again with no more luck a little
later. Finally, she gave up and watched Tibir instead.

Later that evening she accompanied Tibir to the great
library, built on an island in the harbor. To her delight, he
released his bodyguard and Sword-Bearer to wander freely
while he visited Lord Kladdur and the historians and reviewed
their work. The Angul baturs went down into the courtyard in
search of a rumored barrel of wine, but Sibby hung out a
window four stories above the harbor, and lost herself in the
wonder of sunset reflected from the brilliantly mirrored walls
of the fabled city. She felt so totally at peace that she did not
even turn at the first hissed words behind her.

"Show me your face. I must be sure I am not mistaken."
She did not turn until the words had been repeated, and then
she turned slowly.

Blankly, she met the eyes of the man who had watched her
so fiercely that afternoon. If anything, his face was now even
fiercer, and after a pause she asked politely, "Were you?" He
stepped back as though she had hit him in the stomach. She
waited for enlightenment.

"How long—how long have you served the Angul lord?"
Before she could answer, he went on. "Has he forced you?
Are you his prisoner? How long has he had you in his
power?" He was approaching her, a wild expression on his
face, and Sibby shrank back against the wall. She drew
herself up to her full height, which was only an inch or two
less than her questioner's.

"There is some mistake," she said. "I am the Sword-
Bearer of the Agan. What do you want of me?"

"Sibby!" he cried and she started at the sound of her
name. There were tears now in the corners of his eyes, and
his body was trembling. He looked quite mad. "Sibby!" he
cried again. "Why did you leave me? I thought you were
gone forever. I thought—and now . . . now . . . here you are

with the Conqueror of the World—'' He fell back against a
table piled with manuscript, his face in his hands.

Enlightenment was slowly coming to Sibby. She had no
idea what he was doing here, but she could make a pretty
good guess at who he might be. She smiled and held out her
hand.

"I'm sorry I didn't recognize you," she said. "You must
be Leron."

from The Song of Tibir

Into the garden of the Chama
Under a moon like white paper
Where the blossoms drug the air with odors of pleasure
The Falcon has climbed the wall
He has entered the arbor
He has taken her into his arms
Whose body shines like the moon
Her face is as fair as the moon
Her long black hair hangs down, eclipsing her beauties.

They were young
They thought it no shame to lie down in the grass
No one who saw them could say which one was which
Which one was fairer
Alike in their beauty they sigh in the grass and sleep.

She wakes, the Lord of Zamarra asleep in her arms
The weight of the world on her body
She wakes, a sword shines in the moonlight
Singing of death in the dark
She holds up her hand, catches the blade in the moonlight
Her blood runs out in the dark.

She turns the blade from his neck
It pierces his shoulder
As it was written,
      He will lose an arm to love
      and a leg to war.
The Eagle of Almadun wakes

The Hawk of Zamarra leaps and strikes
The Falcon seized the enemy's sword
And a dark head rolls in the grass.

And when they are far from Samida the Chama will curse
The Falcon has stolen the moon, my garden is dark.
But in Zamarra the Golden, Queen of Cities
Tibir the Hawk has wed the Angulidan Moon.

PARTIAL
ECLIPSE

Chapter Thirteen

THE WEDDING

I

Ibrasa, Marricson and Tamara followed Sikin's army for want
of any better plan. When General Sikin met up with his
father's forces, they fell back a little further—lingering like a
discreet shadow, several days to the rear. Their clothes and
faces were powdered with yellow dust and their horses stumbled on the heavily trodden ground. Behind the army there
was a sorry collection of stragglers and camp followers. It
was from their gossip that Ibrasa learned the startling news of
Clerowan Ajur's rise to favor. At Tamara's insistence, he also
ascertained that the Emperor's Sword-Bearer was still the
mysterious northern sorceress, Subi.

Tamara was all for following the imperial army into Gagan-
ala to see some of its wonders for herself, but Ibrasa flatly
forbid it. The army was headed north of Gagan-ala to winter
over, and there in the confusion of the new camp they would
attempt to contact the Karif.

Marricson, still puffed up from his success at castledown,
spent the evenings practicing his new art. He did not discard
the baraka, but carefully packed it away. "I have used that
dodge one time too many," he said "Now I must practice
some new ones. I will learn to play games for a living." He
still sang to amuse Tamara, but she was just as fascinated to
sit by his knee and watch his large, clever hands flash over
the casting stones. Soon he could throw any number he
wished, over and over again, and Tamara could not detect
anything suspicious no matter how closely she watched. He

also practiced more outrageous cheating, moving the pieces
themselves on the board, while keeping up such a clever
patter that she was convinced her memory of the gameboard
was wrong. He bounced with his own success at this, but
Tamara shook her head.

"Just don't try that on the Agan," she said. "I have heard
that he remembers the placement of every piece and every
move in every game he has ever played for the last fifty
years."

Marricson was not cast down. "If he plays, he can be
fooled," was his only answer.

As they neared the imperial city, the sky was disturbed by
flashes of light, bursts of glittering stars like sparks from a
giant log, explosions of red and gold. The sky along the
western horizon flickered, and after the light the sound came
dimly to them in booms and dangerous cracklings. It was
small and far away, but terrifying; Tamara's first, sickening
reaction was that the city had been set on fire and all who
accompanied the Emperor destroyed, in some sort of fire from
heaven. But Marricson reassured her, and explained about the
artificial fires of the Samidans, and the Samidan custom to
make these loud noises and lights whenever a great celebration was at hand. She was reassured, but still put her head
under his cloak and let him pat her back while the fury along
the horizon continued. The false lights made her friendly old
stars look as far away and powerless as she felt.

Craftsmen had been at work north of Gagan-ala for months,
building Tibir's new winter camp of Tibiridan in the wilderness. Although only meant as a base for his next great
campaign, Tibiridan was to be as magnificent as haste would
allow. The highroad had been extended north from Gagan-
ala, built of smooth, red, kiln-fired brick; cut blocks of marble
and granite lined the sides and hastily planted trees in tubs
provided shade along the way. There were also fountains cut
in stone for the refreshment of travelers and their beasts.
While Tibir and the royal household lingered in Gagan-ala,
there was heavy traffic on the new north road as Tibiridan
prepared for the Emperor's visit. Ibrasa's party had to move
slowly despite the breadth of the highway, their way blocked
by lumbering carts of goods and foodstuffs, trains of pack
animals, gangs of laborers. In such a crowd, their privacy
was easy to preserve.

Between the walls of Tibiridan and the harbor, they found a cheap teahouse that smelled of smoke and new lumber. Sap dripped from its boards, and some of the uprights still had bark. But the owner had had an itinerant painter decorate the bare walls with scenes from Tibir's campaigns, and the massive brass urns gleamed from polishing. There were no rooms left for rent, but the owner offered them quilts and cushions in a private corner in return for help with his small livery. Ibrasa ate his pride and went to work with the mules, donkeys and broken-down saddle horses. In exchange for an evening meal, their own horses were put to hire, although Tamara struggled with tears at the thought of Faras being rented out. She only quieted when Ibrasa told her shortly it was that or sell him. Horses were born to work for man, he said, and added softly that Karabdin warriors were not.

It was Marricson who became the major breadwinner, taking his gaming board with him to teahouses and public baths, cheating so cautiously his winnings seemed nothing more than modest luck. His round face looked so honest. Ibrasa took to sleeping with their money under his pillow and a dagger in his hand.

As Tibir's great procession approached, the crowds swelled into the market squares and filled the villages outside the walls. Their teahouse became breathlessly overcrowded. The organization of Sikin's army could be seen everywhere, however; the streets remained clean and all services were maintained.

The old Emperor himself had no interest in cities. He rode in one gate, through the streets and out another, leaving some of his family to settle and take up administrative duties. His own encampment was on a low, flat hilltop, just visible to the east at the edge of the plains. A wooded cape of great natural beauty commanding both harbor and city had been summarily dismissed by him when suggested by the builders as a good site for a pavilion. To one who disliked ships and the sea, and who was a master of land armies, this was not a scenic spot but a natural trap.

Tamara wormed her way through the crowds for a glimpse of Tibir as he rode through. Her heart rose in her throat when she saw the familiar figure of the Batur Subi riding behind him. The silver wires on the Enku caught the sun, and the light glittered as well on Monkey's new bridle, completely

silver-wrapped. Subi looked well but somber-eyed, and riding
ahead of the royal household, the Empress could also be seen
on horseback, as well and as strong as ever. Part of Tamara's
fears were laid to rest.

Something in the way one of the bodyguard sat his horse
made her think of the Karif, but the soldiers were all in gold
and silver armor, with nosepieces on their helmets shadowing
their faces. Her interest flagged after the Emperor and his
family passed, but the procession continued, division after
division. Only the center and the rear guard came through the
city, the wings having already spread out to make camp in
positions defensive to the region. As Tamara watched Sikin
ride past at the head of the rear guard, she giggled at what he
would think if he knew his runaway groom and nursemaid
were so close. Now that the children were safely distant,
Tamara could think of them somewhat fondly.

She was unprepared for the wave of maudlin sentiment that
washed over her as she remembered Sikin embracing his
children. She thought of summer evenings, walking or riding
in the garden in Tredana, Leron with Geret on his shoulders,
her hand in his, Liniris with the baby in her arms. She really
should have been nicer to Liniris. Poor Liniris, who had tried
so hard to make Tamara love her, and had always been so
patient with her temper and rude behavior. Poor Liniris
couldn't help being so boring. Tears of self-pity and loss
began to well up in Tamara's eyes.

Her mind was so full of her father that when she saw Leron
on horseback she thought she was dreaming. She actually
rubbed her eyes so hard that colored spots leapt out. He was
still there when she looked again, riding a fine horse in the
train of the Emperor. He was more richly dressed than she had
ever seen him, and his curly hair and beard glistened in the
sun. There was a gold circlet around his head, something that
startled her, for he had always said that crowns were silly and
barbaric. He looked tense and unhappy, so unhappy that she
wanted to push her way through the crowds and throw her
arms around his neck.

A countrywoman standing next to her nudged her with an
elbow. "That's the captive king of Tredana," she said. "Fancy
that, a king from over the waters. They say Tibir is going to
make him one of his governors. He seems to like these
outlanders. The wedding is going to be quite the celebration."

"Wedding?"

"That batur of his, the Sword-Bearer. You must have seen her. She has pleased the Emperor so well that he is giving her the king of Tredana, and a fortune as well. The feasting starts next week. There will be more food and wine and gold and silver and gems and music and fresh-gathered flowers in Tibiridan than anyone has ever seen together in one place in the world. Ah, but it is a great thing to live in the city of the Fortunate Lord."

Tamara nodded, struck completely dumb.

II

The woman had not exaggerated. For the wedding festivities, Tibiridan was filled with food, flowers, dancers and music through the generosity of the Agan; all private debts for the period of one week were paid from the public treasury, and for a like time all taxes were cancelled. But the wedding itself was to take place in true Angul fashion, among the tents of Tibir.

Since Tamara was not sure whether or not Ibrasa would agree to her going, she did not ask. She left him a note written with great care and attention to the niceties of courteous expression, as taught by Alric and Dansen. Then she joined the foot procession of curious onlookers, going to gawk at the ceremonies and marvel at the gifts and food, some perhaps hoping to catch a gold coin or gemstone tossed into the crowd in Tibir's reputed fashion. Tamara decided she would believe that when she saw it.

Tamara knew that there were aspects of human behavior that she did not understand. She did not really understand why adult human beings were so capricious in their friendships and their love affairs, warm one week and cold the next. But she was certain that in this matter her father was simply bowing to the inevitable, a decree from Tibir. The unkind things she had often thought about Liniris haunted her, and she hoped devoutly with fingers crossed that her stepmother and the children were safe somewhere.

She also had the greatest difficulty imagining the Batur Subi as a bride, or, indeed, in any sort of womanly role. She

had liked her very much as a companion, but she felt about
her much as she did about Ibrasa, not as another girl. It had
been a shock to her when they were both in the bath and she
had seen that the batur had a real woman's body—probably a
body that men would find attractive. Tamara wasn't sure how
these things were judged. She had seen her father kissing
Liniris when they thought they were alone, and wondered
why he ran his hands all over her body. The Batur was
shaped similarly to Liniris, though taller and more muscular.
Then she thought about Shadith and how the Karif had loved
her, and before that Ibrasa's father, the fierce old Tayyib.
And Shadith had been just a quiet little woman, thin and
intense, with the figure of a boy. Maybe it didn't matter what
you looked like. She tried to clear her head. After all, what
did it matter about the Batur? Leron obviously had had no
choice in this matter.

Two miles from Tibir's encampment, the honor guard started:
silent men in armor, ten ranks deep, sitting their quiet horses.
Except for the tossing of heads, the swishing of tails, the
occasional snort and pawing front leg, the horsemen might
have been statues. Their armor was inlaid with gold, and they
wore the red and white silks of Tibir. The wide way that lay
between their facing ranks was covered with crushed flowers,
flowers gathered and rushed in by galloping messengers from
all over the surrounding countryside.

The path of flowers led all the way to a great silk pavillion
covering the central part of the camp. The poles supporting it
were as thick as a man's waist, twisted with wires of precious
metal and fluttering with colored silks. Carpets of silk and
fine lamb's wool covered the ground. In the center were
thrones for Tibir and, a little lower, the Empress. They faced
a platform draped with colored gauze. The central area was
empty, but the musicians were already playing and flights of
white doves were released from time to time—many of which
returned to settle on the ropes and poles around them. There
were two great fountains on either side, built of marble and
made to work by a hidden mechanism. The water did not run
over continuously but shot upward in bursts. Brilliantly red,
ripe pomegranates danced in the foam that filled the basins
below. Tamara wormed her way through with the impunity of
a child, receiving the occasional elbow in her ribs and shov-
ing back in return. Near the front of the pack she halted,

sheltered between two massive old men, and looked out from
under their sleeves. She felt hot and faint.

The restless crowd hushed as Tibir was brought in on his
litter and assisted to the thorne. The Empress was also carried
in and placed on her lower, cushioned seat. They were dressed
as Tamara had never before seen them, in white silk so
embroidered with diamonds that it hurt to look at them directly. Tibir wore his helmet, with a white horse's tail hanging down from the crest; the Empress a tall headdress of
golden leaves and gemstone berries.

First there was silence. Then a vast number of doves were
released, so many that the flapping of their wings drowned
out the music. Then two more litters brought in the affianced
pair; if Tamara had not known who they were, she would
never have recognized their masklike faces. They were seated
on the gauze-draped platform and lifted their arms mechani-
cally to have their dark outer robes removed. Underneath
they were dressed in fine white linen; bare-armed and unadorned, they sat there stonily with unchanging faces. More
music played, and the first of the ceremonial robes were
brought in, white ones for the color of the east, made of
splendid silk velvet, cut in patterns, embroidered with pearls
and diamonds and opals. The couple were dressed, and then
attendants carrying heaped platters of gemstones poured river
pearls and silver coins over their slightly bowed heads. Then
they passed around the perimeter of the crowd, tossing handfuls of coins and gems among the people.

The crowd naturally broke up at this, and scrambled on
hands and knees. When some order had returned, the banquet
cloths were laid down and covered with a variety of foods in
white, cooked and plain, sweet and sour, fruits, meats, baked
goods. Bowls of white wine stood with white flowers twined
around them. Everyone was invited to eat. Tamara was far
from hungry. She picked at a handful of pale green grapes,
listened to gossip and tried to keep an eye on the stony figures
of Leron and the Batur Subi. Many people, she noticed, were
stuffing food into pockets and bags of cloth they had brought
with them. And she realized from what they said that this was
just a start, and that the wedding would probably last for three
days, or six, or nine.

The Emperor and the Empress were carried out, as were the
wedding couple. The crowds continued to eat and drink until

they grew sleepy, then wandered away to find places to lie down. Tamara hunched against a pillar, and was still not fully asleep when torches were lit and music started up again. There were more players this time, the music was more cheerful and the doves that were flying around now had their long tail and wing feathers dyed blue. When the Agan and his wife were brought in, they were dressed in dark blue robes embroidered with sapphires; the wedding couple were brought back in their white robes, which were ceremoniously removed and replaced with ones of similar richness in blue. Sapphires and beads of lapis were poured over their heads this time, and then distributed among the crowd. The second course of the meal was blue, grapes and berries and fruit-glazed meats. The wine was deep purple and the flowers were all in shades of blue, the color of the north.

It was quiet until dawn, when the musicians reappeared in greater numbers than before. The color of this celebration was yellow, the color of the west. Yellow silk and velvet, embroidered with topazes and amber, hung with coins of pure gold. Gold and topazes were poured over the newly robed royal couple, and the gold that was scattered through the crowds drove them wild. The food was saffron rice and curried meats, garnished with yellow fruits and berries; the wine was pale yellow and sweet.

Later that afternoon the color was that of the south: black. Black-dyed doves, black silk and velvet, beads of polished jet and onyx. Tibir and Soria sat with unchanged expression, but the wedding pair were pale against their new robes and seemed to droop under their weight. The food was glazed with burned sugar and decorated with blackberries and nearly black plums; the wine was dark and strange.

After two days and a night of celebration, the next night started peacefully. For several hours Tamara slept heavily, then jerked awake. Drums had been added to the music—deep, booming drums that made the ground shake and woke the sleeping crowds. Red-dyed doves were fluttering over their heads, and falls of red silk were unrolling, changing the inner color of the great tent. Bronze braziers filled with coals had some powder sprinkled on them to make red smoke. Everything was to be the color of Almadun, the Heart of the World.

The Agan was brought in wearing red velvet, encrusted

with rubies and garnets. Instead of his helmet he wore a tall
hat of red felt, pinned in front with a ruby as large as his fist.
The Empress was similarly dressed, and this time the lesser
wives as well, also in scarlet, filed in to take their places and
do honor to the wedding. The marriage couple's platform was
draped in red gauze and sprinkled with rubies and garnets
before they were brought in, still dressed in black. The red
robes that replaced the black ones were absolutely stiff with
rubies and inlays of gold wire. The red food dazzled the eye
and the palate, and tiny rubies were sprinkled over the banquet like salt. Pomegranates, apples, sweet red berries, red-
glazed meats, beets and radishes, boiled sweets, deep red
wine. Some in the crowd were now so drunk that they were
eating the rubies rather than pocketing them. Tamara tried to
shrink out of the way.

Her evasive behavior brought her up against the end of the
table where the marriage cup stood, heavy gold, with four
handles and inset with rubies. Suddenly inspired, Tamara
ripped her glass ring from its string around her neck and
flipped it accurately into the deep red wine. It sank with
hardly a ripple. Then she stood back and waited.

The wedding couple sat stiffly, as though propped up by
their new red robes. For the first time since Loresta City,
Tamara saw Arbytis, almost unrecognizable in his rich robes.
He was helped by two young students, and carried the scarves
that the couple exchanged with inaudible vows. Then the cup
was picked up and brought over to the dais, the first food or
drink to be offered publicly to the couple. But before it was
presented to them the chief of the bodyguard was beckoned
forward. Normally, only the Agan or one of his sons would
require a taster at a banquet, but today the wedding pair were
temporary royalty.

Tamara did not recognize the bodyguard until he stepped
forward out of the shadows behind the dais and stooped to
grasp the marriage cup between his hands. The torches gleamed
on his long, pale hair as it swung forward. He did not wear it
braided. As he touched his lips to the cup, his hand moved
with the dexterity of Marricson cheating at castledown. Tamara was certain no one else saw the flash of blue as the ring
was scooped out of the cup.

Next, the couple's hands were interlaced to grasp the handles properly. First Leron offered it to Subi, and she barely

wet her lips. Then she held it for him and he drank deeply. Now the crowd became raucous, laughing and making rude jokes. Servants took up the married couple and carried them bodily toward the wedding tent through a long, silk-draped passage. It was smoky with incense, soft with pillows and rich fabrics. Tamara wormed herself all the way into the bedchamber, and while all eyes were on the ceremonious undressing and bedding of the couple, she hid herself between the inner hangings and the outer wall of the tent. The atmosphere was so thick with scented smoke that it was all she could do to keep from coughing. On the far side of the curtain, the laughter had taken on a loud coarseness that frightened her, but already the servants of the Agan were pushing the crowds out. It seemed to take forever, but finally she was alone with her father and the Batur Subi. She only wished they still had their clothes on, and were not in bed together. It was very hard to figure out what to say.

The couple did not remain bedded for very long. The Batur Subi threw back the covers and crossed the chamber in a few long strides, a flash of pale skin and long dark hair, to dive into a quilted robe that lay in a heap on the floor. She belted it around her with little angry jerks, her eyes vivid in the fatigued pallor of her face. "I suggest you get dressed," she snapped, "and you can keep your hands to yourself."

From her position behind the curtains, Tamara could see only part of the bed; her father's face was hidden. His voice sounded tired but amused in a way Tamara had never heard before. He sounded a little like a stranger. "I am obeying the commands of the Emperor. I thought you were sworn to obey him also."

"Within reason." Subi was standing with her arms folded, looking down at the bed, not in the least amused.

Tamara heard a grunt and a rustle of bedding, then Leron's upper body heaved into view, naked. He scratched his beard. "I don't think we were stripped and bedded just to have an argument," he added mildly. "You might at least sit down. I am too tired to keep looking up at you." He dropped his face into his hands and rubbed his eyes. "Too tired to obey the commands of the Emperor."

Subi sat down on a pile of cushions, several feet away from the bed. "I hope you're not too tired to get out of my bed.

I'm too tired to spend what is left of the night sitting on the floor of my own tent.''

"Your tent? We were both put in here.''

"It was my tent before you came and I hope it will still be mine after you leave. I may not remember you, but I do know quite a bit about you. And I know that you have a wife and children to whom you ought to be trying to return.''

Leron massaged his curly head and failed to meet her eyes. "I only learned of the Anguls and Samida a year ago,'' he remarked evasively. "I should be flattered they know so much about me.''

"I don't have any idea how much they know about you. My information comes from the Karif.''

Tamara was startled at this, but not so much as Leron. Her shock made a barely perceptible movement behind the curtain, whereas Leron's head snapped up so quickly the bed cushions shook. His pale face grew even whiter, his pleasant features twisted. With a hoarse vehemence that Tamara did not recognize, he said, "Again??''

Tamara shrank back against the tent wall, making herself small. She had no idea what was going on, but it was obvious that this was neither the time nor the place for an interruption. Inside the tent, the little flat oil lamp sputtered and made shadows dance. Outside the tent walls she could hear the first birds, and she wished she were somewhere else.

Leron's head had dropped onto his chest, and when he raised his face there was a glitter of tears in the corners of his eyes. "Does he dare still call himself my friend?'' he said. "You are more than a cousin, you are like my twin, a part I need to be whole. Three times fate has brought our lives together. You saved my boyhood quest, you returned my kingdom to me, and today the Emperor of the World joined us in marriage. And once again this arrogant, outlandish tribal chieftain tries to break the contract fate would have us forge. Can you not see what is happening? He is an agent of our enemies. He chose well when he took the name Clerowan, for he is at heart that same wandering rogue destroying what he cannot have. How did he find his way here?''

Subi spoke quietly, her voice tired. "The Anguls attacked in the desert. Tamara was stolen. He followed her here.''

"A likely story,'' he said fiercely. His apparent lack of interest in his daughter's fate made Tamara's heart sink even lower. He went on. "Somehow, he must have learned that you were returning to us, and he came to interfere. But I have won as I won before. We were married under the laws of Tredana and now we are joined according to the customs of the Anguls. Look at me! Take my hand! You have loved me since you were a child, can you deny it? Will you say you have forgotten?"

He scrambled forward on his knees and grabbed for Subi's hand, catching a fold of her gown in his fist. She started to pull away, then looked up over his shoulder into the dark. It was probably just the effect of the lamplight shadowing her eyes and cheekbones and throat, but to Tamara she suddenly seemed transformed from an ordinary person into a woman of great beauty. Behind her, a familiar voice spoke.

"Cover your nakedness, Leron of Tredana. Surely we have had enough vulgar displays this week." And the long form of the Karif squatted down on its heels next to the Batur Subi, smiling coldly at Leron.

"What are you doing here?" cried Leron desperately.

The Karif raised an eyebrow. "I live here. But I will give you my bed. In the antechamber." His deep voice had dropped even lower, soft but intense, "Leron of Tredana, there is much we have to talk over, plans we have to make. But to argue tonight will serve no purpose." He nodded his head at Subi. "She is asleep already as she sits here. You have been awake two days and two nights. Sleep now. We will talk later." He picked up a robe that lay on the floor and held it for Leron, who swiftly pulled it around himself, scowling angrily. As Leron tied the sash, the Karif held something up before his eyes. Once more Tamara saw a sparkle of blue. "And although you did not ask," he went on softly, "she is here."

Leron's ugly expression vanished and his eyes lit up. "Where?"

Ajjibawr shrugged. "Nearby. Doubtless she will reveal herself."

Tamara almost responded to this by throwing the curtains back, but second thoughts prevailed. It was more than likely that the scene she had just witnessed, fascinating as it was, was not the sort of thing the actors would care to share with her. Outside, the sky was lightening. She could see why the tent walls were curtained inside: the ground was so uneven that there were gaps along the bottom edge, which the inner hangings concealed. She dropped quietly down onto her knees and took a look out. No one in sight. She slipped under the edge and moved along the outer wall several feet to where the antechamber joined the main tent. Here, she once more slipped under the edge, although it was a tighter fit. She found herself behind a miscellaneous pile of harness and armor in various stages of cleaning, a few feet from where the curtain to the inner chamber hung. As she watched it lifted, and Leron came stumbling through to collapse on an untidy pile of bedding, burying his face in the pillows. Behind the curtain, the lamp was suddenly extinguished, and in the absence of that little light the outside brightening became much more apparent. The birds were also louder. But Leron was already mumblingly asleep, and Tamara curled up snugly behind the armor, also to sleep.

She slept until late in the day, but even so she was the first to awake. She was not used to awakening stiff: she was up stretching and yawning before she remembered where she was and looked down to see Leron sleeping heavily in a pile of blankets. Last night was a confusing dream. He was here, he was safe; but first, curiosity had to be satisfied. She stepped quietly past him and peeked around the edge of the curtain.

The Karif had laid himself down, still dressed, on top of the bed, and the Batur Subi was curled in his left arm, her head against his chest. His hand lightly held her shoulder and his right arm lay across his chest, a strand of her long hair twisted through his fingers. They looked very peaceful. She watched them for a few moments, then squatted on her heels next to Leron's pillow and touched his shoulder.

He came to slowly, speech thick, eyes closed. He muttered her name like a statement, seemed to doze, then jerked awake. "Tamara!" His face had none of the queer look of last night. He hugged her and kissed her and held her head against his beating chest while he stroked her hair and repeated her name over and over. Finally she struggled free, filled with happiness, to sit beside him and hold one of his hands. "You've grown up so," he said. "My little girl is gone."

"Tell me about Tredana," she said. "Why are you here? Where's the rest of the family? Is everyone all right?"

"I know very little. Alric came with me. He is in Gagan-ala. Liniris and the children were safe when I left Melismala. They were guests of Arrod. Dansen has been forced to come to Samida to share his learning with the Anguls. I have had no news of home since I left, nothing, except that the Emperor has told me he desires my loyalty and that of Tredana as a faithful client state."

"Is that why he made you marry his Sword-Bearer?" Leron colored. He cleared his throat.

"Tamara, what I am going to tell you is difficult to explain. I don't understand it myself. Neither does she. But the Sword-Bearer, the Batur Subi as she is called, is very far from being a stranger."

Tamara waited, hardly able to breathe, the hair prickling on her arms already. Leron failed to meet her eyes. He pulled her against his chest once more and spoke into the air over her head.

"She is your mother. Sibby."

Of course she had been expecting it, but actually hearing the words made her stomach turn. She felt like fainting or being sick. Then she forced herself to swallow, breathe deeply, open her eyes. She relaxed her grip on Leron's upper arm. "It is impossible."

"It is unlikely. But it is true."

The image she had carried so long in her heart, the goddess and queen, mother and heroine, displayed itself in her mind's eye one last time. In her imagination she quite deliberately folded the picture up and packed it away. She closed her eyes again and felt like crying. It was one thing to put away the childhood image; it was quite another thing to have to face the replacement.

Murmurs and soft sounds from behind the curtain seemed to indicate that the rest of the party would soon be joining them. Tamara's heart hammered and Leron looked suddenly tense. The curtain fluttered from movement inside and Tamara's nerve broke, for the first time in her life. She squeezed Leron's hand one last time, pulled free and bolted out of the tent.

She bolted straight into the midsection of one of the Empress's guards, who steadied her by the shoulders and went on a few steps, then recognized her as the missing hostage and wheeled just in time to catch her by the sleeve. He shook her and scolded. "You have caused us much trouble. Were you hiding in camp all along? The Empress has been worried for your safety." When he scowled, his narrow Angul eyes almost disappeared, but nothing could erase the basic good nature of his broad, high-cheekboned face. He exchanged his grip for a firmer one on her pigtail, and steered her ahead of him toward the royal household. Tamara felt oddly relieved.

The servants of the Empress clucked and scolded and stripped off her clothes, forcibly bathing her like a baby and redressing her in a freshly aired shirt and robes that had been beaten dust-free and then rolled in pungent spices. That made Tamara sneeze, but she felt much better, and when she was brought into the presence of the Empress, she was genuinely contrite. The Empress neither scolded nor questioned. She looked her over critically, examined her for health, cleanliness and appropriate attire, then motioned for her to sit at her feet.

"I have heard where you were discovered," she said at last. "Have you spoken with your father?"

Tamara nodded.

"I have no objection to your living with him, if that is what you wish. It depends, of course, on the Batur Subi. What does she say?"

"I don't know. I mean, she was asleep."

The Empress looked at her keenly, as though reading her mind. "I see. She might not have thanked you for interrupting her wedding night? But no decision can be made without her. And here she is to tell us herself."

Tamara looked up, startled. From the safety of her spot at the Empress's feet, she examined her mother critically. Sibby had lost the look of peace she had shown asleep. Nor was there any sign of the beauty that had revealed itself so vividly in the night. Tamara saw a tall woman of athletic build with long, unruly dark hair and arrogant black eyes. Her complexion was faintly golden, where it was not tanned from the sun and wind. In her face was all the angry tenseness of the preceding night. The Empress frowned.

"You do not look like a woman just risen from enjoying the embraces of her husband." Her hand dropped onto Tamara's shoulder. "Or is it that you have been unable to agree with him about his daughter? She may stay with me if you prefer."

Tamara studied her boots as long as possible, then slowly raised her eyes to meet her mother's compelling look. "Her father and I," said Sibby, carefully choosing the words, "would like very much to have her with us."

Tamara felt the Empress tighten her fingers on her shoulder. "A certain jealousy on the part of this child," she said, "is understandable. It will be best if she stays with me for the next few weeks. Understand, she is a prisoner no longer, but an honored guest. When things are more peaceful under your roof, you may send for her."

Sibby bowed and prepared to go out, submissive in gesture but not expression. The Empress still had her hand on Tamara's shoulder, and Tamara was surprised to feel it trembling as though with age. "Batur Subi," said the Empress, "your bodyguard has been reassigned to the Agan's own corps. Please inform him. His valor has found much favor in the eyes of Tibir."

Sibby's face paled and her eyes looked enormous. Tamara felt such a rush of sympathy that her legs trembled. But she did nothing, only leaned back against the Empress's knee and dropped her lashes so she could watch Sibby go out without meeting her eyes again.

There was silence for a few moments, then the Empress spoke to Tamara, very softly. "Where was the Batur Clerowan last night?" Tamara looked at her boots again. There was fancy stitching around the ankles in bright red thread. She had to answer and could not think of any alternative to the truth. "In the tent," was her final choice.

"Was he alone?"

"They spent some time talking together, all three. I fell asleep."

"Where did you fall asleep?"

"In the antechamber." Tamara was suddenly inspired. "Clerowan has his bed there, too, but there was room for me by the pile of harness." She was pleased with the cleverness of her statement, but the Empress out-generalled her.

"And who slept in the bed of Clerowan?" Tamara hung her head and felt her shoulder being patted. "Do not feel badly, child. Your father is not a warrior. It was too much to expect for him to face down two such formidable opponents. But I think he will be able to handle one nicely. When all is

well between your father and the batur, then will be the time
for you to join him.''

Tamara dropped her face in her hands, seeing the image of
Sibby asleep in the arms of the Karif, and, further back,
memories of Liniris, laughing at some word of Leron's, his
arm around her waist. They all needed help, but she had no
idea where to start first.

Chapter Fourteen

THE SCHEME

Tamara enjoyed the protection of the Empress. It was good to have a wall, or at least a curtain, between herself and the surprising and unpredictable mixture of passions from which she had fled. But she could not forget that the protection was temporary. Nor was it easy always to be avoiding the Emperor's Sword-Bearer, his new Batur, or his faithful vassal the king of Tredana. She could feel their hurt and reproachful gazes burning through her hunched shoulders as she scuttled to safety in an imperial tent or among a group of royal children. The Empress was very pleased by the sudden intense interest Tamara showed in Taan's lessons. The interest was genuine, if convenient. Tamara had found a new friend.

She had met Danyas briefly when they were both little children and Dansen had made his first visit back to Tredana with the Lady Arrod and their eldest son. Tamara would never forget the whipping she had received from her nurse when she was discovered sitting naked with her new friend examining the fluttering gill lines at the base of his neck. The dissatisfaction she had felt then at having neither the equipment to be a boy nor the apparatus with which to breathe underwater had been buried very quickly by resentment at the unjust punishment. True, she had never seen that nurse again, for she was dismissed that night. But it was not because she had whipped Tamara. It was for also slapping and shaking Danyas, nearly killing him. Tamara had learned very quickly the delicacy of the Dylalyr on land, with which they paid for their mastery of the undersea.

Danyas must have remembered their last meeting also. His

shyness was quickly past, however, and soon the two of them were giggling and annoying Taan, and generally disrupting study sessions. In Danyas she found someone to share her problems, and at the end of their first long talk she felt as though she had known him forever. In many ways he was like his father—kind, careful, unexpectedly humorous. It was easy to forget that he was not entirely human.

On a cold and sunny afternoon, a few days after the great wedding, Danyas and Tamara took a lunch of bread and olives and walked a distance out of camp into the hills. Below them they could see the ceaseless activity of Tibir's forces, readying for the great march on Paradon. Danyas was sorry to think he would not be there. "Taan promised that I would be returned to my family by spring. He tells me that father's work in the library will soon be done. Then we will be sent back to Melismala together." He took an infinitesimal bite of bread and began the laborious task of chewing. When he had to eat landsmen's food, it took him ages to finish the smallest portion; he told Tamara that he had to chew it until it dissolved and lost all taste, or he could not swallow without gagging.

Tamara took a healthy bite of her portion and eyed her friend's olives. He placed them in her hand. "Please," he said. "I can't face them today."

She accepted happily, then asked, "Why do you want to see the war on Paradon?"

He shrugged. "The warlords caused so much misery in my country. They killed so many of my people, even my mother's brother, whom she dearly loved. I think that's why the forces of Tibir had such an easy sweep in Melismala. They said from the first that they were planning a campaign against Paradon, and my people have dreamed of such a revenge for many years. They do not want to be ruled by Tibir, but they will accept it if it helps them humble an old enemy."

"That's fine for now," said Tamara, "but what about later? When Paradon's finished? Tibir will probably still keep forces in Melismala."

"That's what Father said, in council. But the others did not listen, or did not care. They said there are worse things than the rule of a strong Emperor. And I suppose they are right. Tibir has not been cruel to the islands. Just a little greedy."

Danyas took a second pinch of bread and eyed it with

distaste before inserting it in his mouth. "If it weren't for Father, of course, it wouldn't affect my family. All of us are more Dylalyr than human. We could just have taken to the waters. At first, when we didn't know what was going to happen, that's what Father told us to do. Mother was very angry with him. She said if he continued to talk like that she'd pull him in the water and hold his head down and be done with it. In any case, she had her guests to take care of, too: your stepmother and the children."

Tamara heaved a sigh and dropped her head in her hands. "Danyas," she said, "I think I have a very big problem." He listened soberly while she brought him up to date, only a fluttering at the base of his neck betraying surprise when she told him who the Batur Subi really was, and how the relationships stood between her and Leron and Clerowan, who was really the Karif. "And furthermore," she said, "I was told in the desert, by someone who was probably well informed, that Leron isn't my real father anyway! And that he knows it. Or suspects it."

"That would probably explain some of what you overheard."

"Well, it does not explain why my mother is pretending that she never heard of any of us. If she didn't remember, how did she manage to get back together with the Karif so quickly? And if she's always felt like that about him—if he is my father," she had to choke down a lump in her throat as she said the words, "then why did she marry Leron and let him believe that I was his daughter *and* go away and leave him with me to take care of? That wasn't very nice, or fair. And he has tried to be a good father to me, really he has." She found to her embarrassment that there were tears in her eyes, and that her nose was getting stuffy. "What's going to happen to him now, if I tell him that he isn't my father? After all the trouble that he's been through? His wonderful Sibby says don't touch me and his miraculously recovered daughter says, sorry, but I don't think you're my father!"

Danyas gave up on his morsel of bread and discreetly spat it out. "There's only one solution: forget about the past. The queen is still in Melismala with the children. There's no question of whose family they are. Leron should return to them."

"But he's gotten all droopy-eyed and quivery seeing my mother again."

Danyas made an extravagant gesture with his hand. "We will use force if necessary." Coming from one of the Dylalyr, that was a joke, and Tamara laughed gratefully, clearing her nose and throat.

"Do you think we can get him on a boat to Melismala?"

"We can try." Danyas stared into the distance. "And we can probably get the Karif to help. Anyway, it might save the king's life. He's bound to get into big trouble with the Karif if he stays around. I saw them, you know, the Batur Subi and Clerowan. Just this morning. They thought they were concealed behind one of Taan's windbreaks. I don't think they're ready to separate yet."

Tamara tried to look casual. "What were they doing?"

Danyas raised his eyebrows. "They were dressed and standing. But there was a lot of panting and gasping and wandering hands. Tibir's bound to find out sooner or later. They wouldn't have noticed me if I'd jumped up and down and flapped my arms like a bird. Are you going to ask him if he's your father?"

Tamara felt her cheeks grow hot and red. "I couldn't."

"The only reason I ask is, you'd better decide whether you want to come back with us to Melismala, or stay here with your mother."

Tamara closed her eyes and pictured Liniris smiling sweetly and uncomprehendingly at her, her arms around Geret and the baby Anith. Leron standing behind her, smiling down fondly. She couldn't place herself in that picture, not comfortably. But she didn't say so.

Taan had called Danyas a memory on legs, but in the next few days the boy showed organizational talent and original thinking as well. The project to return Leron to his wife and children became an obsession, and he made provisional plans and contingency plans and alternative plans with all the zest of a frustrated general. Tamara was given assignments. Her first assignment was to infiltrate family headquarters, and so she reluctantly made herself ask the Empress for permission to visit her father in his tent. As she walked toward the pavilion, she felt like a condemned man approaching the swordsman.

An unfamiliar bodyguard stood outside the tent. Inside, all was in order—no untidy litter of weaponry and saddles. The antechamber had a new rug on the floor, and little hard pillows lined the walls. The inner chamber had only the bed and a low, carved chest, and a small heap of Sibby's fancier clothes. Leron sat cross-legged on the floor, some papers spread out on the chest, reading intently. He did not look up until she had been there several minutes, and when he saw her his face lit like a lamp. He did not even say her name, just rose and folded her in his arms. "My dear," he said. "My dear little girl."

He drew her down to sit next to him and look at the papers. "See here—the engineers of the Agan have drawn up complete plans for the restoration of Tredana. Look at these drainage ditches! Remember how the market square always floods in the spring? It is the old sea drain that causes the problem. Look at this—" He traced a drawing with his finger, something that looked like a complicated serpent with sharp-edged turns and many little offshoots. "They have come up with a solution. Tibir wants me to approve these renovations. By the time I return, the city will be rebuilt better than ever."

The drawings meant nothing to Tamara, but she had a vivid mental image of the master drain builder taking orders from an Angul engineer. "Who will oversee the project? Uncle Gannoc?"

Leron paled and his lips trembled. "My dear, I thought you had heard. He—he did not survive the first attack on the city."

She looked at him blankly, feeling the tears spill down her face without any awareness of having burst into tears. She did not want to say it, but asked anyway: "Aunt Mara?" He shook his head. She turned her face away and let the tears run down freely, feeling the whole top of her shirt grow wet as the grief flowed silently out. "How can you sit there gloating over drains?" she finally choked out. "I'd rather have the market square three feet under all year round, than—than not have them. And what about Liniris and Geret and Anith? Anith will be walking by now. When are we going home to them?"

Somehow through her tears she had managed to bring in Danyas' third-ranked suggestion for raising the subject of the family; she was amazed at how easily duplicity came to her even in the midst of overwhelming sorrow.

Leron was caught unguarded. "The Emperor has made me a new alliance," he said softly, "not knowing he renewed an earlier tie."

Tamara gritted her teeth and made herself say it. "It seems to me that my mother has also renewed an earlier tie." She forced herself to raise her eyes to Leron's, and they regarded each other soberly. "I think that we should go back to Tredana," she said. "But I also think we should take the rest of the family. Your real family."

She could not mistake the small lifting of tension in his face when she said *we*. "Do you want to go home?" he asked.

She nodded.

"And your mother?"

She shook her head. "To me, she is the Emperor's Sword-Bearer. She doesn't belong in Tredana."

He took her hand in both of his. "Perhaps you are right," he sighed.

They were sitting silently side by side when the Batur Subi came in. The Enku was on her hip and she wore light battle armor. Her eyes were bright and her cheeks so pink that Tamara recalled what Danyas had told her and found herself blushing. Sibby halted in the doorway.

"Tamara! I'm so glad you are here." She came over and sat down by them, giving Leron a small smile. "Are you ready to leave the royal household?"

Tamara shook her head.

"Do you want to talk?"

Tamara shrugged.

"What would you like?" she asked patiently, and Tamara felt trapped.

"I don't know," she mumbled, and felt vaguely satisfied by the expression of irritation on both faces. Then to her alarm Leron got up.

"You have not had any chance to talk," he said. "I will leave you alone for a while." He went out, and Tamara wished she had the nerve to demand he take her with him. She was finally alone with her mother, and one of them was going to have to say something.

Tamara sat silently regarding her hands, which were folded in her lap. Her mother slowly got up and began taking off the mailed helmet, light breastplate and meshed gloves that formal attendance on the Agan required. When she unbuckled the Enku, she pressed its hilt briefly against her lips before setting it down; Tamara felt a shudder of revulsion. She forgot Danyas' carefully worked out progression of questions and statements.

"You really don't remember me, do you?" It came out in a more unpleasant tone than Tamara had intended. Her mother dropped down in front of her, looking very much younger in her long, belted linen shirt. She shook her head.

"Tamara," she said softly, "let me tell you some of this story from my point of view. I was dropped here out of the middle of a life in which I belonged—not the happiest, perhaps, but not so terrible either. I am a practical person. I accepted that this was something I could not understand, and tried to make the best of it. You have to try and believe this one thing: I have done my best to remain the same person I have always been, even though I was placed in a new setting. And now—now I am confronted by people who say they know me, say they are related to me, say I have obligations to them. What would you do in my place?"

Tamara met her eyes. She had been steeling herself to resist some unwarranted protestation of affection or concern, and it took a minute to relax. But the question was genuinely interesting. "Do you believe us—I mean, these people?"

"The weight of evidence seems to be on their side. But as for memory, I feel nothing."

"Even for the Karif?"

Again, she had lost control over the tone of her voice, and her mother flinched. She answered slowly, choosing her words with great care. "Tamara, there are some things that are hard to explain to someone who is younger. I don't expect you—I wouldn't want you to understand how passion works. All I can tell you is that when I first saw this man, whom I now know is the Karif, I was very strongly moved. I found him disturbing. If I have ever felt like this about anyone before," she laughed a little bitterly, "I do not remember it. I love him so much that it is almost not enjoyable, because it all means too much, is too important."

Tamara cleared her throat. "Does he love you the same way?"

"I doubt it. He loves me, but his nature is more detached—or less obsessive. There is only one thing that means more to him than anything else. And that is you."

Tamara felt the shock of that in her stomach. "What do you mean?"

"I mean that you're his only child. He wants you to have whatever he can give you."

Tamara got to her feet, feeling angry tears in her eyes that she could not control. "It's a little late, don't you think? It is such a wonderful chance that I feel like a fool to pass it up. Just consider, I can give up being the princess royal of Tredana and accept a generously minded outlaw as my very own, real father!"

Sibby stood up too, overpowering her with her height and presence. "If I ever hear you talk like that again, I will be only too happy to act like a real mother. Who do you think you are? Are you going to tell me that you are the only one who is suffering? Why do you think the Karif has not tried to speak with you? He knows you would be better off in Tredana. He gave us his country and his people and came halfway round the world on foot and horseback, and now he isn't even going to speak to you because he wants what is best for you. Don't you dare tell me that gift is worthless!"

Tamara bit her lip, forced back her tears, straightened her features and turned to face her mother. "And what about you?"

"What about me?"

"I'm your only child, too. Do you want me or don't you?" She heard her voice ringing much too loudly, and felt that she was betraying Danyas' careful work.

Sibby stepped up and took her by the shoulders, examining her features carefully. "Tamara," she said, "when I first met you I was fascinated by you. I thought you were delightful. I do not usually pay much attention to people your age, but I couldn't take my eyes off you. When we were attacked in the horse pasture I was sick for fear you would be hurt or killed. My instinct was to risk anything to protect you. I felt the same way outside the gates of Yokan. I may never remember having had you, but I cannot prevent myself from reacting to you like a mother. Yes, I want you—but not as a prisoner. It has to be your decision."

Tamara shrugged herself free of her mother's hands and sat down on the edge of the chest. "I have to think about it," she said coldly. "But in the meantime I have a project for us to work on. It's about Leron. Will you help me try to get him back to Tredana?"

Sibby made a face and sat down at her feet. "With pleasure, madam. What's your plan?"

Tamara told her about Danyas and his projects, and Sibby
approved, with a few suggestions.

That afternoon, Tamara was eager to report to Danyas, but
she was not able to speak with him alone until the following
day. The only thing of interest during the rest of that long day
was seeing the Karif sitting on a horse and talking to a group
of men. She liked seeing him in his desert robes better than
the livery of the Agan, but he still was the most handsome
man she had ever seen, and it made her feel very proud as she
studied him from a distance, admiring how straight he sat, the
length of his legs, the paleness of his hair in the winter sunlight. She wished there were a mirror somewhere so that she
could examine her own face for any trace of his commanding
look. As she admired him, he slowly turned his head in her
direction. She made a little worried smile and he nodded
briefly in response, no change in his expression. She hurried
on to the Empress's tent.

Next day, when she met with Danyas late in the morning,
he smiled approvingly. "Good work, Captain," he said in his
best Angul accent. They both laughed.

"How did you know?" she asked.

"Taan—I should say Master Taan, he is always correcting
me on that—Master Taan told me this morning that my return
to Melismala might be a bigger affair than a simple trip
home. He said he had heard that the king of Tredana might be
sent back to his country to oversee the rebuilding and to help
establish permanent routes of trade—from Gagan-ala through
Apadan, to Tredana and Rym Treglad. He told me that there
might be a great sailing from the new harbor in Tibiridan.
Your mother works fast."

"She made an improvement on your suggestion. She said
that Tibir is especially fond of indirection. That's why he's so
good at castledown. So her idea—and she's obviously already
done it—was to tell the Agan that the best way to fool the
warlords of Paradon into complacency was to appear to send
a major part of the army overseas. We know there are spies in
camp, so this should make them think Tibir's northern campaign is now delayed."

Danyas nodded. "Very, very good. Excellent. And, of
course, since there really is going to be a northern campaign,

Tibir still has to have his Enku and his Sword-Bearer, so she stays here as we planned. Any problems there?''

"I don't know. I haven't spoken with her today. She said she was going to have her work cut out for her trying to convince the Agan—and the Empress—that sending Leron home was not her personal wish but a sound political decision.''

"I will be interested to hear her technique. Master Taan is waiting for me now, but report to me tonight if you can, after you have seen your mother.'' They saluted each other and Danyas marched off to find his teacher.

Tamara found the Batur Subi sitting at the feet of the Empress, in earnest conversation. The Empress beckoned her over. "Child, this concerns you. Your father is being sent back to rebuild Tredana. The Agan wishes for you to stay here with us, as a pledge against his obedience. You accept his command?''

Tamara bowed at the old woman's feet. "I will do whatever you wish,'' she said sincerely, and the Empress smiled.

"Very well,'' she said. "You may visit freely with your father during the next two weeks. But I want you by my side when he embarks. There will be no more hiding and playing games. It would not please me at all to have to treat you like a captive.''

Tamara bowed again, almost light-headed with relief. Now she would not have to be petted and loved and crooned over by Liniris. Now she would not have to try and answer embarrassing questions about Leron's adventures. Only the thought of Geret and baby Anith brought a little stab of longing, quickly stifled. The Empress patted her head and sent her out with the Batur Subi.

As they walked together through camp, for the first time Tamara noted the respect and awe with which her mother was treated. She tried to match her for length of stride, but her legs were still a little too short. Again she found herself wondering if there were any noticeable resemblance. People had always remarked on how much she looked like her father. Perhaps it was because Leron and Sibby themselves looked so much alike. Closer than cousins, just as he had said. She sighed, and her mother looked at her questioningly.

At the remount string she selected two horses, and they rode out into the hills without a questioning word from anyone. As soon as the horses were warmed up, Sibby set a

flying pace and they galloped onto the hills overlooking
Tibiridan and the sea, in a spray of dust and little pebbles.
Here they dismounted and loosened the girths and let the
horses nose around for weeds and wisps of winter-killed
grass. Finally, Sibby spoke.

"As you can see, your friend's plan—with my mod-
ifications—has been successful. Outstandingly successful."

Tamara smiled a little smugly, then realized with concern
that there were tears shining in her mother's eyes. "What's
happened?" she asked.

"Tibir is sending a force of men with Leron, as you know.
They are to be led by the Batur Clerowan." Sibby had her
face turned away, but her voice trembled.

Tamara felt like screaming. After all her work, for things
to go wrong now! "How strongly does the Agan feel about
it? I mean, did he say he wouldn't send Leron back unless
Clerowan went too, or was it just something that happened?"

Sibby was leaning against her horse's saddle, and her voice
was a little muffled. "I don't know. The thing is, he volunteered. Clerowan."

Tamara's first reaction was to wash her hands of the whole
business and let the adults fend for themselves. Then she
reflected on the mess they were making, and decided that the
only honorable thing to do was to continue and help them no
matter how stupidly they behaved. She took her mother's
sleeve and tugged until she was facing her, then asked her to
sit down. "Catch your breath," she said commandingly,
"and tell me the whole story."

Sibby laughed at this and wiped her face on the bottom of
her shirt. "I don't know the story, not yet. I waited on Tibir
this morning while he sat with his generals and heard their
reports. One asked about the composition of the bodyguard,
and he told him that it was being restructured, because Clerowan
was leaving. Of course I was startled at this, and he looked me
in the eye and I swear spoke truly when he said, 'Clerowan
wishes to return to his own country. He has asked to lead the
army of occupation, and I have said yes. He will doubtless
prove as valuable to us there as he has in our present
company.' "

Tamara spread her hands in despair. "Do you mean to tell
me that you believed that? What did you think he was going to
say? He knows perfectly well how you feel about the Karif,

and he has done the obvious thing. So obvious that I am embarrassed we didn't guess he was going to do it.''

Sibby sighed. ''I'd like to think that. But it doesn't explain why the Karif avoided me this morning.''

Her head dropped onto her drawn-up knees, and Tamara regarded her quivering shoulders dubiously. Finally, she leaned over and gave them a tentative pat of comfort. ''I'm ready to go back any time you are,'' she said. ''I really think you should try and have a word with the Karif before you get yourself all worked up.''

Sibby managed a sound that could be taken for agreement.

When they arrived back in camp, there was word that the Agan requested the presence of his Sword-Bearer at once. Still slightly red-eyed, Sibby hurried off. Tamara went to her mother's tent to await her return, and found an unlikely pair to be deep in amicable discussion: the king of Tredana and the Karif of all the Karabdu. She smiled at them both a little tensely.

Leron smiled happily in return, while the Karif smiled distantly, looking at a point above her head. ''My dear,'' said Leron, ''soon we will be home. You have heard the news?''

Tamara folded her arms. ''I think I'm more up to date than you are,'' she remarked. ''The Agan is keeping me here, as hostage for your good behavior. The Empress told me this morning.''

She had the satisfaction of seeing them both startled. Leron's head jerked with surprise, while the Karif's pale face flushed a little and his heavy lids dropped to conceal his eyes. The frustration she had felt when Sibby started crying now turned into rage at the stupidity of these men. She could see now that they had been making plans, too, conniving at her safe return to Tredana under their protection, never mind what she wanted or who she wanted to be with, never mind what happened to the woman they both pretended to love. She was furious. She stood up shaking.

''Don't look so worried,'' she said. ''I know you'll have a lot to talk about on the trip home. Maybe Liniris can find a nice girl for the Karif. Nice and obedient.'' She enjoyed seeing the Karif jerk back at that. She put her hands on her hips, really enjoying the warmth of her anger as it grew inside her. ''Go home to Tredana, both of you,'' she said. ''We don't need you here. I'm going to stay with my mother.''

LETTER

as recorded in Taan's The History of the World Conqueror

PADESHI
WARLORD OF PARADON, BROTHER IN VAZDZ TO
ARBAB, MIMBASH, SAHLAR, SEHAR AND MULKE,
LORD OF THE NORTH SEA, CHAMPION OF VAZDZ,
PROTECTOR OF INIVIN

to Tibir
Warlord of Almadun

The EYE OF VAZDZ sees all, Outlander. You are permitted to humble the unbelievers and take to yourself the wealth of the impious. Vahn, Treclere, Tredana and Rym Treglad alike have renounced the truth of Vazdz; Vazdz makes you the instrument of his severity against them. Further, you are allowed the country of the heretic Chama, and the drear lands of the godless Anguls.

No further north may you go, Outlander. It is forbidden by Vazdz himself. You may not visit the islands of Melismala nor come to Paradon, nor may you march into those northern lands where Vazdz allows none but the people of Tammush the pious Angul to encamp.

You have had some little success, Outlander, but only as Vazdz has willed it. Admit Vazdz, prostrate yourself before his name, and someday you too may be allowed to view the splendours of Inivin.

Heed my warning, Outlander, or learn the taste of humiliation.

Chapter Fifteen

THE REVENGE

I

Leron could not believe his good fortune. To be returning home again unscathed, restored to the throne of Tredana, soon to be reunited with his wife and children. . . . He did not spare Tibiridan so much as a glance over his shoulder. For company he had the faithful Alric, as well as Dansen and his son. And he would not have to speak with Ajjibawr again until landfall in Melismala, since the meddlesome Karif was safely disposed of on another vessel, a large one filled with soldiers.

The *Sea Rose* was an ordinary ship by Tredanan standards, but to the Anguls she was a prize. Their many skills did not include any mastery of the sea or boats. Samidan shipwrights, under the orders of Tibir, had redecorated her in a manner befitting Leron's rank. Leron had never enjoyed such luxury. Velvet hangings, a deep-piled carpet and down-filled cushions transformed the stern cabin. His own wardrobe reflected the Emperor's generosity. It had not taken long to grow used to the weight of the golden circlet on his head; it was slender and beautifully made, a fine example of Samidan craftsmanship. The robes, too, while a trifle ornate by Tredanan standards, were delightful in the quality of the fabric and ornamentation, comfortable to wear.

Now he had to decide how to explain matters to Liniris. Tamara had helped him pick out rich clothing for her, as well as presents for the children. She had written her stepmother a loving note, too. She was a good girl, a credit to her upbring-

ing. He would miss her company and her advice, although he
knew Liniris would be secretly relieved not to have to deal
with her. If only she were not growing to look so much
like—like an outlander. Under the old Tredanan law, Tamara's claim to the throne was ensured by matrilineal succes-
sion, whatever rumors might circulate about her fathering.
But the law was now changed. There was one code only for
the widespread empire of Tibir, the ancient law of the Anguls.
Leron had studied it and had found no fault in it. Women
could earn positions for themselves, or they could inherit rank
from their fathers or their husbands: but all such inheritance
came through the male line only. Had Tredana been under
Angul law when he had married Liniris, Tamara, the first-
born child, would have lost her rank to Geret, the first-born
son.

Now it only remained to make known to the Emperor the
existence of his other marriage and children. In Angul society, multiple marriage was common; Leron regretted not
having been more open with the Emperor. Finding Sibby so
suddenly had really addled his wits, and now he would have
to pay for having kept Liniris and the children a secret. Leron
sighed and rubbed his tender chin. The Emperor had requested
that he remove his beard as a sign of leaving barbarian
customs behind, and his skin was unused to the razor. He
turned away from the rail and saw Dansen quietly waiting.

A little less than middle height, a little more than middle-
aged, Dansen never seemed to change, except that the grey in
his sleek hair was beginning to overtake the brown. If his
patron the Angul prince had been generous with him, his
clothing did not show it. He was dressed in simple Melismalan
fashion, brown homespun belted over unbleached linen. Only
his cap was velvet, and that well-worn.

"I did not care to disturb you, my lord; you seemed so
deep in thought."

Leron drew the older man to him. "Come below, my dear,
and see the gifts Tibir has bestowed on his newest vassal-
king." In the cabin he sat Dansen down in the padded
window-seat and poured him a green Samidan wine, then
gestured with his hand. "What do you think of the honors
shown to Tredana?"

Dansen shook his head. "Chains do not honor the captive,
not even chains of gold."

Leron laughed and took a sip of wine. "Dansen, my dear Dansen, what are you saying? Tibir is Master of the World, the whole world—except for Paradon. And from what I hear, Paradon will soon feel his strength. We must deal with the world as it is, not as we wish it were. Tredana has been fortunate—I have been fortunate. And so, too, with you and your adopted islands."

Dansen set aside his wine untasted. "We are alone, my lord. There are no Angul spies hiding in the walls. I beg of you, speak with me freely. We are facing the greatest challenge of our not unadventuresome lives. I crave your honest counsel, as I will give you mine."

"Dansen, I do not dissemble. Tibir has won my loyalty. I will serve him to the best of my ability."

Dansen's normally placid face tightened and he stood up, brushing invisible dust from the skirt of his gown. "Then all my years of scholarship are nought, if I have failed so greatly in my most eminent pupil. Tibir leads us all to the edge of the abyss. Will you shut your eyes and blindly stumble in?"

"Tibir Agan, World Conqueror, Lord of the Fortunate Conjunction—he has united the world under one rule, one code of laws. Force has been used, it is true, and many good and innocent lives have been lost. Is it Gannoc's death that so upsets you? I will never cease to grieve for our dear and loyal steward, or for his wife. But I think Gannoc himself would not have grudged his fate, had he known what we know now."

"And what is it that we know?"

"We know that there will be peace everlasting under the Angul Empire. A man will be able to travel the length and breadth of this world in safety, under Angul protection. Trade and learning will prosper, wars will cease. I am proud to be a vassal-king to such an empire."

Dansen sat down again and took a gulp of wine, screwing up his face at the acidity. "My lord," he said quietly, "how many years lie on the Emperor's shoulders? Seventy? All that and more. How many sons survive him? How many grandsons? What love do they bear each other? What generals serve him who would sooner serve themselves? How many vassal-kings proclaim him as loyally as yourself? Think on it. Answer these questions in your mind, then say truly what a lifetime of bloodshed and conquest has bought for Tibir Agan.

I will not deny that he is a great man. He has done what no one else has ever done, not since the history of the world began. But it has taken him a lifetime to do it. Who will build on what he has accomplished? Who will turn his extraordinariness into ordinariness? I am one who prefers to consider the past, not predict the future, but I tell you now the center will not hold. Only for a very short time will the world be as one.''

Leron felt the warmth of the wine rise in his face. Dansen looked genuinely distraught; he attempted to soothe him. "Dansen, peace. Of course what you say may come to pass. But I prefer to consider the good possibilities, not the evil ones. What would you have us do? Go into exile as we did years past? Become, once more, wilderness adventurers? I am too old, Dansen, and so should you be. If I sleep on the damp ground, my bones creak in protest. And our case is not as it was then, with a diseased madman and a cold-hearted whore usurping the throne. The generosity of Tibir Agan has made it possible for us to return to our place in society, to rejoin our families, to go on with our lives. If the Angul Empire falls apart, so be it—we will deal with it then. But as for me, as for now, I will faithfully serve the Emperor.''

Dansen stood up again, and bowed his head briefly. "I will not argue with you, my lord. I am sorry if anything I said has offended you. Should you require my services, you have only to ask. Now, if you will excuse me?''

Leron nodded, then took another sip of wine. He was hurt at Dansen's coldness, but on reflection he realized that it had been foolish of him to think they would be able to resume the easy familiarity of years past. They were no longer teacher and student; Leron was no longer a young, idealistic prince.

He drowsed a little, images of past adventures drifting through his mind. Dastra, the prisoner princess of Glass Island, with her bright blue eyes and silvery lashes and sweet, lying voice . . . the mysterious city of Treclere, suffused with the power of Simirimia . . . that strange, half-remembered journey north with the child Sibby. For some reason, he pictured a silver snake around his neck, his memory playing tricks. . . . Then the years of exile in Rym Treglad, such lonely years before Sibby returned. He suddenly realized, as he never had before, that Sibby had not agreed to marry him until the moment they both thought the Karif dead. He still could see the bloody head as it tumbled from the outlaw's bag, he still could feel relief and revulsion mixed. And if that had been Ajjibawr's head, rocking on the floor, how would his life have been different? He toyed with that not unpleasant thought, and was almost asleep when a scuffling sound by the door brought him fully awake.

There was a boy standing there, thin and poorly dressed. He dropped to his knees and held out his hands imploringly. "Mercy, my lord," he whispered hoarsely. "Do not give me away, I beg you." Fair lashes veiled his brilliant eyes.

"Who are you?" asked Leron sharply, trying to sound gruff. He stifled an impulse to feed the poor starveling first before asking questions. The boy dropped his head.

"I cannot lie to you, my lord. I hid myself away on your ship in hopes of making a safe return to your continent. But I've done nothing wrong! I was enslaved by an Angul captain. He brought me away from my country. I don't want to cause any trouble. I just want to go home!"

There was fruit on the table, as well as wine. Leron poured another glass and cut a big slice of melon. "Come," he said kindly, "eat and drink. Then tell me your story."

The boy ate greedily but with good manners, and drank to Leron's fortune with his first sip. His face was fine-featured and reminded Leron of someone he had once known. He was not a Tredanan, however. He explained to Leron that he was one of the settled Karabdu, from a village at the edge of the great desert.

"Shall I give you into the keeping of the Karif?" asked Leron. "He sails on one of the other ships, but soon we will anchor together in the Melismalan Islands before proceeding to the mainland."

The boy shook his head and once more dropped his eyes. "There is a feud between his family and mine. Some question of honor—I think concerning a woman. I am afraid he would return me to my Angul owner. The Karif has little to do with the landed Karabdu. We are not his responsibility."

"What shall I do with you, then?"

The boy once more dropped to his knees. "Let me serve you, sire. I will be your page, your bodyservant, whatever you require. When you need my services no longer, then I will return to my country."

Leron was touched by the boy's deference. "Get up, lad,

and answer me this. What is the king of Tredana to you? Why are you so eager to serve me?''

The boy stood slowly and raised his blue eyes to Leron's face. "In serving you, my lord, I start to fulfil the pledge I made to my mother on her deathbed. She wanted me to make something of myself, to be a greater man even than my father. Fate has put me in your power. Let me be your servant, not your slave or prisoner.''

The answer did not make much sense, but Leron liked the boy's looks and obvious sincerity. He summoned Alric and overrode his protests at the irregularity, seeing to it that the boy had clothes, food and a place to sleep. Not until Alric asked did he learn his new page's name. An outlandish Karabdin name it was: Faras.

Tibir's fleet had good weather for the crossing to Melismala. The days were sunny and warm, breezy enough to keep the sails full, yet quiet enough for comfortable sailing. Faras, the stowaway page, made himself useful to Leron in many different ways. In particular, he served as a messenger between Leron and Dansen's small party. Dansen, his son and his scribes were all polite enough, but Leron found himself uncomfortable in their presence. With Faras as go-between, he was able to share the Emperor's plans for Melismala and Tredana without being drawn into any more awkward discussions.

Nevertheless, Dansen did come to him once more to speak in private—the very day the Melismalan islands appeared as a dark bump on the horizon. His kindly face was worried and he seemed at a loss for words.

"My lord," he said at last, "I could not let you go ashore without speaking. You must understand I am sharing suspicions with you, not facts. But they are so well-founded I cannot keep them to myself. You know, I think, that my son was taken from me for a while, to share his knowledge with Master Taan, the Emperor's chief historian? But I do not think you know that he became reacquainted with your daughter at this time; indeed, he became quite friendly with the princess.''

"I did not know that. I am glad she had his company.''

"It was a good thing for them both. And since they are both children, they spoke freely with each other in a way they would not with one of us. Danyas heard from Tamara all the details of her capture by the Anguls. How much did she tell you?''

Leron flushed. "Very little. I did not—"

"I thought as much. She did not tell you about the young boy, the spy, the one who arranged her kidnapping? The boy who claimed to be Dastra's missing son?"

Leron sat down suddenly. "Dansen! This is impossible. You must have heard how Dastra's boy ran off into the wilderness when she died. The Tregladan guard spent weeks in search of him. How could he have survived that barren waste, let alone come to power among the Anguls, in such a short time? He was only a child."

Dansen shook his head. "Only a child? Own son to Dastra and the Arleon! Consider how quickly the Arleon rose in power, after he came to our world. Consider how easily he removed Dastra's husband from out of her way and how easily he stepped in instead. If the son is like the father, he has as many lives as a cat, and the same ability always to land on his feet."

Leron poured them both a little wine, and this time Dansen did not hesitate to drink. "So where is the boy now? Among the Anguls?"

"Tamara thought so. But Danyas thinks he sees him here with us. Your new page, Faras."

Leron laughed. "Does he know him by sight?" Dansen shook his head. "On what does he base this conclusion?"

"Tamara described Lerdas well—his face, his mannerisms, the new scar on his forehead . . . his fanatical devotion to the memory of his mother and his fanatical determination to avenge himself on you . . . nothing definite, I grant you. But when I mentioned your page's name to my son it started him thinking, and finally he layed his suspicions out for me to examine. And I agreed to come to you."

"Is the name Faras so full of portent?"

"It is the name of a horse, my lord; not any horse, but the one given to Tamara by the Karif. Faras, in the Karabdin tongue, is a binding promise, an oath, a vow. Just such an oath as Lerdas apparently made to his mother."

"A coincidence, Dansen! In Tredana we name our milk cows and our horses and our pet hounds with the names of men and women; why should it not be so among the Karabdu? What does it signify that this poor lad has the same name as my daughter's horse? I would rather ask why her horse was given such a name. Ask your son if he knows the answer to that!''

Dansen rose abruptly. ''My lord, I have simply told you my son's suspicions. I can only warn—but I beg of you, be careful. Now, for happier thoughts. Soon we will be in Apadana. The letter of the Agan will assure you all honor, and a suite in the governor's house. Shall I bring your family there to you tonight?''

Leron shook his head. ''I will visit you tomorrow and speak with my wife. The Emperor is not yet aware of my family. We must make our plans carefully.''

Dansen nodded and withdrew.

The *Sea Rose* led Tibir's fleet into the harbor, but the other ships did not approach the deep-water docks. The army of occupation's fleet dropped anchor in the entrance of the harbor and sent only one boat ashore. Leron had already been greeted by Talyas, saluted by the Angul guard and accepted the hospitality of the islands by the time the longboat beached and Tibir's general stepped ashore—Batur Clerowan with his few retainers.

Ajjibawr saluted Leron with formal courtesy, but there was an unmistakable arrogance in his face. Leron might be vassal-king of Tredana, but the Karif was Tibir's viceroy for the entire continent; the men who accompanied him were only the first of many soldiers to come. He informed Talyas that there would be no shore leave for his troops, the better to preserve the safety of the islanders, and Talyas thanked him with genuine warmth. Then he informed Leron that they would hold private council on board the *Sea Rose* in three days' time, excused himself and went to hear the reports of the Angul guard, never asking if Leron would find such a time convenient. Leron restrained his tongue. It would do no good for them to fall out among themselves. He smiled at Talyas and thanked him for his courtesy in the name of Tibir Agan, Conqueror of the World, then followed him in to supper.

On shore, Leron missed the many small attentions of Faras. The boy had begun feeling ill as they approached land and was still on the *Sea Rose*, in bed with a sleeping draught mixed by the ship's doctor. Leron had been assured there was nothing seriously amiss, but it did make him aware how useful the boy had become. Next morning he washed, dressed and shaved with unusual care and made known his wish to visit Dansen's house. An honor guard accompanied him through the town's quiet streets and out along the shore road. The island was so small that more people walked than rode; Leron had been offered a horse but he preferred stretching his legs after days at sea.

Dansen's estate was low and pillared, with lawns stretching down to the sea. Between the house and the water a shady retreat had been made under a bower of climbing roses and wild grapes. Leron left his guard by the gate and was shown through the house by a quiet servant who left him under the arbor, then went to summon Liniris. He did not wait long.

Her arms were around his neck and her face was against his neck. "Your beard!" she cried in surprise, then stopped as he closed her mouth with kisses. Tears rose in both their eyes as they clung and kissed and murmured endearments. Before he could ask, she had assured him the children were well. It was just that she had wanted to see him alone.

For a while, the morning passed sweetly. Leron half reclined on the bench with Liniris in his arms, warm and fragrant against his body. The taste of her skin, the softness of her hair, the soothing familiar words of love . . . but at last the moment came for kisses to give way to words. Now he had to explain his position; worse, he had to explain her lack of one.

"But I don't understand. What does it matter whether or not Tibir knows of your wife and children? He has made you vassal-king of Tredana. Doesn't that mean that things will be as they were? Tibir is far away. If you proclaim loyalty to him, what more is needed? Explain yourself, my dear."

Miserably, Leron tried to do so. Even with Liniris, whom he loved and trusted, he could not tell all the truth. He could not tell her the true identity of the Batur Subi. He explained the Emperor's penchant for matchmaking and how he had joined the vassal-king of Tredana to his female Sword-Bearer. Leron did his best to make Sibby sound strange and formidable; he stressed her strong attachment to another warrior in the imperial bodyguard. But he also stressed the inviolate nature of the bond, from the Emperor's standpoint.

"I confess to you my cowardice. I did not tell him of my family. I thought—I thought it would keep you safe. The only one of my family he knows is Tamara, and she is his hostage, a pledge for my obedience here. She is not unhappy—you will see from her letter that she is well treated. But she is not allowed to return. As for the woman the Emperor thinks of as my wife, she must stay at his side through the next campaign, the war on Paradon. I assure you, she likes this match no better than I. But I do not know how to proceed. For now, I think you will have to agree to live with me as a—as a companion. Everyone in Tredana knows you are really my wife. It is just a ruse to please the Emperor.''

Liniris stood up, angry tears in her eyes. Her voice was choked. ''As a companion? If you mean as your mistress, why not say so? What else have you done to please the Emperor? You have cut off your beard, left your eldest daughter in bondage, repudiated your wife and children. If you want a mistress, perhaps you should look for someone younger—and unaccustomed to being a wife.'' She ran inside.

II

The ships of the Angul Army had made their repairs and taken aboard all necessary supplies within three days of their arrival. During this time, the Batur Clerowan had paid close attention to everything from the quality of the sailcloth to the saltiness of the beef. He had also made time each day for a meeting with the elders of Melismala, explaining to them the requirements of the Emperor and hearing from them their problems. All this Leron learned from Talyas.

Dansen had kindly consented to carry Leron's presents and letters to Liniris and the children, but there had been no second meeting. She had asked of him a proof of loyalty he could not give. If he and the *Sea Rose* stayed an extra week after the main fleet's sailing, she and the children would return to Tredana with him. She knew he had orders to stay with the army. She did not understand why he would not do such a simple thing for her as break his word to the Emperor.

On the day Ajjibawr had appointed for their private meeting, Leron woke with a headache and a savage temper. He had slept aboard his ship and the slap of water against the hull had kept him awake rather than soothing him to sleep. Faras unpinned the curtains to close out the light and brought him a pain-killing mixture from the ship's doctor. It helped a little, and Leron was soon feeling well enough to see to the arrangements for the meeting that evening. Of his staff he kept only Faras, sending Alric and most of the crew ashore. Two guardsmen stayed on deck. This was to be a strictly private meeting.

Ajjibawr left his guard behind and entered Leron's quarters alone. Before he sat down he removed his helmet and stripped off his gloves and Leron was shocked by his pallor. "Are you unwell?" he asked, and the other shook his head.

"It is nothing," he said. "A little trouble with a recent wound." He pulled down the edge of his shirt and Leron saw a red and swollen scar across the side of his neck. It was oozing fluid and Leron suddenly understood why Ajjibawr stood and sat so stiffly. Something else caught his eye and quelled the little sympathy that had been rising in him. Tamara's glass ring, looped on a leather thong around the Karif's wounded neck.

"My wife used to wear that bauble," he said hoarsely. "And after her, my daughter. For which one do you wear it?"

"For both of them," said Ajjibawr evenly. "For the daughter I can never acknowledge and her mother—the girl to whom I first gave it twenty-four years ago. Do you envy me this trifling remembrance?"

Leron reddened. "You admit it? You admit fathering Tamara on my wife? When were you planning to speak up? Were you waiting to see the world laugh at the revelation of a Karabdin bastard on the Tredanan throne?" His words were choked off as Ajjibawr took hold of his shirt and jerked him from his seat.

"Unsay those words, Leron of Tredana, and we may yet be friends."

Leron pulled himself free and straightened his shirt. "I spoke in anger, and for that I apologize. But if you wish to claim Tamara and she is willing to accept you, why hesitate? I have a son. I will not keep your daughter from you."

Ajjibawr held his eyes with his own, then dropped his heavy lids. "Why hesitate?" he asked softly. "First, because of a promise to her mother. Second, because you seemed to love her, and she you. Third, because I thought I had nothing to give her. Can you give up your child so easily, Leron of Tredana?"

"She is not my child," Leron said gruffly, and felt an odd relief as he said so.

Ajjibawr sighed. "Then I did wrong to leave her. At least she is with her mother and well protected."

Leron opened the wine that Faras had put on the table and broke a hard crust of bread in half. "Karif, let us settle our differences here and now. Eat and drink with me. It is in our best interest and that of Tibir, whom we serve. I have been jealous of you, it is true, but all that is in the past. My cousin Sibyl has rejected me, Tamara needs me no longer. I have my own life and you have yours. Instead of arguing with you here to no purpose, I should be thinking of a way to convince Liniris and the children to come home to Tredana."

Ajjibawr accepted the bread and wine and sat again, stiffly. As Leron explained his problem, Ajjibawr shook his head. "I will be happy to send the Emperor a report of the *Sea Rose*'s need for trifling repairs, enough to delay her sailing some few days. I will leave two ships for her escort as well, the two that carry reinforcements for the Tredanan guard. Then I can sail on directly to Treclere. Will this be of help?"

Leron shrugged. "I can only try." He dropped his eyes. "Whatever I may have said, Karif, however I may have acted, Liniris is my true wife, the mother of my children. I do not wish to return to Tredana without her. I hope you can understand, and forgive me."

"There is little to forgive," said Ajjibawr. "And I understand your feelings all too well." He fumbled in the front of his shirt and pulled out the glass ring on its cord. Below it hung a small silk pouch. He opened it slowly. "I know you think me a cold man, Leron. Perhaps you are right. But in one thing I am as sentimental as any moonstruck boy." A long curl of dark hair wound around his finger; he touched it to his lips and put it back in the pouch again. "I stole it while she slept," he said. "My dignity would not let me ask for it. Now it may be all I ever have." He held out his hand and Leron clasped it strongly. "Do not let foolish pride keep you from your wife and children." Ajjibawr stumbled on the last words, then lost his balance and fell forward against the table.

Leron reached to help him and found himself staggering also. There was no strength in his arms, his legs were buckling. As he slumped against his chair he felt hands steadying him and dimly, through darkening eyes, he could see Faras. "Good lad. See to the Karif. I'll be all right."

Leron was dimly aware of being helped to his bed, his feet lifted onto the cushions. "You're a good page," he murmured and closed his eyes. "Dansen was wrong." He felt a light touch on his arms, his throat.

"Wrong about what, my lord?" Faras was bending over him.

"Some foolishness," Leron muttered. His tongue was heavy in his mouth. "An old matter. Doesn't concern you."

"But it does, my lord." Faras had spoken loudly and Leron forced his eyes open. The boy held a thin cord in his hands and his eyes were the same light blue as Dastra's, framed by the same sparse silver lashes. "It does concern me, *Father*. I have just heard you casually relinquish a daughter. But your treatment of Tamara is a model of kindness compared to mine. I'll show you what kind of son your savagery brought forth. You will never call my mother a whore again. Look at me, false prince. I am Lerdas!"

Leron tried to raise his hand to save his throat, but his arms were pinned to his sides. His head was spinning and his eyes would not stay open. As he forced the lids open again, he saw Ajjibawr stagger forward a few steps, then fall to his knees as the boy hit him on his wounded neck with a wine bottle. Leron managed to unstick his tongue and weakly cry out. Lerdas laughed.

"There are only two guards and they have drunk the same wine." He picked up the cord again, then put it down. "Strangling is too quick. My mother suffered for years at your hands, and even her death was slow." Lerdas pulled the lamp from its holder and poured some flaming oil on the floor, igniting the carpet. "I will fire the ship as I leave. Burn you or drown you, it matters not to me. In Apadana I will give the alarm, but I'm afraid it will be too late. . . ."

Leron struggled to sit up, but his head was much too heavy. He could smell scorched wool. He drew in a ragged breath and coughed as the acrid smoke filled his lungs. Another deep breath and his head seemed to clear a little. The cabin's rich hangings were in flame and the heat hurt his skin. Then he felt the Karif's hands on him and a sharp knife scratched his arms, cutting the cords. Leaning together like drunkards, they staggered to the door, but its panels were hot to the touch and something was wedged against it from outside. They turned and stumbled across the cabin to Leron's bed and, reeling from side to side, falling and picking themselves up again, they climbed onto the couch and wrenched open the heavy stern window. A crescent moon glittered on the choppy water below and the little lights of Apadana made streaks in the distance. A tongue of flame licked at their feet. Despite his drugged stupor, Leron managed to wink and the Karif grinned back as they pitched themselves over the side and fell spread-eagled into the cold, dark sea.

Chapter Sixteen

THE OMEN

There was no war in winter: throughout the world it was the custom to start campaigns in the spring. It was typical of Tibir to plan his unconventional first offensive against Paradon for late winter. No ordinary general would think it possible to keep an army in the field supplied at such a season. But Tibir had made careful plans.

The Empress still expected Tamara to keep to her studies. Now she was Taan's only pupil. The royal children had been left in Tibiridan with their mothers, and Danyas, of course, had been reunited with his father and sent home in the fleet that carried Leron and the army of occupation back toward Tredana. Nevertheless, the Empress allowed Tamara some liberty during the day. She could ride behind her mother—dressed in boy's armor and carrying a light sword. Her orders in the event of attack were absolute, however. Tamara was to join the Empress, and by no means take part in any fighting. That suited her own taste quite well. It was better to wear a sword than to use it.

A bed had been made for her in the antechamber of her mother's tent and she slept there most nights, except when the Agan required his personal attendants to sit up late with him. Then Sibby insisted on putting Tamara to bed in the larger part of the tent; Sibby slept outside, rather than disturb her by stepping over her in the middle of the night. Tamara was unable to convince her that nothing much was likely to wake her up in the middle of the night. It obviously made Sibby feel good to try and do something motherly for her, so she accepted the arrangement gracefully. When she nestled down into the cushions, she tried not to think about the Karif and his abrupt departure.

Ibrasa had managed to send her a word of farewell before embarking for home on one of the Karif's ships. She had not had a chance to speak with him. And Marricson, she knew, had joined in the motley collection of families, tradesmen, entertainers and petty criminals who had followed the army from Gagan-ala and Tibiridan and were now doing their best to stay with it as it marched north. The army was so vast, and its followers so many, that as long as he avoided a direct confrontation with detachments from Sikin's army he felt perfectly safe. Despite her loneliness, Tamara did not dare draw attention to him, but Marricson occasionally found the chance to share a few words with her on the road or during an encampment.

It would have been quicker for Tibir to put his armies on shipboard and bring them to Paradon by water, sailing through the islands of Melismala. His chief batur, Clerowan, had suggested just such a plan. But Tibir was a land warrior and had no love of ships. Therefore, he marched his men several hundred miles up the coast to where it curved around westward, and the easternmost tip of Paradon could be seen across a narrow strait. Their progress was slowed by the short, dim days and long, black nights. More time was spent cooking and eating and telling stories than could be spent on the road. And every few days a messenger galloped in and then galloped out on a swift remount, bringing the news of the empire to the Agan.

They had been marching less than a month when the Empress discovered that Marricson was traveling with the camp followers, and demanded that he wait on her that night. Tamara was sick with worry for her friend. She felt cold and shaky as she sat huddled in her furs below the royal dais, shivering despite the stuffy warmth of the tent. But Marricson bounded in as foolishly entertaining as ever. He prostrated himself at the Empress's feet and swore that he had been following the army in the vain hope of seeing her beauty again, and she smiled. He begged her forgiveness for having fled during the panic outside Yokan, and she forgave him. He begged her to tell him what he could do to please her, and she told him. He was appointed to be her chief entertainer, to be available whenever she summoned him, and he thanked her with becoming gravity. Tamara wiggled out of her furs and settled back to enjoy his singing. A few times he winked at her and made her blush.

The next night Sibby was able to leave the Agan's court earlier than usual, and she joined the Empress and her daughter to listen to the singer. Marricson played up to her outrageously, and the Empress was even freer than usual with her red wine. The great tent grew warmer and warmer. Awareness of how cold it was outside made everyone reluctant to end the evening. Marricson put his baraka into Sibby's hands, and she laughingly protested that she could not play it, her words slurring a little. Tamara was given her mother's wine bowl to hold and she stuck her tongue in cautiously, then sipped it up in little swallows while she watched her mother fumble with the strings. Suddenly a tune came out of the baraka, a few notes, a few more, then a run of clear sounds. Marricson nodded and started singing the words, Sibby joined in with pauses and sudden rushes of confidence.

> *A lady on an eastern shore*
> *Seasons pass and the seed is sown*
> *Two only were the babes she bore*
> *Sing for all the singing birds are gone*

Tamara knew she had heard that song somewhere. The tune was hauntingly familiar, the words a little less so. But as the song went on, Sibby seemed to remember more and more of it. She had a pretty voice, light and young sounding, and Tamara closed her eyes to listen. Before the song was through, she had fallen asleep.

In the night she awoke, still in the Empress's warm tent, lying rolled in her fur-lined cloak, her mother's arm over her. In the great bronze firebowl the coals were glowing red, and other members of the Empress's court were lying asleep on the floor. The wind was howling outside, promising snow. Sibby stirred and drew her closer, then coughed and changed her position. Tamara whispered, "Are you awake?" A mutter indicated yes. "It's not fair that Marricson can't stay here where it's warm. Do you think the Empress would be angry if I asked her?" Sibby muttered *no*. "Good. I'll do it tomorrow. When did you learn to play the baraka?" Silence.

Tamara rolled around to face her mother and saw she was looking puzzled.

"What's a baraka?"

"Marricson's instrument. The one you were playing."

"Oh. It's a lot like some we have in my world. The tuning was just a little different."

"Then how did you know his song?"

"Was I singing?"

"Yes, and you knew the words. Are you going to tell me that came from your world, too?"

Sibby sighed. "Honey, I don't remember the song. We'll have to ask him about it tomorrow. Now try and sleep." She turned over on her side and Tamara buried her face in the furs that were wrapped around them.

Next day the snowstorms came, and everyone who could, stayed indoors. Tamara could picture the makeshift tents and shelters huddled along the far reaches of the encampment, and felt guilty to be so comfortable herself. She timidly voiced her concern to the Empress, and Soria graciously sent for Marricson to join her household. Seeing her friend warm and safe helped Tamara sleep.

Some evenings Arbytis also joined them. Tamara had learned through cautious eavesdropping how the Emperor's own physicians were seeing to the health of the fabled High Priest. Now, on rare occasions, Arbytis was able to leave Sharkim's close custody for the relative freedom of the Empress's tent. He smiled at Tamara and her mother, but sat silently near the royal dais without speaking directly to either of them. He looked much older than he had in Loresta. Occasionally the Empress questioned him and, if in a serious mood, she would debate points of fate and morality with him for hours.

It was near the deepest part of the winter, the time of the shortest day and longest night, that Marricson introduced another type of amusement to the evening's entertainment. Outside it was now so cold that the herdsmen were losing stock for lack of water; snow covered the tents and the army had made no attempt to move forward for more than a week. Inside the great tent it was smoky and smelly from unaired clothing and poorly cured sheepskins. Tamara was lying contentedly with her head pillowed against the side of an enormous Angul guard dog—muscular, hairy, broad-headed, brave and stupid. She loved him and he had appointed himself her protector, since she had started saving scraps for him. When the weather broke, she knew he would probably return to his shepherd, but for now he was hers. She called him her batur to everyone's amusement.

Her head was on the dog's back and her feet were in her mother's lap. As they listened to Marricson, Sibby absent-mindedly massaged Tamara's ankles. The song was about a hero who went on a quest for knowledge, strange words, but a pretty tune.

> *He journeyed east, he journeyed west*
> *he journeyed south and north*
> *and when he came to Tremyrag*
> *he bid its lord stand forth.*

> *Stand forth, stand forth O Zenedrim*
> *and show me what you have*
> *Look where you will, the hermit said.*
> *All roads lead to the grave.*

> *Speak up, speak up O Zenedrim*
> *and tell me all you know*
> *I cannot speak the hermit said.*
> *But I have much to show.*

> *He led him through the mountainside*
> *he led him higher and higher*
> *he led him to the chamber where*
> *the god stood wreathed in fire.*

Sibby's knees shifted under the weight of Tamara's feet; she began rubbing her right hand first against her knee, then with her left hand, as though it hurt her.

> *Look in the cup the hermit said*
> *the truth is writ in water*
> *look in the cup and you will see*
> *the goddess and her daughter.*

> *He went to where the Jawmir stood*
> *and took it in his hands*
> *inside it held sun moon and stars*
> *its rim had seven bands.*

He read the meaning of the past
the meaning of today
he looked into the future
and then he went away.

The last note still hung poignantly quivering in the air as
Marricson effected a complete change of mood. "Why go
into the wasteland, or to Tremyrag, wherever that may be? I,
Marricson, Prince of the Entertainers, can show you the
future as well as sing about it." With a flourish that Tamara
recognized, he drew the stones from his pocket, and as he
cast them he covered his eyes. "It will fall a seven," he
intoned then opened his eyes in feigned delight at the sight of
the four and three before him. The audience was entranced.
From the pillows next to the royal dais came a dry laugh.
Tamara saw Arbytis turning his blind face in Marricson's
direction, shaking his head slowly from side to side. In
return, Marricson was staring back, frank puzzlement on his
features. Arbytis lifted a tall silver cup, covered with a cloth.

"You speak of the Zenedrim and the Jawmir, singer, then
offer tricks with casting stones. I cannot claim this cup is as
true as the Jawmir, yet many have been known to see strange
sights herein. Think what you would like to see, future,
present, past—and it may appear. Who will try it?"

The Empress nodded. "This is easily tested. Hand it to
me."

The old man bowed before her, and she lifted it to her face,
pushing back the linen that covered it. The light from its
surface shone on her face in ripples. "Think," he said softly.
"Ask, and it will answer."

Her hooded eyes looked down into the surface and her thin
lips moved, making a soundless request. Color slowly moved
over her face, brightening her skin from pale to gold, filling
the streaks in her hair with black. The lines in her face filled
and disappeared, and to Tamara's sleepy eyes she looked
suddenly beautiful, more so than any of the Agan's young
wives, glorious in fact. She smiled as she looked into the cup,
nodding her head in agreement with the vision. Then the light
dimmed, the color faded, and Soria was once again the old
Empress, Tibir's wife of fifty years. A faint smile still lifted
one edge of her lips as she covered the cup again. "A good

trick," she said tersely. Arbytis smiled and Marricson leaned forward, staring intently at him.

Several others looked into the cup after that, and all professed themselves satisfied. Some stated their questions out loud, some murmured softly to themselves. Then Tamara was roused from her rest by Arbytis gesturing in her direction. "Wake up and tell us what you would see."

Tamara spoke without much reflection. "I'd like to see what my father is doing," she said, and wondered which father the cup would show. Perhaps they were both together. She got up and went over to kneel by the cup. It looked unexpectedly dark inside, and the torches in the tent made a strange reflection on the limpid surface. She repeated her request softly, under her breath, and watched the cup intently. Then the dark liquid spread out, growing larger until she was looking down at a dark and swirling sea, flecked with whitecaps. She was looking out over a sill and under her feet she could feel a ship move up and down. "I am seeing what he sees," she thought. "But which one am I? If I could see my hands I would know." Before she could lift her hands to her eyes she felt herself falling out into emptiness, hard onto a wave which lifted up to smack her breathless and roll her under. Green water rushed over her head, stung her eyes, filled her nose and throat; she gasped at the cold and choked and tried to cry out. Then she was back in the tent and her mother was pounding on her back.

"Are you all right? You started to choke. Here." A bowl of red wine was thrust into her hands. She sipped it and the panic subsided in her mind.

"I'm fine," she lied, "I just swallowed wrong." Sibby nodded dubiously.

A few more wanted to look in the cup, and more wanted to test Marricson's ability to foretell the casting stones. Inevitably, a castledown or sitranga board appeared, and soon Tamara could see that Marricson was still supporting himself in high style, though he seemed distracted by his curiosity about the High Priest. The waves had subsided in her head, but the horror of the fall and the choking remained. She wasn't sure now what she had seen in the cup. The memories were muddled. But it was filling her with a sense of foreboding. She turned around and lay down with her head in her mother's lap and her feet on the dog. Sibby smoothed her forehead with a cool hand.

"Do you feel better? What did you see?"

"Sea water. It made me choke. I felt like I fell in."

"It must have been a very powerful image. I'd like to know how he does that."

"Who? Does what?"

"How the old man makes you see those pictures."

"Old man? I told you, that's Arbytis the High Priest. And anyway, it isn't him, it's the cup." Tamara closed her eyes as her mother lightly caressed her face. Above her she heard a chuckle.

"It might be the cup, darling, but I doubt it. And I have my doubts about high priests. I think he is a very clever man and I am curious about what other tricks he may have up his sleeve. Right now I don't believe him any more than I believe in the honesty of your friend Marricson. Tricks always work if you don't know how they're done. I just wish I could be sure that the magic of Paradon is at this same level. If it is, we will not have much trouble. But if there is real power on that island, we will need more than a gamester with quick hands and an old man with a magic cup."

Tamara drifted off to sleep hearing her mother's voice still murmuring above her head.

from Dansen's The History of Our Islands

As may be seen in the foregoing account, our peaceful islands were brought into the Empire of Tibir with only a small show of force. Among the islanders there was little resistance; most, indeed, counted themselves fortunate to take part in the Emperor's great plan to humble Paradon. Nevertheless it was with dread we saw the Imperial Fleet assemble in our harbor, and it was with relief we heard that there would be no shore-leave for the Emperor's troops. Only the Emperor's new Vassal-King, Leron the son of Mathon, landed with his attendants.

One would not expect so remote a place as Apadana to have much influence on the affairs of the World Conqueror. But it was in Apadana that sly and shocking murder was planned, against both Leron and the Commander-in-chief of the Emperor's army of occupation. Thus it was the Emperor's plans were changed without his knowledge, and thus it was that Leron added to his title of Vassal-King the greater rank of general, Commander-in-chief of the army of occupation.

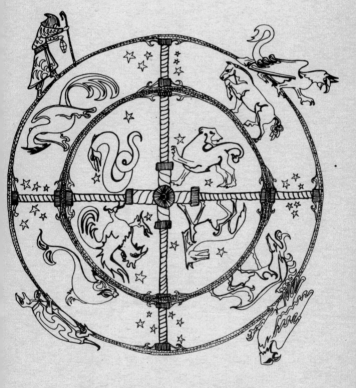

THE WHEEL TURNS

Chapter Seventeen

THE CROSSING

I

A thaw came in the deepest part of winter. The sky was blue and the air seemed warm. The Anguls shed their heavy furs, but Tamara could tell from her nose and her fingers how cold it really was, however soft the air might seem. It was all an illusion.

Now for the first time she saw the barges on which the crossing to Paradon would be made. Huge and flat-bottomed, they had been caulked tight with pitch, which had shrunk and become brittle in the cold, leaving gaps between the planks. Fires were lit in the barges themselves and new pitch was softened to improve the seal. There was some excitement when one of the barges burned through carelessness. Tamara hung around enjoying the smoke, flames and general activity, until her feet got too cold from standing. The smell of the raw lumber burning was intoxicating, and there was no harm done, except possibly in the punishment awaiting the guard who had been tending the fire.

At their narrowest point, the straits were less than a mile in width. Tibir's simple solution had been to build enough barges to make a loosely linked bridge over the turbulent water. Across it he could march his men and horses in their hundreds of thousands.

Tamara spent several days readying Faras for the grand invasion. He looked more like a ganoose than a horse, with long tufts of hair curving out of his ears, a wispy, goatlike beard and a line of silky curls down the back of each leg—

curls just the right length to wind around her finger. She lovingly groomed all these winter adornments, and unpicked the tangles in his impossibly long mane and tail. An Angul groom had showed her how to make the intricate knot with which they tied up their own horses' tails to be out of the way during combat; on Faras, the effect was particularly elegant, making his muscular haunches appear even more beautifully round. She also braided together the ends of his mane, and into the bottom, to weigh it down, she tied a silver charm that Marricson had given her out of his illicit winnings. By the time they were ready to embark, he looked very pretty.

The servants of the Empress took as much care with Tamara as she had with her horse. On the day of the great ride over the water, Tamara's skin tingled from scrubbing, and her scalp, still wet, ached with cold. Her clothing was lined with the finest and most supple sheepskin, and her boots were of embroidered leather over felt liners. She had silk next to the skin and a middle layer of soft woolen cloth. Faras, too, had a new saddle liner of bright white sheepskin; like all the better bred horses, he wore a winter bit of hard leather. The metal bits froze and pulled off bits of skin, a discomfort which the more ordinary horses had to learn to accept.

Monkey wore no bit at all, since Sibby had trained her to go as well without a bridle as with one. She had put on weight while they were snowed in, and her fluffy white undercoat made her look even rounder. Her ears were so woolly that they looked almost circular, and the bright halter of red and green yarn was buried in the thick fur that covered her face. Even her long eyelashes were tripled by winter growth.

She stood patiently, head hanging, while the fancier blood horses snorted and bounced around. Her look of calm was deceiving, however. With the onset of cold weather, Sibby had found that, when she wished to, sweet little Monkey could buck like a fiend. But today she was resigned to waiting.

The first barges had been rowed out into the morning mist that boiled up off the water. They were soon lost in the fog, except for a stray sparkle and gleam from the armored men aboard. One after another they were maneuvered onto the sands, pushed out a little way, loaded, pushed clear of shore. The vast resources of the Emperor made the undertaking seem almost ordinary, as a hundred men pushed, another hundred pulled, and a hundred more waited their turn.

By midday nearly all the great barges had been linked; Tibir had ordered eighty of them built, and with the sixty-fifth, the bridge of boats was nearly complete. The last few were poled into place and the connecting ramps dropped and secured; the long sweep of boats undulated and creaked, writhed and vibrated like a snake in its last agonies.

When all was ready, Tibir rode up on an old bay stallion who had seen twenty years campaigning. The horse was lumpy in the legs and gaunt in the head, but he arched his neck and clattered his feet proudly as he carried his master up the wooden causeway. Sibby rode at his heels, with the rest of the royal bodyguard and then the center of the army; Tamara had to wait until much later, to cross with the Empress and her party.

Faras was not amused by the hollow sound of the planking under his feet, but the other horses gave him the courage to go on. He snorted and curtsied and bumped the horses next to him, who answered with flattened ears and bared teeth until he quieted. Tamara was too entranced with her surroundings to pay any attention to his foolishness, or even to correct it. On either side as they rode there was undulating water; sounds carried clearly across to them. There was a strong smell of salt, and it seemed a most unlikely and magical thing to be crossing the water on horseback rather than boat. Her horse agreed it was unlikely.

Then Faras set foot on Paradon. It was a pebbly beach no different in appearance from the one they had left, yet Tamara felt a shiver of apprehension. A few hundred yards ahead chalk cliffs gleamed white in the winter sun. But their way led south for a distance along the beach, to a breach in the hills. They stayed well clear of the overhanging cliffs for the sake of safety, yet there was no sign of any life, no defenders, no attackers.

The first night they made a simple camp and Tamara slept huddled in her mother's arms for warmth, her back seared by the heat of the fire, her face buried comfortably against her mother's breast. Sibby's back must have been cold, but she did not mention it. Near them, the Emperor reclined in his litter, surrounded by his bodyguard and covered with furs. Tamara wondered if on nights like this he regretted the formality which kept him and his wives apart in public. But then, she thought, perhaps he is so old that he prefers being alone.

It took two weeks for the army to complete its crossing, but the carts and tents were well established within the first few days. All that was not essential had been left behind, and Tamara discovered to her sorrow that this included the special tent of the Batur Subi. They were given a place at the fires of the Empress, as before. Unusually, however, the Empress and the Agan had their tents set up adjoining, the reception chambers separate but the sleeping chambers linked. The bodyguard frowned on this unsafe arrangement, but none could question the wishes of the Agan. Personally, Tamara was relieved. She liked to picture them lying warm in each other's arms, peacefully, the way she had seen her mother asleep on her father's chest. She also liked to picture her mother and father back together again, the way they should be when the Karif was able to return from his campaign. She was sure she would be able to bring them back together if they persisted in being difficult. The problem of Leron was not so simple, but time and separation was in her favor.

Despite what Tamara assumed to be the greater comforts of his personal arrangements, Tibir did not look well. In the first days after their landing his stern face grew even harsher, his infrequent smile disappeared entirely, he spoke little and then only to rebuke or correct. His impatience increased. In the evening Sibby left his side with relief, to seek the court of the Empress and listen to Marricson singing and fooling. Then, one night, the Empress did not join her guests, and Tamara watched her mother sit brooding, chin on hands, staring into space. "Is something the matter?" She had to ask twice before Sibby turned and met her eyes.

"I don't know. It's pretty obvious that the Agan is sick, but no one knows or says anything. I think he is using all his energy now just to manage his pain. He can hardly sit up. I tried to speak with Sharkim, but he has not left the Agan's quarters."

"Tell him you're a healer, then he'll see you."

Sibby smiled at her. "They know that healing has worked through me, once or twice in the past. They also know it's not my power to control. If something is making Tibir sick, I think he'll need more than a friendly laying on of hands. If he is really sick, we will all need as much help as we can get."

Tamara sobered at this, and for the first time wondered what would happen if Tibir were not in control.

They were not left long in suspense. The Batur Subi was sent for to bring the Enku into Tibir's presence, and Tamara of Tredana followed along like a silent shadow. The inner chamber of the Agan's tent was as austere as the outer. On a low brass stand stood a sitranga board in mid-game. A large robe of furs was spread over a low, hard mattress, and the rugs on the ground were old and worn. The only luxury was the number of firebowls crowded together, heaped with coals, filling the air with a close heat. "An old man cold in winter," Tamara remembered, then bowed before the Emperor of the World.

He lay on his side, his skin paler than usual against the black sheen of Sharkim's bared arms. His lids were heavy and, with the loss of vitality, his face was suddenly ancient. Tamara had never seen so old a face on so young a body. The terrible marks of his early injuries wreathed his right shoulder in a knot of dull red scarring. The scars distorted his clan tatoo as well, the hawk that stretched from his right shoulder to his left breast. The blue of the drawing was vivid against his pallor. Another artist, less skilled than the first, had added a full moon to the picture, just within reach of the hawk's open talons: "The hawk of Zamarra has stolen the Chama's moon."

Tibir made no movement when Sharkim pushed back the fur robe that covered his legs, and then Tamara realized that he had been drugged. "He is as iron as his name," whispered Sharkim, "but even the Agan has limitations." The right hip was exposed, the twisted hip from which hung a useless right leg. The contrast was shocking: a live leg and a dead one, juxtaposed. Tibir's left leg was as well-proportioned as his arms and chest, excessively muscular perhaps, but smooth and remarkably young looking. The right leg was shriveled and crooked, useless; a shocking deformity. Where the hip bone jutted out there was a great putrid sore, the size of two spread hands.

The Empress joined them. "He has not had the full use of his leg since he was fifteen and took a spear high in the thigh. There has been a sore on his hip for the fifty years I have known him. But it has been a small place, usually smaller than my palm, sometimes less than two fingers in width. He told me before we crossed the water that his hip pained him a little, and I wondered because he never speaks of such things. But he would not show me. Then, last night when he uncovered himself, I could not believe what I saw. He told me it grew suddenly, that it was not like this before, but I do not believe him. Tonight he asked for the Enku; then, as he spoke, he was in such pain that I commanded Sharkim to give him powders. And he was in such pain that he took them."

Sharkim touched the edges of the sore gently. "I can treat its surface, but there is something inside which defies my skill. I have even tried the charms of my people, but it is stronger than any craft I have. It grows as we look at it."

Sibby touched the Bloodstone on her shoulder and looked at the Emperor's face. "How long will he sleep?"

"He is a difficult patient. I gave him enough to keep two strong men asleep for half the night. With him, I expect he will waken within the hour."

Sibby unbuckled the Enku and laid it on the ground, then knelt and touched the edges of the sore. Even in his drugged sleep Tibir flinched, and sweat formed on his face in huge drops. "I do not think he asked for the Enku," she said softly. "I think it was the Enku-dar." The light in the tent suddenly caught her red amber pin and filled it with glowing colors. She closed her eyes and for a long time all was still in the tent. Her fingertips rested lightly on the Emperor's hip.

When Sibby spoke again her voice was soft and her lips hardly seemed to move. "I am trying to go in," she said. "There is something in my way—it is cold and hard but I am pushing, gently, gently—now I am through." She paused and her face looked puzzled. "What now—there it is, the passageway leading down into the rock . . . down, down, down. It is all rock, it is cold, it is hard—" Her head turned slightly. "There is water in the stone, I can hear it running. Further now, the walls are so close . . . oh, at last! I am through." She smiled and lifted her face. "The sun is shining down here. I was afraid it would be dark. But it is too bright." Her eyes squinted at the imagined light. "I can see all is not well. There is something hiding here, in the stones." She tilted her head and smiled again. "I see you, friend hawk. There is someone here who needs your help. My friend and yours. What? It is where?"

She stooped forward until her face was inches from the

weeping sore, and Tamara's stomach rolled over in disgust. Tamara had closed her eyes before Sibby's lips touched it, but she opened them again as the Emperor's body suddenly heaved and jerked and twisted. No sound came from him, but his lips were drawn back in a grimace that made his face look like a death's head. Then his chest heaved two or three times in a spasm of exhalation and he lay still. Sibby raised her head, eyes still closed, then her face contorted and she spat violently into the air. Something small and black and wriggling seemed to fly out, and Tamara would never forget the awful cricketlike screeching it made as it burst in a tiny flash of light and was gone.

Sibby put out her arms in a vague effort to catch herself, but she fell sideways onto the floor, white as death, with a dark smear of bloody matter on her chin. Tamara did not dare move. Then Sibby's eyes fluttered and she made a face of disgust, scrubbing at her lips with the back of her hand. She rinsed her mouth with the wine that the Empress held for her and spat it out on the carpet, then drank deeply.

Soria took her by the arm. "Where did you go?"

Sibby rubbed her face. "I'm not sure. It was bright. The hawk was there. Tibir's hawk." Her head drooped again and she spoke very faintly. "He showed me where the thing was hiding, he caught it and killed it for me. Or showed me how. I'm not sure."

She turned and looked at the Agan, on whose hip the sore had suddenly paled in color, still large but less enflamed, no longer angrily running with blood and water. "There were evil things there," she said. "They were hiding everywhere. It would have been dangerous without the hawk." She drank a little more wine. "I think we were very silly to think we could land here unopposed. We expected an army, so we brought one. But I think the warlords of Paradon have already started their attack."

In the first hours following Tibir's strange cure, no one but Tamara seemed to have any concern for the health of the healer. Sharkim and Tibir's servants, the Empress and her people, all clustered about the Agan. The Batur Subi had collapsed again, and was so cold that Tamara despaired of ever warming her. She managed to lead and drag her out to a place by the fire in the Empress's nearly empty pavilion, and held her wrapped in furs. As her mother's face grew paler and paler, her breathing slower, her skin colder, Tamara felt panic rising in her throat. She wanted to go get help, but she didn't dare leave her mother alone. She clutched her more and more tightly, looking around desperately for anyone.

When Marricson came in from outdoors, Tamara cried out to him with relief. He lumbered over and picked up Sibby in his arms, then sat down carefully, holding her like a baby. Tamara knelt next to them, still holding her mother's limp cold hand. She was too distraught to hear the light step behind her, but Marricson looked up past her shoulder and smiled as Arbytis sat down beside them.

"Greetings, my son," he said to Marricson. "Your eyes did not deceive you. I have been forced to save my strength or I would have greeted you sooner." He touched Tamara's cheek as surely as though he could see her. "Courage, little one. Your mother is only resting." He leaned forward and gently laid his hands on Sibby's face, his expression like Sibby's when she touched the Emperor's wound. He looked concerned but not worried, and there was a touch of satisfaction in his voice when he spoke. "So. It has started at last."

After a moment his hands gently began to vibrate on Sibby's face, the fingertips stroking her closed lids. Tamara could see color return under his touch; her mother's eyelids fluttered and her breathing became deeper and more regular. The eyelids opened and Sibby muttered a few unintelligible words, then said clearly, "Arbytis?"

The old man nodded reassuringly, and Sibby's eyes closed again. She seemed to fall into normal sleep, and the High Priest's hands dropped by his sides. He turned his blind face to meet Tamara's questioning eyes.

"Yes, child, she begins to remember. We have reached the arena wherein the last act is to be played; now the players can drop their masks and speak their final lines."

Marricson smiled at her from over Arbytis' shoulder. "The first mask to drop shall be mine. Before I was a wandering singer I was, for a little while, a king. Your father and mother knew me well before, when I was Odric."

Tamara nodded, too numb to react properly. "But she didn't know you!"

"She will," said Marricson.

Arbytis added, "There is a price on her memory. It is a high one, so high I did not dare to name it before. But now I think she will pay it.'' Then Sibby opened her eyes again, and sat up despite Marricson's gently restraining hand.

''I'm sorry,'' she said in an embarrassed voice. ''I'm afraid I passed out.''

Arbytis bowed his head before her. ''Daughter, you must forgive me for not having acknowledged you sooner. I was once High Priest in Treglad; while you and I both live, I will try and serve you.''

Sibby passed her hand over her face. ''High Priest? Priest of what?''

Arbytis laughed. ''Priest of a temple that was destroyed a thousand years ago. Priest of the Double Goddess. And later, when Simirimia left to practice black arts in Treclere, priest of the fading goddess of old Treglad, Rianna. Now, of all that was once the glory of the temple Ornat in Treglad, there is left only the feeble remains of the High Priest Arbytis and Simirimia's half-human daughter, Sibyl. Therefore, such as I am, I am your priest.''

Sibby sighed. ''I have heard of you, but I do not remember.''

''Daughter, you *will* remember, when it is time.''

''Is there any purpose in my remembering? Am I here by chance only, or is there a design?''

Arbytis smiled. ''How you love to fight your fate. You are well named Sword-Bearer.'' He sighed. ''Of course there is a design. There is a design in everything. You are the one with eyes. Tell me what you see that is random.''

Sibby rubbed her eyes again. ''I am too tired to argue.''

''Do not say that, daughter. There is no time for rest in the days to come. You will argue for everything you hold most dear, and everything will depend on the skill with which you make your arguments.''

Sibby reached out and Tamara felt the cold fingers touch her. She interlaced her own warm ones and squeezed her mother's hand reassuringly.

''With whom must I make these arguments?'' asked Sibby.

''The formal challenge will come soon, now that you have turned aside the first secret attack.''

''Surely any challenge will come to the Agan.''

''Yes, but the challenge will concern his Sword-Bearer. You will see.''

II

Tamara wanted to listen more, but the conversation was hard to follow. She found herself yawning. Then Marricson—no, Odric—patted his knee invitingly and she climbed into his arms as though she were a little child, Geret's age or younger. She put her arms around his thick strong neck and buried her face in his soft beard and he hugged her until she fell asleep.

In Odric's arms she jerked awake twice, feeling herself falling, and both times he soothed her and she settled into sleep again. But even in sleep she continued to fall, down and out, spinning and turning in the dark. She was still falling as the darkness lightened, fading from black to dark blue to steel blue to grey. There were stars around her, huge and filled with color, sparkling. Planets too, but they were round and glowing. She passed the planets. They disappeared behind her and she continued through corridors of stars wheeling and spiraling around her until they paled and disappeared in the growing light. She was still falling when she awoke and it was morning.

The Empress's tent was empty except for her and Odric. The fire had been allowed to die down. As Tamara yawned and stretched she heard a thumping, and then from a pile of furs her shaggy batur rose, stretching fore and aft, yawning, tail beating the floor. Odric also rose and stretched and then the three of them went in search of company and food.

There was a crowd in the antechamber of the Agan's tent, waiting to see Tibir. Odric snared some stray handfuls of bread and cheese for Tamara, himself, and the dog, and then they settled in to wait. At length, the Empress appeared with several of her women. Then Taan with Arbytis. Finally, Sibby, the Enku strapped on her hip, and after her the litter of the Emperor, carried by two of his bodyguard.

Tamara could not believe that this was the sick man she had seen in the night. It was probably more force of will than recovery, but he sat straight and impassive, only his eyes a little heavier than usual. The restless crowd in the audience chamber quieted, respectful and relieved. Some indeed slipped unobtrusively out, to return to the tasks they had dropped at the rumor of the Agan's illness. Others went about presenting their daily reports and inquiries as though nothing had happened. Tibir listened, nodded, made judgments and then, through his captain, gave the order for tomorrow's march. The audience was over.

The officers dispersed, leaving the Agan alone with his court. The captain of the bodyguard had not yet left when a clatter of galloping hooves grew louder and louder outside, approaching. There was nothing unusual in this, except that the sound of galloping did not slow down, and suddenly and shockingly invaded the tent. Even Tibir looked up, though no expression appeared on his face. Batur stepped purposefully out in front of Tamara and growled, head lowered, hackles raised. The drumming increased, many horses now, making the ground seem to tremble underneath them. Then the unseen herd passed out through the far tent wall and the noises dwindled away.

Tamara's heart was pounding, but except for the drawn sword of the captain, no one else showed any change of expression. A look of irritation passed over Tibir's face. "I have not traveled this far," he said drily, "and put myself to this inconvenience to be entertained by the tricks of an illusionist. I hope there is a real army here, and not just the sound of one." He gestured to his captain. "We march today, not tomorrow. They have sent us the sound of a few men galloping. We will show them the sight of many."

They struck camp and fell into battle order, armor gleaming, weapons at hand. In order to leave the coast, their way wound through narrow clefts in the ragged cliff face that fringed the shore line. Tamara felt more alert than usual, and under her Faras bounced along with tense little steps, ears flicking, nostrils wide to catch the first hint of any unfamiliar scent. Even the imperturbable Angul soldiers showed their unease at moving inland, farther into the famous island of sorcery and power. The cliffs seemed threatening, the stony ground sterile; the air was dry and cold. A light, sleety rain began to fall, wet enough to soak clothing, frozen enough to be painful, coating many surfaces with sharp-edged ice.

They traveled a few miles through the hills, then climbed up onto the rolling grasslands that seemed to slide out over the top of the cliffs overhanging the shore. The army spread out into normal formation, the wings ranging out in long lines that reached many miles from the center. A hundred thousand

horse soldiers and their support troops slowly rode forward
into Paradon, and the sleety rain, increasing, hid them from
themselves and slowly drew them into a brilliantly white,
swirling and impenetrable fog.

At first Tamara could see far across the downs. She rode in
the center, behind the Emperor and his Sword-Bearer, and the
long, rolling sweep of snow-dusted grassland shimmered before her eyes as the air filled with damp. The air thickened
and closed in on them, obscuring the farthest soldiers. Tamara was watching Monkey's hindquarters a few horse-lengths
ahead; her tail was silver-white against her charcoal rump,
and the tail shimmered as it swung from side to side, tied in
an intricate knot above the hocks. Sibby had also knotted the
end of her own long braid, and her black tail of hair swung
from side to side on her shoulders in the same rhythm as her
horse's tail below.

Tamara blinked and tried to focus her eyes. Sibby was
almost lost in the mist and Monkey's tail was a vague shape,
no longer a white plume against a black background. Tamara
could see the soldiers riding on either side of her clearly, but
everything further away was hidden in the mists. Despite the
cold, Faras was in a sweat of nervousness, and her nostrils
filled with his pungent odor. She looked down at Faras' neck
and the brightness of his golden mane was hidden in the fog.
She could hardly see her own knees, and the riders on either
side were now hidden entirely. In some curious way the fog
covered up sounds as well as sights, and Tamara could not
hear the other riders, either. Suddenly Faras broke and bolted,
running between the Emperor and the Sword-Bearer, bouncing against the rump of the Emperor's horse. Scared and
embarrassed, Tamara tried to rein him back, but his jaw was
suddenly rigid, his neck inflexible. The fog rolled apart and
shafts of light poured out of the sky, illuminating the army
with which she rode—all strangers, except for the Agan.

She clutched at Faras' mane for support, then recoiled at
the scratchy feel. She was on a mealy-coated large pony with
a bristling black mane. The rider on her right turned to look at
her, laughing. He was tall and dressed in dark armor and his
helmet made his head look like a boar's. The rider on her left
was helmeted like a stag. She looked around a little wildly
and they were all fantastically armed, with horns and antlers
and bestial faces made of metal hiding their own.

Two of them pushed their horses together between her and the Emperor and their tall forms blocked the Agan and his horse from her. Now the sun was shining fully, and the air was extraordinarily clear and limpid, like water in a pool. The grass was green underfoot, the air cold but not wintry. There were birds in the sky. The rider on the right laughed at Tamara again and she pushed her chin up, angrily, and laughed back at him. She sensed that he was startled, despite the mask that concealed his face.

The rest of the riders veered off to the left, the Emperor riding in their midst. Tamara's escort pushed in on either side, until their armored knees jostled and bruised her legs. With her pony squeezed in between their larger horses, she was forced forward up a green hill, in sunlight so dazzling it made her eyes water. The smell of bruised grass and damp earth filled her nostrils. She could see now that all their horses were wet to the belly and, turning in the saddle, she saw a broad, flat river behind them, forded by columns of this strange new army. The far bank was shrouded in fog. On either side the land was green, a green she had forgotten during her days in the wastelands of Angulidan. Despite the lushness it made her recoil, and she felt a desperate homesickness for the wide brown sweep of the steppes.

At the top of the hill, a heavyset man stood facing away from her, hands clasped behind his back. He stood with his legs spread wide, and the furs trimming his knee-length coat made him seem even bulkier and more overwhelming. She was helped down from her pony, not ungently, and given a little push that made her stumble. The man turned slowly and looked coldly down at Tamara from under heavy grey eyebrows. His full beard was grey and red mixed, his massive head was balding; he had small eyes and a smaller mouth with very pink lips, which he moistened with his tongue before speaking.

"I am Padeshi," he said. "Chief among equals, the first of the Seven Warlords of Paradon. I will take you inside. We were not expecting anyone else from Tibir's party to join us." He smiled and showed the tip of his tongue. "I knew your mother when she was no more than the hostage queen of Tredana. You resemble her somewhat. I hope you will prove a more amenable guest. Then when the time comes, you can encourage her to be the same. Come.''

He gestured to a low opening in the hill, and moved aside so that she could step down into the darkness first.

Chapter Eighteen

THE UNDERWORLD

I

Sibby's weariness was so great that she hardly noticed the fog closing in around them as they rode. She was half asleep in the saddle when Monkey leapt sideways and whirled around to make a threatening face at the horse crowding her. Sibby's eyes snapped open and she made a clutch at Faras' rein, grabbing the wild-eyed horse as he tried to push past. His saddle was empty.

At the same moment there came a shout from the Emperor's bodyguard. The mists rolled aside to reveal one of them leaning over in his saddle, holding the Agan's horse by the bridle. Like Faras, the bay stallion was suddenly riderless. Sibby swallowed and shook her head, aware for the first time in her life of a fear that numbed her legs and made her hands heavy at her sides. The forward guards threw up their hands to signal a halt and Sibby dismounted, her legs almost buckling under her as she touched ground. She pressed her face against Monkey's neck for strength, then walked forward to examine the Emperor's horse, Faras trailing behind her. The saddle was empty, that was all. It was still warm to the touch, and the sweaty place below it where Tibir's useless leg rubbed was still smeared with foam. She covered her Bloodstone with her hand and her palm tingled with energy, but no picture came into her mind. She looked around vaguely and saw they had ridden right up to the edge of a broad, dark, sluggish river, whose width could not be judged because of the overhanging fog. On the bank a single horse stood waiting for them, a black horse in black armor.

The strange horse whinnied at their approach and turned sideways, so that the left stirrup dangled invitingly before their eyes, daring a hero to mount. The bodyguard drew back. With a feeling of inevitability, Sibby walked forward slowly, and the horse turned to her with ears pricked. His black eyes were fathomless.

"Stop here," Sibby said to Tibir's captain, and she was surprised by the firmness of her voice. "Pitch your tents and pasture your horses. I will go on alone. Send for the High Priest Arbytis, tell him what you have seen. If anyone can give advice, it is he. Wait three days for me. If I return, I will meet you here."

The black horse wore no bridle, but he stood while she mounted, then whirled on his hind legs and leapt into the stream.

He plunged through the river like a dolphin; the blood-warm water flowed past them on both sides in waves. She could not tell if her legs were wet or not. Then she blinked and ducked her head as they broke through into hard, sunny, brilliant air. The horse plunged up the grassy bank ahead, cantered up the hill then halted abruptly, putting his head down to pull at the thick green grass. It was not winter here.

Sibby slid off and touched first her amulet, then the hilt of her sword. No warning tingled in her fingers. The cool breeze struck cold on her wet legs. As far as she could see in three directions, there was nothing but rolling grassland and the shadows of high fluffy clouds chasing across the hills. Behind her was the river, its far bank hidden in mist. She sighed and stepped forward to the cavelike opening of a low swelling in the ground just ahead. A voice spoke in the darkness.

"You cannot enter here. You are not of this world. Any price you pay would be meaningless. Return to your own world, outlander."

Sibby closed her eyes and leaned against the rocky wall. "I do belong to this world," she said softly. "What must I do to prove it?"

"You must let the door be closed through which you have passed so many times. You must let the keeper of the First Gate clean the otherworld memories from your heart. You must place yourself under our laws, if you would descend to the Underworld.''

Sibby nodded slowly and the darkness opened for her. She stepped in.

Inside the air was colder, and reminded her of the Angul tombs. A few steps in and the passage turned, cutting off the light as abruptly as a knife. She closed her eyes and trailed her fingers along the wall, and took her cautious way down. The passageway was so narrow that the tip of the Enku scraped its sides behind her as she turned. Sibby could not tell if it was a return of light that finally showed her the scene ahead, or some accurate interior vision, but the passageway gradually opened, revealing a cavern with vast ribbed sides and a high rocky ceiling. The way ahead was barred by a jewelled gate, sparkling dimly in the dusk.

Before she could knock on its panels, the First Gate opened a crack and its guardian stepped through, armored in black, helmeted like a tortoise, with a harsh, beaked face. ''You cannot enter here,'' he croaked. ''Give up your sword, Sword-Bearer.'' Her cold fingers fumbled with the belt and the guardian ripped it from her hands. ''At last,'' he cried harshly. ''The Enku has returned to the Underworld.'' He placed its tip to her breast. ''I will take your promise now,'' he said and the iron burned into her chest. Pain cracked across her ribs and dropped her, breathless, to her knees. As the guardian pushed her through his gate, faces and images of her past life whirled up before her eyes, losing their meaning, fading away. She stumbled on through the dark as though drunk or asleep.

The Second Gate spanned another dim cavern, and here the guardian was helmeted in the likeness of a cock. He did not speak, but pointed at Sibby's helmet and clacked his beak together, making a jerky, lifting gesture. She took it off and shook out her coiled up hair; the keeper took the helmet and opened his gate for her to pass.

Once more she was descending in the dark; once more the passage eventually broadened into a vaguely lit cavern. Another gate, another keeper, this one wearing a helmet like a stag's head. He gestured to her golden breastplate and when it was removed, took it from her and opened the Third Gate. The guardian of the Fourth Gate was helmeted like a lion, and the toll he demanded was her heavy felt robe and stitched boots. The frosty air cut through her linen shirt as she went on, and the rocks were cold and sharp under her bare feet.

The downward path was long and uncomfortable, her feet were cut and sore by the time she came to the Fifth Gate. The keeper hissed like the serpent he was armored to resemble; he plucked the amulet from her shoulder and seemed to swallow it. In her mind she could hear him welcome the Bloodstone back to its proper world. The keeper of the Sixth Gate was helmeted like a boar, and as she waited for his demand, he rushed at her in silence and his tusks raked her breast and shoulder, knocking her to the stones. The brand of Tibir was obliterated. He shoved her through his gate and locked it behind her.

She had nothing left but the shirt she stood in and her silver ring. There was less light in the seventh cavern; that, or her sight was dimming. She collapsed against its sharp, encrusted surface, legs trembling, feet bleeding, chilled beyond warming. She hammered on it with her hand, and left bloody marks on its surface. "Open for me," she cried. "I will pay your price."

The air she breathed seemed to make her weaker. When the gate finally opened, she had difficulty lifting her head. The keeper of the Seventh Gate looked at her for a long time. He was helmeted in the likeness of a ram. He pointed at her hand and she covered the ring protectively for a moment, then pressed it against her lips. It was the hardest thing to give up because it had never been a burden. The keeper took her ring and made her finger bleed as he pulled it off. She steadied herself against the gate and walked on, dressed only in a linen shirt like a shroud.

The passage made another angled turn, and she was out in the light again, but it was a cold light—greyish, bluish, sharply edged. She looked around, puzzled, and saw that she was on a hill like the one where the black horse had left her, but under a moonlit sky. The horse that now awaited her was skeletal and white. She pulled herself up, wearily, and let herself be carried down the hill.

This horse carried her softly over the ground, grass turning to stone, stone turning to sand, sand turning to a hard clear surface like black glass. The horse's hooves never slipped and made no sound. In the shimmering distance a shiny black fortress arose, formed of the same material as the ground.

These walls, too, had a gate, but it stood open. The horse stopped under the archway, and as Sibby's bare feet touched the ground the cold stabbed up through her legs and almost made her cry out.

She forced herself to stand upright before she walked in. There seemed to be hooded beings ranged along the walls, looking at her. She felt the weight of their eyes upon her, but she could not see them clearly. It was all she could do not to stagger under the heaviness of their regard. The inner court-yard was dimmer but empty. It led to an audience chamber, pillared, lined with mirrors, darkly luminescent. There was a throne at the far end, in which a woman leaned back lazily.

Except for her long straight hair and greater height and strength, she might have been Sibby's reflection. Silver brace-lets were on her arms and she wore a long, pleated garment of mulberry-black silk. She smiled as she looked Sibby over.

"Welcome," she said, "At long last, welcome. Of your own choice you have paid the price to visit where few come willingly. What is your mission, here in the land from which no traveler returns?"

"I have come for Tibir Agan."

"The Emperor is much in demand. Vazdz himself has tried to take him from me. He wishes him to come to Inivin, to play at castledown. But first he had to send someone to me to pay my price."

"What is your price?"

"A ransom often asked and seldom paid. For one of my guests to leave my table, another must come to take his place—willingly."

"I will take the place of the Agan."

"Consider what you say, little one. In this place I am queen; none may resist me, not even Vazdz. Once I was a queen in the upper air, but all my plans were brought to ruin by you. I have waited many years to welcome you here. And now, of your own free will, there is no escape for you anymore, no convenient return to the otherworld. Sit down, daughter, and consider well what you are saying."

Sibby was finding it hard to breathe; the cold had filled her lungs and was pressing on her throat. In the emptiness of her freshly scoured mind new memories were forming, visions of past journeys in strange realms. She found the strength to bow her head, and managed an ironic inflection as she spoke.

"I beg pardon for not recognizing you at once, Great Queen. My memory has been clouded." She sat at Simirimia's feet, trying not to collapse. "Tell me what I must do to free the Agan. Willingly I have paid the price to visit your world. Does that not entitle me to answers?"

"You may ransom the Agan, but it will not be to send him back to his people. He must visit Vazdz first, to play at castledown. It is one game he is unlikely to win. You understand? You accept the terms?"

"What if the Agan wins?"

Simirimia threw back her head and laughed, her throat white, her long hair swirling like a cloud around her. "If the Agan loses I will have you both. If he wins, I will let him choose which of you returns to stay with me forever. Now, do you wish to pay so great a price for so poor a victory?"

"I will pay it. But my place is with the Agan. Will you not let me stay at his side while he visits Inivin?"

Simirimia held up her hand and Tamara stepped out of the gloom, calm-faced and empty-eyed. The queen flicked her hand and Tamara awoke, her horrified expression telling Sibby more clearly than any mirror how she must look.

"Your loyalty to the Agan is touching. More so than your sense of motherhood. You will give your life to save the bloody murderer of millions, an infirm man of seventy years, and leave to me your little daughter? Youth such as hers is highly prized among us here in the Underworld. Are you certain you have chosen correctly?"

Sibby closed her eyes, but Tamara's sweet face would not be shut out. She could still see Tamara bending over her, eyes filled with concern, her warm hand clutching her own cold one. Then in her mind's eye she saw Arbytis also, leaning over Tamara's shoulder.

"Is the Great Queen so hungry for flesh," she asked, "that she wastes her time with this little girl when her greatest enemy lies within her grasp?"

"Who is this great enemy?" hissed Simirimia.

Sibby spoke firmly. "My High Priest Arbytis. The priest who despises you, and who denies the rule of Vazdz. He waits in the upper air above with the army of Tibir, ready to see your ruin and the humbling of Vazdz. Send Tamara to fetch him. He will come to you gladly. Or are you afraid to face him? In that case you are safer preying on children."

"*Your* High Priest! He is mine, and has been for more than a thousand years. I have had his eyes, and now I will have his soul." Simirimia rose and stretched her white arms above her head. Under her gaze, Tamara drooped and her face grew blank again. "I will send her as you say, to summon the old man forth. But not until he comes will I release you even to Vazdz."

Sibby raised her eyes to Simirimia. "How will Arbytis pass the gates?"

"They will stand open for your daughter's replacement. But he must find his way here within the next seven days. After that the gates will close, and they will not open again to let you out, not even so far as Inivin to watch the Agan play his final game. Pray that the old man comes."

Simirimia drew her silver collar from her neck and it turned in her hands into a small, slim serpent.

"Come here," she said, "I have waited many years to correct this error."

Sibby bowed her head before her and felt a band of ice encircle her neck. As it tightened, her breath stopped and her vision blackened. Through the rush of blood that blocked her ears she heard Simirimia's mocking reminder of seven days.

II

At first she was only aware of blackness. She was walking through blackness, breathing black air. Then she stumbled and fell to her knees, and her groping hands felt an inert body on the stones in front of her. Cold as she was, he was so much colder; her hand felt the age-sculpted face, the braided hair, and she recognized the Agan. Had she not paid enough to buy his release? She held her hand over his face and felt no breath, no warmth. The collar around her neck tightened but she fought the rising faintness and laid her face against Tibir's chest. She could not hear or feel a heartbeat, but his chilly flesh warmed under her touch. She lay down next to him on the icy ground and put her arms around him. The necklet tightened cruelly.

In her arms, the Agan began to writhe and choke. His breath came suddenly in loud harsh gasps, and slowly he was transformed into a rough-coated animal rippling with muscle, with gaping jaws, hot stinking breath and sharp-nailed feet. His claws ripped across her back and sank into her shoulders, but she held him down to the ground, even though his jaws were snapping next to her head. Blood ran down her back and she felt her strength run out also. Then the Agan heaved again in her arms and rippled into a long and limbless, cold and muscular creature. She heard him hiss and felt the flick of his tongue before his fangs stung her neck and the venom spread burning through her veins.

Sibby held on and the Agan flapped and beat the air around her, transformed into a fierce eagle, ripping at her belly with his talons, slashing at her face with his beak, hissing and shrieking in anger. She pinned him to the ground with her body and he was suddenly a man again, uncrippled, with strong arms and legs that overwhelmed her strength. He rolled her over and crushed her against the stones and she saw him in his battles—armed with a sword, an axe, a spear. Blood flowed over his booted legs, heads rolled at his feet, the horses he rode trampled bodies into the mud of number-less battlefields. Smoke swirled around him from burning cities and the shrieks of murdered innocents filled the air. In her horror, she finally loosened her grip, but in this final transformation he was the one with strength and he held her. Tight as his arms were, her collar was tighter. She could not fight it any longer and her conciousness faded away.

The only reality was cold. It slowed time so that her thoughts wandered on long journeys in the space of a single, squeezing heartbeat. She was neither sitting nor standing nor lying down, but it took an infinity of slow thinking before she realized that she was hanging with her arms bound above her head. She was so out of touch with her body that it did not seem a very interesting discovery.

It was dark as well as cold. After a long time stars appeared in the darkness, very near and bright. It was no longer possible to say what was up or down. The stars, like the dark, were all around her. There were planets also, glowing with color that reminded her of life, of all the joys and pleasures she would never see again. She would have wept but the effort was beyond her, and tears would have frozen in her eyes.

From her place among the stars she watched with scant

interest the curve of earth overhead, or possibly underfoot. The shapes of land and water meant nothing to her, until she realized that anything she looked at increased in sharpness and detail as though she were adjusting a lens. Zamarra sparkled blue in the desert like a gemstone set in yellow gold. Its domes were lovely, and she had trouble remembering why Tibir was never going to see his city again. From above, she could see where Yokan had stood, its foundation stones clear under the river that swirled over it. And the sparkle of Gagan-ala was such that no detail could be seen, only a flash of brightness at the edge of the sea.

Darkness curved over the edge of the land and hid it from her. It was turning, she was turning; she could not tell which. Six times the world turned dark then light over her head, and as it turned her eyes failed; even the stars and planets near at hand lost their brilliance. It was so hard to remember now what it was she had feared leaving, feared losing. Something to do with holding and being held. As the stars darkened and went out, she knew herself to be back in the courts of the Underworld. It was completely dark, and the circlet bit deep in her neck.

There was a flash of brilliance before her eyes and she suddenly remembered having been in an icy underworld where flame had danced in reflection on the ice. The image teased at her memory as she hung there, hearing from afar the voice of the Great Queen as she ordered the Seven Gates shut. The deep reverberation of their closing rocked the chamber in which she hung. She could hear the Queen of the Underworld counting, but there was a long pause after six. Then the Great Queen shouted aloud with triumph. "Arbytis! Have you come to serve in my new temple?"

Sibby thought she had forgotten pain, but the searing agony that burst into her lungs and heart as she tried to breathe was greater than any pain she had ever known. Then she felt a ripping at her throat and she was able to draw a deep breath. She opened her eyes to see a small brown hawk hanging with beating wings in the air before her face. A silver snake writhed in his curved bill. He caught it in one foot and severed its head, dropping the pieces to the floor as he rose in the air to hover above Arbytis' bent head. Arbytis raised his robed arm and the hawk disappeared in his hand like a conjurer's dove. "I have come to serve you and your daughter," he said at last.

He walked past Simirimia's throne and stood by Sibby's dangling feet. He held up a small wineskin and poured a few drops on her ankles. The trickling wine felt like liquid fire and made her writhe in her bonds, until the thongs loosened and she fell to the floor in a heap. Arbytis lifted her chin and a mouthful of wine burned the cold out of her throat; he then produced a morsel of bread, which he crumbled between his fingers and insisted that she swallow. "Eat," he said. "It comes from the land of the Upper Air." Her heart gave a great leap in her chest and beat wildly and hard for several minutes before settling into its usual steady rhythm. She rolled over onto her face and forced herself onto her knees. Then, with Arbytis' help, she stood up. She was alive; the cold dank air smelled delicious.

Simirimia had resumed her throne. Her chin was resting on one hand as she watched them. Arbytis turned to face her and bowed deeply.

"As once long ago you wished, I am yours to command."

"How will you serve me? The Queen of the Underworld does not need a priest. I left the ambitions of the Upper Air long ago."

"Simirimia, you may use me as you will. I will be your priest if you wish it. Or I will sit at your table in place of the child who summoned me here."

"How can you take her place? In the world above you were famous for one thing only after your skills and wisdom had faded; the inability to die."

"And if I lose that famous inability, then you will know your master Vazdz has completed his term of rule."

Simirimia shook her head. "Vazdz is Lord of all, Lord forever."

Arbytis shook his head. "He is Lord of Some and only for a little. With the New Age, all will change. Have you forgotten everything you knew when you were one with Rianna? The stars dance even here, in the Underworld. The Great Wheel turns."

Simirimia stood up and took hold of Arbytis by the front of his gown. "Do you still persist in this foolishness? What connection can there be between the progression of the stars and the power of Vazdz? You have soothed yourself with this fantasy of the Great Year ever since Vazdz and I broke the power of the Double Goddess, a thousand years ago. And he was lord a thousand years before that."

"Lord for the term of the Serpent, but lord no longer. The Firebird rises in the east, and he will snap the Serpent as easily as that little hawk broke your charm."

Simirimia laughed and released the old man contemptuously. "When you tricked me out of my kingdom, you thought yourself clever. And then, when the petty kings of Vahn resisted submission to Vazdz, your faction thought Vazdz must be powerless. Now you have seen him humble the so-called Conqueror of the World."

"We have seen him challenge the World Conqueror. We have not seen him win. Your famous Vazdz does not even dare let him keep his Enku or his Enku-dar. Of what is he so afraid?"

"Afraid? Lord Vazdz fears nothing. Sit down, priest, and wait at my feet. We will watch him win together."

Simirimia's cold green eyes looked straight at Sibby for the first time, and her lip lifted slightly in distaste. "It will give me great satisfaction to destroy the memory of my one mistake. But I can wait for my pleasures. You may go back to the land of the Upper Air, but you must stay within the enchanted realm. Go to Inivin. You have eaten the bread of life and drunk its wine. You will have the strength to go as far as that. And when the game is lost, Tibir will choose and we will welcome you back."

She turned to Arbytis. "Too bad, priest, you saw so little of her future. You might have helped her save herself. She should have left a token of herself behind, a charm to draw her back to the land of the living. You should have warned her, priest."

Sibby tried to touch Arbytis, but he shrank away as though he could see her hand. "You may not touch me now," he said softly. "Never again. Touch nothing, take nothing, go your way with my blessing. It may be you will find there is a token to draw you home."

Sibby raised her eyes once more to the Great Queen's face. "How do I find my way to Inivin?"

"Inivin will find you. My guides wait above. And in Inivin they are impatient for your coming." Sibby hesitated, eager to go, unable to leave Arbytis without a word of farewell. He smiled and gestured with his hand. "Begone, my child, your work is only starting. They are playing a great game in Inivin. And when this is over you must remember to give my blessing to another dear friend, my brother in blood these forty years past. Salute the Karif for me."

Sibby stumbled out through the gate and the doors shut behind her, leaving her in the dark.

No horse waited to take her across the glassy plain. She slipped and fell on her knees and cut her palms, then scrambled to her feet and slipped another few steps. Eventually she reached the rocky hillside where the passage of seven gateways led to the Land of Upper Air. The journey out was all uphill, all black. The gates opened for her, but she did not see them until she struck them with her hands and sometimes her face; she tripped and stumbled on the rocks and once more her feet were blistered and bleeding. When the last turn brought her into daylight, she fell forward on her face and buried her hands in the grass, pressing herself into the ground, crying. The black horse snuffling the back of her head reminded her of her duty.

When she stood up, she was shocked to see how thin and white her legs looked, poking out from under the ragged hem of her bloodstained shirt. Her arms and hands also looked gaunt and unfamiliar; she felt her face and the skull was prominent under the skin. The only color she had was blood and bruises. Although the horse stood as patiently as before, it was almost beyond her strength to pull herself into the saddle.

The sun was as bright as before, the air as clear. The horse cantered comfortably over the grass, so lightly that she had no sense of any variation in the terrain. For a long time they traveled south, the river on their right hand, until they reached a boggy area of stagnant streams and brilliant green islands. The horse slowed slightly, picking his way through the treacherous ground. The river curved around before them, widening as it flowed into a sea inlet. The fog that marked its opposite bank coiled up into a great bank of clouds. The horse stood on the shore and looked across the water, ears pricked, nostrils snuffing the wind. If he had said "Inivin," she could not have understood him more clearly.

Sibby slipped to the ground and her hand trailed over the ornamental saddle. The habit of years could not be denied. "I don't think you can possibly be a real horse," she said, "but that doesn't keep me from treating you like one." She unfastened the girth and tipped the heavy saddle off onto the ground. As the harness fell off his body, the horse exploded into an enormous buck and squealed with delight. And as he squealed he disappeared, slowly fading into nothingness. Sibby shrugged and pushed at the saddle with her bare foot. It was still solid and real. She walked down to the sea's edge and it was real, too—cold and foamy. She felt light-headed now, and silly. She walked out into the water and looked at the scum forming around her ankles. "I sure hope this is the way to Inivin and not a permanent path back to where I just left." She launched herself forward into the cold green water.

She was too weary to swim more than a few strokes, but those few strokes carried her out into a strong current where she turned and floated on her back, arms spread, savoring the heat of the sun on her death-chill flesh. She washed death off of her skin and out of her hair, she gulped up mouthfuls of sea water and spit it out again, rinsing her teeth and mouth clean. She was still cleaning herself when the current bumped her onto the farther beach.

The sun was hot here. She wished more than anything to just lie on the sand, baking. In her head she argued with herself, asking what on earth she thought she was doing lying there when there was still work to be done. She groaned and rolled over and once more heaved herself onto her feet, brushing the sand from her rapidly drying body. Inivin seemed to be a place of trees. Scrubby woods started just past the high-tide mark, and thicker woods could be seen beyond. When she turned and looked back across the inlet, low clouds hid Paradon from sight.

Boots crunched on the sand and she turned slowly. Several tall men in armor were looking at her, their expressions hidden behind their full helmets. These helmets, like those of the guardians of the Underworld, were fantastic in design, with animal faces, horns and antlers. One of them held out a surcoat of red silk, which she slipped on. The belt went around her twice. They gestured and she had no choice but to follow, flinching a little as her bare feet stepped on sharp stones and prickle-leaved weeds, hurrying to keep up with their long, heavy strides. She missed the feel of the Enku on her hip.

from Arbytis' Concerning the Prophecies of Ornat

I was born in the last days of an earlier age, the Great Year of the Grey Wolf. I remember well when the Serpent came to power, for in his rising he put aside the Goddess and destroyed the Temple Ornat where I had been High Priest. He cursed me, then, and his curse has been my blessing as well as my burden. Alone among men I have lived to see the end of the Great Age that I saw begin. Alone among my fellow priests I have lived to see the truth of our Oracle.

> *Even the deathless ones of high descent*
> *Even the daughters of the Great Mother*
> *Even these Goddesses of most excellent aspect*
> *Even these shall not escape the Yinry.*

> *The law binds all from lowest to most high*
> *The sun is bound by day, the moon by night*
> *Bound in their dance the stars and wandering planets*
> *Bound are the seasons to their turning wheel*
> *O Petitioner, even you are bound*
> *Run if you will, but none escape the Yinry.*

The Yinry are the servants of the Underworld, the hooded watchers who fly abroad in search of lawful prey. I have seen many who thought to escape them, but none who were successful. The Great Queen Simirimia put her trust in Vazdz but when she broke the law the Yinry took her to serve below as she had served above. Vazdz could not shield her from their eyes. Nor can he save himself once the Great Wheel turns.

Chapter Nineteen

THE GAME OF CASTLEDOWN

At first Sibby saw nothing on Inivin to suggest the trappings of a great god. Scrubby trees and low bushes pushed their way up through sandy soil; the beach was littered with brown and white shells and pebbles of granite and quartz. Crabgrass and drying seaweed ornamented the shoreline. Gods, even false ones, should live on lofty mountains, or in marble courtyards, or under the sea. Not in a wrack of weed and driftwood. Sibby laughed at Inivin's unimpressive shore until her escort turned their hidden faces on her. They were sobering.

They led her up a low hill, three warriors on either side, to where the seventh man waited at the top. His helmet was unadorned. "Welcome to Inivin," he said. His voice was vaguely familiar. "You are resilient, Queen. In my own way I, too, have returned from death. I knew we were well matched when we first met. I should have pressed you then a little harder."

Sibby stared into his shadowy visor. "I have never been in Paradon," she said.

"True," he answered. "And this is your first meeting with the fabled Padeshi, whose place I have taken since I came to Paradon." He gestured to his left. "Here are Mimbash, Sahlar, Mulke." He waved his other hand. "And here are Arbab, Dallal, Zehar. The warlords of Paradon never change, though mortal men come and go as they take the roles. Before I was Padeshi of Paradon I was Master of Vahn, and once you knew me well."

Sibby drew herself up, proud in her weakness. "I had heard Bodrum was dead," she said.

"No more dead than my bastard boy Odric, whose blood I can smell at the distance of ten miles, even amidst the crowd in Tibir's camp. Like the Queen of the Underworld, I, too, have waited to wipe out the great mistakes of my past. You must tell me sometime, if you live, how it was she let you go.'' He drew her forward by the sleeve. "But the lord of Inivin awaits you, and I and my brothers in Vazdz have a pleasant task before us.'' He spread his fleshy hands wide and an army revealed itself around them on the hillside, armored in black on black horses. "The last soldiers of Tammush have gathered their forces at the bridge of boats. The leaderless army of Tibir is in panic in the mists of Paradon. Now my brothers and I ride to trample them into the ground. The historians will only know this, that the World Conqueror took a hundred thousand men to invade a little island, and that he and his men were never seen again.''

The warlords mounted their chargers. "You may tell this to Tibir, if you can take his mind from the game.'' When they rode away she heard nothing; they flickered and were gone.

Sibby stood alone on the hilltop, looking about her. She examined the crabgrass about her feet: it looked, felt, even tasted real, sharp-edged, stringy, salty. But she was no longer sure that anything on Inivin was as it seemed. She stood with her back to Paradon and stared toward the unremarkable center of Inivin. Then she closed her eyes and covered them with her hands. At first there was nothing but darkness. Then little flashes of light, gold and purple, and circling through the flashes, a small dark figure like a bird. She walked toward him, and her bare feet felt a smooth surface underfoot. She sensed rather than saw a flight of stone stairs before her. She had not climbed more than a few steps when the warmth of the sun was cut off and she knew herself to be somewhere inside. Slowly, she opened her eyes.

She was on a winding stair made of highly polished marble, pale and greyish. Walls of the same material vaulted overhead, meeting in a central seam high above that was striped with gold. Light shone through the walls. The stair appeared to circle as it climbed, but the lack of any point of reference made judgment difficult. Was she really climbing? Sometimes it felt as though she were on the level, or even descending, though to her eyes the steps always went up. Was she turning, or going straight? How long had she been climbing? There was nothing to do but lift her feet and place them down, again and again and again. Her sore knees hurt and trembled, the weakened muscles in her thighs were burning. Her breath came harshly and her heart pounded in her chest. Several times she tried to count, but before she could reach a hundred she would lose her place and start over. She was not sure how many times this happened.

The stairs did have an ending: an archway filled with light was finally before her. She stepped out onto a platform so high above Inivin, the clouds were below the railing that encircled it. In the center there was a low table made of some gleaming metal, and on it a game of castledown was in progress. Tibir was in widegame: he raised his hand to cast the stones and his arm shook with weariness. He was still in his battle armor, his pointed helmet lying on the smooth floor by his feet, the meshed gloves next to it. His eyes were hooded with fatigue but his narrow mouth was shut firm. In him, she could see neither the beast nor the butcher—neither could she see any remainder of the strength he had seemed to possess in the Underworld. But perhaps that had all been Simirimia's illusion. His throw was a good one, but it took him longer than usual to set aside the stones and move his piece with his left hand, his right arm twitching uselessly by his side.

Tibir's opponent was a young man with curly brown hair, casually dressed in gold-embroidered white. His youthfulness was in cruel contrast to Tibir's age. He had no beard, and his eyes were a strange light blue, like colored glass. He considered Tibir's move for a few moments before turning in his carved chair to look at Sibby. He laughed delightedly. "The Emperor's Sword-Bearer! Or the Enku-dar, as our Angul friends would say! Have you come to watch Us win?"

He turned an apparently guileless face on her, but with her inner vision she could see all his other faces flowing over this one like waves making patterns in the sand. They were old, middle-aged, young; they were fair, dark, yellow, brown, black; there was no kindness in any of them. She shook her head.

"Without suspense there cannot be a game."

She walked over to Tibir and placed her hands on his shoulders, gripping hard. The armor was between them, but at her touch he straightened and drew a deep breath. "You are welcome again to me, my daughter."

Vazdz looked at the board again, then leaned back in his chair. Once more he addressed Sibby over the head of the Emperor. "You will learn much here," he said, "but it is of little account, since you will not be able to pass your knowledge on. Your Agan plays well at this game, for a child of seventy years; but I was a master at castledown a thousand years before he was born. You have heard the story of Chanaga Gagan, and how he was bested by a blind beggar in his own camp, and humiliated before his men? I was that blind beggar. I have been many things in many stories, and always I have won.''

''A notable triumph,'' said Sibby shortly. ''I am surprised that the minstrels do not sing of it. But perhaps your minstrels do.'' She still had her hands on the Agan's shoulders, and her breath was coming hard as she tried to force all her strength and power into his failing body.

Vazdz finally made his move and bettered his position a little. ''This is our final game,'' he said. ''We have each had a victory. But the third game tells the tale, and the third game will be mine.''

''What is the prize?'' asked Sibby. ''Or better yet, the price?''

Vazdz smiled at her little joke, showing clean white teeth. ''The prize is winning and the price is losing,'' he answered, laughing now at his own wit. ''The Agan is no longer a penniless young adventurer, playing castledown—pardon, sitranga— in the hope of a prize of money! And what is there of value in the whole world I could offer him? Except, of course, his life.''

Tibir was still in widegame: he had to make at least another throw before he could return to the main part of the board. His features had not changed listening to Vazdz's banter, but as he shook the stones in his hand he made a remark to no one in particular. ''I always heard that the great Chanaga Gagan was middling poor at sitranga. He never sat and thought if he could be up and doing.'' He threw a nine and deliberately moved his general back into the battleground. ''I, too, might have been as impetuous as Chanaga Gagan,'' he said. ''But a kindly fate put a spear through my hip, and from time to time I have been forced to sit and consider the shape of things, the pattern of events. I am only half a man, but I have conquered the whole world. No whole man has ever done half so much.''

Vazdz looked at the board and his eyes shone brilliantly. Sibby felt Tibir straightening under her touch, while she herself felt weaker, so much so that she now was leaning on him. ''Perhaps,'' Vazdz said nastily, ''a spear through your other hip would have given you the time to learn to read. The

Conqueror of the World: an illiterate, unable to read, unable to write, unable to count, unable to calculate. For all your vaunted conquests, you have never mastered the simplest lessons.'' He moved a piece, his fingers straying doubtfully over the board.

Tibir smiled. "A man's lifetime is not long enough for all lessons. I chose to master the difficult ones. Tell me, how many years did it take you to gain a passable mastery of the board? Five hundred? I do not think I played a truly masterful game until I was well past—twenty.'' He moved a minor piece, off to one side, and sat back satisfied.

Vazdz studied the board and his puzzlement was clear to Sibby, even though the course of the game was not. Vazdz looked up and his light blue eyes glistened at her. "And what is your purpose in coming here? A Sword-Bearer looks oddly useless without a sword. Where did you leave it? In the heart of an enemy?''

Sibby tried to straighten her shoulders as she answered wearily. "I gave it to the guardian of the First Gate.''

"Of course—when you paid that little visit to your mother. I do not think the Agan is aware that he has had the daughter of a goddess fetching and carrying for him. Surely he would have enjoyed the rightness of it, that the daughter of the Queen of the Underworld should carry the arms of one who has been the Angel of Death to so many.''

Tibir never took his eyes from the board, waiting for Vazdz to make his move. But he was listening. "It was clear to me,'' he said, "when first I saw her, that more than mortal blood flowed in her veins. I confess I did not suspect a relationship with the Dark Goddess. Now I understand the source of her strange healing powers. It is ironic that she has used her skills to disappoint her mother.''

"Disappoint?'' cried Vazdz. "Not at all! Once, it is true, she spent her time weeping over hurt animals—berating others for taking part in passages of arms—but how times change! Now she takes her place in the bloody shadow of the World Conqueror, carrying his sword, helping him count his skulls, warming herself by the heat of burning cities, burning bodies.''

Tibir frowned, but whether it was at the board or the words of Vazdz, it was impossible to say. His hand strayed toward the board, then rested again as he considered the moves. "She carried the sword of the great Gagan as she was intended,'' he said, "but she did not use it. And now it seems she has given it back to his keepers.''

Vazdz suddenly stood up, locking his hands behind his back, walking around the board to stand by Sibyl and view the game from Tibir's side. His body emanated cold to the same degree a man would shed his warmth. "A fine distinction," he hissed. "Listen to our illiterate casuist! Has not every moralist in every era agreed that the armorer shares the guilt of the warrior?"

Tibir did not let his eyes stray from the board. "If one did that," he said, "one would have to blame iron for existing. Iron has many uses, but it is no accident that in my language Tibir means blade, as well as the metal from which a blade is hammered. When I was a child I heard a prophet telling of Vazdz, the Avenging God, and he said, 'the glittering blade of the Angul is the instrument of his severity.' I thought he referred to me by name."

Vazdz slowly returned to his side of the table, and made a move. Tibir laughed. "Vazdz, for more than fifty years I have been the instrument of your severity. Now it seems I must also be the agent of your destruction." He made another seemingly insignificant move, and leaned back slightly in his chair. His hand was trembling more than ever, and there was also a slight twitch under one eye. Vazdz leaned over the board, examining the pieces, while around them the sky darkened and the air grew colder. The air trembled around them as though threatening thunder, and Sibby blinked as the pieces seemed to rearrange themselves before her eyes. She thought it was her fatigue, but Tibir clicked his tongue disapprovingly.

"For shame," he said in a voice deeper and more commanding than the god's. He tried to rise to his feet, and with Sibby's assistance managed to hold himself partially upright. "For shame," he said again. "I have killed many men, but I have never cheated. It is well that the New Age is at hand. The sun must be weary of rising in your house."

Vazdz sat down in his chair and examined the board calmly. "So you are another of those fantasists who believes my power has some connection with the revolving stars?" He spun his hand around. "The stars turn constantly, but no one has ever proved a connection with the affairs of gods or men. This coming year will be a disappointment for you. I have no plans for the lessening of my powers. If you cannot even win a simple game against me, how can you hope to take away my strength? Sit down, little king, and make your move.''

Tibir made no move to sit, still leaning heavily on Sibby's arm. ''I have made my move, trickster, and I have won. Return me to my army as you said. I claim no other prize.''

Vazdz's face darkened and he looked older; there was grey in his hair. ''The game is not finished,'' he said. ''Sit down and play.''

Tibir deliberately leaned down and moved three or four pieces with his left hand. ''This is the truth of the board, before you worked your illusions. I have won. Return me to my men.''

Vazdz pressed his lips together and went to the parapet, looking down into the clouds. ''You have been away longer than you think,'' he said. ''Your men are no longer where they were. The warlords of Paradon have routed them utterly, ridden them into the dirt. Whoever lived to flee to the bridge of boats has been cut down by the soldiers of Tammush, waiting on the other side. They crave revenge for your murder of their prince, and I have given it.''

''The execution of Tammush was long overdue. And his men will fight for whoever pays them and take no heed of revenge. Do not lie to me any more. My men have not wavered in the worst campaigning. Return me to them.''

Vazdz raised his hand as though he would strike, his face contorted with rage. ''I tell you they have fled. You are a conqueror with no conquests, a general without an army; your only retainer is a weaponless Sword-Bearer. I have beaten you on the gameboard and I have beaten you in the field. Go see for yourself, lame one! I will spare you the stairs, for you will need all your strength to drag yourself out of my country. The sons of Tammush await you. But do not think they will kill you as quickly as they have killed your men.''

The thunder that had been threatening in the distance rumbled overhead. Sibby ducked under Tibir's arm and tried to hold him upright as the cold wind blasted against them and the icy rain followed after, in solid sheets of water. She closed her eyes, slipped and found her balance again, then recoiled as her bare foot struck something yielding and the stench of death filled her nostrils. Lightning snapped in the air and lit the battlefield where they stood—a battlefield strewn with corpses as far as could be seen in the rain and dark. The standard of Tibir lay just before them, ridden into the mud.

Chapter Twenty

WAR'S END

I

As the noise of the fighting came closer, Tamara tried to bury her aching head under the pillows. The Empress's tent was no longer the island of safety it had always seemed. It was easy to imagine the sword of the enemy ripping through its silk sides, cutting down its poles and lines, trampling its inhabitants to death. When Tamara first had come back from her puzzling sojourn in the dark, Arbytis had seemed to be waiting for her. He had heard her story, unsurprised, and set out confidently into the night like a sighted man on a well-lit road. Tamara had been ashamed at the relief she felt to stay safely behind in the light, with friends. She no longer felt so privileged.

At the Emperor's command, the Empress and her party had remained encamped on the shore, protected by the rear guard and part of the center. The disappearance of the Emperor had stretched their nerves taut; much of the eagerness with which Tamara had been greeted lay in their hope of some word on his fate. Tamara had disappointed them. When the first fighting started she had felt the tension in the Empress's party increase, and now, after several terrible days, she knew that some of the guard were deserting, fleeing back toward the bridge of boats. The Empress had put on body armor and had given Tamara a short sword and a shield. Odric had saluted the one, embraced the other, and left to join in the battle. The noise of the fighting increased.

Tamara flinched at the touch on her shoulder, then sat up

shame-faced and bowed her head before Soria. It was the middle of the night, and the battle was louder than ever. "Put on your breastplate," said the Empress. She herself was dressed in armor, and her helmet hung from one hand. "They can kill us, but no man will ever be able to say he dishonored the Agan in his own tent. We will give them no prisoners." Tamara's fingers trembled on the straps. She felt so cold it was hard to hold on to the sword the Empress pressed into her fingers.

Side by side they sat in the antechamber, in the dim light of the embers that lined the cooling firebowls. Tamara wondered if the bodyguard had fled, but could not ask. As flurries of galloping hooves surrounded the tent she looked up questioningly, and the Empress softly answered her with a shake of her head. "The left wing has broken. But the right will hold. And no one has ever got the better of the center. They are the Emperor's men."

Shortly before dawn a fierce storm swept over them, rattling the sides of the tent in violent gusts that filled the chamber with freezing air. Lightning cracked overhead and thunder made the ground rumble underfoot. As violently as the storm had come, it passed over. But the cold dawn brought no peace. There was no lessening of the terrible sounds of fighting. At the Empress's bidding Tamara got up stiffly and went to the entrance. A light rain was falling, fine and intense, too thick for her to see anything. The sound of fighting confused her, though—it seemed to come from both north and east, not only from the fields where the Emperor had disappeared, but also from the shore where they had disembarked from the bridge of boats. The Empress joined her and put her hand on her shoulder. "At least there will be no more rout," she said. "There is to be no escape from this accursed island. We have been surrounded." Tamara squinted up toward the veiled sky. She had never before been awake at dawn and felt no lifting of spirit. The sun was rising and it did not matter, because it was going to be her last day on earth.

The rain lessened a little. The clearing air revealed dead men, dead horses, confusion, destruction; and beyond it all, the noise of fighting was undiminished. From the direction of the mainland she could faintly hear the sound of Angul drums and trumpets, and she was too tired and confused to wonder that troops in rout should indulge in such a display. When she heard troops galloping toward them from the east, she shrank back into the tent and tried to grip her sword with authority. She had it over her head, held tight in both hands, when they invaded the tent.

The first men stumbled in and threw themselves on their knees, supporting themselves on stained swords, the points digging into the carpet. As they hung their exhausted heads, their captain came in behind them, bloodied and filthy. He stood in the doorway loosening his helmet, then smiled at Tamara as he dropped stiffly on one knee before the Empress. Soria closed her eyes and drew a deep breath as she held out her hand to him. "Welcome, Batur. We did not expect a rescue."

Tamara lowered her sword and looked at her father in bewilderment. Ajjibawr smiled again, crinkling around the eyes, and before he could get to his feet she had thrown her arms around his neck and buried her face against his. He stank of sweat and was shaking with fatigue: she rubbed her face against the stubble of his cheek and hugged him as hard as she could. He brushed his lips against her forehead and gently pushed her back. "Sweetheart," he murmured, "our troubles are far from over."

Soria was looking at them with raised eyebrows. Ajjibawr briefly inclined his head once more. "Your pardon, Agana. It was not possible to tell you before. She is my only child. By a twist of fate she was raised in Tredana, but her patrimony is the desert. Before I left home to play at outlaw, I was Karif of all the Karabdu. This has been a year for many roles. As leader of the army of occupation I left you; now I return as leader of the army of liberation."

"God willing, there will be time for your story later. What was the condition of our troops at the bridge?"

Ajjibawr raised an eyebrow. "Poor," he said briefly. "They met a small force there, the last of the armies that were pledged to Tammush, and such was their broken condition they could not hold battle formation. They were being cut down by a smaller and less well-horsed force when I arrived. Fate favored us and we turned the battle to our favor. I have left the bridge under guard and we now march to reinforce the center and the left. What news of the Emperor?"

The Empress shook her head. She told him of the disappearances, and Tamara filled in with what little she remembered of her journey into the dark. Of what happened after she had followed the warlord into the hill she recalled little, except for a long trip alone through dark passageways, and a strange awakening face to face with her mother and another woman, whom she did not know. She had been told to find Arbytis and she had; why, she did not know. Ajjibawr nodded as he listened.

"Arbytis will explain all when we see him. Have you seen your mother since?"

Tamara shook her head and, from the corner of her eyes, saw the Empress's tired face suddenly lift in lines of understanding.

Ibrasa appeared at the entrance in full armor, and his eyes lit up at the sight of Tamara. Then he bowed to Ajjibawr and said that all was in order for the advance of the troops. "You should be safe here," said Ajjibawr to the Empress. "As safe as any of us can be. I regret to tell you that supplies are not in order and I see no prospect of improving the situation here. There is flour and meat and wine in our stores on the mainland. Do you prefer to await us there or stay here?"

"We will stay here," said the Empress firmly. "We await your message that the warlords of Paradon have been driven back into the mists that spawned them."

Ajjibawr bowed to the Empress, then took Tamara's face in his hands and kissed her forehead again. "Be of good heart, my daughter," he said. "This morning has brought us the first day of spring, and the sun has risen in the House of the Kermyrag. Surely a new age has dawned, and the terrors of the old are past."

Tamara had her hands dug into the leather coat covering his battered mesh armor. As he gently pried them loose, she twined her fingers in his. "I am coming with you," she said, and he smiled ruefully.

"I could never tell your mother anything. I don't see why I should expect you to be more obedient. Wear a helmet."

The rain thinned into needle-fine spray as they followed the well-worn path to the battlefield. On either side of the main road lay the dead and dying, the wounded crying for help. Tamara forced herself to stare straight ahead, though the sights and the smells made her stomach clench and her eyes water. She concentrated on sitting up straight like the Karif, and raised her chin another notch. As they approached the plains, Ajjibawr signaled to his officers and sent small groups to rally the huddled and dispirited forces of bewildered, leaderless men. She heard them signal with trumpets and play the great war drums, and sensed that the army was pulling itself together after a period of stark terror.

By noon they were on a hill overlooking the plain where the center had made its stand. There was nothing but carnage to be seen: even the great standard of Tibir was buried in the morass of mud and death ahead. The Karif turned his horse around, his face white. "They were faithful to the end. How goes it with the right?"

A familiar figure on a tired horse jogged up, and Odric saluted; he had a bloody bandage tied around his thigh. The Karif pushed his horse alongside and embraced his friend from the saddle; they pounded each other on the back, and Odric choked with emotion. "The warlords caught us with their darkness and their illusions, yet all stood firm, except for the left. And when the left broke, it rode through the center and broke their line. The enemy followed after. But the right turned them again, and the vanguard chased them back toward the river. Along the waterside, they disappeared."

The Karif raised his eyebrows. "When we have cleaned away this mess we will organize a proper advance and sweep the island. We have men enough. Paradon will be a land of mystery no longer." When he set his jaw he looked remarkably like Tibir. He turned in the saddle for a last look over the place where the center had been lost, and suddenly stood up in his stirrups, squinting his eyes. He pointed with his whip. Tamara could see some movement near the river, but what it was she could not tell. Suddenly the Karif had gathered his horse under him and was galloping down the hill. He was already on the grassy surface below before she had started out after him.

Her horse was not clever with his feet. Tamara had to pull him down to a walk to negotiate her way through the battlefield. She was still several hundred yards from the river when she saw the Karif's horse coming back toward her, bright-eyed and streaky with sweat. His neck was arched as though he knew he carried the World Conqueror in the saddle. Tamara slipped off her horse and bowed as Tibir rode past, and he acknowledged her with a slight nod as he rode back toward the remnants of his army. Tamara remounted and rode on to find her father and lend him her horse.

When she reached the place where Tibir's standard had stood, she once more dismounted, then held onto her horse's bridle for support while he rubbed his sweaty forehead against her arm. With great satisfaction, she watched her parents embracing. Time passed and they showed no sign of separating: only the position of the hands changed. Finally, Tamara's impatience grew too great. She dropped the reins, stepped forward, and boldly pushed herself between them. She was crushed against her father's armor, while her mother cradled her face in her hands and kissed her. Then she heard her mother's bones creak as her father's arms tightened about them both. Sibby started laughing and tried to pull free.

"Ease up," she said. "Let go!" Tamara listened with great satisfaction as her father muttered "Never again" from somewhere over her head.

II

Sibby was able to stay on her horse long enough to ride out of Paradon, over the bridge of boats, back to the main Angul encampment. She caught a glimpse of Tibir and heard vaguely that he was organizing a grand review of the army, but for once she did not even stop to puzzle over the source of his remarkable energy. Someone steadied her for the few feet from her horse to the flaps of an invitingly empty tent. She staggered through and fell onto the quilts.

Sibby slept through the grand review, which lasted for three days. She slept through the pacification of the armies of Paradon and the surrender of the surviving warlords. From time to time, someone prodded her awake and she must have talked lucidly for several minutes at a time, even taking a few mouthfuls of food, but these were moments only. For the most part, she slept. The Anguls had all left Paradon, except for civil administrators and a few troops of light cavalry, and the camp was being dismantled around her for the journey south, before she came fully awake.

Odric was sitting near her, a bandaged leg stretched out before him. His baraka lay quiet under his idle hand, and he was watching her with an expression of deep concern. "Odric," she said and his eyes lit up. She sat up and ruffled her hair with her hands. "I guess I was more tired than I thought."

He laughed and put his instrument to one side. "It is so good to hear your voice. My dear, you looked as though you were dead."

"I think I was," said Sibby briefly; she did not elaborate. But she reached over and took his warm hand and squeezed it with what strength she still had. He was patting her hand with his free one when Tamara stuck her head around the edge of the curtain. She bounced in and threw her arms around her mother's neck, kissing her enthusiastically.

"At last!" she breathed in dramatic tones. "Ibrasa says that the army thinks you're dead. Won't they be surprised! And the Agan wants to see you, too. We're supposed to be underway by noon. He's impatient to reach Zamarra. He has another grandson. But he didn't want to start until you were well enough to travel. The Empress says that this is the first time he has ever delayed a march for anyone. She even—"

Sibby gently covered her daughter's mouth. "Enough. Help me get up. You can tell me the rest in the bathhouse."

As Sibby soaked and scrubbed, Tamara told her all, breathlessly, her words tumbling over themselves. More than once Sibby had to stop her and ask her to explain more carefully, with fewer pronouns and more proper names. Sibby learned that Ajjibawr and Leron had settled their differences in Melismala and parted friends, after a narrow brush with death. It was a boy who had nearly killed them, Dastra's son Lerdas, and a boy who had saved them, quick-thinking Danyas. In a sense, Danyas was responsible for their good fortune on Paradon as well, since it was the news carried by his sea-born relatives that made Ajjibawr leave his army under Leron's command and sail swiftly to Paradon with a picked company of baturs. Ajjibawr was still on Paradon, making sure of the last details of Angul administration there: he would join them on the mainland soon.

As Tamara continued to talk, Sibby dressed, rejecting the trappings of Sword-Bearer for a plain silk shirt, quilted overdress and soft felt boots. Then walking together, mother and daughter, they went to wait on the Emperor.

The troops showed the results of the grand review. Their armor sparkled down to the smallest stud and buckle. All smooth leather was glossy and polished and the nap on rough leather had been scrubbed smooth. Horses were groomed and the warriors' own hair was slicked back, greased and braided. Several men smiled on recognizing the Batur Subi, and saluted her as she walked past.

The Emperor was on horseback, overseeing the formation of his troops for the march south. He acknowledged Sibby's presence, then smiled at the sight of Tamara standing behind her mother. He beckoned to her and she walked confidently up to his horse to receive a brief caress on the top of her head; Sibby could see that her daughter had been making herself popular during the last few days. The Emperor was assisted in dismounting, and seats immediately appeared, made out of rugs thrown over packing cases. Sibby caught Tamara's eye and her daughter discreetly withdrew to pat the Emperor's horse on the nose. The Emperor watched her walk away with a faint smile still on his lips.

"The Empress has explained why there is so great a similarity between you. Be assured that I have no wish to separate you from your child or the child's father. And even if you did not wish him to stay, it seems I could ill afford to lose the most loyal and effective of my generals." Sibby murmured her thanks. "I am told," Tibir continued, "that the king of Tredana has promised to remain a loyal vassal in all respects, except his recent marriage. This does not displease you?" She smiled and shook her head. "Tell me, what does the Sword-Bearer wish, now that she has returned the sword to the Underworld from which it came?" Tibir asked the question very simply, and Sibby raised her eyes to meet his.

"Lord Tibir," she said, "I will be loyal to you as long as I live. But I do not wish to stay in your court, unless you absolutely command it. Let me return to the ardan of Soktani Agana. If you wish to be generous, give me some tents and horses."

Tibir frowned. "Soktani Agana pastures her flocks in the east. Why do you wish to go so far from the Batur Clerowan? I have commanded him to stay here and look to the administration of Paradon. What if I put the ardan of the traitor Tammush into your hands? These are good lands. You can graze ten thousand horses here, if the weather is kind." He permitted himself a slight smile. "I will expect a little better order of loyalty from these regions than I have enjoyed in the past."

Sibby looked out across the flat grazing lands that stretched to the distant horizon. "It is all I have hoped for," she said, and amazed herself by dropping to her knees before Tibir and pressing his hands to her forehead. He withdrew one hand and patted her much as he had caressed Tamara.

"You have performed your duties and have earned your reward. But do not think I give these things away lightly. To you I make a gift of these pasture lands, and responsibility for the families that Tammush has left leaderless and broken through his manifest crimes. Also, I give you a certain number of horses, sheep and cattle. But control of my northern forces I leave with my new general, the Batur Clerowan; to him also I have allocated the greater number of riding horses to be found here, as well as promising him a certain number of desert animals now presently at grass near Zamarra. You have the lands, and he has the horses. I will leave it to you to make whatever further arrangements are necessary."

Tibir got slowly to his feet, and as he leaned on Sibby's arm, his eyes met hers. "Come bid farewell to the Empress, and wish us a good journey south. I will send you some courtiers for your amusement, from Tibiridan and Gagan-ala. But you will find there is much to do here in the north. I know for a fact that Tammush's adventures have kept the fields unplanted two years in a row. Speak with Clerowan. He has a little experience in these matters. Next autumn I will hold a grand review in Zamarra. Then you can report to me on your progress here."

Tamara held his stirrup and he pulled himself on his horse with a strength that never failed to amaze Sibby. He nodded and rejoined his guard, who waited at a respectful distance. Sibby smiled at her daughter, and put her hand on her shoulder.

"I think Tibir has just made another of his state weddings. He has given me the lands of Tammush, but all the horses here now belong to your father."

Tamara grinned.

The vanguard of Tibir's army had disappeared into the distance when Ajjibawr returned from Paradon. Tibir had drawn in the wings of his cavalry to ride in close formation on either side of the center, and was waiting impatiently for a last word with his general before he left. The Empress was also on horseback. Ajjibawr dropped to his knees before the

Emperor as though he were in the practice of making obei-
sance, and bent his stiff neck before the Emperor of the
World. He received Tibir's gifts graciously, but even at a
slight distance Sibby could sense the smile that quirked the
edges of his mouth. He stayed on his knees until the royal
party had ridden past, then stiffly rose and brushed the dust
from his knees. He looked at Sibby's tents and carts approvingly, then smiled at her.

She felt her heart turn over as easily as it had when she was
Tamara's age and first saw the Karif smiling at her in the
sunlight. His hair had been a pale gold then; now it was
nearly white and showed considerably more forehead. But the
tight skin still creased in the corners of his bright blue eyes
when he smiled. He was still the most attractive man she had
ever seen. Something in her face must have given her thoughts
away, for he stepped up to her quite confidently and put his
hands on her shoulders.

"Now that you remember all," he said, "what do you
think?"

She pulled away, not quite ready to capitulate. "I think
about many things," she said evasively. "When do you
return to Paradon?"

He laughed and rubbed the edge of his nostril as though he
had just taken a pinch of snuff. "I have left Ibrasa in charge.
I heard there was work to be done here, with the people of
Tammush. Tibir has left us Odric to amuse us, and promised
us some scribes and chroniclers from Tibiridan. We must not
forget to keep track of all our actions. We are accountable to
the Emperor."

"We? I think you assume a great deal." She felt his hurt
and made herself stick to her purpose. She crossed her arms
over her chest and tried not to look him in the eye. "It is
hard for me to forget," she said firmly, "the eagerness with
which you left here, not so long ago. I will not deny you have
a very attractive smile, but before I smile at you in return I
would like to have some idea whether or not you plan on
staying."

To state it so baldly made her feel like a fool, but she had
the satisfaction of seeing him flinch. They stood silent for a
moment, then Ajjibawr took her arm and firmly steered her in
among the tents. He pushed her into the nearest empty one
and pulled the flaps shut behind them.

She was not sure what she expected, but the last thing in the world was the sight of the Karif dropping onto his knees. "Get up!" she said and pulled at his shoulders.

He kept his head bowed though, and spoke so softly she had trouble hearing. "It is not easy for me to make an apology," he said. "I have not had much practice in accountability."

She sank to her own knees so that she could hear him better. "I'm not asking for some kind of confession," she said. "I just want to know whether I matter to you or not. If I don't matter, all I ask is a little distance, for my own protection. Is that so unreasonable? I'm not trying to force myself on you. I know you're not exactly the sentimental type. It's just that you mean too much to me for me to be able to say goodbye to you again without pain."

He did not answer her directly, but reached in the front of his shirt and extracted a small bag on a string around his neck. From the bag he pulled out a long, thick curl of black hair.

Sibby felt tears rising in her eyes. "When I last saw Arbytis in the Underworld," she said, "he charged me to greet you for him. And in answer to Simirimia, when she said I should have had some token left in the Upper World to charm me home, he said that someone might have such a talisman. How did you come by this?"

"I may not be sentimental," he said softly, "but I stole this while you slept, the last night we were together. I have had it by my heart since. I thought then it was all of you I would ever have. I never thought it would help bring you back to me. I will stay as long as you wish it, my dear. It was simple cowardice drove me away. If it were anything else, I would find it easy to talk to you. But I have not had much practice in confessing fear."

Sibby put her hands on either side of his face and he kissed her hand as she touched him, but still failed to meet her eyes. "Fear? Of what?"

Ajjibawr laughed bitterly. "Of the Emperor keeping his word. He told me I could take an army to Tredana as a whole man, or stay with his forces not quite so—intact. It was also suggested to me that the terms of his proposal not be shared with anyone, especially the Emperor's Sword-Bearer." His pale face had colored considerably as he spoke.

Sibby pulled his head against her breast and kissed the side of his face. She was unable to keep from crying with relief. "I thought you wanted to get away from me," she explained, and Ajjibawr laughed shakily as he turned his mouth to meet hers.

"I'm sorry," he said again when they were able to talk. "There was no way I could explain why I ran away. It is fortunate I was able to please the Emperor when I returned. Otherwise, I might be under the surgeon's knife at this very moment."

He tried to make it sound like a joke, but Sibby just wrapped her arms around him and held on tight.

Sibby shut her eyes and felt her heart knock in her chest, in the same rhythm as his. "I give you permission," she said, "to pasture your herds of horses on my land. But I give you fair warning: if you try and leave this country I will make the Emperor's threats look like a mild rebuke in comparison to mine."

Ajjibawr tightened his arms around her until she could hardly breathe, and his answer might have gone further if Tamara had not come in search of them.

from Tibir's Victory-Book

From the land of mists and sorcery the Agan brought home his troops in good order, and for the first time in the period of written history Paradon was rejoined to the world of living men and the lord of Zamarra claimed the loyalty of its warlords, now vassal chieftains.

Tibir Agan was in his seventieth year, the fiftieth of his campaigning, and he passed through the streets of Tibiridan and Gagan-ala to the acclaim of his faithful troops and loyal subjects. But the Wheel of Fate, which in its revolutions had seen fit to humble even the Great God Vazdz before the might of our Agan, now dashed his triumphs to nothing.

For less than thirty days was Tibir Agan truly Conqueror of the World. Before his army had reached Almadun the Emperor fell sick, and nothing might warm him. They made a halt in the border town of Odar, little knowing that the servants of death awaited him therein. Our lord was put to bed in the palace there, much though he protested it, and fires of such magnitude were lit to warm his chamber, a part of the roof was burned. But nothing might warm him. The skill of the physicians was as nothing, and the sorceress who had healed him before was far away in the north.

Indeed it was said by some as Tibir lay dying, that this was the last act of the demon whose power he overthrew in Paradon, to wit, the false god Vazdz. It was said by some that Tibir's life had been forfeited in some contest of skill with Vazdz; it was said by others that Tibir had won (as indeed he won all contests in his life) yet for his own reasons chose to agree to the forfeit.

Sharkim the Zanidan practiced all his arts, but the Agan continued ill some three days. Then he opened his eyes and sent for his wives and sons and grandchildren, and to each of them he spoke in private. Then he asked for the Empress to stay by his bed, for as he said himself, of ministers and favorites never had he one and a deathbed was not the place to start. Another day he lay talking with his queen, until he fell insensible, and after another day he died, never to see his city of Zamarra again with living eyes.

The Empress caused him to be embalmed after the customs of the Samidan Empire, and to mark his final resting place in Zamarra she sent to Gagan-ala for a stone of pure quartz seven feet in length and broad proportionately, and under this stone Tibir now lies, in the city he loved better than anything else in the world. And before the ceremonies that marked his interment were complete, the breaking up of his empire had commenced, leading to all that unrest we have known so well in our time.

Airs, Ancient and Modern

BANORIE O BANORIE

There was a lady in a tower Banorie O Banorie....

TWO HUNDRED HORSES

It was summer in Tredana and the ----

THE QUEST

He journeyed east, he journeyed west, journeyed south & north, and when he came to Tremyrag — he - bid its Lord stand forth

ABOUT THE AUTHOR

Joyce Ballou Gregorian's father is an Armenian who fled Iran as a child, her mother a descendant of early New England settlers. She grew up entranced by tales of travel and adventure, some from her father's own life story. She is involved with the family business of buying and selling oriental rugs, and has traveled widely teaching and lecturing on the subject. (One reviewer compared the complexity of her plots and imagined civilizations to the intricacies in the patterns of the rugs she knows so much about.)

Ms. Gregorian is married to an architect and lives on a farm in Massachusetts with five cats, three dogs, and forty horses. *The Great Wheel* is a sequel to her earlier books, *The Broken Citadel* and *Castledown*.